The Call to Arms:

Euwae said nothing as her eyes bored into visions of retributions yet to be dealt. Brand looked at her face and scowled.

But, softly he said, "Euwae... I told you before: I need you focused. Right here, right now. If you go out there like this, you'll kill a lot of them before you die – But you'll never see the hit that kills you, either, because you're too shitesan angry. If you can't get your head back into this fight, you've not only killed us, but you've killed everyone left alive in that village.

"So, if you don't want to hand Summerfords over to cu'Kullah on a plate, then look at me and take a deep breath – Help me save those people down there."

Dedication:

To James White: may all of us find the honor and harmony that you teach, live and enjoy. Thank you, sir, for having the faith and courage to do so.

The
Ree's Tale

First Printing – January 2016

Copyright © Timothy A. Gilkes 2016

ISBN 978-0-9822812-6-0

Cover Art by Aaron Addison, Timothy Gilkes and Juliana Sheinheit

Published by WhiteBelt Productions, LLC

39 James Street, Greenfield MA 01301

Printed in the USA.

Table of Contents

Common Glossary

Some elements of the Cord'Or language which are used throughout the tale that follows:

SOCIETY

Ard'Ree – the mythical high king of the Cord'Or

al'Aith – a member of the royal or noble caste

> **ree** – the leader of a province (similar to a duke in status, although the term is gender neutral)

bua'Theu – the commoners of Cord'Or society

> **ath'Ale** – a warrior (usually of the bua'Theu caste)

cuhm'l – the name of Cord'Or currency; it is also a derogatory term for a refugee or a prisoner of war

dicenn – a derogatory term for an outsider or a member of society who has been stripped of a torc

CULTURAL TERMS

en'Och – personal honor, but also one's status within their caste and the Cord'Or society as a whole

geas – a personal stricture which cannot be broken or the person will die and are typically assigned at birth

hiel – a Cord'Or epithet

twoth – a region of the Cord'Or overseen by a specific ree

weaving – to create a magical effect

OBJECTS

aes'ree – quasi-magical heirlooms are objects which are used to perform deeds of renown; they are attributed with the success of that act and granted a unique name for which the object acquires its own en'Och

bara'Ba – the traditional Cord'Or sword (a sword with a heavy blade that curves downward, similar to the falcata in design)

tathlum – an ancient weapon of the ree, who used the heads of their enemies to inflict grievous wounds upon those who knew the deceased

torc – an item of jewelry that proclaims one's caste and status within Cord'Or society

Ancient Forest

The noise of the camp fractured his dreams like an iron chisel, hewing away his refuge of sleep until consciousness collapsed in upon him. As Brand opened his eyes, his head was still pitched forward towards the ground, his arms still bound behind him; the whole of his body, from his neck to his hips were a single knot of contorted aching muscle. When his face contorted as he opened his eyes, the man sitting beside him took a fistful of his hair, pulled his head back and looked at him intently.

The sudden motion sent an obvious cascade of pain through Brand, his breath escaping as a pitiful moan. The guard nodded in satisfaction and dropped the prisoners head, sending broken convulsions through Brand's body as it sought to wring out the contents of his long empty stomach. He rolled to his side and pulled up his legs as best he could, trying to bring some release to the acid fire in his muscles... But kept his mouth clenched shut in a furious display of repulsion at his own weakness.

The warrior watching him smiled in dismissal as he rose and walked off towards the fire.

"Angus," he called out with respect as he approached the large man standing keeping watch over another, who sat on his haunches in the ruddy light moving fist sized stones across the dirt with a long stick.

"It is I, o'Keil."

"Aye." Angus nodded.

"He is awake." o'Keil added dutifully.

Angus looked at the man kneeling in front of him.

"My al'Aith?"

In response, cu'Kullah moved a second stone into the shadow cast by the first, thrust the stick into the soft earth and rose to his full height. The fire played across the thick bronze torc on his neck with a sinister flicker as he retrieved the long, tattered bundle that had lain beside him. He turned his back to the fire and walked the short distance to where the outlander lay.

"Everyone thought you to be dead, you know." He said conversationally in a southern brogue as he looked down at the man laying before him. "Dead you should have stayed. Now, the twoth of the River Prince will have the stain of disgrace to add to the color of its defeat."

Brand's eyes slowly climbed to the man's face, but he said nothing.

"It hurts, eh? To be the spoils of anothers glory." Cu'Kullah nudged Brand's arm with his boot, leaving a scuff of dirt across it. "But not there.

"You were a warrior: *the* warrior." he continued. "The mightiest ath'Ale of the River Prince's swordsmen in all the twoth'Shan'n. The mightiest in a generation – Maybe more."

Cu'Kullah shrugged. "But men such as us, we know the body's pain better than we know its pleasures, eh? And you were wise long ago, as I was, that wounds mean next to nothing."

The barrel chested warrior bent over Brand until his long blond hair nearly brushed the prisoner's face and lowered his voice so that only the prisoner could hear.

"But the cuts you are feeling now are in the heart, eh? Wounds of defeat and shame. You will never know the warrior's death, now... Never find glory to fill the ache in you.

"I own you now, Brand Eastlander..."

Then cu'Kullah chuckled. "But luck is with you – If it was not, you would have lived on a slave and reveled in the scat of my dogs in our hall as we feasted your loss – And counted yourself curst until age brought the geas of men down upon you."

As cu'Kullah rose, Brand kept his dark eyes fixed upon the emerald green eyes of his captor, but the larger warrior only smiled even more broadly. "You doubt your luck, then?" he crooned in amusement.

"Cuhm'l such as you are not allowed to look men in the eye," he said blandly. "Surely your service to the River Prince showed you as much. But I have a fair notion that you will not be doing so much longer, and such is the way of it."

He grinned and stroked the bundle under his arm.

"In that wise," he continued as if lecturing a child, "it was not you that we set out to be bringing to glory. Had you sense of any sort, you would have known as much. As I said, you *were* dead to us." He chuckled again.

"But this, now..." He gazed at the bundle under his arm with reverence. "This prize is worth more than even the skull of the greatest warrior of our lifetime."

Brand's eyes flickered to the bundle, which cu'Kullah slowly disrobed as if it were his most prized woman. From within, the hilt of thu'Ked shone, the ancestral sword of the ree of twoth'Shan'n radiant even in the darkness. When cu'Kullah gently wrapped it once more, Brand's gaze tumbled back down into the dirt.

Cu'Kullah's smile was brilliant with his triumph. "But I must now admit, cuhm'l, that your skull being here may well change my own courses just a bit."

Then the imposing nobleman turned back to the fire.

"Angus!" He called out merrily. "Come, set him loose. We will be having no further trouble with our prize, now that he knows the way of it!" Cu'Kullah strode with gusto back to the warmth of the fire. As he passed o'Keil, he clapped him heartily on the back and both men let out a guffaw of satisfaction.

Angus stroked his full, ruddy beard as he walked over to Brand. Drawing a long, straight bladed knife with a sharply angled chisel point from his belt, Angus looked down at the prisoner.

"This is a goodly knife, you had upon you," he said quietly, thumbing the edge appreciatively, "and no mistake. I shall take good care of it now, as you will be having no need of it."

Muscle tremors quaked through the prisoner's body as Angus slowly cut the ropes from his arms. Although he was no longer physically bound, Brand continued to lay in the dirt at the center of the camp, making no attempt to pull his gaze away from the wretched earth to which he had fallen in the shadow of cu'Kullah of twoth'Fhee.

*   *   *

The war band traveled another three days before reaching the red stone markers which gave warning to the geas that surrounded the black waters of the lake Ers'Elb. There, cu'Kullah directed his men to make camp a hundred paces up slope of that boundary, in a flat cull-de-sac between the arms of the chalky hills of the lakes western shore. While the warriors set out their gear, cu'Kullah himself went down to the henge and sang songs of remembrance.

From the camp, Brand could catch only traces of the song although he could easily see the surface of the water down the slope from them. Even in the early evening, the sky cast no reflection upon it: the waters seemed to pull at the light in odd ways, but no glare from the heavy sun shimmered or danced on the surface.

Angus noticed Brand's stare and hastily trotted over to the prisoner.

"Look NOT upon Ers'Elb!" he scolded in a fierce whisper. "You will be bringing the ire of the wraith out of the water and no mistake!"

Brand shrugged and looked at Angus listlessly.

"You know what?" Brand said. "We stood side by side against marauds and now you're worried about a dirty lake?" He waived out at the other warriors. "What happened to all of you?" He looked pointedly at Angus.

"What happened to *you*?"

When the other man failed to respond, Brand shook his head.

"If there's a spirit in the lake, I'm betting it would take more than a glance from up here to get its attention."

Angus took a step forward, his right hand on the hilt of his sword.

"Stupid dicenn!" he hissed. "Even in your backwards land, can people be so blind?" His left hand made a vague gesture towards the lake, but his right never came away from his weapon, nor his eyes away from Brand.

"Long ago, a great priest came to Ers'Elb, well loved in the court of Ard'Ree and tasked to create a place of peace, where all could enjoy it.

"Then, the waters were clear as the sky; a pair of lush tors lay like a bosom in the waters and a pool which healed any wound lay between them..."

Brand shook his head.

"Does this priest have a name?" he asked coolly. "'Cause I don't think they did that good a job."

Angus drew back, spat three times on the ground and wiped his beard clean with the back of his free hand.

"You ARE an idiot!" He choked, trying to keep his voice as low as possible. "Even *you* cannot be so ignorant. That is no longer a sacred pool that lies beyond those rune stones. That is *death*. Those who fail to pay the ancient tributes are doomed to suffer forever –"

"You just said it was death, Angus. How can you suffer forever once you're dead?"

"Oh, there are mysteries, even in death," a deep, low voice responded slowly.

Angus went pale and jumped as a hand fell onto his shoulder. But the soft chuckling burr of Genna Highstaff, the magician who had long served as the war band's druid, set him at ease. With a chiding look Genna stepped forward and clicked his tongue.

"You might complain about the dicenn's ignorance, but you are doing little better Angus. Set aside your fear: wraiths cannot trespass outside the stones standing watch along the shore, save that they are given cause and obligation to do so."

Then his voice dropped to a more serious tone.

"Cu'Kullah is laying out the tales of his en'Och to satisfy the oaths of the rune stones. Until he returns, he is not well served by any of us speaking ill of Ers'Elb." He reached out and took Angus' hand away from his weapon.

"Do you see this wise?" Genna asked calmly.

Angus started to shake his head, as if to clear his sight from a waking dream. With only an uncertain nod as an answer, he turned from Brand and Genna and made his way back to the other ath'Ale in the camp.

Brand watched Angus with idle interest. Once the big warrior was out of earshot he posed a question to the magician.

12

"He said wraith. You said wraiths," Brand asked conversationally. "Which is it?"

Genna simply shook his head in the negative, touched his sapphire studded torc in an ironic salute and walked away.

Brand sighed and looked at the ground while he scraped at the chalky earth with the toe of his boot.

"It's not wraiths," he said to himself distractedly. "Even the most enchanted waters'll poison the spirits of the dead..."

He kept his face down but lifted his gaze back to Ers'Elb. Around them all, the setting sun cast the last of its ruddy light upon all but the black waters of the lake, a gaping wound in a land stained with hues of watered blood.

*   *   *

A red moon was just hovering into the night sky before cu'Kullah stopped singing and walked back up the short rise to the camp. The rest of the men went silent in expectation, but their leader waived his hands in dismissal and they fell back to their idle tasks as he passed. At his tent, cu'Kullah spoke quietly for a long moment to Genna, but his eyes remained fixed on Brand before he ducked inside.

The druid shook his head with unspoken disagreement before he went to the fire and dished out a large bowl of stew with a wooden spoon. Then he took the steaming food to the slopes of the cul-de-sac, where Brand sat alone in the darkness.

"What's this, priest?" Brand asked cautiously, hanging bitter sarcasm on the magician's formal title. "I've already had my portion for the day."

The campfire behind him shadowed Genna's features as he passed Brand the bowl and shrugged the strap of his wineskin over his head. Handing it to the prisoner as well, he rocked his head back towards cu'Kullah's tent. Brand took the bowl and the wine, then looked up at Genna.

The druid simply shrugged.

"There is more, if you want it," he said, as if in explanation.

"And if I don't?"

"If you choose to refuse our hospitality, then so be it."

Brand snorted sarcastically as he scooped the food into his mouth.

"Believe what you will, Brand of the Condotterai, Master of Horses and Champion of twoth'Shan'n..." Brand stopped and clenched his jaw, but said nothing; Genna continued, his voice smooth with an odd tone of formality.

"You, who are the victor over the marauds that faced down the twoth'Fhee at del'Ath; who threw down the Pyrbound corsairs; who led the host of the River Prince and over matched the red caps of twoth'Ba - And for which was granted the honor of service upon the en'Och of thu'Ked; who led the guard of Caer Shan'n so that your ree might escape the might of cu'Kullah, though the River Prince fell smitten amongst the dead; you, who wandered the land nameless for six years and sought battle with any beast, without honor in the name of any lesser cause –"

At that, Brand set aside the food and stood up before Genna. They were of equal height, but Brand was the broader built and the gleam in his eye made him far more formidable as he emerged from the others shadow.

"That's enough, witch. I served twoth'Shan'n and its ree in honor – Something the *men* of cu'Kullah hardly practice, if they even know how. The only dishonor you've got on me is that after you repaid the River Prince for our help with treachery and murder, I wasn't able to do the same to you."

Genna smiled broadly, obviously pleased with Brand's response. Brand ignored him and continued coldly.

"No matter what cu'Kullah thinks, I won't serve his shitesan twoth, in life or death. I *swear* by the Banner of the Citadel of Fallenway, by the bones of my fathers and the rule of the Ard'Ree... Twoth'Shan'n will be avenged in blood against those who spilled it."

A chill wind sent whispers through the distant trees and stole across the waters of Ers'Elb. Brand bent down and picked up the food and drink to pass it back to Genna, but the druid raised his hands palms out and backed away.

"Brave words, dicenn," he said with surety. "But remember, outlander: such an oath may well have served your cause in your distant home. Even here, words brave as those *might* have attracted the very eye of Ard'Ree and no mistake – Save one. With no torc to hold en'Och to you, all your doings are no more than the breeze, whisking the very word of them away into the darkness as soon as they are made plain."

Genna shook his head in scorn.

"Eat while you may, Brand Eastlander. Drink, if you have a mind. Better yet, get drunk." He said in mock sympathy.

"Come the setting of the moon, you will be wishing you had enjoyed the hospitality of cu'Kullah just a wee bit longer and that is the way of it."

Genna turned and walked back to the fire to rejoin the others. Brand sat back down and turned his gaze to the horizon, where the moon slipped inexorably towards Ers'Elb. Then slowly he began to eat.

*   *   *

"Get up, dicenn." Hissed Angus quietly.

Brand had once again fallen asleep sitting up. He opened his eyes, before he raised his head. Across Ers'Elb, the moon was almost to the tops of the trees. Brand looked at Angus, who shifted anxiously and stepped a pace back.

"It's time?" Brand asked calmly.

Angus nodded and gestured emphatically for him to rise. Brand did so without shifting his legs, coming smoothly to his feet despite the awkward position in which he had been sitting. He took a step forward, but Angus stretched out a hand and placed it on the center of his chest.

"Hold up, there." He commanded. "First, I will be needing you to take off that fine shirt you are wearing."

Brand scowled, but Angus' hand strayed towards the hilt of his sword. With a shake of his head, Brand pulled loose the lacing at the collar of his shirt and drew it over his head. He offered it to Angus, but the other man refused to take it. So Brand folded it instead and set it gently upon the ground.

To spite his captors impatience, he also brushed off the chalky clay from his hands as best he could, the pale dust leaving a ghostly stain from his fingers across his trousers as he finally followed Angus down the slope towards the standing stones on the shore.

At the henge, two more warriors stood on the near side. On the left, the man's gloriously long blond hair betrayed o'Keil, the warrior from the north county. On the right was Genna; the druid walked up to Brand and positioned him so that he was facing the shore directly.

"Now, kneel." He ordered.

Brand continued to stand, so the magician turned to the other warrior.

"O'Keil?" He asked politely.

The large man walked behind Brand and kicked him hard behind his right knee. Brand started to topple, but Genna and Angus caught him and helped lower the prisoner into a kneeling position.

"Thank you, o'Keil." Genna said smoothly.

"Yeah, o'Keil," Brand parroted through gritted teeth. "Thanks a lot."

Brand heard motion behind him and tensed for a second kick, but Genna raised his hand and o'Keil withheld the blow. Genna and Angus stepped away from Brand; the druid moved up to the nearest of the red stones, standing to the right of it, while Angus stepped behind Brand and out of his peripheral vision.

The sapphires on the druid's torc gleamed as he began to speak softly. Brand could not make out the words, but the effect was obvious: first, runes of gold began to glow upon the surface of the stone; then ripples not born of any breeze began to stir the surface of Ers'Elb. For the first time, the men were able to discern the reflection of the sky in the surface as those small waves wrinkled the skin of the lake.

After a moment, Angus let out a muffled cry. "On all the skulls! It *is* true..." His voice faded weakly.

Brand looked out across Ers'Elb and saw two hills set gracefully upon the water. A gleam of the ruddy moonlight marked the course of a stream, running like a vein down each slope and into the cleft between them.

"Of course it is true." Spoke cu'Kullah behind them proudly. "And, soon lads, I will show you more than you would ever think to be dreaming."

The leader of the war band moved forward so that he stood to the right of Brand.

"A sight that has not been marked since the turn of the age..." he said respectfully as he gazed out over the water.

Brand looked up at him.

"If it's such a rare sight – Care to join me?"

The big warrior looked down at him and chuckled. "No, Brand; your place in this is yours by right and no mistake. Now hush, until the priest has finished."

Brand shook his head.

"With all respect to your wizard, shouldn't you be doing the talking?"

Cu'Kullah shook his head.

"We each must play our part, eh? Now, please – Show some respect."

"I'm not so sure – "

The nudge of o'Keil's boot in the small of his back silenced Brand's retort. They all waited while Genna's chant wove around them and the moon slipped ever closer to the tree line across the shore. A breeze carried up soft fragrances from the water. Soon a path began to shimmer in the moonlight, leading from the red stone across the shore and down into the black water, continuing on until it was lost in the depths. The priest staggered back from the red stone and nodded to cu'Kullah.

"The time is now," he said wearily, wiping a heavy sheen of sweat from his brow. "Or you will be waiting a year again for this night to come."

"Now it is." Said cu'Kullah. Then, he turned to Brand. "Walk with me."

As he rose, Brand glimpsed the naked blade of thu'Ked clenched in cu'Kullah's right hand, despite the other man's attempts to hold it out of sight from his captive. With a deep breath, Brand stood and slowly followed, favoring his right leg.

Cu'Kullah walked confidently following the shining path to the very edge of the water. Being very careful to stay within that boundary, Brand did the same. Once they stood side by side, the big warrior pointed towards the pair of hills with thu'Ked; the reflection of the red moon slid across the thick blade of the falcata like an ember in the darkness.

"Have you heard the truth of Ers'Elb?" He asked, flicking the sword tip towards the distant island.

Brand clenched his jaw and shook his head no.

His captor nodded. "There is no shame there, to be sure. Few, even amongst the Cord'Or, know the way of it." He lowered the sword and stepped back slightly, affording Brand the full view of the dark lake stretching out towards the island before them.

"Long ago, in the days before the Power broke the spine of the worlds spirit, the Cord'Or lived without the hand of Ard'Ree or the wisdom of druids such as our priest here to guide them. Every twoth stood alone against the enemies at our gate and was at the throat of every other, besides. Life was sharp and swift; the passing of a court from ree to ree went more often to the strongest hand in it than the son or daughter of the one on the throne.

"But, even in such times, none were like to follow an al'Aith with the blood of his master staining his blade. So, when a ree passed on or came to grief, such nobles as were remaining would in accord disband the court for a time; a challenge was set before those so interested to travel here, to the red stones.

"In that journey, they would seek out the greatest champions and overthrow them in battle. They would search for the most renown aes'ree and seize those relics worthy of their own name as best they could; those who were less able would gather all the wealth that could be got. Then, with those captives and such treasures as they could amass they would arrive to the shore and await with the rest for the redding of the moon.

"On that night, all would feast as kin... Then one of their number not seeking the throne would speak to the stones and open the way to the shores beyond once the moon rested upon the crown of the Ancient Forest itself and the moment had come."

Both men turned their gaze upwards, to the moon hanging just moments away from the touch of the tops of the tallest trees on the far side of Ers'Elb. Cu'Kullah moved behind Brand and placed his left hand on the prisoner's shoulder.

"Then, as one, those who were worthy took their glorious treasures to the shore and cast them into the water; those who were mighty took the heads of those who had been beaten and kept them, though the bodies were let slip into the black waters as well."

17

His hand pushed down on Brand's shoulder, but his prisoner refused to kneel.

Cu'Kullah ignored his reluctance and continued his tale.

"Once such sacrifices were done, there would come a sign from *that* very island. Out across the water, one name would be called and one alone. That warrior would then come to the very edge of this shore and take a knee...

"Then, from the bosom of the waters would rise a torc, fashioned of the very wealth that had that night been cast away. So the new ree of the twoth would be known to all as the rightful heir to the court that awaited them."

Brand stared resolutely ahead across the water. "And you think that you're worthy?" he spat out the question coldly. "The Ard'Ree dispenses the twoths now... Not this – Place. If it ever did."

Cu'Kullah's voice remained low and confident, unshaken by Brand's scorn.

"On another day, I might agree with you," he said with assurance. "But *you* forget, yourself. There is a twoth, right now, that has gone fallow for near on six years... And which Ard'Ree in all wisdom has seen fit to ignore."

Brand's fists closed in silent rage as cu'Kullah continued.

"I have brought its champion – the greatest warrior of our day, it is said! – to his knees before the red stone. I have brought its treasures to Ers'Elb to craft for me the finest torc that has been seen in the eyes of a host of grandfathers. And," he said with complete confidence, "I do to have this."

He brandished thu'Ked and held it out past Brand's shoulder so that he could gaze upon the shining blade one last time.

"You swore your oaths to the River Prince on the heirloom of Shan'n, did you not?" He said softly, leaning forward so that he hovered just above Brand's shoulder. "Upon the aes'ree thu'Ked?

"It is sung that this blade was ancient, even in the age of those who lived before the Power and the rule of Ard'Ree... That there were but twenty brothers and sisters like it forged with a true name, though thu'Ked's kin have all been lost to the long ages since their birth.

"I know your oaths have strength to *you*, dicenn. You swore to serve the master of this blade... And, in that wise, your oaths have earned you one final glory.

"Time has stolen what honor *you* possessed, outlander; your past is nothing more than a song on the wind of a mercenary whose words proved empty... It sings of you, now cuhm'l to a true warrior of Cord'Or, who will expend you for the glory of en'Och that shall burn in living memory forever.

"Your ree has fallen. The ath'Ale who followed you into battle are dead or scattered. The twoth you hoped to call home is lost. And at the last, champion, you shall pass the throne to me in joining them."

Cu'Kullah stood back and released his hand.

"Kneel."

Brand closed his eyes. Slowly, he settled onto his knees just short of the water upon the shore. He took a long, slow breath and opened his eyes... But his gaze focused on nothing. Cu'Kullah raised the sword and drew it high behind Brand's neck.

"Ah – My al'Aith?" Angus said timidly. Cu'Kullah kept his pose, but his shoulders sagged.

"Angus..." He growled.

"What if he's not – Not worthy?"

That caused cu'Kullah's head to turn.

"What?"

"You said, my al'Aith, that he has never known a torc. He may be a great warrior of his kind: but he has never been of the folk of Cord'Or and has long been free of his past honors. *Is* such a one worthy of the sacrifice? Will his death prove you a worthy ree?"

Genna nodded.

"And did he not," the priest added superstitiously, "swear to Ard'Ree that he would never serve you as his master, in life *or* death? You said you know his oaths have strength..."

Cu'Kullah rolled his eyes and then shook his head.

At the waterline Brand waited on his knees, his breathing steady. Cu'Kullah looked down at him and nodded. He lowered thu'Ked and looked at the falcata with regret.

"I said, his oaths have power to him." He said reproachfully to the others. But then, he looked down at Brand and scowled.

"The greatest champion of our age not worthy?" Cu'Kullah asked to himself, grimaced and sighed. "Yet the time of the sacrifice is nigh..." He continued absently, "there will be no hope for it after this night, should we fail our offerings now; there is nothing to be had for not seeing this quest through and that is the way of it."

With regret touching the edges of his tone, he looked up as the red moon sat like an eye upon the crest of the tallest trees.

"Ers'Elb," he cried aloud, "I have come for all that is to be mine! Take what is yours!" He brought the sword up swiftly over his head. "I give you this greatest of gifts – The aes'ree thu'Ked!"

With that he hurled the weapon over Brand's head, high into the air above them out towards the waters of Ers'Elb.

For Brand, time ceased to be.

Thu'Ked had already begun to arc into the sky as he became aware of what cu'Kullah had done. Brand raised is head and watched the weapon rise far out of reach into the air, his eyes shifting from wide with horror to narrow with concentration as the sword hung at the apex of the throw, then began to spin downward towards the water where it would land just ten feet from shore.

As cu'Kullah howled in triumph, Brand tensed and leaped out over the water, his arms outstretched.

The blade glinted in the night as it spun inevitability downward.

From the far side of the henge, o'Keil and Genna began to sprint towards the men at the waters edge.

Brand pistoned his right arm out in a last attempt to save the ancestral weapon of the River Prince.

Cu'Kullah's eyes grew wide as his cry of victory slipped to a tone of shock.

Genna tried to move around cu'Kullah but stumbled; he caught himself by flailing his arm forward against the ground but it landed in the sand well beyond the border of the glittering path.

O'Keil reached the edge of the black water but drew up short, as well past the shoreline Brand's hand closed around the hilt of the aes'ree and he collapsed towards the water.

The outlander came down onto the surface of Ers'Elb... But rather than plunge below the surface, the glassy reflection was as hard as ice. He hit on his left shoulder and grunted as his body snapped forward with the weight of the impact and drove his head down onto the left temple. He rolled a half rotation, sliding twice his body length before coming to rest on his back upon the waters surface, with thu'Ked cradled like a child under his right arm.

And then, he lay still.

Genna screamed. O'Keil ignored him and jumped out onto Ers'Elb after Brand. When he came down on it, however, he did not stand, nor did he make a splash. Instead, his golden hair spread around him like a cloud as he simply dropped away, as if there were nothing but shadow beneath him. And then o'Keil was simply -

Gone.

Genna fell onto his back, clutching his left forearm. Before his eyes, his left hand was consumed by a crusty pallor, the fingers half clenched and frozen in a rictus of pain. A faint dust rose from it as the limb was suddenly wrenched backwards by an invisible force and the priest was dragged bodily behind it back towards the henge.

"Cu'Kullah!" he cried pitifully. But the large warrior continued to stare at Brand, lying motionless upon the face of Ers'Elb as if it were a black mirror, his shadow merging with his dark reflection.

Genna rolled and tried to dig his heels into the earth as he passed the stones, but his calcified hand dragged him like a hooked fish through the henge and back towards the camp. There, the ath'Ale were starting to rise, weapons in hand, but confused as to the commotion from the waters below.

Angus saw Genna's distress and acted out of instinct, grabbing his comrade in an attempt to keep him from being pulled any further. But the force was too great; both men were dragged up the bank another eight feet before Angus was shaken free.

With a howl of rage he scrambled to his feet and chased after Genna, his sword flashing out of the sheath and biting deeply into the druid's left arm at the elbow. The priest screamed again in pain as his blood splashed them both. But Angus continued to strike. With two more blows the limb was severed.

Genna cradled the stump of his arm and sobbed as Angus pulled off his sword belt and wrapped it above the wound to stop the bleeding. The severed forearm continued to slide off at the same inexorable pace, up the slope of the hill and through the camp, where the men jumped aside at its passage. Finally, the limb reached the chalky earth where the hills washed into the end of the cull-de-sac; there, it was wholly absorbed into the ground as if the appendage was water on a dry sponge.

While the men in the camp watched the grotesque demise of Genna's hand, they had their backs to Ers'Elb. On the shore, cu'Kullah had dropped to his knees in frustration, when the waters in front of him churned and rose up like a hooded cloak, inside of which the drowned corpse of o'Keil could just be discerned. The bodies' right arm shot forward, sliding around cu'Kullah's throat. The big warrior tried to get off his knees, but the waters flowed up the arm and joined the two men like the scarf of death, wrapping in increasing layers about cu'Kullah's neck until his mouth was wrenched open in a silent scream and his bloodshot eyes fluttered shut.

When the grip of Ers'Elb slipped away at the last, cu'Kullah fell on the path and – like Brand – lay still in the darkness as the last vestiges of the red moon slipped away into the trees.

*   *   *

Brand opened his eyes.

He lay on a narrow strip of dark sand, where the water had washed the soil free of the grass above. Wincing as he moved his left arm, he steadied himself and stood up in the shallow waters. Turning back towards the lake, he shaded his eyes from the sun as it shone off of the blue waters. He was able to discern the henge of red stone on the far shore, at the bottom of the track that led back to the narrow vale where the ath'Ale of cu'Kullah had camped. But there was no sign of them now.

With a frown he looked back at the water, which sparked brightly in the morning light. Nearer to shore, it looked pure and inviting, but Brand shook his head.

"Ers'Elb," he said cautiously, "I don't like this at all."

Only the wind whispered a reply as he turned and looked up at the nearer of the two hills, upon whose shoulder he had lain. The grass swayed in the breeze; no track other than the course of the bubbling stream from its crown was apparent.

With a frown Brand shook his head and walked through the shallow water where it lapped against the bluff, until he came to the trough between the two hills. There, he found the sodden pilings of a long collapsed pier. Where the line of wooden pillars ended, an overgrown cobbled track led onto the shore. Making sure to walk between the sets of posts, Brand stepped out of the water and walked onto the ancient road. He paused to listen for a moment, but there was no change to the timbre of the breeze or other sign of danger. With a shrug, he resumed his walk across the cleft between the two slopes.

After a short while he came to the place where the two rivulets from each of the hills joined at their bases. The ruin of a bridge arced over the water, but the collapsed span was narrow enough that Brand could jump it with little effort. The conjoined course continued on, following the slight downward slope until it gathered in a clear pool at the center of the island.

Here, the last of the cobbles was lost to the grass. Brand paused before he reached the end of the way, taking a moment to look over the slopes of the hills and the far side of the shallow valley.

"Well, Angus," he muttered, "this doesn't look like the lair of a corrupted sorcerer. No towers, no ruins..." He shrugged dismissively.

Again he paused, listening to the wind, but there was still no change to the languid flow of air.

"Well, I guess that settles that." He said warily.

Brand turned and walked back to the ruins of the bridge. Stripping off his wet pants and boots, he set them out to dry on the warm stone. Then he padded up to the top of the broken span and sat down, looking over the grassy cleft between the hills with a thoughtful expression.

Once his clothes were dry, Brand stretched and redressed. The wind had finally loitered away, leaving a calm stoicism about the island. With some reluctance, he walked to the end of the old track and took a deep breath. Then he stepped off and into the ankle high grass.

When nothing changed, he exhaled for several seconds in relief. With an abashed grin, he walked over to the pool and looked into the water. But that, like the rest of the lake, held nothing more than clear water laying over a stony depression, with the sun shining on its smooth surface.

"Huh." Brand muttered, somewhat crestfallen. "So, this little pond heals any wound, eh, Angus?" He shrugged. "I think you're gonna be disappointed."

With that, he turned away from the pool and started up the slope of the hill where he had first come ashore. On the crest, he found that the water spilled out of an overturned cauldron of verdigrised brass, half buried in the earth. Out of curiosity Brand ducked down to look inside, but it was no deeper than it appeared; the water simply bubbled out in an unending flow.

"So..." Brand commented with concern, "there's more to this after all."

He stood and looked across the cleft to the crest of the other hill. There, a golden cauldron lay in a similar state. Brand stroked his chin.

"All right, then... The waters flow from a brass cauldron and a gold one? Brass for the al'Aith, gold for the druids. Got it. The question is..." He looked around.

"How does that help me? Shitesat metaphors." He stroked his chin.

"Then, lets see. The torcs of the nobles are brass; the torcs of the druids are gold.

"Brass; gold. The torcs of the freemen are silver. So, where's that?"

With his eyes locked to the ground, Brand searched the hill until the sun was caressing the tops of the forest around the lake. Bathed in the wine-red glow, he made his way back down the hill to the pool below. With frustration, he dropped himself onto the grass and ran both hands through his hair.

"Shitesat Cord'Or magic." He muttered. "I would have thought for sure there'd be a silver basin around here somewhere."

He rubbed his shoulder and grimaced.

"So, what've I got? I jumped up to grab thu'Ked. Now I'm on the island, no sword, but Ers'Elb looks like the holy place Angus described...

"Hmm. I guess I managed to do something right –" He scowled. "Or cu'Kullah did."

Brand stood up and began to pace.

"That doesn't make sense, though. If he pulled it off, I'd be dead. Not here.

"So, what then?" He let out a sarcastic chuckle. "Of course, I *could* be dead... The Cord'Or are *pretty* sure that there's a pretty harsh fate waiting for the dead who *don't* have torcs." He looked around at the island. "But this doesn't seem like any of the nastiness I've ever heard of."

With a sour face, he walked back to the edge of the pool and sat down on his haunches, looking at his reflection. The water was perfectly still, but in the twilight the water reflected more of the sky than the man gazing into it.

With a sigh, Brand reclined on the grass and watched as the first of the stars begin their dance in the night sky. As the evening breeze began to stir once more through the grass the landscape finally lulled him to sleep.

Brand slowly awoke to the light of the nearly full moon casting short shadows though the valley. Favoring his left shoulder, he sat up and looked about. The wind had all but died off once more, draping a mantle of heavy silence across the island. He rubbed his stomach with his right hand and started to stand, when his brow furrowed as he looked at the pool in front of him.

"Huh." He muttered in self reproach. "That'll teach me..."

Brand's face almost seemed to glow in the silvery light of the pool, shimmering silver in the moonlight. Remaining in a crouch, he moved closer until he was poised directly above the water. It did not reflect him, however, or even the moon. Instead, it appeared as if the fluid was mercurial rather than being a mere trick of the light.

With a quizzical expression, Brand slowly reached out towards the pool, so that his hand cast a shadow upon it in the moonlight. But there was no other change to the surface. Lowering his hand further, he touched it gently.

Wide ripples spread out from his hand and spread across the pool. As the waves moved across it the silver sheen seemed to be sucked away, leaving only the water behind them. Brand watched as the ripples struck against the edges of the pool and were slowly lost on their return towards the center of the water. But the silver sheen did not re-appear.

Finally he rose and crossed to the far side of the island, to gaze across the lake towards the forest beyond.

"That's gonna be quite the swim," he said, shaking his head remorsefully. "Looks like I've got my work cut out for me tomorrow."

At that, the wind stirred and gently stoked through his hair as it slipped off the surface of Ers'Elb and stole across the island. He turned with the breeze and made his way back to the pool. With a last, thirsty look into the clear water, he laid back down on the grass and went back to sleep.

Just before dawn, Brand thrashed about on the grassy hillside before he struggled back to consciousness. Stumbling to his feet, he looked around wildly before he bent over, placed his hands on his thighs and took several long gulps of air.

Standing straight, he ran his right hand over his mouth and kept it on his chin as he swallowed painfully, his eyes locked on the pool below him as he struggled in vain against his thirst. Fruitlessly running his dry tongue over his lips, he walked stiffly to the edge of the water and dropped to his knees, leaning out over it to stare at his haggard reflection... Closing his eyes, he reached out and dipped his right hand into the cool water.

After a short pause he pulled it back and opened his eyes again. There was no change in the water. No trace of a wind. With shallow breaths he slowly lowered his face to the water to drink out of the pool.

With a shudder he took just enough to wet his mouth and refresh his stomach, then rocked back into the grassy bank, his body stiff with apprehension. Although the sky slowly grew lighter, the wind was no more insistent. At last he moved back to the edge of the pool and wholly slaked his thirst. Tension sloughed out his body as he sat back again, bringing his hand to his mouth to wipe away the water from his chin...

His eyes grew wide with apprehension.

"Oh, shitesan..." He uttered in shock. The water on the back of his hand was an opaque black.

A wracking cough shook Brand as he shuffled on his back away from the water which began to churn out a thin fog. From the center of the pool came a hiss as frothy gray bubbles crusted across it. Brand tried to stand, but his arms shot to his stomach as wracking pain drove him back to his knees. Still, he could not look away from the pool as the thick fluid in the center slowly arched up and a body floated to the surface.

Convulsive spasms shuddered out from Brand's stomach; his mouth opened and his head rocked forward, but nothing was expelled from his agonized body. The cadaver in the center of the pool sat up. The dead eyes of o'Keil fell upon him.

Uncontrollably, Brand dropped forward as the corpse stood up in the shallow pool and hobbled its way up the bank towards him. The air was being choked from Brand's lungs; his eyes began to roll back in his head as the corpse of the ath'Ale reached down and easily flipped him onto his back.

To Brand's delirious mind the corpse towered off into the very heavens, where the wind seemed to take on a voice of its own.

"Death is upon you," the wind whispered to him, "you have trespassed upon the sacred isle: now you shall be brought forth and judged for all that you have done..."

Unable to further resist the wracking pain, Brand's eyes fluttered shut as his mind was broken by the darkness. The unliving thing standing above him bent over and flipped him back onto his stomach. It cruelly bound his hands behind his back and slipped the end of the cord around his neck in the executioner's noose. That final task completed, the remains of o'Keil seized the fallen man by the ankle and dragged him back to the pool, where both of them were embraced by the black waters as they passed away beneath them.

twoth'Ba

Euwae and Una circled each other around the pell post. Although Una was obviously the older, there could be no doubt that these two ladies were the delight of the same parents' eyes: both of the lithe women had the same heart shaped face, the same pout of concentration as they kept their swords at a perfect angle to deflect the blows of the other; each had the same competitive gleam in their dark brown eyes as the sisters studied each other, searching for an opportunity to take advantage of any mistake; each had her red hair wound about her head in a thick braid as additional padding for the linen hood under the chain mail coif they wore as their only protection during the duel.

Una shortened her step for a pace and Euwae almost fell for the ploy, when the following longer step almost brought her a strike to the arm for her lack of attention. Rather than parry, Euwae turned into the blow and brought her own blade down and out for a jab at Una's legs. Una skipped to the left and laughed; the circling resumed.

From the fence of the cattle pen, Finara watched his older sisters with fascination at their exchange. He was a decade younger than Euwae, but his wild red hair and dark brown eyes were a match for those of the two women now engaged in swordplay. As the circling resumed, he made a sour face and pouted.

"Why do you ALWAYS walk in circles?" His brogue held a plaintive note of anguish.

"The ATH'ALE fight in lines. Why is it you cannot?"

Una laughed brightly.

"The ath'Ale fight in a line to look towards each other, Fin," she explained patiently. "But we al'Aith – "

"Even so bold a nobleman as *you* -" Euwae interjected.

"Al'Aith lead the ath'Ale in battle... We must be ready to fight no matter when nor where we may be." Una finished without missing a syllable or a step. Finara was unimpressed by either.

"When can we ride the horses?" He asked again. "Can we ride them now? You have been going about in circles *all* day."

At that, both Una and Euwae stopped and looked first to each other, then at their young brother. Euwae shook her head and leaned her blade against the pell post.

"He will not be stopping until he has won the day," she said with the conviction of countless other losses of that particular battle. "But he has the way of it: we are none the closer to settling who will ride with him today."

Una laughed again, taking her sister in her arms and giving her a quick embrace.

"I will see to the little ree, Euwae. I've a mind to take in some of the strand after the last storm – And the roan mare has not been given her own reins in a week now."

Euwae reached out and took her older sister's sword.

"Give me that, then and your war bonnet besides. I will see to them while you are off to the shores of the sea."

Una nodded. "A fair exchange, to be sure." She doffed the coif and pulled the braid loose from her head, then straightened the ornate bronze torc on her neck

"By the moon and sky, that is so much the better!" she sighed in relief.

Finara jumped from the fence in excitement.

"Time to ride?" He asked with a blissful expression.

"Aye, you wee pest." Una chided. "Time to ride, indeed."

Heedless of the jibe, the little boy ran off towards the stable.

"You had best be after him, Una," Euwae grinned, "or it will be father's warhorse he will be tearing off upon and no mistake."

She laughed as Una rolled her eyes and ran after their brother, her skirt hiked up to give her long legs room to propel her off in her pursuit. As the two of them disappeared past the stable doors, Euwae gently set her sister's sword and mail on the ground outside the circle of dirt that surrounded the pell post. Then she drew her own blade once more and turned to the thick pole.

Extending her arm so that only the last few inches of the wicked point of her falcata touched the post at the height of her own head, she began the age old exercise of striking pairs of blows on each side of it: two at head height, two at the waist, then crouching to land a final pair of blows at the height of her knees. As she worked her way back up the post, Euwae fell into the long familiar rhythm of the blows and started to sing softly in time to each strike of the steel into the wood.

As Una and Finara emerged from the stable, the young boy looked back at Euwae's exertions, then respectfully up at his sister behind him.

"Is Euwae angry again, Una?"

Una followed his gaze and shook her head no gently. "No, Fin. But she is always happiest when she is singing to her blade... And our swords need the practice, too, if they are to serve us well."

Finara looked back at Euwae, her sweat gleaming like dew in the sun.

"Father will give her a named weapon some day, Una, will he not?"

Una looked from Euwae to Finara. "The gifting of aes'ree is for the druids to decide, Fin."

He nodded solemnly, but Una smiled.

"You look just like father when you do that, Fin." She admitted with playful respect.

Finara beamed with pride. Una tapped the flanks of the horse and turned the reigns towards the gap in the bluff that led down to the shore; behind them, the steady beat of Euwae's pells followed as best the wind would allow.

When Euwae's song ended, she gratefully lowered her arms and rose from her deep stance. As she sheathed the weapon and shook out of her chain mail hood to wipe the sweat from her brow, she was startled to hear another person speak.

"Euwae," her mother said respectfully, "have you seen Finara?"

Euwae turned to face Meeruen. The queen of twoth'Ba was dressed in a long green gown with a high collar designed to accentuate her thick golden torc, capped with serpents who each devoured a large ruby, which guarded her throat. Like her children, her hair was red, although it smoldered at her temples with the first touches of age. But that brush had yet to engrave itself into the noble features of her face and she looked every inch a worthy ree of the largest twoth of all the Cord'Or.

Euwae bowed her head in respect before answering.

"Yes, mother. Una took him to the shore, on the back of the roan mare."

Meeruen began to walk towards Una's sword and armor, but Euwae stepped forward quickly and scooped them up first.

"I promised I would see to them," she said quickly. Her mother smiled knowingly and touched her on the shoulder.

"I am sure you did, my dear... As I am sure you will."

Side by side, they turned and walked back to the great hall of twoth'Ba.

*   *   *

Well after the evening meal, Euwae sat at the trail head which led down to the sea of isle'Eh. The sun was just about to set, casting a great shadow from the cliff across the strand and waves beyond. The young woman's loose hair whipped around her head and face in the evening breeze; heedless of that nuisance, she raised her chin and sang out to the sea:

As I sip mead from a clay mug
Two scents entwine
Mead wafting in the wind
And yours from my memory

As I lay in my sleeping furs
My dreams entwine
For now, the mead is gone
But your memory remains

While she sang, a pair of shadows rose on the right bank of the pass as two people walked into the furrow between the hills and down the trail. Una, clad in a blue dress with a low bodice led the way, with their brother Kelleu walking close behind. Dressed in a padded gown, he carried the long staff of a shaman across his shoulder as he made his way down the path behind Una.

When Euwae began to end the song with a reprise of the first verse, her siblings joined in, carrying the harmony to her strong alto voice. Once the last notes faded away on the wind, the three of them looked out across the waves as twilight threw a cool blue cloak across the world.

Una moved behind Euwae and put her arms around her; their hair mingled in the wind as she gave her sister a sympathetic hug.

"Do not be worrying, Euwae," Una said comfortingly, "to be sure, father will be back soon."

"But will it be in time?" Euwae asked plaintively. Turning to Kelleu, she continued. "You said the red moon would be tonight. Tonight!"

Kelleu nodded.

"It will... I have seen it in the leaves of the alder –"

"And the alder moon only comes *once* a year." She added mournfully.

"That may be, Euwae," her brother continued. "But the summer is barely upon us. When the alder moon comes late upon the spring, it is sure to come early for the next two years to come. Even if –"

"Hush on it, Kelleu!" Una scolded. "Father has never failed in his word to anyone, al'Aith or freeman. It is sure that he will not be failing his own flesh and blood in so great a matter as this."

Kelleu started to reply, but a heavy lidded scowl from his older sister bludgeoned it from his lips.

"That is so," he agreed instead. "And the al'Aith of the Confederation do not make their lair so far away as they once did, after twoth'Ba laid them so low two years ago."

Una mouthed a silent 'thank you' to Kelleu, but said aloud, "So there, then. If your brother the druid says it must be true, then true it must be. The sight *is* upon him; you know that."

Euwae turned from the sea to look at her brother. Her brown eyes locking firmly with his green ones, she swallowed and spoke hopefully, "Is it true? Has the sight shown you that father will return in time to treat with the priest and hear the word of Ard'Ree?"

Kelleu's hand went to his golden torc. He turned away from his sister and looked out across the sea as night shrouded it.

"You *will* have an aes'ree, Euwae." Kelleu said, his tone quiet and restrained. "I have seen it. And not a mantle or a ring: a named weapon of wide fame and reputation, indeed."

"A sword," Euwae sighed. "Oh, Kelleu – Thank you!"

She slipped free of Una's arms and gave her brother a great hug. His arms raised slowly as he reluctantly returned her gesture; his wide eyes looked up at the moon, then sought out Una's and he shook his head 'no' after his younger sister had charged in with her celebratory embrace.

Una chewed her lip for a moment, then gently freed Kelleu from Euwae's embrace.

"Come, now," she said gently. "Mother will be putting Finara to bed soon and you know as well as any what a battle that will be on the night father is due to return."

Euwae released her brother and laughed.

"So true!" She smiled. "Come then, the two of you. I will run you back to the hall!"

Euwae sprinted off, but Una shook her head.

"You go," she prodded Kelleu. "I will be no match for her in my gown and that is the way of it."

Kelleu rolled his eyes, but ran after his sister none the less.

As they cleared the lip of the gap, Una turned once more to face the ocean.

"Do not dally, father," she said sadly. "You have never failed your word – To anyone..."

Pulling her hair out of her eyes and freeing it from the horse heads on her thick bronze torc, she followed his sister and brother back up the trail, but she turned and raised her hand in a final farewell to the sea as she crested the rise.

*   *   *

Kelleu's eyes shot open in the deep shadow of dying embers.

In the room around him, his family slept peacefully. He could discern Una amongst the sleeping furs near the fire; Finara slept on his raised pallet with two of the hounds at his feet. Across the chamber, his mother lay on the large sleeping bench, her arms outstretched towards the space his father would fill once he returned from the voyage to collect the tribute of the Confederation.

He tugged at the gold torc around his neck, idly rubbing his thumb across the emerald eyed stags head caps after freeing his long blond hair from underneath it. Then he sat up in his own furs, slipped into his soft boots and padded out of the room and into the great hall.

Here, the warriors of his father's court who were not on guard slept on the benches pulled back against the wall. At the head of the high table, his sister Euwae slumbered beside the ree's high seat, her head tucked onto her forearms and her hair spilling like flowered honey across her face and over the table's edge.

Making as little noise as he could, he padded across the room, past the trio of ath'Ale who stood sentry at the outer door and breathed freely in the cool air of the courtyard beyond.

The night was quiet; he could even hear the sounds of the waves on the shore, far beyond the lowing of the slumbering livestock outside the court proper. Turning to the west, he noted with curiosity the red moon which blazed low above the turf roof of the hall of twoth'Ba.

Another door yielded in the darkness. Soon Kelleu was joined by his mentor, Raf'Em. The old shaman maneuvered unerringly to the younger druid, who still looked west into the sky.

"You dreamed of it." The old wizard said quietly.

"I saw the Ancient Forest..." Kelleu agreed. "And - A deep lake, whose dark waters were bound by stones carved with the old *runes*. I felt hunger and thirst, although I knew I was sated. I was touched, although I was alone. And I knew – I knew..."

Raf'Em nodded.

"When I saw the weavings of the druid within you, I knew that the traditions of the shaman would open your eyes to the world." He said proudly. "And rightly so: you were already well along in knowing the songs all the world whispers to the keepers of the ancient ways.

"But, now..." his eyes were wide with realization and he whistled softly. "You have wandered deeply into the Ancient Forest, tonight... Deeper than most will ever go; trod ways so old that only Ard'Ree knows the truths of them all. But I know of the waters you speak. In fact, I have with my own eyes looked out beyond the stones that keep watch over the banks and beheld Ers'Elb."

A start shot through Kelleu like he had been doused with water steeped in ice.

"Ers'Elb..." The young man said, his voice quivering.

Gravely, the old druid nodded.

"All the folk of Cord'Or know the three deaths that await us; these three taboos that we cannot break are our privilege to bear, as those who stand proud as the Folk have always done. One is given us when we come of age; another when we are chosen by our torc and shown the glory of en'Och."

"And the first" continued Kelleu, repeating the familiar rite "is that which is whispered to each babe by a shaman when we are born."

"Just so," Raf'Em beamed, "and of the three, this one geas – this one taboo – is unknown to all but the most bold among us, who choose to undergo a rigorous pilgrimage and seek to discover it for themselves."

He smiled but shook his head with conflicted emotion.

"Like all those who believe themselves strong enough to carry such burdens, I sought to know what secret doom awaited me; what geas had been seen at the moment of my birth that would be my death, should I ever break it. As a shaman, whose magic is rooted with the knowledge of the Ancient Forest, I believed my skill and insights would shelter me from the perils of that journey." A sad smile crept onto his face. "Such are the wisdoms of youth."

Kelleu let out his breath sharply and shook his head. "Yet you succeeded."

"Hmm?" Raf'Em shook off his reverie. "Oh, yes. I found Ers'Elb. But I did not succeed.

"My prince, the wellspring of our geasa does not bow to the idle fancies of men. The power there stems from places beyond our understanding. I knew the old words; I knew I could pass the stones and trod the moon path down the shore. I had my sacrifices prepared and the need to know my secret bane burned like coals in my heart."

Kelleu's green eyes shone as he studied his teacher's face in the moonlight.

"Yet you did not." The prince said at last.

"No..." Raf'Em agreed. "No, I did not." His gaze threaded the long paths back across the years as he spoke.

"I saw that no trees grew near the stones, nor upon the shore. And I thought that odd... For what has the Ancient Forest – which has grown ever stronger, even in an age as dark as this – to fear? The trees could have reached to the waters had they wished, of that I was certain."

As his narrative continued, his voice began to take on an odd tone which Kelleu had not heard from the old man before.

"I recalled the tale of the noble druid who, beloved of Ard'Ree, was gifted the healing springs of Ers'Elb but betrayed that trust by poisoning the land with the dark fruits of servitude to the Power of the south."

"That is but legend." Kelleu interjected.

Raf'Em nodded. "So it is. Yet, gazing upon Ers'Elb, I heard the whispers rustling through the Ancient Forest around me. I saw, stretched before me, the black waters. And in my heart my magic wove itself sadly, while my mind put words to the tune:

Beyond mortal days

Lost Hopes' artesian artery

Draught and wine of Fate

Kelleu shivered again.

"That is what I heard," the younger shaman whispered fearfully, "in my dream."

The elder druid nodded almost imperceptibly, with a trembling in his beard that was not caused by the wind.

"I began to see in this the way of it, that Ers'Elb was seeking *me*." He continued at last. "And now waited... Waited for the words to blind the stones, for my body to warm the path with my presence... To feed the black water with my sacrifice."

He exhaled heavily under the weight of that dark realization.

"That place is awash in tides of things long forgotten and days bathed in fires and darkness not of this world's making. Men have no place – no right – to cast ourselves in such depths." His ancient eyes looked at things that Kelleu was relived he could not yet perceive.

"That the waters there *are* the birthplace of every doom of the Cord'Or may well be." He continued at last.

"But I understood at that moment Ers'Elb's mysteries are such that opening ourselves to even one of them is far worse a fate than not knowing all there is to know about ourselves."

Kelleu turned back to the red moon, glowering low on the horizon.

"Even if that mystery is the secret of how we will die?"

The old druid let out a snort.

"Even so." He said with complete conviction.

Kelleu looked back into his mentor's eyes.

"Then why did I see this?" He asked with concern.

Raf'Em reached out and clasped his shoulder reassuringly.

"The Ancient Forest calls to its stewards for many reasons." He said calmly. "But not one of them is to seek to do us harm.

"Whatever is in those winds, Kelleu, rest assured that this vision, if it *is* a mystery, answers a question you simply have yet to ask."

Despite the comfort of his words, the older shaman did not remove his hand from the shoulder of his student as they stood together in the darkness, watching the red moon sink out of sight behind the hall of the twoth'Ba until the last glow of it was lost beyond the western horizon.

*   *   *

The moon had long since set as Bayl'Ors Eye slid smoothly onto the shore, the warriors at the oars gave a final strong pull before slipping them from the locks and heaving to. The al'Aith of the vessel started calling out orders, though the crew, long accustomed to such tasks, already moved across the strake in the center of the ship to secure the heavy linen sail. Lohvtreu, ree of twoth'Ba, pulled his gray-red hair back from his face and close cropped beard as he respectfully watched those sailors who jostled like dancers across the narrow spaces and confines of the long ship seeing to their collective tasks.

Konner rose up from the bench in the stern of the ship and stood beside the ree.

"They are happy to be home at last," he said with a smile.

"That is the way of it, for any whose path leads across the waves of isle'Eh." Lohvtreu replied with certainty, turning to gaze back out upon the bleak gray sea as it churned restlessly under the stars. "We have had a lucky voyage, Konner: the Confederation was quick enough to pay their tribute this year, with none of their usual bluster. Better yet, the skies held nothing but wide views and favorable winds.

"Yet I am gladder still to be back to the halls of twoth'Ba at last and no mistake."

"Aye," Konner nodded. "Remind me I shall be needing to thank old Raf'Em for his insisting we leave early for the isles this year... His word was as true as song."

Lohvtreu grinned as he turned back to Konner.

"Fair words for your old rival? This voyage *was* wondrous, indeed!"

"A priest is expected to dispense the truth, my al'Aith," he said in feigned injury, "even if that truth goes less than well with us."

The ree clapped the druid on his upper arm and nodded.

"And you do so fairly, Konner" He said with conviction. His brown eyes locked with those of the priest. "It was most well, having your companionship across the span of isle'Eh. But sure, your good wife and your new son are of a different mind, eh?"

The ree smiled kindly. "The captain and I can see to the rest of it." Then he rocked his head towards the wide trail leading up the bluffs.

"Get going, you. On my word, I will not be calling on you before the next full moon has ridden twice over upon the hall. Until then, I shall see to it that none venture over the moor to disturb Konner Knot-Spender in the Halls of Summersford."

Konner started to reply, but Lohvtreu raised his finger in a sign of dismissal.

"Go, lad. Give our best wishes to your bride."

Konner closed his mouth but the corners of it rose slightly.

"Aye, my al'Aith."

Konner started forward across the deck, but turned to wave farewell to Lohvtreu who then turned back in dismissal, watching the waves as they boiled fitfully across the bay. Shaking his head while his broad grin gave birth to a full smile, the priest disembarked. By the time the ree turned back to the shore, Konner was already halfway up the track towards the top, jostling through the ath'Ale who made their way down the slope to escort their ree and his treasure back home.

As those warriors made their way across the beach, Konner turned at the gap and tossed a salute back towards the ship. Lohvtreu returned it – Then swore loudly.

The captain turned and strode back to the stern.

"Is there some problem, then?" He asked with concern. But the ree shook his head.

"No, Fergus," he reassured the captain darkly. "All is well here."

Fergus continued to look concerned, however, so the ree continued balefully.

"But I shall be coming home to less than a heroes' welcome and that is the truth."

"I do not see the wise of that, my al'Aith."

Lohvtreu rolled his tongue through his right cheek and across the inside of his lower lip and shook his head, his eyes fixed on the gap in the hills where Konner had slipped away.

"Before we took sail, I pledged to my daughter a matter of some importance – But I fear I will not be keeping it."

Fergus spoke reassuringly. "I am sure that al'Aith Una will understand. She is, after all, a worthy lady in her own right – And acts to earn that respect, with all the folk of twoth'Ba."

The ree let out a quick breath of satisfaction.

"Aye, that is truth, captain. And I thank you... Yet my word was given not to Una, but to Euwae."

The captain followed Lohvtreu's gaze and chewed his lip.

"Ah." He finally managed.

The ree shook his head again, then gave the captain a nudge on the shoulder.

"We had best get to this, Fergus," he said with consternation. "We both have a bit of work ahead of us yet and no mistake."

Once the casks of treasure had been passed to the warriors on the shore, Lohvtreu took his leave of the captain and allowed his folk to see to their tasks as he made his way alone up the trail. At the crest of the rise, he caught his breath: the hall of twoth'Ba, with its ancient stone walls and turf roof stood like a fortress of the hearth in the torch lit courtyard and never failed to stir him so after a long journey.

The ree breathed deeply, his eyes watering; but he brusquely swept away the moisture and strode purposefully across the open pasture and through the gate into the flagstone paved courtyard. At the pell post across from the stable, he paused and looked it over thoughtfully before he continued on to the three ath'Ale dutifully guarding the ornately carved doors. They nodded in respect at the ree's approach; he responded in kind and they stood back to allow him to enter the great hall beyond.

His eyes, accustomed to the nighted darkness, took just a moment to take in the span of the room. The benches along the walls were in slight disarray, as the men had hurried out to see to the arrival of Bayl'Ors Eye. Only one figure remained.

Euwae's shadow filled the space at the far end of the hall as she arose at the head of the feast table. She stood, her hands clasped together, her eyes wide with joy.

Taking a deep breath, Lohvtreu, ree of the twoth'Ba, bane of red caps and marauds and vanquisher of the Confederation, walked slowly into the calm before the storm with his shoulders set and his jaw clamped tightly shut.

*   *   *

Meeruen slipped behind Lohvtreu and wrapped her arms around his thick waist.

"Sure, but there was nothing to be done, my ree." She said quietly. "It is no fault of yours that led you to return so late. Had you been in your halls,

Euwae would have reminded you of the rites of the aes'ree and that is the way of it."

The ree's hands slid down her arms until they covered hers.

"But the deed is done," he said sadly, "and my own blood is the worse for it."

Meeruen squeezed her husband. "It is, sure as not, something she shall be forgetting soon enough once some new fancy takes her eye.

"And she knows you love her as greatly as any – And no less, for being kept so."

Lohvtreu turned in the lady's arms, so that he could wrap his own around her.

"You are wise in a great many things, my love," he said quietly, "but in this I think you are mistaken.

"There is fire in the en'Och of Euwae the likes of which I have rarely seen, in all those I have come to know." He chuckled sadly. "She feels that the priests are all but bound to pronounce her worthy of aes'ree... And I would to be struck dumb should she be wrong in it. You have seen her at the pells –"

"Aye."

"And in battle there is en'Och enough for five men in that heart of hers, young as she is... She has never failed to prove it."

"But Lohvtreu," the lady said gently, "you yourself said she put up not so much as a ill word when you told her the way of it."

"No, she did not... She simply said 'So be it.' and went to bed straight away."

"There, then. Do you not see this as the end of it?" Meeruen said reassuringly, as she leaned back and tugged at his heavy bronze torc so that the braying mouths of the horses rested equally on either side of his throat. "It is not to be worried over, then."

The ree pulled back and looked deeply into his wife's eyes.

"You do not, in all honesty, believe that..?"

Meeruen swallowed and rocked her head slightly to the left.

"No." She said at last.

Lohvtreu let a sad smile escape him and hugged Meeruen tightly once more.

*   *   *

"SO – " chunk.

"UN – " chunk.

"FAIR – " chunk.

Euwae's sword bit deeply into the pell post with each syllable as she circled it like a shark stalks a lost sailor. The usual crowd of warriors had gathered to the practice field. All but the youngest of the ath'Ale paid her little mind, their furtive glances speaking volumes about their experience with the princess and the black moods that consumed her.

"SO – " chunk.

"UN – " chunk.

"FAIR – " chunk.

Through the outer press of sparring combatants, Una and Kelleu made their way to the pell circle. Kelleu was contrite, his head down, but was swept along none the less by strength of his sister's presence as she approached. Euwae had already been at the pells for a good while; the log was deeply rent by the strikes of her falcata and she was drenched in sweat. Her eyes tracked the approach of her siblings, but she gave no sign of recognition once they reached the edge of the circle.

"SO – " chunk.

"Euwae..." Said Una quietly.

"UN – " chunk.

"Euwae..." She repeated directly.

"FAIR – " chunk.

"Please."

But Euwae did not stop, until Kelleu stepped beside Una and confronted his sister.

"I am sorry." He said earnestly.

Euwae's sword stopped in mid-swing. Her head swiveled to face him as if it were locked to her shoulders, cold fury graven into her eyes. Yet Kelleu did not flinch or back away.

"Do not *speak* to me." She said quietly, lowering her sword.

"But I *am* sorry, Euwae. More than you could know."

Euwae let out a quick, wild shriek and spun on her right heel. Her left foot whipped up and the kick came close enough to Kelleu's face to leave a spatter of mud across his cheek; it hit the battered pell post with enough force to crack it.

"I SAID – " she screamed.

"EUWAE!" Shouted Una. "How *dare* you threaten our brother so!"

"Brother!" spat Euwae. "He is not *my* brother."

Euwae stepped forward so that her face was just inches from Kelleu's.

"He is just a hostage – Sent to father by some pitiful al'Aith who has not the wits to defend his own twoth and keep the deer in the meadow from making off with it all." She poked her brother in the chest.

"Too weak to stand alone; not enough en'Och in his blood to dare try." She poked him again, hard enough that he winced. "Too – "

"Euwae!" Una said in a low, dangerous tone. "*That* is enough."

Euwae was unmoved. She stared up into Kelleu's eyes, her nose almost touching his chin.

Kelleu blinked. "What I told you was true..." He said with quiet determination. "You will – "

"LIAR!" Shouted Euwae, pushing Kelleu hard enough with her free hand that he stumbled to the ground.

"Oh, you think yourself so *wise*."She sneered. "The mighty shaman of the Ancient Forest. You who can see so many things, eh? But what good are the visions of a man who will not speak the *truth*?"

She took a step forward, her sword raised. But Una stepped up behind Kelleu, her jaw set.

"If you make to strike him, Euwae, you will be the worse for it and no mistake." Una said coolly.

"Are you of a mind to defend him, then?" Her sister replied, with her eyes still locked firmly on those of Kelleu.

"As much as you are, should you wish to see him harmed."

With a shout, Euwae leaped over Kelleu and threw herself onto her sister.

Una deftly stepped to the side and manged to knock the sword from her hand, but Euwae landed a counter punch that knocked Una onto the flat of her back, then dove on top of her.

When Kelleu stood up and fled for the hall, the ath'Ale around them could no longer ignore the brawling al'Aith. The warriors of twoth'Ba dropped their own weapons and rushed over to break up the fight.

Two took Euwae by the arms and pulled her off her sister. The first of them took her heel to his groin and sagged over breathlessly. She spun and swept the legs out from under the second, toppling him onto the first.

Una rolled to her feet and rushed into her sister. Catching her by the stomach she wrenched left and put them both into the dirt around the broken pell. But Euwae's hands were quick and Una was unable to land any strikes before her sister's legs snaked up and caught her under the arms and pulled her off.

Euwae attempted to dive on top of her sister, but again the circle of warriors around them interfered. A woman took her by the wrist and pulled her off to the side. Euwae fell to the ground and pulled the woman down with her, putting the heel of her right hand against the woman's chin and forcing back her head until the princess was able to land a wicked strike to the side of the warrior's head with her left that sent the warrior's helmet spinning as she fell senseless to the ground.

Una had made it to her feet before someone took hold of her shoulder from behind, but she threw a back fist and hit the warrior's nose with a crunch, smiling with grim satisfaction as her sister rose to face her.

They circled each other for a moment, waiting for any opening on the part of the other. Una threw a few testing punches towards Euwae, before her sister managed to seize her arm and twist it savagely. Thus engaged, two more warriors jumped forward to Una's rescue; one grabbed Euwae by the hair from behind while the other locked her free arm into the same hold that she was using on her sister.

Euwae released Una and kicked back at the man on her arm, hitting his knee and drawing a yelp of agony as he sank down. She swung her arms about in a futile bid to grab the woman who had her by the hair, but the ath'Ale leaned back to keep out of reach. Finally, the princess spun so that she was facing the woman, who quickly then let Euwae go and retreated back into the crowd, her hands raised in admission of defeat.

Panting, Euwae and Una locked eyes again and failed to observe that the warriors around them suddenly began to thin like dry leaves caught in the autumn winds; their circle broke entirely as Lohvtreu and Meeruen advanced relentlessly upon the princesses. At the edge of the track around the pell post the rees finally halted, their shadows falling starkly between their two daughters as the rulers of twoth'Ba looked at the five warriors laying about them.

"Enough." Lohvtreu said with finality.

As one, the two princesses turned with a motion so familiar it seemed to be choreographed when they faced their parents. Una dropped her hands and walked off proudly towards the hall without a backwards glance. Euwae's chest heaved as she stared at her father.

"Euwae – " Meeruen said gently, but to little purpose. Her daughter raised herself haughtily and wiped at the blood in the corner of her mouth before she turned her back on them and strode off towards the gap in the bluffs.

The rees exchanged a meaningful glance before they called to the others to help attend their injured.

*   *   *

The music fought a losing battle against the raucous conversations boiling up from the tables arranged along the walls of the great hall, as the ath'Ale regaled each other with the tales of their deeds while they had been away with – or from – the ree. At the center board, Lohvtreu sat next to Meeruen. To his left sat Una and Kelleu; to the queen's right, an empty chair stood between her and that of Finara. Despite the jovial atmosphere, the family of the rees seemed somewhat detached from the festivities celebrating the success of the voyage and the warriors' safe return; only their youngest member seemed to be enjoying the same moment as the retinue of the court of twoth'Ba.

After the singers had finished and the musicians moved to the center of the hall to take up a merry reel, Finara glanced at the empty seat.

"Mother," he asked around a mouthful of roasted boar, "when will Euwae come out to eat? She did to promise me a dance when father came home."

For the fourth time, Meeruen took a shallow breath and composed herself before she turned to face her son.

"Your sister is feeling not her best, this evening." She replied kindly. "Surely, were she able, she would be the first to take your hand and step out with you."

"But mother," Finara replied, "should she be taken ill, cannot Kelleu but give her a potion to make her right?" The young boy leaned across the empty seat and looked at his mother with gravity. "He is a right wise shaman, now and that is the way of it."

Meeruen's smile shone, despite herself." "Is he, now?"

Finara nodded with importance. "Oh, aye!"

He leaned closer and said conspiratorially, "I have even heard Raf'Em say it was so."

Meeruen nodded gracefully.

"Well, then, my thanks to you, Finara. You are indeed wise to the ways of things." She said with amused formality. Finara beamed.

"So, shall it be done?" He asked earnestly. "In truth, were she to attend the feast even so, I am certain that she would be the better for it..."

Meeruen bit her lip, but her smile never faded. She nodded in solemn agreement.

"I am certain that you have the way of it and no mistake." She said gently.

Finara studied her face, but two servers came past the table with sweet cheese and when he called for some, his eye was drawn back to the swirl of colors and noise as the folk began to dance. While he chewed in time to the music, Meeruen leaned on the other side of her chair; as always, her husband leaned towards her to take in her counsel.

"She should have been changed into her gown long ago." Meeruen said quietly, her eyes focused on the dancers and not on the face of her husband to hide her concern. "Would you care that I see to her?"

Lohvtreu's head rolled loosely on his shoulders as a small frown furrowed his lips.

"No, my love – Our daughter she is, true enough – But a child she is no longer. The night she ventured into the barrow of our ancestors and took up her torc, she stepped out past the chiding of youth. If Euwae is set so upon this fury of hers that she is obliged to show such scorn to all who love her, then there is but little we can do to change that now.

"And more's the pity... For it is her who will be living with the ghosts of such choices in the days to come."

Beside him, Una's head bobbed in time with the rhythm of the music, but her hand continually strayed to the swelling on her left cheek and the deep brown-blue circle under her eye. Kelleu took a sip of mead and made a repentant face.

"I am sorry, Una... She dealt you a solid knock, there, indeed."

Una's head swung towards him, but she kept her voice low, beneath the noise of the revels around them.

"*You* are sorry?" She said incredulously. "After the hurtful things that she said to you, it is I who am sorry. This - " she rubbed her eye "will heal. But to utter such things about your kin..."

Kelleu pursed his lips and smiled.

"No, Una. Rest easy, then. Our father has never been loathe to tell me of my past, nor to turn my eyes away from it."

Una's eyes opened involuntarily. "Turn your eyes away from what?"

Kelleu let free a quick exhalation.

"In truth," he responded quietly, "my father is not a ree, yet nor is he as weak as Euwae would to claim. But a hard al'Aith he does to be and – I fear – one who's en'Och is less than it might be."

"Father told you this?" Una said, her voice thick with surprise.

"No, not that last. Of that, I came to know the way of it amongst the whispers of the Ancient Forest."

Una sat there, stunned. Kelleu reached out and touched her arm gently.

"It is not a shame I bear, Una." He said reassuringly. "I may not be of your blood, but I am proud to be the son of the ree of twoth'Ba... I stand now as your brother and that of the wild Euwae besides. And I shall ever be so, no matter the rages that test our sister in this wise."

Una's eyes started to water, but she let out a small gasp of surprise as Finara tugged at her sleeve.

"Una," the boy said meekly, "Euwae said that she would dance with me."

She looked into his disappointed face.

"Well, then." Said Una brightly, "The al'Aith of twoth'Ba are not ones to be breaking our word, are we?" She rose and lifted him onto the table. "You find us a place to stand and I will be on the other side of the board straight away."

With a gleeful yelp Finara climbed up his chair, stepped over the plates of food and leaped to the floor on the other side of the table before his sister could catch him. With a fond sigh as he dodged through the outer ring of dancers, Una turned, reached out and squeezed Kelleu's shoulder before she slipped out from behind the chairs to join her little brother in the innermost ring of dancers who gathered in the middle of the hall.

As Una rejoined Finara and took his hand amongst the other revelers, Lohvtreu leaned back in his chair, his jaw set in thought until Meeruen touched his arm.

"My al'Aith?" she said quietly. "The court awaits you."

With a scowl, Lohvtreu realized that the room had gone silent. The three rings of dancers now stood arranged, wanting only for the pair who stood both at the center of the reel and their society; all eyes rested upon him set within various masks of urgency and understanding.

He sat up straighter in his seat and swept them all with his own self assured assessment, before Finara stepped away from Una's side and called out to him.

"Father," he said, innocently unaware of the cause for the silence around him, "can the pipers play the March of the Ba now?" He turned towards the crowd and beamed. "That is my favorite, and no mistake!"

With a proud smirk, Lohvtreu and Meeruen rose from their seats with the union of intimate experience. His lady held up her hand, the ree took it and with gentle pressure escorted her from around the seats and table to the center of the room, where the pipers stood at near attention. With a twist of his head, he looked towards Finara and said, "Call the beat, lad."

The young prince swelled with pride.

"Pipers!" He cried. "The al'Aiths and rees of twoth'Ba stand assembled for the March of the Ba!" The pipers smiled at each other and nodded their approval before taking a deep breath and filling their bagpipes with air. As the drone began, Finara turned ceremoniously to his sister and began to count the measure.

"One! Two! Thr –" His eyes grew wide as he looked towards the back of the hall.

Behind the tall chair of the queen stood Euwae. She wore a red dress with a high bodice of rich green that shimmered in the polished eyes of the horses on her bronze torc. Her hair was pulled off to the left, falling over the side of her face, but failed to hide the ugly bruise on her jaw or the badly swollen and split lower lip.

With all of the eyes of the court turned upon her, Euwae took a deep breath before she walked around the ree's table to stand beside Kelleu.

"Brother," she said resolutely, without looking directly at him, "it is not seemly that you stand rooted so and are taking no hand to dance to the reel."

Kelleu looked at Euwae and pursed his lips. "And you, sister."

Shifting her eyes to her father, Euwae clenched her jaw, but raised her hand. With a covert grin, Kelleu took it in his own and led them to stand with the rest of their family in the ring of dancers closest to the ree and his wife. As they made their way to the center of the chamber, Finara looked at his mother and said wisely, "I knew Kelleu would make her better."

Meeruen looked down at her youngest son and smiled in response.

Once the pair had taken their place, the prince again called the tempo out to the musicians. Soon, all of the court were dancing merrily, keeping to it until the last of the mead flasks were finally exhausted and the hearth held nothing but embers.

As the dawn started to chase the faintest stars from the sky, Lohvtreu excused himself from the few revelers who had stayed at it to the last and stepped into the doorway to the outer courtyard.

"It is a long vigil you have been made to hold this night." He said to the three ath'Ale guarding the doors.

The warriors nodded in response, but respectfully did not reply.

Looking into the wan light above isle'Eh, the ree noted simmering darkness beneath it: the first storm of the summer was finally blowing in from across the sea. Turning back to the guards he gestured towards the eastern horizon.

"You have done your turn, here, lads." He said with honest regard. "Get you to the stables and pens. See to the beasts, then take your rest." He added gently. "You've more than earned it, to be sure."

As the three men gratefully took their leave, the ree leaned against the heavy frame of the door and ran his left hand through his hair. He breathed deeply as the warm breeze carried the scents of the ocean and the animals past him and closed his eyes as he slowly exhaled.

"Rest," he said to himself, "aye. Earned it indeed."

At the opposite end of the hall, Euwae sat in the shadows beside her father's chair, motionless save for the flickering gleam in her eyes as she marked the places of the sleeping revelers around the room. One last, dying flare of the hearth showed her lips were tight, her jaw clenched with raw determination. When the deep red glow had faded completely away, her eyes focused at last on her father. But the light never touched her right hand, slowly clenching and unwrapping around the hilt of the sword she had tucked away carefully beside her chair.

twoth'Shan'n

As the sun dropped below the western hills. Euwae dismounted and led her horse between the pillars demarcating the ruins of the overthrown gate.

"Easy, there, Courser," she coaxed gently. "There's none left to find us here and that's the way of it..." She looked at the sad state of the open grounds around them.

"I hope." She added dubiously.

The courtyard was laid out much like that of twoth'Ba, if less grand in scope. She slowly led the horse towards the collapsed timbers that were once the stable and tied off the reigns. While her mount bent at the neck to pull at the tufts of long grass, Euwae drew her sword and stalked across the open space towards the collapsed great hall at the center.

Signs of long lost battle lay about her. Shields, gouged by wear and weather, lay abandoned in a loose orbit that spiraled inwards towards the great hall. The staves of broken spears and the occasional knife lay closer still, but there were no swords or pieces of armor to be seen.

Euwae chewed at the inside of her lip as she moved up the steps and peered through the shattered portal of the feasting chamber. Fire had ravaged the interior, scouring away the beams and trellises until the turf roof had fallen down upon the room below. Near the walls, she could see the blackened timbers and charred treasures that had once adorned them.

"By the skulls of the blessed..." She swore fitfully.

Even in the failing light, the al'Aith could see bones. So *many* bones.

She backed away from the door and turned towards Courser. With ragged breaths she jogged to the horse and unwound the reigns. As she placed her foot in the stirrup, however, she heard a weak voice cry out from inside the remains of the stable.

"Potest aliquis exaudi me?" It whispered hoarsely.

Euwae froze in place, half raised into the saddle.

"Placere adiuva me..." The voice continued. "Perii..."

Euwae dropped back to the ground and slowly drew her sword. Keeping the blade of the bara'Ba reversed along the length of her arm to hide the sheen of the light along the length of the blade, she advanced on the wreckage of the door and peered inside. The roof of the building, like that of the great hall, had suffered a collapse from fire; its turf now formed an inverted dome inside the thick stone walls, where water now collected like a great bowl.

Struggling in the shallow pool was a half naked man. A thick leather cord was wrapped around his neck and bound his hands behind his back in an

47

upward position; a fading bruise darkened much of his left shoulder. His body was thick and muscular, painted with the scars of the veteran warrior; his wet, long black hair hung down obscuring his face as it caught in the stubble of his beard.

Her own face a mask of concern, Euwae lowered her sword and clambered up onto the grassy interior of the building. At the sound of her arrival his head rolled back awkwardly.

"Quae citadel tu veni ex?" He croaked anxiously.

"Just lie still there, ath'Ale. I have to cut you free, before you go off and choke or drown."

She slowly brought her sword around and his eyes went wide. His pupils were so dilated that they seemed to be more like holes boring into his skull, but he did not panic; instead, he lowered his head in a gesture of acceptance.

"Good enough, then." Euwae said comfortingly. "Don't move..." She slipped her blade between the man's back and the cord; with her left hand she gripped the leather above the blade to keep the pressure off the man's neck.

"Would that I had myself a knife!" She muttered as she began to saw away at the tough material. She had no choice but to put more pressure against his bound hands, pulling his arms back further, but the man made no sounds of discomfort or protest. At the last, her sharp weapon made quick enough work of it; once the longer raw hide cord was cut, she unwound it first from his neck and then from around his wrists before she gently helped move his stiff arms back to their natural position.

Once she had freed the man, she rolled him gently onto his back. He locked her eyes with his and nodded once.

"Gratias ago vos..." He said with a raspy voice. "Non turbabit vos amplius." He tried to stand, but his arms and legs refused to support him.

"Uh, you are welcome, most certainly." Euwae said coolly, her face a mask of exasperation.

With effort, she pulled the man out of the water, made her way out of the ruined building and back to her horse. Courser hadn't wandered far; she led him back to the post and tethered him again, freed her pack from the saddle and went back inside.

The al'Aith pulled a blanket from her satchel and placed it over the stranger. Courser let out a brusque whinny; Euwae rolled her eyes, went back outside and saw to the grooming of the horse. By the time that chore was done, the sky was dark and the wind from out of the hills was starting to whistle through the debris in the abandoned estate. She wrinkled her nose and looked back at the great hall.

"No ghosts tonight, if you would be so kind." She said with little conviction. "I will keep to your courtesy and stay but the night and in the stable besides; once the sun rises to grace your court again, I shall be the more thankful for your kindness the evening agone."

With that she levered herself back into the doorway and onto the fallen turf roof.

"Well, that is a good sign, then." She said as she observed the man had turned and wrapped himself in the blanket. His breathing now lifted the cover with regular motions of sleep.

"Rest will serve you well, after what you have been seeing to." Euwae said softly as she went to him, pulled the pack open and rummaged out some food.

"You had best not be snoring, though." She added sarcastically as she ate her meager ration.

With her meal taken, the al'Aith took out her sword again and climbed up to the corner of the old roof, where it still butted against the highest corner of the wall. Setting her back to it, she stretched out her legs and laid the sword across her lap.

"Rest well, the two of you." She said to the horse and the man that she had freed, before she drew her cloak around her and settled into it, getting as comfortable as she could for the night ahead.

*   *   *

Euwae pried open her eyes in the nighted darkness as the cold hand wrapped itself across her mouth. She whipped her sword up and held it to the throat of the man that she had rescued, but he shook his head no; his left hand was raised with a single finger across his lips.

When Euwae nodded that she understood, he moved beside her and placed his back to the wall.

"Just what the –"

He shushed her again and held out his right hand in a closed fist, with the palm facing down. Then he moved it in a circle.

Euwae's right eyebrow shot up.

"We are surrounded then?" She whispered coolly.

He nodded and pointed once at her sword. She shook her head no and held up a single finger. With a grim nod, he took a shallow breath, turned and slid over to the doorway, keeping the raised edge of the turf roof between himself and the gap in the wall; Euwae slid after him and peered out into the darkness.

Three dark clad figures were standing near Courser; a fourth lay beside the horse, having obviously been trampled by it. For the moment they

49

kept their distance, speaking in a guttural language as they pointed at and about the animal, laying their plans to attack it. Off in the distance, two more could be seen prowling about the entry to the great hall. Satisfied, Euwae slid back out of sight down the slope.

Her companion did the same, repeated the fist down gesture and raised three fingers which he pointed towards the far end of the old stable. He lowered one finger and pointed at the remaining two, off towards the gate of the enclosure. Euwae nodded.

"You may not know a civilized tongue, but it is a blessing indeed that you know the hand-speak!" She said quietly.

The man looked at her quizzically, but said nothing. She smiled and shrugged in response to her own comment.

"It is well, ath'Ale." She said and nodded to him.

She raised her left hand and pointed towards herself, then at the back of the stable. She raised three fingers, lowered one. She joined the remaining two and motioned towards the three near Courser; keeping them together she swung her hand in a circle towards the back of the stable. Finally, she pointed at her companion and motioned towards the gap in the stable wall where the front door had stood, extended her thumb and ran it under her throat.

He smiled and nodded once in confirmation of the plan.

Euwae quickly moved to the end of the stable roof. She waited for just a few seconds, then launched herself into the air and over the rear wall with a high piercing wail.

Immediately, the three by the horse ran around the right side of the stable towards the rear of the stable. The man spied a short bow and arrows on the saddle near the horse; he leaped up and ran towards Courser, but the horse was well trained and moved to defend itself. The ath'Ale immediately stopped; he raised his hands to his sides slowly and stayed within the horse's line of sight before he resumed his advance, this time walking slowly and calmly directly at the horse ignoring the fallen body beside it.

He could hear the others closing on his flanks from the gate and the great hall, but he kept his eyes locked with those of the horse until it finally lowered its head and whinnied once. But, having calmed the horse there was now no time left to secure the bow. Instead, he stepped in and pulled a studded wooden club from under the body, giving it a few swings to test its balance as he turned to face the oncoming foes.

Still, he was startled as Euwae vaulted around the corner of the stable at a dead run.

"RED CAPS!" She shouted as she ducked past him and freed the reigns of her horse. "Get on!" She gestured at her mount. "We can outrun them!"

He shook his head in the negative with a pair of quick jerks.

"I can't." He said his voice still rough and hoarse.

"Fine!" Shouted Euwae, as she vaulted on to the bare back of the horse. Then, she looked down at the man.

"Wait." She stammered. "What?"

But there was no more time for conversation. The thick limbed goblins pounded around the corner of the stable but drew up in a line at the sight of a second opponent. With a grin they spread out to surround them both.

"GO!" the man shouted and slapped the side of the horse. Courser took a pair of quick side steps, but stopped as Euwae slid from his back.

"Three are better than one," she said in a hard tone as she watched the other red caps come running across the courtyard to join their fellows. The man said nothing as the eleven misshapen foes closed the ring around them and like a rising tide began an uneven but inexorable advance.

Euwae stepped towards her only ally, but he shook his head.

"Stay with the horse," he said coolly, "they'll be after it first." She shot him a dark look, but returned to Coursers side just as the first of the red caps ducked foward to strike the rear leg of the horse outside Euwae's reach.

But the stranger was quicker. His club knocked the attack wide; as the red cap stepped out to regain its balance he brought the club all the way around and struck it in the exposed knee. The creature yelped in pain as it fell onto its back and scrabbled away to rejoin its companions.

Another came for the foreleg on Euwae's flank. She gauged the creature's leap, tucked and rolled forward so that its momentum carried it into the strike of her bara'Ba and tore a gaping wound across its chest and abdomen. It collapsed in a heap in front of Courser, who reared and crushed it.

Euwae's eyes were wide as she quickly regained her feet.

"They bleed!" She said with astonishment.

"They'll bleed," the man replied with a hard look at the monsters in front of him, "and they'll die."

Three of the red caps fell back and huddled into a frantic conversation while the others began to circle their prey. Euwae stepped back and took up her position beside Courser. Her companion made sure to keep the one that he had injured in sight; soon, its limp was all but gone and he nodded darkly.

"Shitesan," he muttered. Then he called out "Al'Aith! This club won't stop them. I can slow them down, but your blade or the horse will have to finish them!"

"It is well!" Euwae called back. "Do your worst to them; Courser and I will see to your aid, ath'Ale!"

The man rolled his eyes, but kept his tongue as two more red caps charged together. Rather than come at the horse, they ran directly into the man and let their heavy bodies carry the three of them to the ground. The club was dislodged from his grip, rolling underneath the horse and out past Euwae, where another red cap scooped it up before it had come to a stop.

Euwae's eyes were wide when she called out, "Are you well?"

"Just see to – The horse..." he responded through clenched teeth as the three of them jostled about on the ground. Euwae turned and sprung back onto Courser and cried out, "TWOTH'BA!" The horse reared up to its full height and she swung her sword about her head.

"Glory and skulls for twoth'Ba!" She called again.

The three red caps that had broken away to confer looked up at her, their dark eyes gleaming. As the horse dropped back to the ground they looked at each other.

And then they ran for the gate, crying out unintelligibly as they fled.

After a few seconds, most of the others followed, save for the two that still wrestled with the man on the ground. He landed a solid kick on one, but there was little indication that the blow was of any use against his attacker. Euwae threw herself off the horse and into the press, pulling back at the hood of the nearest one and raising her sword to strike it.

But she stepped back and felt her gorge rise as she realized that the creature wore a hat woven from the tanned flesh of a human face.

Sensing her distress the red cap jumped up towards her, but Euwae was far from desperate. She waited until the beast nearly had its hands upon her before making a pair of savage slashes across its belly and spilling its guts across the ground. Stepping around the mortally wounded foe she stalked towards the one which still wrestled with her companion. But it saw her approach from the writhing body of its fellow; rather than risk death itself, it freed itself from the man's grasp and ran with alacrity after the others.

Euwae looked down at the man with passing concern.

"Are you hurt, then?"

His chest was heaving, but he shook his head. "No – No, I'm good." He said. He set his hands on the ground to lever himself up, but Euwae extended a hand to him.

"Euwae," she said with a nod. He took her hand and rose quickly to his feet.

"Thanks." He said in return.

Euwae stepped around and in front of him. "That is no right response, then, is it?" She said with a trace of indignation. "After all I did to save your life this night and that is the truth of it."

"You didn't save me from the red caps." He growled. "I could have handled that."

"Really now?" She said hotly. "With your hands tied behind your back and all?"

The man scowled, looked at the chafing on his wrists and his eyes closed as his head rocked down and to the left. He took a deep breath and looked back at Euwae.

"No," he said in a repentant tone. "Not then."

He balled his right hand into a fist and struck his chest over his heart.

"Thank you, for that."

With a smug air, Euwae smiled. "That is better then." She bobbed her head.

"So, now. I am Euwae. And, you, ath'Ale? With whom do I have the honor of besting the red caps with this night?"

But the man moved brusquely away and back towards Courser. He ran his hands over the flanks of the animal, ducking down to check the legs above the hooves for injury. Euwae balled her fists in frustration.

"Why do you not answer, hiel?"

The man's expression was hard enough to cool even Euwae's frustration.

"Because I don't know." He said bitterly.

"What was that, then?" Euwae asked dubiously. "How can a man not be knowing..." She trailed off as he continued to fix her with the same cold set to his face.

"I..." He shook his head and turned back to the horse.

"He's got a pretty good knock, here. You won't be riding him for a while."

Euwae moved next to him and ran her hands over the knot on Coursers right foreleg.

"Aye," she said quietly, stealing a glance at the warrior's face. "It would seem as if we are bound to stay for a bit longer, indeed."

She turned to face him fully.

"I have known of ath'Ale, to be sure, who lost more than a few of their wits after a solid pounding. It is sure that you know a great deal of horses – Enough that Courser, here, had the sense to see you as a friend, even. There are few amongst the ath'Ale who are gifted with a steed, and fewer still the skills to see it stays hale.

"Are you an al'Aith, then, and not a common bua'Theu?"

Suddenly, her eyes went wide with horror.

"Oh!" her hand shot to cover her mouth. "Your torc! It is gone!"

But the man shook his head slowly.

"I..." He drew his lips back in a deep grimace. "I don't know. I think that is why I am here..."

"To get back your torc?"

"Not exactly." He shook his head. "That doesn't seem right, somehow."

"What, then? Do the red caps have it?"

Again, he shook his head. "No. I'm certain they don't."

Euwae leaned back on her haunches, lifting a hand to Coursers flank for balance.

"When I found you, you spoke an outlandish tongue. I thought then that you might be a corsair of the Confederation, until you showed knowledge of the hand-speak: it is sure that none of the Cord'Or would be teaching that to the pirates!"

Her eyes ran across his body and face. "I have never seen the like of a man like you..." She said quietly. "Do you remember aught of who you are?"

The ath'Ale stood and looked back at the ruins of the great hall.

"I belong here." He said quietly. "All of this –" he gestured towards the ruined and abandoned court and said with dark wonder, "I shouldn't be back..."

Euwae's brow lowered in consternation.

"*You* are of twoth'Shan'n?" she asked dubiously. But the man didn't respond. Instead, he walked off slowly towards the collapsed skeleton of the great hall. Euwae followed, her brows still locked in a deep frown.

He made his way across the right side of the hall, towards the furrows in the hill which once sheltered the doors into the private chambers of the ath'Ale who had lived there. The fire that had devoured the structure left the entries impassable. But he stood there and stared at them, his eyes moving as they followed things that Euwae couldn't see.

At last, she reached out and put a hand on his shoulder. His body went rigid with surprise.

"You know more of this than you are telling, to be sure." She said gently. He closed his eyes and shook his head.

"It's a dream, al'Aith... It's all just a dream, now."

"It is Euwae." She said gently. "You have no need to be so formal with the likes of me."

He turned to her and opened his mouth, but his eyes focused on something behind her before he replied. The man stepped around his companion to get a better perspective in the darkness beyond them and his eyes went wide.

"Shitesa!" He called out and trotted off towards the tumbled edge of the courts well. Reaching down amongst the rocks, he started prying loose a long metal bar.

"What is shitesa, then?" Euwae asked curiously as she followed him at a walk.

"Shitesa?" He said distractedly. "Ah, it's – " He turned and looked at her briefly, then shook his head. "It's not a *polite* thing to say, al'Aith." He pulled the object free.

Euwae grinned ironically at his modesty as she studied the object he had found with curiosity: a metal bar, more than four feet long; at one end, smooth, stained leather wrapped around the base as a handle. At the other end, two protrusions were set at right angles to the bar. Once was a thick oval which reminded her of a large pickle, carved with the face of a bird. The other side was a broad knob that looked for all the world like a flat steel mushroom.

"And *this* is shitesa?" She said after examining it. "It is the worse for all the weather it has seen, to be sure. But for all that there is not but a dew of rust upon it. It is well made for a simple tool."

"This is no tool." Her companion said with near reverence.

She looked into the ath'Ale's beaming face with a mingling of curiosity and distaste.

"What is it, then?" She asked cautiously.

"This" he said with pride "is mine."

"Yours?" She nodded and circled her right hand to prompt him on. "Your... Your what?"

"This is Crows Call..." He said, turning it over and examining it carefully. "It's my aes'ree."

Euwae's mouth dropped open.

"This..?" She stuttered in disbelief. "This – Is named?"

He nodded and began to closely examine the old, brittle looking leather of the handle.

"But... How can THAT be?" Euwae stammered. "Are you but a bua'Theu then? Some carpenter?" She looked at Crows Call in distaste. "And what manner of name is the like of Crows Call for some – Pry bar?"

At that, his head shot up and he locked his eyes on hers.

"This isn't a shitesan tool," he almost growled. "This bec de corbin has served my family for..."

"For..." A look of panic crossed his face as the memory fled and was gone.

"AHHG!" He shouted with sudden frustration.

Euwae rocked back on her heels and crossed her arms. The sarcasm on her face was deep enough to cause the man to clutch the steel object to his chest in a gesture of total retreat.

"Crows Call, eh?" She said, rolling the words in her mouth.

"And you, then. This aes'ree has served your kin since the time of your father's father?"

He nodded uncertainly but instinctive pride still lifted his chin.

"Fine then." Euwae concluded. "Then it is Bird Club I will call you, save that you find better which suits you more."

The ath'Ale rolled his head slightly to the right as he thought about that. At last, he nodded.

"I can live with that." He said in his odd accent, his voice still pensive.

Euwae shook her head and looked away with amused disappointed at his consent to her jibe. She started to walk away, but realized that he wasn't following. She turned and looked back at her companion, whose eyes were still locked on the weapon as he studied it intently.

"Come then, Bird Club," she said haughtily, "and let us see what we can find for fare here abouts. I have enough food to keep our bellies quiet for a short while, but I had not planned as to be stopping on my ride, let alone feeding two besides."

She turned and walked off again. This time he followed, but his fingers continued to wrap around the smooth leather on the handle of his aes'ree with long familiarity as he quietly followed her lead.

*   *   *

The pair decided to move away from the gate and into the shelter of the earthen sheds near the well, before they started to cast about for food. The sun was well into a cloudy sky after they had collected what they could from the fallow gardens. Euwae had the better luck, as the man's broken memories continued to plague him in fits and starts. But he never mentioned it, so she pretended not to notice. Once they had enough to create a fair soup, Euwae set him to preparing the vegetables as she took her small cauldron to the well to fill it. When she lowered it into the well, however, it reached the bottom with a hollow clang.

Euwae looked over the side of the well, shaded her eyes and squinted into the darkness below.

"Bird Club," she called hesitantly, "there is something here in the well..."

Slowly he put aside the tubers and walked over to the well.

"I cannot quite make out the way of it," Euwae said as she continued to look down the shaft. "But whatever lays below us, it is in the way of the kettle and no mistake." She shook the pot at the end of her rope and it rang like an off key bell.

"Just a minute, Euwae." He cautioned, then walked back to their fire and took out a long piece of kindling. Setting it alight, he carried it back to the well and held it over the edge.

"I still can't make it out," he said, pursing his lips.

"Toss it in, then."

He looked at her, shrugged and let the long piece of wood fall into the well. It clattered off several obstructions before it hit the water and sizzled out.

"Well, at least there's water down there." He said cautiously. "But there is definitely something else, too."

"Could you see what it was?"

He scowled. "No." He reached for the rope.

"What are you doing then?"

"I'm going to see if I can pull it up."

She smirked and snatched up the rope, slipping away to the far side of the well.

"It is my mystery, Bird Club and that is the way of it. You just head back to your kitchen... I will do the fishing here and no mistake."

He looked at her across the well and shrugged.

"No mistake." He muttered as he went back to finish preparing the food.

Euwae swung the cauldron about towards the bottom of the well for almost thirty minutes with varying degrees of failure as her companion watched with a grin while he finished skinning the vegetables. Finally the rope grew taught in her hands. With a practiced lift she gingerly she moved it away from the edge of the well and drew it back towards her hand over hand until the weight at the end was close enough for her to see.

"Bird Club!" She exclaimed with delight. "Come and see!"

The ath'Ale rocked to his feet and ran to the side of the well.

Below them, hooked across the rope was the handle of a rusty falcata.

"It is a sword!" Euwae exclaimed excitedly. She started to draw the rope up vigorously, but he reached out a hand and laid it on her shoulder.

"Euwae, don't." he said sadly.

She stopped and looked at him in exasperation.

"But, why? There are aes'ree that you may be finding at the bottom of such a well as this –"

"Not this well."

"And what is it that makes you so sure, now, Bird Club?"

A cool wind stalked across the courtyard and pulled at Euwae's hair.

"Let it go."

I will not. I will lose my cauldron."

"Euwae, please. *Let go of the rope.*"

"And who are you, to be ordering about the likes of me?" Euwae demanded. "You, who claims that your ditch pick is an aes'ree and who is like as not never known the en'Och of the Cord'Or?"

"Euwae –"

"I will not."

The ath'Ale moved towards her, but she kept the well between them easily and took another two pulls on the rope. He stopped circling towards her and raised his hands.

"Euwae, look." He said earnestly. How do you think that sword ended up in the well?"

"Someone tried to hide it, like as not."

"Not, Euwae. You've looked around here. You've seen what happened."

"I *know* what happened, here, Bird Club. The River Prince of the twoth'Shan'n was a close friend to my – " She paused uncertainly.

"To someone I know. A great loss it was, when he and his were taken at night by the Marauds and put to the sword."

He opened his mouth, but ended up waiving his hands in futility as the words failed him.

58

"No!" He cried at last. "This was no maraud raid. They don't leave the dead behind – "

"Oh and you are to be knowing now about the marauds, too – You who have no name?"

"*HE HAS A NAME,*" called out a harsh whisper on the wind, "*AND IT IS A FOOL'S MIND TO BE SURE TO QUESTION THINGS THE LIKE OF WHICH YOU KNOW LESS THAN HE WHO HAS FORGOTTEN IT.*"

"A fool's mind, is it!" Euwae cried out indignantly. "Show yourself, then and I will show you who is more the fool!"

"Euwae!" Cried her companion sharply. "Don't!"

But the challenge was answered.

Courser reared back and screamed, broke free of his hitch and fled across the courtyard.

The wan sunlight struggling through the clouds faded to late evening as the wind howled across the far end of the courtyard. Euwae's eyes grew wide as she stared off towards the ruins of the great hall. The rope slipped forgotten from her fingers, but neither the cauldron nor the sword could be heard as they vanished into the earth.

From the space where the doors to the inner chamber once opened from the ruined hall spilled the pale shimmers of the dead.

Following the paths they had in life, the gossamer forms gathered at a swift pace from the great hall to surround the pair at the well. The ath'Ale moved around the edge of the pit to stand beside Euwae, holding the steel hammer diagonally across his body with his hands spaced wide apart on the shaft. Euwae reached down and drew her own sword, but held it low towards the ground in a less provocative stance.

The dead were hard to gaze upon; their features seemed to shift like a reflection on a quiet pond which slipped from an almost lifelike visage, through a moment of agony while their form wavered to that of a desiccated corpse. They moved so closely together around the pair that there was no clear passage between them through which they could escape.

"Bird Club," Euwae said with a thick voice, "it would to seem I am owing you an apology."

He shook his head. "Not to me." He said with a calm voice. "But I'm not sure what difference it'll make now."

Suddenly, the wind plunged away into utter stillness; the only sound was the heavy breathing of the last living people in the court of the twoth'Shan'n as the dead slowly flowed in upon them. Euwae shrieked as they reached out for her, but the ath'Ale rushed between them and the dead moved slightly away.

"*WHAT IS THIS?*" The wind whined. "*BY HER HAND AND WORD SHE HAS FORSWORN ALL CLAIM TO AUGHT BUT A VERDICT.*"

But he shook his head.

"If the al'Aith is a villain, I haven't seen it." He said quietly. "She didn't call you on purpose."

"*WE ARE NOT HERE AT HER CALL,*" the wind hissed, "*BUT FOR YOURS.*"

At that, he drew back but Euwae slipped in front of him.

"No!" She cried. "It was I and none other, who made to pull the blade from the well. If you must make to strike one of us down, then it should be none but me!"

The man reached out a hand and pulled her back as the dead began to circle around them and swirl into the air. The last of the light faded around the pair, leaving them abandoned in a vengeful darkness lit only by the glow of the ghosts around them.

"*SO BE IT...*" The wind intimated submissively. "*HARK YOU THEN:*

THE EAST WIND BLOWS

IT ALONE KNOWS

OF TWOTH'SHAN'N'S LOST FAME

FROM IT DISCERN

AND THUSLY LEARN

THE NOW FORGOTTEN NAME

WITH THIS ANON

DRUIDS THEREON

SHALL OPEN THE CAIRN'S GATES

WHERE BROKEN RINGS

OF EACH TORC SINGS

WHOSE GEAS THAT AWAITS

AND ONLY THEN

TWOTH'SHAN'N

MAY FINALLY BE FREE

THUS DARKNESS FAILS
AND BLOOD AVAILS
THE CHAMPION AND REE

And with that the al'Aith and the ath'Ale flinched and threw their hands over their eyes to shade them against the unfettered light of the cloudy day, which was free once more and blinded their shocked eyes...

Of the dead there was no sign.

*　　　　　*　　　　　*

Despite their reluctance to stay so near a place of the unquiet dead, the threat of the red caps and the injury to Courser kept the pair in the relative safety of the courtyard, although they made sure to stay well clear of the great hall for the rest of their stay. That night, Euwae sat forlornly beside the fire. Her companion fed another piece of the old animal pen into the flames, then settled down across from her.

"You've hardly said a word since you went fishing in the well," he said with dark optimism. He studied her across the fire.

"You want to talk about it?"

Euwae said nothing. After a moment, he nodded.

"Fair enough. It must be pretty bad, if an al'Aith as proud as you are isn't proud of it."

She looked at him; the growing flames threw shadows across her face like the stains of old blood. She snorted.

"You are not one to be judging me. Memory or no, you have never known the whisper of the torc, nor felt the fires of en'Och burning through your blood. So keep your tongue to yourself, if you have a mind to be keeping it."

A grin split his face.

"Are you – Threatening me?"

Euwae's voice was as cold as the darkness beyond the comfort of their fire.

"You have no idea what I am capable of, *dicenn*."

He leaned back and shifted his gaze into the coals between them.

"Dicenn," he said, rolling the word over in his mouth. "Once." He nodded, meeting Euwae's gaze directly.

"Once." He repeated calmly. "But not any more."

She snorted.

61

"No? And how, if you will, does that come to be? You do not look to be a babe to me... So how else is it that you might be reborn into the blood of the Cord'Or?"

His focus shifted, past Euwae and into the black recesses of his own thoughts. Finally he closed his eyes and shook his head in resignation.

"I wish I could tell you." He said regretfully.

Euwae's face slowly softened at his tone.

"I am sorry," she said at last. Her own eyes drifted away from his and deep into the embers of the fire.

"In truth, I am. I should have no quarrel with the likes of you, Bird Club... It was not you who brought me here, nor who caused even the bitter dead to look down upon me so. You are more than a worthy ath'Ale; in truth, I am the better for your company."

His mouth crept upwards in an unwilling grin.

"Are you sure you don't want to ta-"

"No."

"Fair enough."

"Indeed."

"I was only –"

"You need not only, then. The apology was mine to be making. But I will take this talk no further than that."

"Fair enough."

"Indeed."

He looked at her across the fire. Finally she looked up too and realized he was staring.

"What is it, then?" She asked crossly.

"It's nothing."

"Truly? Nothing?"

"Yes."

"Fair enough." She said, mirroring his tone.

"Indeed." He replied in imitation of her thick eastern brogue.

After another moment of staring, they both broke out into laughter.

Once the fit had passed, he leaned back. His face slipped into the shadows, although the light still played in his eyes.

"Ere the rising of the dead, you spoke of the swords in the well." She said quietly, her composure locked back into place. "To what were you referring, then? If it is, as you say, not marauds who brought fire and ruin to twoth'Shan'n?"

His eyes rose and shifted to the corpse of the great hall behind them in the darkness, then closed in concentration.

"It's – There's something to do with a sacrifice. I can't remember what, or why. But this wasn't done by the marauds." His tone sharpened at the memories. "*Those* shitesannus I remember – I can still see them... As likely to drop on a fallen warrior and eat them as to move on to strike at the next in our line. I don't think they understand death, other than it gets them more to eat.

"When I saw the bones in the great hall, I knew it wasn't marauds."

He sat back up and held out his hands towards the fire.

"It could have been red caps. They don't bury our dead, and don't eat them, either. But when you pulled the sword up in the well, I *saw* something."

"What was it that you saw, then?" She prompted gently.

He stared into the coals, but finally shook his head no.

"What, then?" She said, more insistently.

He looked up at her.

"Are you always like this?"

She pursed her lips in a scowl, but nodded affirmatively. He let out a quick snort and shook his head.

"I saw a sword being thrown away. Not any sword, either; an aes'ree."

"In truth?" Euwae started and stared off in the direction of the well.

He sighed heavily.

"Yes, Euwae. But it's gone, now. It's – Yeah, gone."

"And just what, exactly, is that to be meaning? Gone? As in, lost down the well?"

"NO." He said forcefully and rose to his feet. "Not down the bloody well! It's –" His hands moved futilely through the air as he sought to unearth the words locked in his mind.

"It's gone, shitesat. It's been given – It's been cast away into the..."

His breathing calmed as he looked at the ruin of the great hall.

"Sacrificed. To – " He swallowed with difficulty. "Something dark and old... Something the Ard'Ree put down before any of us were born."

Euwae paled.

"*The Power*?" She whispered in horror.

He shook his head.

"I don't think so, Euwae," he said, without looking at her. "I've heard that the Power strikes away the senses, drives you mad. But this was different."

The al'Aith's right hand moved defensively to her sword.

"You have lost your name, Bird Club, to be sure..."

His shoulders dropped as the tension drained out of him.

"Yeah, I have," he chuckled under his breath, "can't argue with that one."

He turned slowly, his eyes running down her face to her right hand.

"But I haven't gone crazy, have I?"

Slowly, her hand slid back into her lap.

"No," he finished, "this was just... Old. And it wasn't something that wanted *me*, if that makes any sense... It was just – Waiting." He shrugged.

"Truth be told, Bird Club, it makes less than little sense to me. It has the sound of weaving to it, though; that is certain."

He nodded. "I can't argue with that, either. But I'm pretty certain that the magic wasn't anything a druid just calls up."

Slowly the wind stirred around them and whispered across the courtyard. Both of them turned towards the tumbled walls of the great hall.

"We should get some sleep, Euwae." The ath'Ale suggested at last.

As they prepared to settle in, she stopped and looked at him across the fire.

"I have a last thought for you, Bird Club."

"Hmm?"

"If in truth all of the weapons here-about have been cast down into the well – the aes'ree even – then how is it that yours came to be left on the ground beside it, rather than cast down with the lot of them? It would seem to me that such a –" She looked at his weapon and chewed on the name of it.

"Bec de corbin."

"Ah, yes. Such a fine weapon as your bec de corbin there would have been the first to go, as it were."

She looked askance as he sat down with his legs crossed and drew her blanket about him like a cloak, rather than lay down to sleep.

"It's the weapon of a dicenn, Euwae." He said without concern.

She scowled as much at his sleeping position as his answer.

"I can see that, sure enough. But what has that to do with it?"

"We're not Cord'Or..." He replied through a yawn.

Finally, he added, "Not worthy."

Soon, he drifted off to sleep, despite the fact that he was still sitting up. But Euwae lay with her cloak pulled about her and was up through most of the night, unable to slip out from beneath the weight of the thoughts that dueled in her mind.

*   *   *

"FATHER!"

Euwae surged upright, her right hand blindly groping for her sword. With wild eyes she looked about, then after a moment of realization struggled to get her ragged breathing under control.

The fog from the moors still lay heavily across the barren courtyard of twoth'Shan'n, stretching curtains of damp gauze across the ground between the surrounding walls. A short distance away, her companion knelt in front of her horse, examining its foreleg. A small fire sent up a few wisps of sparks from beneath her last cauldron. Straightening her cloak as a mask of dignity, Euwae rose and went to the small pot. Bending over it, she breathed in the fragrant tang of the vegetables simmering within as the man finished with the horse and started back towards the fire.

"You should be able to leave tomorrow." He called out, still some distance away. "But it will be three, maybe four days before Courser can travel any distance; even then, you can't ride him for at least a week."

Once he reached the campsite he picked up the blanket he had slept in and shook it out.

"I'm not sure where you're headed, but stick to the river. I don't think that Courser is ready for the forest yet. And you won't meet any red caps down by the water."

Euwae picked up a stick and poked at the coals.

"I've left you the better part of what we got out of the gardens." He continued conversationally. "It should last you until you reach the next twoth, even if you share a treat with your horse on the way."

He folded the blanket and handed it to her. She reached out and took it without a word. He let out a sigh and shook his head.

"Look," he said with an appeasing tone, "I know you don't want to discuss it. I get it. But you aren't headed east. And I need to get to the sea."

She looked up at him. "And what business is it of yours that takes you to the shores of isle'Eh?"

He rocked his head back towards the bulky tumble of the great hall, draped in its tapestries of mist.

"The dead said – if I want to find my name – I need to go to the source of the east winds. That's isle'Eh... And to get there, I've got to go through twoth'Ba."

She looked back into the coals.

"What makes you think I am not traveling east, myself, then?"

"Seriously?"

"I might be. How would you know the way of it?"

He sighed.

"All right. You're an al'Aith." He shrugged. "You can't hide the torc. And I can't remember which twoth closes their torcs with horses, but I don't really have to. You yelled 'twoth'Ba' when we were fighting the red caps, so that's pretty obvious.

"Since you won't talk about your past, I figure you're not headed home any time soon."

Euwae waited for a moment, then looked up at him. He shrugged.

"Is that all, then?" She inquired, almost brightly.

He looked away.

She reached up and waived the stick at him. "It is not, then, is it?" She repeated, but her voice had fallen back into its melancholy. He faced her again.

"No... Not all. You didn't sleep too well last night; you kept saying 'father'... And muttering."

Her eyes went wide, but she quickly knelt over the fire again.

"And just what was it that I was saying, then?"

Again, he shrugged.

"Other than 'father?' A man's name – Kelleu, I think. And a woman's: Una. I couldn't make out much more than that. You were obviously upset about them."

"And why, then, did you fail to wake me?"

"Look, Euwae –"

She turned her eyes upon him; they were hard with raw emotion.

"Did you listen on, to hear wise of that distress then, too?" She said with bitter majesty.

He looked into the fire.

66

"I heard enough to venture a guess. But, if you want my opin-"

"I have no mind to know what it is that you think of me, ath'Ale." Euwae cut in, rising to her feet. "Is *this* why you refuse to let me accompany you?"

"What?" He looked down at her. "No!"

"Then TELL me!"

"Fine," he relented. "But -"

"TELL me!" She waived the stick at him in a proxy of violence.

"So you left your husband!" He snarled back. "That's what your father gets for arranging a marriage in the first place. Let Kelleu go off with Una. Your father will get over it."

Euwae blinked.

The ath'Ale took in her expression, then rolled his eyes in realization.

"Oh, shitesan. You wanted to marry Kelleu, but your father was making him marry Una? Is that why you ran?"

"What?" Euwae countered, unable to pull the mask of shock off of her face.

He reached out slowly and took hold of the stick, swinging it away from his face. The al'Aith put up no resistance.

"Either way, it's obvious you're on the run, now. But the reason doesn't matter to me." He said gently. "That's done, now, Euwae. You can do what you want with your life." He took the stick away and tossed it into the fire.

Euwae watched it fall and begin to burn.

"You're not just a noble, Euwae," he continued, his voice growing softer, "you are noble. That I *do* know. Don't worry about me; once I reach twoth'Ba, I won't mention you – You've got my word on it."

He looked at her in sympathy.

"And you're *good* with that sword," he continued encouragingly, "and brave enough to face down shitesan red caps with a total stranger. I'm sure there are more than a few princes out there who'll be tripping over themselves trying to catch your eye."

Euwae shot to her feet and turned her back to him. She covered her mouth to hide her smile, but her shoulders still shook as she fought the laughter back.

"Euwae..." He said with sincere resignation, "Hey, I'm sorry. You told me to drop it." His shoulders sagged with pity.

"I'll go." He said with reluctance as he turned and scooped up his weapon. Behind him, Euwae's shoulders rocked back and locked into place; her chin lifted as her hands dropped to her sides.

"That goes the long way indeed to show what you know, Bird Club." She called out regally.

"What?" He turned to look back over his shoulder.

With calculated deliberateness she turned to face him.

"We are weeks from isle'Eh, here."

Her lip curled with mischief at his obvious confusion.

"The east wind. It does not blow with abandon in twoth'Shan'n off of the sea, as it does in – " She caught herself and failed to finish her example.

"It gathers its voice on the moors, to the northeast, then dances through the hills before it takes to following the great river through these lands."

He swung Crows Call onto his shoulder as he turned to face her.

"Really?" He asked, his brow lowering as he studied her face.

Euwae tried her best to look innocent.

"Oh, aye. Indeed." She said innocuously.

"I guess it does show what I know, doesn't it?" He asked with tacit skepticism.

Euwae knelt back down and gazed into the cauldron.

"I am thinking your breakfast is all but served, Bird Club," she said nonchalantly. "And I am suredly ready to be breaking my fast."

"Are you not so?"

With a snort that rolled up through his chest, he shook his head and walked off to get their bowls while Euwae continued to kneel over the pot and smiled, singing quietly to herself.

the Great River

The pair slowly made their way down from the ruins of twoth'Shan'n towards the river. They followed the overgrown track that once drew the traffic of merchants and craftsmen to the abandoned realm. The horse navigated the disused road with only slight difficulty, but they both paid close attention to ensure that Courser was able to avoid the hidden ruts and holes.

On their way, the ath'Ale pointed out the red caps that stalked them from the cover of the forest, but – as he had predicted – the goblins did not leave the shelter of the trees and turned back entirely once they reached the banks of the river.

"And what is it, do you think, that the beasts are fearing?" She asked, as the last of the red caps reluctantly retreated into the depths of the wood.

"It has something to do with the Ard'Ree." He replied. "A priest tried to explain it to me once, but I've never really understood all that druid sorcery."

She looked at him from the corner of her eyes.

"Never understood?" She asked slyly.

"No..." He replied quietly. "Never."

"So, your memories are not so far afield as they once were, then?"

He continued to look straight ahead.

"No, Euwae – They aren't."

She waited for him to continue, but he simply walked on in silence.

"So," she asked after a moment, "what is it that you have been remembering?"

"Are you sure you really want to know?"

"Oh, aye, Bird Club... I have no doubt but that your stories will make the miles fly beneath our feet." She chided.

"Fair enough. I think that, as a runaway, you're in good company. I think I am, too."

"You?" She asked brightly. "And from what might the likes of the brave Bird Club be running?"

"I'm pretty sure I'm cuhm'l."

He didn't look at her or break his stride as Euwae nearly tripped over herself.

"WHAT?" She cried indignantly. "You, a slave? Now, that is quite the tall tale indeed!"

69

Since he continued to walk on, she darted in front of him and walked backwards so she could look at him as she spoke.

"But – You are an ath'Ale! I have – with my own eyes – seen you take to battling with the likes of the red caps and get their better. And you have done so before, I will warrant, given all that you have told me.

"How *could* you be cuhm'l?"

He looked at the ground in response as he kept on, forcing Euwae to continue to back pedal before him.

"But – You know the hand sign!" Still he said nothing. "You – You know the ways of the horse!"

Finally, she reached out and tugged at the bec de corbin. "You are blessed with an *aes'ree*!" She stopped walking in front of him and forced him to do the same to avoid running into her. She reached up from Crows Call and placed a hand on his chest.

"Please..." she said, her lower lip trembling, "tell me that this is not the way of it."

The ath'Ale reached up and removed her hand gently; without a further word he stepped to her right side and continued to lead the horse onwards. Euwae stood there, her lips compressed and her chest heaving. After several moments, she spun on her right heel and raised a finger in objection, but he was too far away to see it. She stamped her foot in frustration, then ran after the man and her horse.

She was breathing heavily once she reached them, but he simply kept following the course of the river at the same, inexorable pace. Although she looked at him often, the ath'Ale offered up no further conversation than comments about the footing of their trail or the tending of the horse. If he was aware of how deeply the descent of this uneasy silence between them effected Euwae, he gave no indication of it. The day eroded into evening. The shift of light matched the range of emotions upon her face, as her anger drained away to despondency but ebbed back to a grim determination once the ruddy sunset failed and dropped the world around them into darkness.

After the sun had set, they decided to end the march for the day. The evening was warm and the moon still half full, so the ath'Ale suggested against building a fire and attracting any hostile eyes towards them. Euwae retrieved some food from the saddlebag while her companion saw to the horse. Once he was done tending to Courser, he joined her on the bank as she sat looking out across the eddying water.

"A long time, it has been, since I have ridden Northmoors alone." She said as she stretched out her legs. "Not since my father ascended to – "

She shot a glance at her companion and coolly passed him a packet of smoked fish.

"Thanks." He took it and began to eat. After a few bites, his eyebrows sank down with realization. He turned to face her, but she quickly turned away and looked out again across the river.

"Ascended..? I – " He studied her profile. "I *know* you. And those names: Una; Kelleu."

He faced the far bank of the river as well and reached up to scratch the back of his head. "They aren't lovers... They're your – Family."

"I will buy you then." Euwae responded abruptly.

"What?" He parried with the exclamation at the unexpected turn of the conversation.

"If you are cuhm'l as you say, then I shall be buying you. Then you need not be burdened by the weight of slavery."

He chuckled and took another bite of the ration.

"This is pretty good." He said, raising the fish before he added with dark humor, "I've got a feeling that isn't going to work out, Euwae."

"You are rather free with my name, cuhm'l, if indeed you are knowing who I am."

He scowled. "My apologies, al'Aith. Would you prefer I call you 'highness'?"

"Not in that tone of voice, to be sure."

"But you'd prefer that?" He shrugged. "I suppose... You are a princess, after all."

He continued to eat the fish, while Euwae chewed the inside of her lip. Finally, she shook her head and looked at him.

"Bird Club, your wits are still addled, then. Why would I be buying your *freedom* if I wanted you to treat me so?"

"I don't know," he said without enthusiasm around a mouthful of food, "why would you?"

"That is not so difficult to answer..."

He continued to eat as he waited for that answer. She studied at him, her feet gyrating in frustration. Finally she sighed.

"You still have not a care as to what deeds bring me here, do you?" She asked earnestly.

He stopped eating and turned to face her again.

"Does it matter? A runaway al'Aith has formed a war band with an escaped cuhm'l to see how long they can carve their way through the rest of the Cord'Or." He shrugged nonchalantly.

"Sounds like an epic tale to me."

"Well, if you are to be putting the tale in that wise, it does have a less than heroic cast about it, now, does it not?"

He shrugged and looked back out across the river while he finished his fish.

"Glory and skulls for twoth'Ba," he muttered under his breath as he wiped his hands on his trousers.

"Good. It is settled between us." Euwae countered brightly.

"So, then. If I am to free you," she continued, "you must be telling me the tale of your master. From whom am I to be doing the buying?"

Her companion shook his head. "I don't think he's going to take you up on your offer."

She grinned. "You know not what that *offer* is, Bird Club."

"True. You think it's that good – "

"Oh, rest assured, ath'Ale, it is."

"So, I'm back to ath'Ale, eh?"

A single huff of laughter escaped his lips and he leaned back to rest on his elbows. With a sad smile, his eyes roamed the far shore of the river.

Euwae followed his gaze, until finally her brow furrowed and she asked conversationally, "Have you any notion as to how we might be crossing to Northmoors, now that twoth'Shan'n is no more? Short of walking all the long road back to twoth'Ba, that is?"

He pursed his lips.

"Not yet," he said with conviction, "but I'm sure we'll figure it out."

She looked at him out of the corner of her eye as an impish smile stole across her lips.

"Aye," she murmured, "that we will."

*   *   *

For four days they followed the bank of the great river. Euwae often sang to pass the time; her companion joined in when he knew the tune, or enjoyed the flow of her voice across the swale if he did not. During the evenings, the roles would change; he would provide renditions of the songs he could remember of his homeland, translated them for the al'Aith when she wished or delighted her with the mythologies behind them. The time passed without trouble or interference, save from the insects that lived at the margins of the water or the humble annoyances that follow any who travel along an abandoned way.

However, the forest was now turning back towards the north and drawing ever closer to the edge of the water. Within a day, the track which they followed would leave the river and swing south, into the wood and renew the possibility of another encounter with the red caps.

That afternoon, low clouds were gathering on the eastern sky. They both watched them with growing anxiety and it was well before dinner that Euwae gestured towards the forboding horizon and said in a reluctant tone, "We will be wet, for sure, before this night is out."

"You know, I meant to ask you before why you never packed a tent for your trip."

"I did not leave twoth'Ba in the most expected of moments, Bird Club." She said without emotion. "There was but little enough time to secure the food you have enjoyed and take up the services of Courser, here." She patted the flanks of the horse gently.

"They were both good choices, Euwae," he acknowledged. "Courser is a brave horse, and he's strong. He's not favoring that foreleg; at this point, you'll be able to ride him again, soon."

She glanced down at the horse's leg and nodded.

"I was in haste, but not in such wise that I was blind to all but folly."

"You're good under pressure, all right." He paused, looking at her with an unreadable expression. "Have you been in a battle, before? Before the red caps, I mean."

"You doubt me?" She said with a mixture of surprise and indignation.

"You're good with a sword; I've seen that. But being practiced and being experienced..." He shrugged and drew up on the lead of the horse.

"We should be setting out our food now, I am thinking." Euwae said, her eyes back on the wall of clouds as it built higher into the sky ahead of them. "I have no wish to be wet *and* hungry this night."

He nodded and started to strip the tack off of the horse as Euwae stalked off to the river bank to gather stones to surround a fire. As she set about laying them, the ath'Ale gave Courser a good combing before he used the larger blanket to cover the horse. Once the fire was burning, Euwae retrieved water from the river in her cauldron to cook the last of the vegetables they had managed to gather back in the ruins of twoth'Shan'n.

Once he had seen to the horse, her companion lashed several of the sticks of firewood together to make a crude tent pole for the cloak. All other preparations being complete, the pair settled down in silence to eat their meal.

Despite the threatening portents of the clouds, the rain did not begin to fall until well after dark. The makeshift shelter gave them some protection from the heavy downpour, but did little to keep them truly dry. The ath'Ale sat upright at the higher, open end of their tent, adding a last bit of protection for Euwae, who lay curled up behind him. If the chill of the rain discomforted him, he gave no sign; Euwae often looked up at him, to see his head swivel while he tried to discern any danger in the downpour and the darkness.

Once the fire had gutted out to sputtering coal, Euwae cleared her throat.

"I have seen battle, ath'Ale, in truth. Once the court of twoth'Ba was beset by the pirates of the Confederation; I stood with my sister and mother at the gate while my father and the court saw to the walls. As it happened, the pirates were the fools, and the gate took the worst of it...

"That was the first time blood rusted a blade by my hand."

She fell silent after that. After a moment, she saw his head bob up and down in understanding.

She exhaled softly, her eyes fixing on that moment of time. "I do not know how many I took as I stood to the gap. I was, in truth, frightened as much for my family as myself; I was of no mind to be counting of the faces that stared down into mine that night."

She suddenly became self-conscious of her emotions, burying them behind a forced smile.

"The next battle I stood with my father on the decks of the mighty Bayl'Ors Eye. After the attack on our court, my father swore to Ard'Ree himself the pirates would threaten us no more. For the better part of three years we chased their ships across isle'Eh and followed them to what passed for their meager little forts.

"By the time we had done, we had in truth taken the better part of three dozen islands from them. Now, they pay us tribute each spring under the promise of even greater wrath to be brought down upon them, although I suspect my father has not the desire to bring such about to the pirates, treacherous as they might be. Better they serve to raid those who have fallen to the Power than us, in truth... And this they do willingly, for those wretches refuse to set a hull to the waters of the great ocean and the pirates can come and go against them as they please."

"That's pretty smart." He agreed. "It keeps them at each other's throats and their eyes off the Cord'Or."

"Just so."

"Your father's always been a good leader, Euwae... I've served with him, too, when he led the twoth'Ba down to del'Ath."

Euwae's muscles contracted.

"You fought the red caps in twoth'Fhee?"

"Yeah."

"And my father – Did you serve him under oath of fealty there?"

"No, Euwae. I'd sworn to serve the hand guided by the aes'ree thu'Ked."

"Then, in truth, you are an ath'Ale of the River Prince?" She gasped.

"Guilty." He said with conviction.

"Then, those nights that we did to spend at the court of the twoth'Shan'n – You said that the court had not fallen to marauds, as all contend." She sat up behind him as best she could.

Softly, she concluded, "You survived that night, did you not."

Again, his head bobbed up and down in the darkness.

"Who, then?" She spat out suddenly. "WHO dared raise their hand against the River Prince?"

"Euwae – "

"No, Bird Club!" She whispered harshly. "The ree and his kin were of my blood as well. I have heard the tales of what was to be found there once the court had fallen. And I have seen – no, spoken to! – the restless dead which they have become. If you know whose hand is responsible for bringing this evil upon them, then I bind you to tell me, on the honor of the ree that you swore to serve!"

She thrust her head over his right shoulder and grasped his left to support her weight.

"*Tell* me!" She ordered with furious passion.

He looked into her face as the rain streamed upon it. Even in the darkness, he could see the emotions that burned within her.

"If you knew what you'd find there, why'd you go?" He asked quietly. Her grip on his shoulder tightened; her nails scraped his cool, bare skin.

"That, ath'Ale, is – "

He cut her off. "It is now. When we met, I didn't have a clue who I was, or what the shitesa I was doing. That's not how it is anymore... I may not remember my name – yet – but I'm not lost out in the woods any more.

"I'm here now because the dead sent me here. They know that I won't stop until I've set them free, or I join them. The question is, al'Aith, what about you? You're on the run. I don't know from what and to be honest it doesn't really matter. But I need to know *now* if you're serious about staying with me, or if you'll be taking off again once the horse is strong enough to ride."

75

Euwae slipped past him and stood out in the rain, staring down at her companion.

"You DARE to be questioning my loyalties?" She said hotly.

"Question your – Shitesas, Euwae!" He shot up out of the shelter and into the rain after her.

"I know you're the daughter of Lohvtreu. I know that twoth'Ba lays claim to Northmoors, even if they don't keep much of a presence there because of the trolls and red caps haunting it. If you plan to stay on the run, I'm headed in the wrong shitesast direction.

"So, yes, Euwae. This time, I *need* to know the answer. What were you doing at the court of twoth'Shan'n?"

The water drenched them both as they stared each other down in the black of the nighted storm. To the east, thunder growled, but no lightning yet shattered the gloom. He noticed that her hand had once again strayed to the hilt of her sword, but paid it no mind and kept his eyes locked on her face. Finally, Euwae turned away from him. Her shoulders dropped and sobs shook her. He tentatively raised his left hand towards her, clasping her shoulder in a gesture of comfort.

She raised her own hand to pull it off, but he kept it there with a firm squeeze. She gave it another halfhearted try, then relented and shook her head with enough force to send the rain whipping from her hair.

"I made my way to the fallen court to be finding my destiny."

"Your destiny? How?"

"The shaman have seen that I..." She raised her head proudly. "That I am to be the keeper of an aes'ree of the *highest* lineage."

"You went there to hunt for treasure?"

Euwae spun around and nearly lost her footing in the muddy ground. He caught her and kept her from falling, but she reached across and finally threw off his hand.

"How DARE you? You, whose greatest claim to en'Och and glory is that you are cuhm'l alone? How do you even question such a claim as that which I have to them both? You say that *your* club is an aes'ree. But how would you know? Has it spoken to you, in waking or dream? Has it called out your name and sang of its glories?"

She drew close and pointed a finger into his face.

"You are not of the folk of Cord'Or, Bird Club." She said coldly. "So think not to belittle my destiny with the small dreams of your own."

He took a deep breath.

"You've got some pretty serious issues, don't you?"

"Aargh!" She withdrew her hand. "I had hoped that – slave or no – you might lead me to that which was promised. I have waited since the day of taking up my torc for this glory!" Her voice dropped to a menacing, low tone.

"And better men have sought to deny me this right. No one, now, shall stand against me further save that they are to be of equal mind, or of so little wit I must put them down."

"This aes'ree." He said cautiously. "Was it the sword of the River Prince?"

Lightning flashed, throwing them both into stark shades of blue and white. Euwae's response was lost to the hue of the thunder, but her expression was clear enough to see.

Her companion sighed.

"It's not there, Euwae... thu'Ked: it's not in the court of the twoth'Shan'n."

Her eyes went wide.

"Then – Are you knowing where the aes'ree is to be found?"

He shook his head in the negative. "No, I don't. But I *do* know who took it." Emotions raced across the al'Aith's face as he continued. "So, it looks like we're on the same side, after all."

He reached up and gestured to the makeshift tent.

"Not that this'll make a lot of difference now, but we should get out of the rain. Since I'm out here, I'll check up on Courser. You get back inside."

Euwae slowly followed his instruction, her eyes tracing their most recent dialogue across the darkness. Once he resumed his post at the entrance to their makeshift tent, she sat up and placed her back against his, bringing up her knees and hugging herself for warmth.

"Bird Club," she said confidentially, "I do want you to know – I would have stayed by your side, even had you not known of the Blade of Shan'n." She paused, then added, "You know the way of it, do you not?"

She felt him shrug. "Are you, then, *not* of a mind to believe in me? Save that my destiny does seem to lie along the same course as your own?"

After a moments reflection, he replied. "It may be true, what you people say about en'Och. But I've got to admit, I'm kind of tired of you all calling me ignorant because I'm not wearing a torc. I think I've got a pretty good handle on it, really. But – even if I have no clue about what en'Och really means – I know *all* about honor, al'Aith.

"On that score, I'd like to think you'd stay with me, if only because of what we've been through already." She felt the muscles in his back tighten. "Besides, this is going to be a shitesat of a fight... I could really use a good warrior to back me up.

"The men we're after are hardened veterans. I've fought beside a lot of them. They're not going to just roll over and die for us. And, even worse – "

She felt his head turn towards her left shoulder.

"They're in this for the en'Och, too; all of them. So I suspect you'll have a pretty keen idea of what that means once we find them."

"Oh." Euwae said with dawning realization. "Damn."

He chuckled at her reply.

"Yeah," he responded gravely, "that about sums it up."

*   *   *

The next morning, they arose stiffly from their sodden shelter. Low mists cloaked the area in the gray light; the storm had moved on, but as yet the clouds refused to yield up the comforts of the warm sun to anyone on the ground far below.

Euwae looked down at the pool of water where their fire pit had been the night before and shrugged with defeat.

"There is no hope left for a warm breakfast now and that is the way of it."

Her companion nodded and walked off towards the horse. "It's all right, Euwae," he called over his shoulder, "We might not have had time for it, any way."

"What do you mean by that, Bird Club? Have you grown cold to the thought of my cooking, then?"

"Not at all. Look." He pointed up river. There, through the fog, the mast of a ship could just be seen in the distance.

"Oh!" She exclaimed. "Are you thinking that they will give us passage across the river?"

"I don't see how it'll hurt to ask." He took the soaking blanket from the back of the horse and patted it reassuringly. "So, let's get your kit together.... We should be ready once they get here, just in case they're willing to bring us across."

As the two collected Euwae's gear and wrapped up the wet blanket and cloak, Euwae kept glancing back towards the river. Once they finished, she smiled and pointed back towards the river.

"Look, Bird Club! It is not one boat, but three! Surely they will have no dark concerns for taking on a pair of weary travelers and their loyal steed for the voyage to the Summersford."

He nodded in agreement.

"The first ship'll be here in a few minutes." Her companion observed. "You finish up here. I'll head down to the bank and see if I can signal them."

The al'Aith nodded and began to see to Courser's load as he turned and walked quickly down to the river. Choosing to head a bit upstream to where the river was cutting into a bluff, he soon reached the short cliff and looked out into the fog at the approaching sail. The wind was still blowing gently from the northwest in the wake of the storm, so the sounds from the boat began to reach him before he could call out to signal it.

As he waited, he could make out the gentle creak of the sail in the mast and the indistinct voices of the seamen on board. There was another sound, too... A rhythmic incongruity of the water, which wasn't waves against the hull. He turned his head and listened, his brow furrowed in concentration.

"Bird Club?" Euwae called from further down the bank. "Where have you gotten to?"

"*Euwae!*" He hissed. "*Be quiet!*"

"What was that?"

"*BE quiet!*"

He nodded as he heard Euwae making her way towards him. Once she reached his side, she took his left arm with concern.

"What is it, then?"

"Listen," he said softly, "and tell me what you hear."

She turned her right ear towards the water; her eyes went wide.

"Oars!" She exclaimed under her breath. "Those would to be warships, then..."

"Oars..." He pursed his lips and shook his head. "That's what that is."

"Do you still wish to hail them, or – "

He interrupted with a raise of his hand. Still looking at the river, he reached back, taking her hand off his arm before leading her back down the hill, keeping the rise between them and the sight of the vessels on the river below.

"What is it?" Euwae whispered again, but he made a slicing gesture with his right hand, listening to the voices on the wind.

*   *   *

"What is it, Genna?" Angus' right hand dropped reassuringly to the hilt of his falcata.

The druid raised his own right hand.

"I thought I heard something. A voice, calling from the southern shore."

Angus spun his head to the starboard side of the long boat.

"Lads!" He called softly. "Pull up on the oars!" As the ath'Ale of the war band swiftly followed his request, the boat slid through the water pulled only by the sail. Angus moved to the starboard rail and leaned out over the water, listening. The men, seeing Angus' concern, leaned forward and focused on the southern shore as well.

Genna, however, walked to the stern of the vessel and climbed up onto the steersman's deck. He looked upriver towards the next boat in line, took up a lantern which he waived back and forth, squinting at the other ship. After a moment, the sound of its oars went silent as well.

Only then did he turn to study the southern shore with his own eyes.

Here the banks rose and fell in small hills which dropped in cliffs to the water below. The shore was shallow and would keep the boats from making easy landing; a perfect place for an ambush. With fingers unaccustomed to the task, he unfastened the clasp on his pouch with his right hand and withdrew a collection of thick knotted strings. With the bandaged stump of his left arm he gestured to one of the rowers, who vaulted from his bench at the druid's bidding.

"Yes, my Priest?" He said respectfully, his voice dropping with the mention of the druid's formal title.

"Hold these, then." Genna replied and handed him the fistful of knots. The man's eyes went wide, but Genna shook his head.

"They are not for you," he assured his comrade, "but I have yet to master the use of just my good hand alone." He waived his stump for emphasis.

The warrior nodded, but still accepted the knots gingerly. Genna ignored him and chose a trefoil woven of red and green, with a ruby held fast in the center of the configuration. He took it gently and smiled.

"Ah, there you be, my beauty." Holding up the knot before him, he walked to the starboard rail and studied the far shore.

After several minutes, the fog grew thick again upon the water. Angus left the center of the ship and moved aft to join Genna.

"What do you think? Is it some figment, then, or yet more phantoms that stalks us?"

The druid continued to study the bank as he replied. "Angus, I heard a voice – And no red cap's cry. It was a woman, as sure as I stand here now."

"A woman? Here?"

"Aye."

"A phantom, then, Genna. A ghost of the river, or the fallen court. For sure, no one would be so bold as to take the Old Road with midsummer coming so soon upon us."

"Some might." The druid replied darkly. "We are all but upon it."

"But, Genna," Angus chided with a stroke of his beard, "Ard'Ree has blessed the *waters* of the river, source to sea. No evil may travel upon it, save that they shall face the wrath of the high king of the Cord'Or."

Genna turned haunted eyes towards his companion.

"*No* evil?" He asked for Angus' alone to hear.

As one, they turned towards the last warship in their procession. It continued to row because the wind refused to fill the sails, although the other two vessels caught it with ease. As they looked upon it, that boat was swallowed once more by the unseasonable fog that blew out from twoth'Shan'n... The two men turned away and looked back at each other with haunted eyes.

*   *   *

Once the boats had passed, Euwae closed her eyes.

"What was *that*, then?" She whispered with inhibition. "Were they ghost ships, sailing off to isle'Eh to be damned?"

He stood up and shook his head firmly.

"I really doubt we're going to be that lucky." He said bitterly. "We need to find a way across to Northmoors and fast."

He turned to face her.

"How far away are we from Summersford?"

She shrugged.

"Twelve days. Fifteen at the outside..." She looked downriver after the vessels, now lost in the fog. "Will you be telling me about..." She waived her hand in the direction the ships had taken.

He sighed.

"Twelve days won't cut it. We need to hurry if we're going to catch up with them."

"CATCH them?" She said in frustration. "Catch *who*? You have yet to answer me that!"

He started to walk briskly down towards the river.

"You're right," he said without emotion, "I haven't."

She jogged after him, leaving a long trail of footprints through the wet grass.

"But – You do *know* who it is that just sailed past?" She said with focus. "Your mind has come round enough to recall that?"

"Ooh, yes." He replied with cold urgency. He shook his head and slowed to a walk. "You said you wanted to meet my 'master,' right?"

Euwae gasped. "But – How is that? Who are they?" She took his arm. "Do they walk the world as living men, or dead?"

He shook his head again and turned to face her.

"I don't know, Euwae. But I hope they aren't dead. Yet." He looked into her eyes. "I – *We've* got a debt to pay to them."

She tilted her head, her lips drawn into thin line.

"*We*, Bird Club? Are you so anxious for your freedom, then?"

He shook his head and looked back in the direction the boats had sailed.

"Those are the men who slaughtered the court of twoth'Shan'n."

Her breath caught in her throat as her eyes turned towards the river. The ath'Ale turned to her, watching as a deep flush crimson burn across her face while her chest rose and fell with the fury of her breathing.

"So," she said tightly as she strained to see any trace of the ships, "let the hounds of the just fly and run down the nighted traitor."

"Euwae," he said softly, "first we need to get across the river."

Her head rotated towards him. Very slowly.

He rested his hand upon hers.

"We have no doubt seen what the dead wished us to see." She said, her voice every bit as cold as his had been. "Now we know the truth of the course that they have laid for us."

He shook his head once again.

"My name, Euwae. They told me to find my name."

"The shattered skulls of the dead take your *name*!" She said vehemently. "Evil sails away from us upon the Great River; who knows where it may next set foot to the earth? Would you see them bring the same doom down upon others, as that they laid upon the folk of the River Prince?"

He opened his mouth but she cut him off.

"Well, I will NOT!" She said emphatically.

She pulled her hand away. He let his drop.

"I understand." He said at last with a flat expression. "Looks like we both have to do what we have to do."

Her face drew down with the pinch of anger.

82

"If that is your answer, *ath'Ale*, so be it. In truth, I had expected something better of you, now that the way of it is before us... I *would* have seen you through your quest, were it not for this! But it seems that we are not of a like mind, now that the truth is known and fate flies fast from us."

He looked away from her and out towards Northmoors, where the sun was breaking through the clouds and casting out shafts of light that mortally wounded any of the morning mists which failed to flee across the ground, leaving glittering tails of dew across the grasses where it passed.

"If you must find your way, still," she continued, "then your brand of courage must be of some other stripe indeed, that you can find it within yourself to see such blood cast yet again upon the thirsty earth."

He closed his eyes with a sharp twitch of his head.

"What..?" He asked absently.

Euwae scowled and sucked in a sharp breath.

"A coward, I am calling you." She replied tersely. He opened his eyes and Euwae gasped.

His irises were now a sharp, vibrant blue.

"That... *That* was it?" He said, his voice frosted over with wonder.

"By the skull of the first ree... Your eyes..!"

"Shitesa my eyes." He said with a dark grin. He looked back towards the river as he weighed his options with heavy breath, then looked to Euwae once again.

"Is there still a shaman living in the court of twoth'Ba?"

"A – shaman?" She said with bewilderment, unable to pull her eyes away from his. "Aye... A pair of them."

"Then that works for me." He said with certitude. "Come on, al'Aith; eamus nunc."

He strode away down the hill to where Courser waited patiently. Euwae stared into the space where his face had been, her eyes moving back and forth to the tempo of unasked and unanswered questions that raced through her mind.

Once he reached the horse, he looked back over his shoulder at his companion, but she remained frozen in place, staring off into the fog. With a roll of his eyes he turned to examine the horses foreleg. Courser did not protest as he ran his hand over the small lump, nor did he give any sign when the leg was tested beside, above and below the injury.

"You're a strong old boy, Courser..." He said calmly. "I'll do my best to keep you from working that leg as long as I can, but we've got to pick it up, now."

He checked the load on the horse and smiled in satisfaction at the al'Aith's work; even in haste, she had packed and secured the gear well. Taking up Crows Call from a loop beside the saddle, he swung the weapon over his shoulder and reached for the horses lead, but Euwae stepped up behind him and grabbed the tooled leather straps first.

He tilted his head and shrugged, his brow furrowed as she stared at him.

"What?" He finally asked.

She pulled her head back towards her shoulders and shook it quickly, but couldn't quite manage to wipe the odd, almost wondrous expression from her face.

"What is it with you this morning?" He asked again. "We're headed off to the rescue. Fair enough?"

She raised her free hand to her mouth and ran it roughly over her lips and chin.

"What was it, that you told me?" She asked in a lilting voice. "Shitesan take your eyes?"

He rolled his eyes to the left and looked down towards the ground.

"You ought to watch your language, Euwae." He muttered as he started to walk off towards the grassy space that demarcated the ancient road.

"Oh, is that the way of it?" She retorted. "In truth, I can think of a thing or two that, perhaps, you might be watching of as well were I you."

"I'll try to keep my eyes on it." He responded dubiously, shaking his head in frustration when she only laughed aloud in reply.

*   *   *

The fog had abandoned the northern bank of the river well before noon, but continued to lay siege to the southern shore for the better part of the morning. The wind came around to the west and wound through it slowly, occasionally raising short columns of mist into the air as if phantom scouts were stepping forth from the gossamer veil across the earth.

Here the ground had taken on a sponge-like quality; mosses and ferns grew in abundance and water pooled around their feet as they walked. Despite himself, the ath'Ale kept the pace slow, to avoid making any missteps across the soft ground. By midday they had reached the point where they must now make a choice, to either follow the road into the forest or brave the trackless bank along the southern shore.

Visibility along their route was still a chance thing, but the ground was now giving way to a full marsh and travel was becoming laborious for the horse when they stopped to take some food. Letting go of the lead to allow

Courser to graze, Euwae sloshed her way over to her companion as he tried to discern the lay of the terrain ahead.

"What do you make of it, then?" She asked casually, standing well behind him and to his left. "This ground is not but hard upon poor Courser... Are you thinking that it will be firmer back down against the shores of the river?"

He gave a slight shrug.

"I doubt it." He said at last. "The road would stay down by the river, if that were the case. But, see? It follows that rise, up and into the woods; so the bog is probably worse down by the water."

She moved forward, to stand close behind his left side.

"Ah, I see that, indeed." She said in an obvious, matter of fact voice. "So, then? Is it the road or the river that we shall be following?"

His eyes showed his curiosity over her tone, but his voice betrayed nothing.

"We have to go where the horse can go." He lifted his chin towards the forest. "We'll take the road."

"It is well, then," she said.

"What is well then?" He asked, trying to match her manner as best he could.

"That it is the higher ground we shall to be taking." She grinned and added, "For the sake of the poor beast, of course."

"You realize, Euwae, that the red caps are probably waiting for us in there."

She nodded. "You did say that, yes."

"And that doesn't bother you?"

"The red caps? No. I did to ride this way west, upon my taking leave of twoth'Ba... I saw neither trace nor trail of them, just a week agone."

"That was before you bled them at the court of the River Prince. They may be a bit more interested in you, now."

"It is as you say, of course."

He turned and looked down at her. She stood so close to him that he couldn't gesture with his hands without touching her, so he let them drop inconveniently to his sides as he spoke.

"Are you going to tell me what you've got on your mind?"

The lopsided grin crept further up her left cheek.

"Nothing troubles me, Bird Club, if that is your meaning. In truth, I am somewhat in haste to see the wood... I was of a mind to travel the road, now that the moon is dropping nigh to her sleep and after tonight will take her rest for a time, rather than dancing through the sky."

Despite himself, he looked perplexed.

"You want to travel through the woods and risk the red caps. At night. During the new moon." He ran his tongue over his teeth. "That makes a lot of sense."

She looked up into his eyes and flashed him an honest smile.

"There will be none of the red caps ranging in the woods this night," she said, reaching out and placing a finger upon his chest, "nor any other night until the moon has grown at least a quarter full once more."

"Why not?"

"Because these nights the folk of the land of summers twilight will be out and about upon their errands in the world."

His gaze swung from her face to her hand; slowly, a look of realization spread from his eyes to his mouth.

"Oh, no," he said, backing away two paces. "Ohhh, no." He looked at her sternly. "Euwae, there are *no* such things as faeries."

Euwae let her hand drop.

"Bird Club,"she lectured him gently, "There may well be none of the faer folk where you and yours are born. Of that, I would be not in the least surprised upon hearing.

"But the forests of Cord'Or are alive in the weavings of the most ancient ways... Here, one can yet have an accord with those who dwell under hill, or come out upon midsummer and midwinter to parade in court through the woods we share."

"We're NOT going to run around through the woods looking for faeries tonight."

"Why not? Do you fear that I may be right, and that we shall be crossing their path as they ride?"

He raised both hands and held them palms out towards her.

"We've got enough problems, without going and getting *lost* tonight. You aren't the only one who's been into those woods, Euwae. I've hunted there; I can tell you that there are plenty of things that you can find that've got nothing to do with faeries, but have a lot to do with teeth and claws."

"In truth? You've hunted the wood?" She looked puzzled. "And you've seen naught of the faer folk?"

"Not so much as a wisp or a bell."

Her eyes took on a faraway gaze.

"That is sad... My mother met my father in this very wood, on a midsummer's night. Led together by the faer folk, they were, each following a different elf until they were brought nigh to a glen beside a pool of crystal waters."

"A – Pool." He turned his head away and swallowed with difficulty.

"Aye..." She continued on without taking notice of his discomfort. "There did they stay, until the three nights were past, feasting on nothing besides their love and taking their nourishment from the waters of the pool. And each night, the elfs would come upon them and play them the most haunting music and sing them the most wondrous songs.

"When at last the moon climbed from her covers once more, they vowed to meet by the cliffs of twoth'Ba and be wed. And, so they were." Her eyes refocused on her companion.

"So, then, Bird Club. This is no child's tale, but the way of the meeting of my own parents, the very rees of twoth'Ba. Mind you still such thoughts that there are no faer folk to be found here?"

His brittle gaze caused Euwae to start.

"If you want to believe in faeries, then that's your business. But I need you to promise me: we *stay* to the road. No matter what. Is that clear?"

"What is amiss with you, Bird Club?" She asked in genuine concern. "Why do you act so?"

He stepped forward a pace, menace chiseling his features.

"If there *are* faeries, Euwae, I don't want anything to do with them."

"But – "

"NO!" The word came out like a slap and Euwae turned her head as if he had struck her. He took a deep breath through his mouth and let it go slowly through pursed lips.

"Look – "

"No," she interrupted, but refused to look at him, "you have spoken most plainly. There is no need to be speaking more of it... Your mind is clear on this matter and no mistake."

She walked off, calling to the horse.

Behind her, he jerked his head to the right in frustration and threw a savage kick into a stand of taller grass. The plants dislodged at the blow, throwing a cascade of mud up into his chest and face that clung tenaciously to the long stubble of his nascent beard when he lifted his hand to wipe it away.

"Perfect. Just perfect." He muttered regretfully as he tried to scrub away the pungent mud as best he could.

*   *   *

It took them some time to cover the marshy ground as they made for the road. As the elevation slowly rose they covered the distance with increasing speed, yet it was well into evening by the time they reached the edge of the forest. The cloud cover draped low above them once again, throwing the landscape into the shadow of night well before the sun had left the sky. Together, they decided to make camp beside the road at the edge of the wood, rather than press forward any further for the day and risk facing any threats in the stygian darkness that would soon follow. He gathered wood for a fire while Euwae saw to the horse and unpacked their ration of smoked fish and dried fruit.

Afterward, the evening passed in an uncomfortable détente between them. Euwae focused her attention on tending to the tack for the horse, while the ath'Ale simply sat beyond the inviting warmth of the fire with his back to camp, keeping vigil on the woods beyond. Not long into the evening, she went to bed without a word, wrapped in her damp cloak. Once the untended fire was down the last coals, he slept as well, still sitting up and facing towards the maws of the voids below the faint curtain of trees.

But the ath'Ale did not sleep well. His head nodded up and down toward his chest while he slumbered and he whispered in his native tongue to the images that played through his mind. As the dreams drew on he grew more and more agitated; his muscles worked; his jaw clenched. His voice grew from a whisper to a moan. His hands began to twitch...

He awoke with a start, his eyes wide with apprehension until he could define the lines between himself, the nightmare and the night. Taking deep breaths to calm himself, he began to turn and ensure that his companion still slept soundly when he caught a movement in the trees, just out of the corner of his eye.

Very slowly, he turned his head towards the wood.

Just past the tree line stood a massive stag. Its shoulders rose to at least five feet with antlers which branched out like the boughs of a tree themselves. But most striking of all, the deer was a soft white, as if it were born of the mists that had plagued them throughout the day. In the darkness of the cloudy night, the fur almost seemed to glow, so stark was the contrast between it and the nighted wood.

It studied him with pink eyes, just as surely as he studied it. After a moment, it lowered its head and resumed its forage through the brush at the edge of the wood.

"That's enough food for a month, right there..." He said to himself. As the deer continued to eat, he clenched his jaw and came to a decision.

As gently as possible, the ath'Ale stood up and wrapped the strap of his bec de corbin through his belt. Softly, he walked across the camp to Euwae's gear. There, he stooped and fished about in the darkness until he came up with her short bow. She had only six arrows...

He gave a noncommittal shrug and picked up the bow, stepping through the stave and deftly bringing the string over the top nock. Taking up the quiver and hooking it through his belt as well, he turned and looked back towards the deer.

It still grazed, although it had moved a bit deeper into the wood. The bushes on which it had been feeding now obscured his shot, so he moved forward and right, hoping to stay downwind of the animal and out of the stag's direct line of vision. Stepping carefully to avoid the fallen sticks and louder brush, he slipped behind the bole of a thick oak tree and leaned around it, smoothly setting an arrow to the string and sighting down the shaft.

The stag raised its head, ears twitching. Its tail rose straight up.

The warrior exhaled softly and began to release the string just as the stag bolted off into the forest. The deer ran off about thirty feet, then faltered, its left hind leg failing to support its weight.

"Shitesan!" He swore gently as he quickly made after the animal, ignoring the stabs and scrapes of the thorns that anxiously sought out his exposed skin.

It heard him enter the forest and trotted off in an unsteady gate that he could easily follow. Stringing a second arrow, he slowed as well to minimize the sounds of his pursuit. The stag only trotted on for another minute or so, and slowed to a halting limp when it came to a thick grove of ash trees well away from the edge of the forest. Seeing his chance, he raised the bow and sent the next shaft flying towards his prey.

The arrow skipped off an unseen branch in the darkness and deflected off into the grove with a sigh.

The stag started and bolted from the ash trees back into the open wood, now at an adrenaline burning run. The ath'Ale started to run after it, but after just a few seconds began to slow; he was no match for the massive animals speed. As he started to give up the chase, however, he saw it falter and collapse just at the limits of his vision. With a snort of exertion, he jogged off after it once more.

Upon hearing his approach, the stag levered itself to its feet and lurched off away from its pursuer.

Drowned in the focus of the chase, he now paid scant attention to anything but the quarry that struggled to throw off the hunter. Robbed of speed, the stag sought out ever more difficult terrain instead; this slowed them both but gave the ath'Ale several more clear shots: the first, when the stag came to an unexpected gap in the trees that clearly showed its ghostly white fur and a second when it stumbled amongst a pile of stones as it sought to climb a low ridge that cut across its line of retreat.

The stars finally threw back the clouds and began to wash away the bitter darkness of the night. The stag wheeled right and up a steep hill...

However, its strength was all but spent. Just short of the crest, the animals legs splayed out and it collapsed just beyond the gap where the trees gave way to open sky at the summit and was still.

That same fatigue consumed the warrior chasing it as he labored on the path that wound up the high slope. But, when the deer lay unmoving at the top of the rise, the ath'Ale took a moment to catch his own breath and reached into the quiver. Only one arrow remained, its companion having been dropped at some point during the long last leg of the chase. Still breathing hard, he drew the shaft in a quick motion and laid it against the bow. With the nock of the arrow holding to the bow string like a frightened child to its mother, he slowly resumed his advance up the path.

Although the body of the deer was just out of his line of vision, its antlers were clearly visible in the moonlight, shining like wintered branches of birch at the top of the rise.

Keeping his eyes focused on the prey, the ath'Ale paced inexorably up the path, ready to cast the final arrow into the noble animal and take his prize at last, when a cold wind suddenly howled across the crest of the hill, sending leaves twisting with harsh whispers on their swaying branches. Amidst the din, a dark shape slipped out of the trees and onto the path at the base of the hill. Despite the wan light, a naked sword blade in its hand was plainly visible as it began to move smoothly up the path behind him.

*   *   *

Euwae shivered in the night. The damp cloak gave her scant comfort from the chill and restrained her from seizing the sleep that she sought. Instead, she dozed fitfully on the hard earth, tossing and shivering through the night. At the last, a heavy bladder proved to be the last, unbearable distraction. With a sigh of frustration she arose and stalked off towards the wood to relieve herself.

While so engaged, she heard a stage whisper from the trees off to her right.

"*Euwae! Come here... You have got to see this!*"

She rolled her eyes.

"Just a moment, then! A bit of courtesy, if you have a mind, would be appropriate."

"SHHH!" came the reply. "*Come quickly!*"

She shook her head as she finished. Once she had drawn up her riding trousers she walked off towards the voice as she fastened her belt.

"Now *what* is – So..." her voice died away when a light from deeper in the forest limned the trees around her in a soft, pale blue glow, as if moonlight had been drawn to earth in a great lantern and used to illuminate the wood before her.

"Ah!" She gasped, ducking low. "So! You see?"

"*I do! Come quickly! They are headed off into the forest!*"

She started to move forward, but froze in place with a grin of sarcasm spreading across her face.

"I thought you said that the wood was but too dangerous a place to be treading the ways at night?"

"*But – The faer folk are **here**,*" came the reply. "*Do you not wish to see?*"

Euwae hesitated for a moment more. The light was, indeed, beginning to fade as it moved off further into the trees.

She looked back towards the edge of the wood. She could barely see Courser; it was too dark to make out anything else of the camp.

"*Come on!*" The whisper was fainter now, too.

"Do not worry on, Courser," she said quietly. "I shall be back to you in just a moment." With that, she rose up and hurried after the light.

Drawing nearer, she could see tall, lithe figures basking in the glow, which seemed to be pulled out of the very air around them. They were dancing, but not to any tune or song that she could discern, no matter how hard she listened. The steps were intricately made, accounting not only for their partners as they moved through the wood, but for the trees and terrain as well, as if the whole of the forest had spent long hours rehearsing the choreography that now played out gracefully before her.

After a time, she began to understand that the dance was not just an arrangement of steps, but an opera of motion: she saw in their movements the nature of rees and al'Aith, of druids and the craftsmen and warriors of the bua'Theu caste as well. The forest became an entire court, full of life... Here lovers swooned, warriors fought and nobles received their en'Och from the blessings that their people enjoyed.

With tears in her eyes, Euwae became lost in the weaving of the dance. "Oh, father," she whispered with wonder, "mother... Is this what you saw on that night, so long ago?" She rubbed at the water on her cheeks. "Bird Club, was *this* the thing you were fearing so?"

The dance stopped. Each of the characters was frozen in mid motion; no breath of wind stirred the leaves.

A new dancer leaped from the trees into the midst of the group below. Clad in vibrant red, he looked bruised by the shadows of the blue glow around him. He pirouetted, reached out and touched the closest dancer, who withered fluidly to the ground and lay still; a lithe corpse festooning the forest floor.

The red dancer exploded into motion, shaking the hand of a merchant, placing a kiss onto the cheek of a lover. All of those he touched swooned, fell away and moved no more.

Euwae gasped in horror as other red dancers stood forth from the shadows of the trees. With ugly, clumsy steps they raced through the scene, pushing the other dancers to the ground as quickly as they could. The al'Aith shot up and ran down into the glade where the dancers had gathered, but she was too late. By the time she reached it, the red dancers had completed their charge and withdrawn.

Euwae stood on the edge of the opening in the trees, arterial tears drawn from a wholly different well flooding down her cheeks, when one of the dancers towards the center of the glade slowly spun to his feet. He had the posture of a warrior, although a white mask, blank but for a single tear, covered his face. With heart wrenching grace, he moved his hands around the space as if he were clinging to the fallen spirits as they escaped his grasp. At the last, in defeat, he fell to his knees.

The blue light receded back into the trees and all faded to darkness.

Euwae sensed motion from the dancers as they too withdrew, unseen. Only the last of them remained, locked into his pantomime of grief and loss. Unbidden, she made her way to him; when she reached him he turned his head towards her.

She reached out and touched the tear upon the mask –

"My ree..." The elf said with terrible loss, looking off into the darkness. But the voice was somehow –

Familiar.

"BIRD CLUB!"

Euwae sat bolt upright in the darkness. Courser started and whinnied, turning his head up at the commotion. The fire had long since died away.

Of her companion there was no sign.

She shot to her feet and pulled her sword free of its sheath. Turning towards the forest, she called out his name again. Once the echoes had died away, she heard the faintest of replies, unmistakable but unintelligible in the distance.

Euwae rushed into the wood.

She soon came upon a wide trail that wound between the boles. The path led her through the confines of a thick grove of ash trees, out and along a long dry water course and finally over a low ridge, until she could make out a tall hill in the distance. Starlight now sliced through the leafy boughs and threw pools of cool silver above her, puddles of light in a lake of darkness as she saw a flash of movement at the crest of the hill. With furious effort, she raced on until she reached a point where the trail crooked back upon itself before it led the way up to the summit.

Before her on the trail, her companion held a low crouch, her bow in his hand.

"No..." Euwae murmured, before she began running up the steep slope to join him.

She was less than twenty paces away when he spun on his right heel and pointed the shaft directly at her.

"*Bird Club*!" She hissed. "*I have come to aid you – Save that shaft for the red caps!*"

He immediately lowered the bow.

"Euwae?"

She struggled up the path to him, dropping to her haunches as she gulped for air to soothe her burning lungs.

"Aye." She panted. "And who else would it be," she breathed again, "to be coming to your aid thus?"

He scowled and leaned over her. "Coming to my aid? What are you talking about?"

"I heard you," she said over another shallow breath, "calling out for me."

"No, you didn't."

She closed her eyes and rolled her head as a rebuttal.

"I thought I told you *not* to come into the woods!" He continued.

"Aye, that you did," she said, her voice stronger now, "nor were *you* to venture thus, save that the light of day was well upon it."

His voice dropped to a guilty octave. "Well..."

"Well indeed." She reached out and took his shoulder so that she could lever herself back to her feet. "And yet here you be."

"I was hunting."

"Hunting, were you? In the dead of the night, in a wood brimming with red caps." She took another deep breath and wiped the sweat from her face with her sleeve.

"You don't believe me?" He said with finality. "Fine. Come on and take a look for yourself."

He rose to his full height and walked with long, purposeful paces up the final stretch of the path towards the summit of the hill.

"The deer's right up here." He called back over his shoulder. "And he's a *big* one."

Euwae's shoulders drooped and her head rolled forward, but with a deep breath she summoned the energy to piston her legs up the last stretch of the slope as well.

When she joined him at the summit, she looked at the ground around them.

"So, where *is* this big one that you speak of? I see not so much as a fawn, let alone a great deer worth abandoning the camp for."

"Euwae..." He said, with a tremor to his voice.

She looked up at him. "I see it not, Bird Club."

"Euwae," he repeated, "look." He raised the bow and gestured in a circle.

Before them was spread out the vast, open tracks of Northmoors.

"Ach!" Euwae called out. She spun around, but the way behind them was more of the same.

Her companion pointed off to the right. From this height they could discern the ribbon of the Great River at the very ends of their vision in the sliver of moonlight above. Where there should have been woods on the far bank there was no sign... Only more open plain made up the southern shore.

"Shitesat this."

"This deer of yours... It did not to be a stag, with fur as white as a mountains peak?"

He scowled at her. "Maybe."

"Faer folk!" She gasped. "The White Stag is a powerful fey; it leads you off to any manner of wild adventure!"

He kicked a rock off the top of the hill. "Perfect," he muttered as he watched it roll down the slope.

"But, Bird Club..." Euwae looked up at him again, her face a confusion of anger and excitement.

"What of Courser?" She asked plaintively. "What of my things?"

He shrugged.

"There's not much we can do about that, now." Seeing the emotions spill across her face, he reached out and gave her a conciliatory hug.

"Look," he said gently, "Courser's good enough to run now, and he's a smart horse."

He let her go and looked into her eyes.

"You said you went to twoth'Shan'n by the old road?"

"Aye. But – "

"Don't worry, Euwae. He'll find his way home."

"Do you truly believe that is the way of it?" He nodded, but she continued without solace. "But what of the red caps?"

Her companion flashed a genuine smile. "He's already killed one... He knows how to take care of himself - If he doesn't have to look out for us as well." He added with a chuckle.

She nodded with a lack of enthusiasm.

He looked up and out across the expanse of open ground. "Hey, look over there."

He pointed to the left. In the distance, the failing limestone of a ruined house shone like a lost ring against the barren moor.

"At least we can get some shelter from the wind there."

She nodded again with slightly greater eagerness. He smiled and started to lead her down the hill.

As they walked off, she threw her shoulder against him and asked, "So then. What are you thinking of the faer folk now, eh?"

"I told you," he said darkly, "shitesat this."

"But you must be admitting that they do exist, now."

He shook his head. "Could be. But – either way – you can keep your Cord'Or magic. I don't need to see *any* more of it."

"Is that the way of it, indeed?"

"Believe me: at this point I've seen more sorcery than I've ever dreamed of."

"That may be," she grinned, "but this night I did to have the strangest dream, before I set off into the wood to save you..."

"Something tells me I don't want to hear this..."

"How would you be to knowing that, unless you have first heard the way of it?"

He grimaced and chewed the inside of his lower lip. She made a show of taking his arm in hers as they continued down the path; he looked down at her with a cool expression, which she blissfully ignored. Soon they passed out of site of the top of the hill; the last trace of them was her laughter floating back up the slope, before even that was snatched and swept away by the eastern wind.

Northmoors

While the pair walked across the sparse grasses of Northmoors, Euwae's eyes flashed as she recounted her dream to her companion.

"As I followed the faer folk through the wood, I heard the most wondrous singing and music, until we came to a moonlit glade where they danced about in such a wise as to make the heart ache."

"Sounds like quite the dream."

"Oh, indeed," she said, her eyes lost in the memory of the moment, "I wish you could have been at my side to have seen it."

"In your dream, huh?"

Her vision fell away as she scowled. "You need not be upbraiding me so." She retorted, before her voice resumed its softer timbre. "I could have all but been among them..."

He looked at her out of the corner of his eye, but held back his rebuke.

"At the last, they danced the deaths of a ree and his court," she said sadly. His head rotated around to face her as she continued.

"All but one fell to the attack – "

"Attack?"

"Aye... First by one warrior clad in red... But joined he was, by others so attired. Through the whole of the court they rushed, until all the folk had fallen." He pulled his eyes away from her and cast his gaze to the ground.

"I ran to stop it, but all was lost, before I could..." She sniffed and rubbed her eyes.

"All the elfs had gone, save one. A mask he wore, blank but for a single tear of blue. He looked upon me and mourned the death of his ree, just as I woke from the vision."

Her hand sought his arm in comfort.

"So sad a sight it was, Bird Club..."

He muttered something in response. She looked up at him with a measure of understanding. "And sorry, I am, that you have the wise to live through such a loss as I was shown."

"Shown?" He said, his voice thick in his throat. "You still think it was some shitesat elfs who gave you a dream?"

"And what other?"

She felt, rather than saw his shrug.

"We're here, I guess."

Euwae's eyes watered again, so she turned her face away from his.

"Bird Club – "

"Brand." He interjected.

"What is that?"

"Brand. It's my name." he said with a raw tone. She gasped.

"Brand? That is how you are called, then?"

"Yeah," he acknowledged funereally. "I just thought you ought to know."

Euwae's eyes worked through the doors to the compartments of her memories.

"Brand... Brand – The Eastlander?" She asked with whispered veneration.

He stopped up short and shook off her hand.

"Brand 'the Eastlander' is dead." He said coldly.

"Forget it."

She studied him in the darkness. His body was tense; the bare flesh of his chest and arms was corded by the stress of the muscles underneath. His jaw muscles clenched in time with his breathing as his eyes bore into hers.

Finally, she acquiesced with a nod.

"If that is the way of it..."

The constrictions beneath his skin slowly slipped away as the tide of his emotions ebbed. His breath came more evenly as he looked at Euwae in the faltering light.

"Euwae..." He said conflictedly, then shook his head. She forced a smile to her face through the weight of bitter emotion that clawed at her eyes.

"You need have no worries, Bird Cl – Brand." She corrected herself frankly. "You would have kept my name from being raised had you gone your own way off to twoth'Ba. Honor all but demands that I should to be doing no less – Were the need to be upon me."

A weary smile crept up the corners of his mouth.

"Fair enough, al'Aith... I'd say that's fair enough."

She rubbed away the weight from her eyes and held out her left hand. With a grunt of acknowledgment, he wrapped his own around her forearm. She clasped his and they shook to seal their accord. As the al'Aith released his arm, he drew his eyes away from hers and looked across the open contours of their surroundings towards the old structure, still a goodly hike to the southeast.

"Come on, Euwae... We've still got a ways to go if we want to get any sleep tonight."

She followed his gaze and nodded.

"A long night this has been and no mistake." She said compliantly. "I could do with a fair bit of rest."

"We both could," he agreed straight away. "Come on; let's get moving."

Without further conversation, he started off towards the forgotten building. With a deep breath and a thoughtful expression, Euwae followed his lead.

The structure proved to be in better repair than it appeared from the crest where they had first spied it. Like most Cord'Or dwellings, it had a domed roof of sod, but in this case the roof was broad and shallow, giving the impression of disuse from any distance. Likewise, the low walls that formed a court and pens looked more like tumbled ruins than functional structures, although it was unclear if this was an aspect of abandonment or the design of the folk who had labored to build it.

The outer gate hung askew on hinges of rotted rope as the pair slipped past and made their way cautiously to the door of the main house. There was no sign of any animal life in the old pens, but that was not a sure indication that the structure was empty...

Brand took Crows Call from his belt and rapped three times on the door with the mace head. He waited for half a minute before he knocked again. When there was no reply, he gave the door a solid push and swung it open wide, allowing what light from the night that dared to enter into the space beyond.

There was no sign of habitation.

Brand left the door open as he entered, allowing his eyes time to adjust as best they could to the darkness beyond. That trespass served as the only illumination; the smoke hole at the peak of the roof was covered, as were the narrow slits beneath the eaves that normally allowed light and air passage into the room.

"It looks clear, Euwae... Come on in."

She entered at the same slow pace, while he felt as much as walked towards the center of the room. The hearth still stood, a raised circular structure of stone five feet wide that owned the middle of the chamber. He stooped and felt about with his hands, until he found a pile of split timber and some fire wool. Stacking several logs onto the hearth, he tucked the wool between them and spat upon it. Red embers began to snake through the wool; he blew on it gently until it caught fire.

Euwae surveyed the room as her companion worked to dislodge the cover on the chimney hole in the roof. Besides the hearth and combustibles, the room held only the traditional bench built into the wall of the round room. Once the fire had taken, she closed the door behind them.

"Well, then. This is a cozy home and no mistake." She said honestly.

"Glad it meets your approval, Euwae." Brand replied as he managed to finally leap up and pull on the cord attached to the leather covering as she finished surveying the space around them.

"It has hearth and wood," she continued, "and the roof is sturdy enough: there is no water upon the floor... Nor any sign of scat. The folk who dwelt here knew enough to clear their home of anything that might draw little beasties to claim it once they had gone."

"Hmm. Sounds to me like they planned on coming back."

"Indeed, that would seem to be the way of it."

He shrugged.

"We'll have to thank them later. In the mean time," he sat down on the floor with his back to the hearth, facing the door, "I could use some sleep."

She smiled. "Indeed."

The deep bench along the wall was covered with worn but sturdy leather cushions. Euwae stretched out her damp cloak across an open space of planking and patted the woolen fabric ruefully, sat down next to it and stretched out her legs. "Ah... It feels good to be sleeping up off of the ground for a change."

He nodded. "It's been a while."

The al'Aith looked at him curiously as she swung her legs onto the bench and rested her head on her arms.

"You say that, yet still you sit upon the floor, when you could take better comfort here."

"I'm good, thanks."

"Yes, I can see that."

"I've got a roof. That's more than I've had in a long time; I'll take the luxuries I can get."

"Your folk are curious indeed."

He let out a snort and shook his head, casting odd shadows on the door.

"My folk? They sleep in *beds*."

"Beds? Such as those the pirates sleep upon?"

"More or less."

She was silent for a moment. "Then, why?" She finally asked.

"Why do *I* sleep like this?"

"If you have a mind to tell the tale..."

This time, he was silent for a moment.

"Euwae..."

She yawned. "If you are to be telling me," she said sleepily, "you had best be doing it soon, lest I be back off to the dreaming before you find the words for it."

He glanced over towards the bench where she lay.

"I haven't – I won't..."

He fell silent for a long moment, before his shoulders rose and fell in a defeated shrug.

"Well, then. That was truly wise."

The light behind him kept his bitter scowl deep in shadow.

"The night cu'Kullah and his ath'Ale killed the River Prince was the last time I've let myself *sleep*." He said without a trace of emotion. "After that – Well, after that," he lowered his gaze, "I felt I owed it to the ree not to fail that way again."

Euwae allowed her eyes to close.

"But that was more than six years gone, now." She said quietly. "In all that time, you have not found the comfort of a bench to be slept upon, as you should?"

"No."

Her heavy eyes levered open just enough to allow her to try to study his expressions.

"Surely, that must have gone most hard upon those with whom you have sought comfort."

"Sought comfort?"

"The women you have known."

"Euwae – Believe me. That hasn't been a problem."

"Ah. So they were understanding of your desire to sleep in such a wise?"

"No. There was no 'they.' Or a 'one,' for that matter."

"What, none at all?"

"What part of 'no they or a one' did you miss?" He asked sourly.

She closed her eyes again.

"I am sorry, Bird Club..." She said gently.

His shoulders went stiff.

"In truth," she continued, "I meant no offense. And too, I take back what insult I gave to you back by the river."

His lip twitched. "Which insult was that?"

"I said that you knew not of en'Och... But, most clearly, *Brand Eastlander*, was I wrong. That you have carried the weight of the fall of a ree in such a fashion and for so long a time; in any wise, you are of a station that few even of the al'Aith of the Cord'Or might ever hope to attain.

"It is my honor, to see you keep yourself so."

She waited, but he said nothing more. Soon, she was asleep.

After the fire died away and the room slid into darkness once again, Brand rubbed his palms across his watering eyes and bit the inside of his trembling lip; despite his obvious fatigue, he found no rest until well after the sun had thrown a shaft of pale light through the smoke hole in the center of the roof above him.

*   *   *

The pair slept well into the morning, the dark, cool interior of the house giving strength not only to their bodies, but their spirits as well. Euwae rose and stretched, her stomach gurgling loudly. Still seated on the floor, Brand turned his head towards her, but after seeing her rise rotated it back towards the door and let sleep reclaim him.

With a nod, she tugged her clothes back into position before she gathered up the damp cloak and moved quietly to the door. After a last glance at her companion she slipped outside, being careful to keep as little light from rudely barging past her as possible.

With a guilty smile, she noted the sun was close to the apex of the sky. After another indulgent stretch, Euwae walked to the nearest wall and laid out her cloak to dry. That done, she set about exploring the homestead, moving around the low stone walls and enclosures and peering into each with brazen curiosity.

Some time later, she made her way back to the house, her left arm heavy with tubers picked from the gardens scattered about the grounds, her right holding a mossy wooden bucket. This time, she threw the door open wide, throwing a torrent of light upon her companion. He squinted at her silhouette framed in the opening and nodded.

"Guess I lost track of time."

"Good afternoon and well met to you, as well." She said in feigned arrogance before she walked over to the hearth and set down the bucket and the arm load of vegetables.

"There, then." She nodded approvingly at the food. "We have naught to be cooking them in, more is the pity. But they will be filling our bellies in good form and should keep well enough, until we find better."

She reached down and selected a large carrot. Rinsing it off in the water in the bucket, she passed it to her companion. He took it with a nod of thanks and began to chew into it while she prepared herself a second.

After a few bites, she rolled her head loosely on her neck and scowled regretfully.

"Sad it is, that Courser could not be here to break this fast with us... He is mightily fond of carrot, to be sure."

"I'm sure he's fine." Brand said around a mouthful of his own. "He's probably well on his way back to twoth'Ba by now."

She sighed and ate the rest of her meal in silence.

Once they were done, he set about cleaning the rest of the food while Euwae took the sharpening stone from the scabbard of her sword and honed the edge of the blade.

"Well, then. What are the paths that we shall be following now?" She asked conversationally, without looking up from her task.

"From what we could see last night, we're either well east or well west of twoth'Shan'n." He replied. "I'm hoping that shitesannus deer – "

"White Stag; do not be doing dishonor to those who dwell in the twilight."

"*White Stag,*" he looked at her for agreement, but she continued to stay focused on her sword, "took us east. With luck, we're close to Summersford. We've got at least two days walk to reach the river, so for now we stay headed south. After that, we'll take the northern bank and follow it east until we reach a ford or the sea."

"Are you thinking that we are so close upon isle'Eh?"

He shrugged.

"We didn't see the ocean. But – if we *were* sent east – we may have close to a weeks jump on cu'Kullah."

She stopped honing her sword.

"And what makes you think that *he* has designs to reach the sea, then?"

102

"He and his ath'Ale were in long ships. On the Great River, they could've had any number of cogs; they're easier to sail in the narrow and fords, carry more cargo and are a lot easier to steal than war ships."

"What makes you think that they were stolen?"

Brand looked at Euwae earnestly.

"Point taken." She said and went back to sharpening her sword.

"He didn't have *any* ships, last I knew... And that wasn't too long ago."

"Well enough."

"Anyway, the only reason he'd need ships like that is to take on the ocean. I'm not sure why he's doing it, though. We're into storm season now, so unless he's really desperate to clear out of Cord'Or, he can't be planning on going far."

"What are his hopes, then? If you are of a mind that he is not flying to refuge for his treachery?"

Brand set the last of the food on the hearth and rubbed his hands together in the bucket to clean them. His eyes looked past the surface of the water, towards something far removed from the house on Northmoors.

"Cu'Kullah wants to make himself a ree."

Euwae choked back a laugh and nearly cut herself on the edge of her falcata.

"In *truth*?"

Brand swiveled his head towards her. The laughter died in her throat as she tried to understand the dark emotions that played across his face.

"Shitesat truth. He's got it into his head that he can use some ancient magic to get a ree's torc. The last I knew," he said flatly, turning away from Euwae, "he planned on claiming twoth'Shan'n, by right of conquest and that damned sorcery."

"But... How? Ard'Ree – "

"From what I've heard, the Ard'Ree can't do shitesannus about it; he said something about the magic being older than the Cord'Or, but still a part of your heritage from long ago. Because of that, if he's able to pull it off..."

"He becomes *ree*?"

"That's what he thinks."

She set aside her sword and stood.

"There is more to this tale. I see that much in you." She walked to his side and laid a gentle hand on his arm. He looked down at her hand, but didn't pull away.

"I've seen the ritual... Close up. It's – " His mouth worked as he searched for words that refused to be found. At the last, he looked into her eyes and said quietly, "there's something to it, something ancient he's on to that's way past what your druids practice now.

"I think he's right. It could have worked."

Euwae's hand shot up and covered her mouth, but he shook his head.

"I think it *could* have worked, Euwae. But I don't think it did."

Her hand still covered her mouth, but her eyebrows slid lower as she listened.

"The spell has something to do with – With a sacrifice." he chewed on that thought for a moment before he continued on.

"Something went wrong. It didn't work, at least not the way he intended. Otherwise, he'd be a ree already. But he said something else, too - About going out and raiding others to take their money from them. Maybe *that's* what he's got to do now.

"He's got warships... And I'm betting he didn't just buy them. He could have sailed up river and attacked the northern rees, but while they haven't got a lot of people, they don't have a lot of wealth, either. Since he's headed down river, he's either headed for the sea..."

"Or twoth'Ba." She concluded coldly.

"It'd make sense. The court of twoth'Ba is right on the shore – "

"And we have just gone and collected our tribute from the Confederation."

Brand rocked his head to the right and ran his tongue over the edges of his teeth inside his mouth.

"Yeah... I'd forgotten about that."

Euwae walked purposefully back to the bench and picked up her sword. She first made to sheath it, but stopped, looked at the blade and lifted the tip to her forehead. She cut off a lock of hair and set the weapon back on the bench before she wove the hair into an intricate knot.

After placing the artistic braid upon the hearth, she retrieved her weapon.

"When do we set forth, then?"

Brand looked at the hair she left behind and raised his chin towards it.

"What's that all about?"

Euwae looked towards the hearth, then back at him.

"In all your days, here, have you spent any time in Northmoors?"

"I've been through it before."

"And in your journeys, how often did you enjoy a fire to warm your nights?"

He looked thoughtful. "Not very often."

"Aye, because wood here is in short supply and that is the way of it... Trees are sparse indeed in this land."

"I guess you're right." He looked back at her. "But, what's with the hair?"

She walked back to the hearth and picked up the knot, lifting it so that he could see it more plainly.

"Do you see, here, how it twines so in the middle, to make this long strand? This knot belongs to the ree of twoth'Ba. Should the owner of the house return to find their stores low, I would not have them thinking that they had been robbed while they were about.

"Now, I have left token that we were here; further, should they wish to reclaim their loss, they have but to send this along to the court and the ree there will see to it that they are set right for it."

As she put the hair back on the hearth, he stroked his chin.

"You've got a lot of trust in that, don't you?"

"It is they way of it. I would not see that the hospitality of this home were to go in vain, even though the folk who dwelt here were not about to see it done."

"That wasn't what I meant – But, fair enough."

She drew herself up and threw him a questioning look, but he looked down at the hair rather than continue.

"Are you all set?" He asked at last.

She nodded. "Let me fetch my cloak; we can use it to bear the food on our journey."

She reached across him and picked up the bucket before she made for the door. After she had walked outside, he went to the lock of hair and examined it casually in the sunlight that streamed in from the open smoke hole. It formed a clever trefoil, with a pair of hitches holding the whole of it together at the center and forming the long single strand.

Shaking his head, he started to pick up the vegetables, then gazed up at the roof. With a sigh, he hopped onto the hearth and maneuvered the leather cover back into place.

After gathering the food, he stepped slowly out of the house to join Euwae, being sure to tightly close the door behind him out of respect as he left.

*   *   *

By the beginning of the third day of hiking towards the great river, the food which they had liberated from the empty house was running low. There had been no sign of other homesteads along their way, only rolling ground sparsely covered by thin grasses and punctuated by long pools that filled much of the lowest ground between them.

The area was largely free of insects and animals, as well. The wind, however, was a constant companion to the pair as they made their way south and east. Brand had taken to keeping Euwae's cloak over him to shield him from the sun, but his chest and arms were still beginning to grow a deep red from the constant exposure to the elements.

Their main comfort came from the abundance of water. The pools were all clear and fresh, offering a constant enticement to rest and refrain from the hard pace of their travels.

At last they crested a rise and the soil before them quickly abated to domes of rough, exposed red rock. Below that, the stone stood in ridges, as if a giant had peeled away the grassy earth and hacked calf deep furrows into the sedentary stone beneath. They were surveying the expanse of ridges when Euwae took Brand's arm and pointed east.

There, a trail of smoke was dry brushed into the sky as the winds wiped it away.

"What do you think, then?"

"I'd guess it's more than a camp fire – A hearth, maybe."

"Aye, that was my way of thinking, as well."

He surveyed the area around them, shaking his head.

"They're most likely down by the river, but I don't feel like marching across this," he lifted a foot and brought his heel down roughly on the sandstone, "until we have to. Let's follow the ridge line for now, until we have a straight approach to them."

"That sounds fair enough to my mind."

He nodded and took the lead as they began to follow a course along the northern edge of the escarpment. After several hours, the plume of smoke had shifted from its easterly drift to a location almost due south. However, the ridge line had also risen in elevation and now presented a rather steep climb to the pair as they prepared to scale down to the base of the ridge.

"What do you think?"

"The cliff rises still, further on. Should we continue past, we will be the worse for it."

"Yeah... This is it. What do you think – We take our lunch at the bottom?"

She nodded. "It will be afternoon, soon enough."

106

"Right. Let's get to it, then..."

With care, Brand sat at the edge of the cliff and swung his legs over the edge. He began to roll over to his left side, when the ground beneath him came loose and gave way, dropping him down the face of the escarpment and onto the ridges of rock at the bottom of the slope.

"BIRD CLUB!"

Euwae shouted as she ran to the edge of the cliff, only to have the soil under her feet vanish as well. She tried to spin and catch the edge of the escarpment as she started her fall, but her hands only scraped across the surface of the deep red sand stone as she slipped and dropped away with a desperate cry that echoed off the stones below.

She slid down the sharp angle of the cliff with her forearms scraping across the rough stone, her feet swinging wildly about for purchase but finding none before she struck the ground below. Euwae came down hard on her left leg, wrenching the knee and hip before she tumbled backwards and the back of her head struck an upthrust ridge of rock with a dull thud.

"Euwae. Come on, wake up." The al'Aith's eyes rolled under their lids as Brand cradled her head gently in his lap. "I need to hear what hurts."

Her left eye fluttered open, followed by her right.

"Ughn..."

In the deep red light of late afternoon, Brand shook his head. He leaned over her, looked into her eyes with a scowl, then shaded her face with his left hand. After a moment he pulled the hand away first from her right eye, and then the left as watched for her reaction. With a snort of relief, he leaned back against the cliff.

Euwae's vision focused on the top of the escarpment high above. It had eroded underneath the lip of the crest to a depth greater than her arm was long. A pair of clean half circles marked where the overhang had given way and cast them down to the rocks below. She tried to raise her left arm to shield her face from the sun, but brought it up only a short way before she dropped it again with a hissing inhalation of pain.

Her companion nodded with sympathetic understanding and brought his own hand back up to block out the sun on her face once more.

"You arms are pretty badly scraped up, Euwae. The blood's dry now and I don't have any water, so I don't want to get you bleeding again by poking around. Once we can clean you up, we'll bandage them, all right?"

A wince of a nod showed her consent. After that, no words were spoken until the sun was embedded deeply into the horizon.

"What of you, Bird Club?" Euwae asked through gritted teeth. He looked down at her, his face a mask of deep lines and ruddy shadows.

"I shitesavit my back pretty good," he said slowly, "and scraped up my right knee." In spite of his discomfort, he chuckled. "But, all things considered, I'm not going to complain too much."

"Well, you may not feel that you have leave to be complaining, but I certainly do."

She sat up, her own face graven with the shock of the effort. Her right hand snaked up and behind her head, her fingers running through the crust of dried blood there.

"I am shitesan, all over."

Brand reached out and pulled up his left leg into a more comfortable position. His pants fell away from the tear at the knee, revealing the deep scrapes in the flesh.

"No, Euwae. That's not it."

She looked at him, too weary with the effort to be angry.

"Look," he continued, "if you want to use that kind of language, you might as well use it right."

"In truth – Are you going to lay me low for my speech, after *this*?" Her arm rose stiffly and she pointed to the holes they had made in the top of the cliff.

He waived at her objection with a weak right hand.

"You're right. Forget it."

His hand slumped and he let his full weight rest upon the stone of the cliff behind him. Euwae nodded as he closed his eyes. She looked out across the rows of upended rocks, which seemed to loom dangerously in the long shadows of the setting sun. Then her head rolled gently towards her companion. With pursed lips, she asked curtly, "What did you mean?"

"What?" he said without opening his eyes.

"You said I spoke wrongly. Yet too you said that you were shitesan. How is it that you can be in such a wise, but I cannot?"

"Oh, you can." He half opened his eyes and looked at her as she sat in the deep hues of the dying day. "But you used the wrong word."

"But – " He waived away her objection once again.

"Look – It's like this: 'shitesan' is a *thing*. But, if you want to use it to describe yourself, the word changes; you say, '*I* am *shitesa*.' Get it?"

"Shitesa. So, in truth, you are shitesa."

He shook his head and grinned as well as he could manage. "No, I am shitesa. *You* are *shitesas*."

Tears of pain came to Euwae's eyes as she moved into a crouch and sat beside Brand with her back against the cliff as well.

"I am shitesas?"

He shook his head weakly. "No: if you mean you – yourself – you use the word 'shitesa.' If you mean someone else, then you say 'shitesas.' Does that make sense?"

She chuckled, but the pain that creased her face mirrored her regret for doing so.

"Ah, yes," she said through gritted teeth. "Now I am seeing the way of it. We are shitesas, indeed."

"Shitesant. *We* are *shitesant*."

"In truth?"

"In truth."

She was silent for a moment, before Brand continued. "And if you're talking about a group besides yourself – "

"Brand Eastlander?"

"Hmm?"

"At this time, I am not caring how to speak of it."

He rolled his head towards her and nodded slowly as his own pain swept over him once again.

"Yeah. Makes sense."

Together they closed their eyes and let the darkness of the night overtake them.

*   *   *

The first fragment of the moon was casting tepid light from above them, making their shadows as reluctant to follow them across the upthrust rocks as they were to leave the shelter of the cliff face and begin the difficult trek across the moraine at the edge of the river. Here, no water remained and the only plants were pale lichens that clung to the shadowed lower faces of the stone. The injuries that the pair had sustained made the going all the more treacherous and they often stumbled and fell. However, once they began to walking south there was no even space on which to rest, forcing them on despite their suffering.

Not far away, the river curled away through a series of rocky draws that pulled water away from the main channel. The sky to the east was starting to throw shadows of its own before a house loomed up before them in the darkness. Ahead, they could hear the bleating of sheep; the smell of smoke crawled towards them on the wind that tumbled across the barren rocks.

As they drew closer to the house, Brand seized Euwae by the shoulder and held her fast. She swore under her breath and threw him a smoldering look from her swollen eyes, but he raised a closed fist as he helped her lower into a crouch. She drew a deep breath and looked at the dwelling, her brows furrowed.

With discomfort, she raised her right arm, fist closed, the spread her fingers; he raised two fingers, spread them and rocked his fist up and down twice. With difficulty he rose and moved off to the left. Euwae watched him for half a moment before she began to circle towards the right of the house.

She made good time, once she climbed the low wall around the grassy strand on which it stood. Smoke lay like lace through the courtyard. The sheep, crowded in their pens, put up a hue and cry as Euwae tried to sneak past them. She hobbled forward as best she could to reach the shelter of an outbuilding between the pen and the house proper and put herself into cover.

The domed roof of green turf showed soot streaks which betrayed the locations of the long narrow windows under the eaves; vestiges of smoke still crawled from its low stone walls and the door, snaking across the courtyard as she reached the out building and sheltered behind it, waiting for the ath'Ale to reach his position near the door. As she waited, she heard the door of the small structure creak open slowly. Slipping her hand to the hilt of her falcata, she grimaced as she squatted to lower her center of balance and prepared to defend herself.

Four fingers nearly the size of Euwae's wrist unfurled from the side of the door jam and wrapped around the corner of the building. A sick, bitter taste burned though her nose and throat. But she held her stance, ready to strike as soon as the monster dared come around the corner.

Instead, the stone wall of the building bulged outwards and began to collapse upon her.

With all her might, the al'Aith pushed away to her left and rolled into the courtyard while the troll finished springing its trap and the stones cascaded down onto the ground where she had stood.

While it used those massive hands to dig though the rubble to find her, Euwae sprinted as best she could around the right side of the building and nearly collided with Brand while he rushed to her aid.

"What the shitesan!"

Euwae's eyes were wide.

"It is a troll and no mistake!"

"A troll?" His lips crushed into a straight line as his head shot forward towards his chest. "How big?"

110

A boulder the size of Brand's chest shot over the house and landed fifteen feet past them.

"Big enough." He decided. "Come on!"

He started to move around the building towards the troll but Euwae seized his arm and pulled him back hard enough to make him stumble.

"You cannot mean to take the battle to *it*!" She said in a hoarse tone as he looked at her with irritation. "It does to be *massive*!"

"Yeah, I got that." He said coolly as he stepped past her. Once again she pulled him back; he pulled her hand off of his arm and shook his head fiercely.

"LOOK," he said quickly, "so the troll is big. We *might* have been able to outrun it if we were in *good* shape, but... " He made an awkward gesture with both hands along with an exaggerated shrug.

"Are you so certain?"

He nodded expansively. "Ooh, yeah. I'm cert-"

He was cut off as one of the troll's great hands wrapped about his head and shoulders and jerked him effortlessly up onto the roof. With a shriek, Euwae scrambled up onto the roof after him.

As she crawled over the eaves and onto the lush grass covering the house, Brand shot through the air past her and hit the ground below with an ugly thud. She pulled out her sword just as the massive hands reached out for her, swinging it in an upward arc which lodged it at the front of the troll's hand between its middle fingers. Blackish-green blood spat out at her as the troll howled in pain and pulled back its left hand, wrenching the blade from Euwae's grasp. It instinctively tried to put the wound to its mouth, causing further injury by accidentally dragging the heavy blade across its lips and teeth and tearing a jagged gash in them.

Its howls turned to a roar. The al'Aith dropped beneath a blind swing and rolled off the roof.

"Bird Club!" She called out. "How fare you?"

"Fair enough..." He muttered as he climbed to his feet, pulling off the ruin of Euwae's bow and throwing it to the ground in frustration. "You?"

"It did to steal my bara'Da!"

"It *took* your sword?"

"Aye!"

His head shook in frustration as he jogged towards the roof.

"Stay put!" He ordered. "I'll get it..."

As he climbed back onto the roof, the troll howled again. It was trying to pluck out the heavy sword by pulling at the blade that protruded upwards through the back of its hand, rather than by the hilt that was lodged down towards its palm; more of the thick slippery blood flowed freely from the deep gashes in the fingers and thumb of the opposite hand.

Brand kept his weapon rotated so that the broad beak was towards his opponent as he spiraled away from the edge of the roof towards the monster. When its deep yellowed eyes locked on him, he changed his stance to slip past the charge that immediately followed; the troll's arms closed on the empty air and it tumbled awkwardly by him, rolling off of the roof in a heap.

As it hit the ground, Euwae shot up and sprinted to his side as best she could.

"I thought I told you to stay *put*!" He growled.

"What, with the likes of that troll?"

His cheeks puffed out as he bit back his retort. "Fair enough," he repeated. From the edge of the house, the troll's head hovered into view, its face a mask of rage.

The troll's hands shot onto the roof.

"Get ready..." Brand said needlessly as Euwae sank into a high crouch.

The troll vaulted up, rather than climbing, closing most of the distance in a single leap and sending a creak through the roof like the complaint of brittle ice.

"Move back, Euwae – BACK!" Brand commanded.

Reluctantly, the al'Aith backed away towards the peak of the roof.

The beast focused solely on the retreating opponent, moving recklessly close to Brand's left as it stalked his companion. Brand shifted his stance and turned as it trundled past, lunging out with a wide backhand swing at the beast's right arm. The hammer head cracked into the troll's elbow and the arm straightened reflexively as it howled in pain.

The warrior rolled beneath the troll's groping fingers, catching the beak of Crows Call into the hooked hilt of Euwae's falcata. His inertia did the rest, tearing the blade free of the wound and spinning it freely to the ground as he rolled past the troll down the slope of the roof.

The monster ignored him and pistoned after Euwae in blind rage. As she reached the chimney hole at the summit of the roof, she leaped up and dove for the far side. Behind her, the charging troll was swallowed by an eruption of sparks and smoke as the top of the roof gave way under its weight and plunged the beast into the burning structure below.

The troll's bellows changed to shrieks as it ran blindly through the chamber, seeking to throw off the flames that surrounded it. Brand climbed to his feet and retrieved her sword.

"Did you know that was going to happen?" He called out cynically.

"I have heard tell of men who have fallen to their deaths when their houses caught fire," she explained wearily as she also worked her way to her feet, "so it seemed to be worth the run.

"How fare you, Bird Club?"

"About the same as last time you asked." He rejoined. "Here..."

He tossed her sword across the gap to her feet. As she bent to retrieve it, the troll burst out of the door below them and stood smoldering in the courtyard. Its chest heaved in pain as it wiped its injured hands across its eyes and face, trying to fend off the memory of the heat and smoke. Brand looked down at the creature as it thrashed about.

"Shitesannus, they're tough." He muttered.

Euwae looked down at it, pity softening her gaze.

"Bird Club..."

"Don't." He said coldly. "That thing'll be on us, quick enough."

"Still – "

He shook off her comment with a hard look. "We need to take it down, *while* it's still hurting."

He half staggered to the eave near the right of the troll, gesturing at Euwae to move to the left. With glacial acceptance, she followed his lead. Together, they slipped off the roof and slowly advanced on the troll.

It barked at them pitifully, lunged forward and lashed out blindly at Brand. He deftly raised his weapon and stepped inside the strike, moving Crows Call in an outside arc that brought it back around with the beak striking sharply on the side of the troll's skull.

The monster's head snapped around and its grey-shot yellow eyes rolled back and up in their sockets. With an ungainly flop it collapsed into a sitting position. The head bobbed loosely on its neck as Brand moved in a slow circle around it, closing into striking distance once he was outside of its line of vision. As he raised Crows Call for the final strike, Euwae reached out a hand towards him and called out.

"Brand! No!"

"Euwae – "

"Stay your hand," she said desperately, "please..."

He lowered the bec de corbin and looked at her incredulously. "*What?*"

"The foe is beaten, ath'Ale... You need not strike it down." Her eyes were soft as she looked at the troll.

"Look upon it, if you believe me not."

He raised the weapon again.

"NO!"

Brand stood there, poised to deliver the death blow. Looking at the troll, he realized that the odd convulsions were not stemming from a physical injury, but from something else entirely.

It was crying.

Brand's head rolled up and to the right in frustration. "You've got to shitesas me," he said with painful irony. "*Seriously?*"

The alAith slowly advanced towards the defeated creature, letting her sword hand drop to her side as emotions struggled across her face.

"Euwae," Brand cautioned, "back off. This thing *will* eat you if it gets a hold of you."

She looked at him and grimaced, but backed away none the less. Brand lowered his weapon and retreated to a safe distance before circling to the troll's right and rejoining her. Together, they watched it continue to sob while it rubbed at the burns on its flesh with its wounded hands, smearing blood across its body in confusion and pain.

Brand let out an exhausted sigh, turned and walked away.

Euwae wiped at the moisture in her own eyes as she slowly followed. He stopped at the edge of the low wall enclosing the court yard, looking out across the river. Slowly she reached up and placed her right hand between his shoulder blades, carefully avoiding the deep scrapes in his skin from his fall down the cliff.

"You have fought these beasts before, then, Brand Eastlander?"

He nodded.

"On the southern shores near del'Ath. There were three of them... They attacked our war band one night, coming out of the sea. Two men were asleep when they died; six more were badly hurt before we killed one troll and the other two fled. I can honestly say I've never gone looking for them after that... Once was enough for me."

She ran her fingers up his back to his shoulder.

"I have never before faced them," she said quietly, "although my father did often, when they would come out of the sea to be raiding the flocks of twoth'Ba. Nine such skulls adorn a post by the shore, a warning and ward to any of their kind foolish enough to seek the same glory.

"Yet never have I thought of them in this wise."

He shook his head thoughtfully.

"No, me either. I'll be honest, though... It wasn't pity that kept me from taking that shitesat down."

"If not sadness for the troll's sorry state, than what held fast your hand?"

He turned and looked back at the troll. It had shifted its weight forward and was lurching about, trying to regain its feet. He hefted Crows Call up into both hands, in case it sought to come at them once again. But the troll simply turned its dark shot eyes upon them for a long moment, before staggering off in a wide arc to their left towards the river.

As it trundled away, Brand turned back to the al'Aith.

"I know what it feels like, to be the one who's going to take that hit and can't do shitesan about it."

"What do you mean?" She looked into his face, her thumb running idly across the fingertips of her right hand.

"I mentioned it before... Back at twoth'Shan'n." His jaw muscles worked furiously for a moment. "I was the one on my knees in front of cu'Kullah. And he sure as shitesan wasn't going to let me live."

Her brow furrowed in concern.

"Yet – Yet he *did* let you live, Bird Club..." She said at last. "For here you stand, victorious upon the shores of Northmoors."

Brand turned back to the river as the troll reached the water and surged forward until it slipped beneath the surface. Once again, his jaw muscles were clenched... But this time, he had nothing more to say. In silence, they watched the first shafts of the sun throw dazzling sparks across the cuts in the surface of the water demarking the deliberate flow of the current.

*   *   *

Euwae and Brand spent three days in the ruined farm, taking their rest as best they could. They found no bodies of the family that had dwelt there, but the cellars and grounds yielded numerous testimonials to them. The gardens were well kept, the animals well tended. Toys, a fallen clothes line and storage cellars troubled Euwae's imagination as they took advantage of the farm's misfortune, but Brand had few compunctions about using this bounty to their advantage.

With each day that passed, he grew more anxious that cu'Kullah's ships would come upon them unawares; for her part, Euwae was even more concerned about the troll. But neither threat emerged from the river before they were ready to travel once again.

As Brand prepared the evening meal at the outside hearth, Euwae lay on the grass nearby watching the clouds meander past as the setting sun painted them with fiery crimson and deep reddish blues. She stretched her limbs languorously, a faint smile playing across her face as she began to sing softly.

Nestled by the river

In the forest lee

A tavern lays waiting

All the folk like me

Looking for distraction

With kindred spirits that they knew

And solace with Lady Killigrew

The weather'd door is low

As I stoop inside

Beyond the bar a stair drops

Through the archway wide

Down to the common room

And beckoning everyone who

Does attend the Lady Killigrew

This side of the windows

The air is thick with talk

The scent of curried chicken

And beer as I walk

To my usual table

And settle in without ado

For a night with Lady Killigrew

Soon the verbal sparring
Ranged from tales of war
To resources to vantage
We traded the floor
One subject to the next
And thus all the hours flew
Bantering at Lady Killigrew

'Til chairs up candles out
Final farewells passed
From the great room up the stairs
I took leave at last
Collar up, hood pulled low
A deep breath of cold air I drew
On departing Lady Killigrew

The clouds draped off the moon
Now shadowed the way
Which through wood and fallow field
Like a river lay
And mirrored my spirits
Riding alone all twoth'Ba through
My back to the Lady Killigrew

Past the Green River bridge
The fog hid the banks
Like the hard day cloaked my will
Fatigue the mind blanks
And washed out the focus
On which I dwelt the evening through
With friends and the Lady Killigrew

Now the way climbs steeply

Up through Sachem's Head

And I trust only instinct

On the path I tread

Little seems familiar

'Til my home rises into view

And I bid good dreams to all of you

Brand smiled as he sat down beside her and passed over a bowl of thick stew. Euwae sat up and took it with a bowed head.

"That song," he said respectfully, "was nice... I haven't heard it before. Is it popular in twoth'Ba?"

"In truth, I have heard it only from my mother, who sings it when she works at her weaving on the loom. I know of no tales of the lady of whom the song is sung, so I can but guess that the whole of it is old, or from some twoth of which I know little.

"My mother is the daughter of the ree of twoth'Bur, so it could be too that the song is of her home and that she did but to change the words a bit to lend it to her new life as the wife of my father."

He nodded as he dipped a wooden spoon into the bowl and took a satisfied slurp of the hot broth.

"Whew – That's still a little hot."

"Yet it tastes *most* well, Bird Club." She added as she drank the broth directly from the bowl. He gave her a lopsided grin and the two of them finished the meal in silence.

When it was done, he took up the bowls and set them in a tub of water. Looking at the rapidly closing sky, he threw another two logs on the fire.

"It's gonna get dark again tonight; I doubt we'll see the moon at all."

She nodded, throwing a glance off in the direction of the river. Brand followed it, looked back to her and shook his head.

"You don't have to worry, Euwae." He said with conviction. "I've heard of trolls that can heal up quickly enough – But the greybloods don't get better any faster than you or I do. And we did a number on that one. He'll be licking his wounds for a while."

She turned back to him.

"Bird Club," she asked curiously, "I have been thinking hard upon this... What draws a greyblood this far up the Great River? I have heard no tale that speaks of them dwelling naught but on the broken shores of the islands off the coastlands of Cord'Or..."

He ran his hand through his beard.

"Yeah. I've been thinking about that, too." Finally he shook his head. "Maybe they do go up the river and we just don't hear about it."

She lowered her eyebrows in a gentle rebuke. He shrugged it off.

"I know, it's not really an answer. The whole time I served the River Prince, I never heard of any trolls being south of the river, either... But I've seen mossbacks in the forests since.

"I know that they came down from Northmoors. So I guess it could happen..."

A loud splash echoed up from the river. They both turned and looked in the direction of the water, but it was already being swallowed by the coming night. Brand turned and reached behind the tub of water, producing a pair of clay jugs.

"Here," he said lightly, "take this."

"What have you here?"

"I found them in a cellar by the sheep pen."

The al'Aith took the jug and looked at the wax sealed stopper. "Bird Club..?"

He nodded.

"Yeah. There's a lot more than this down there. Most of the jars have the seal of twoth'Shan'n on them – So I didn't think that you'd be interested in cracking one of those. But some looked to be home brew... And I figured that they might take a bit of the edge off."

She flaked off the wax with her finger and worked the wooden stopper free. Taking a deep breath through her nose over the mouth of the jug, she closed her eyes as the fragrance of the mead washed over her.

"Ooh, that is delightful and no mistake!"

"I'm glad you see it that way, too..." He chuckled as he produced a knife from his belt and pried the stopper in his own jug free. He raised it to Euwae and nodded.

"Memorias defunctorum celebrari." He said solemnly.

Euwae nodded in kind. "To the glory of heroes yet unborn." She replied.

Together, they drank deeply. When they lowered their jugs, Euwae licked her lips with a smile as Brand ran the back of his hand across his own.

"Oh, aye... That will do nicely indeed..."

Brand set down his drink and looked at Euwae with a broad grin. He raised an eyebrow and Euwae nodded enthusiastically. With a salute he rose and left to retrieve more of the earthen jugs.

*   *   *

"You punched out your sister?"

Euwae raised her fist with a triumphant gesture. "It was a grand battle, to be sure. All the ath'Ale of the court of twoth'Ba could not separate us!"

He shook his head. "All because your brother – "

Euwae scowled and interjected "He is not *my* brother."

"Your *brother* told you that you'd inherit an aes'ree."

Euwae's voice dropped an octave. "It is a matter of en'Och, Bird Club."

"Oh, is that it."

The al'Aith tossed aside another jug.

"Aye, that does to be *it* indeed. How comes a man to spend his days in the service of so great a ree as the River Prince and know not of it?"

Brand leaned forward.

"I've seen plenty of men who were willing to die for their pride, Euwae."

"Pride? PRIDE?"

He leaned back on his bench. "En'Och. Whatever."

Euwae slowly rose to her feet. She walked over to where Brand sat and stood in front of him, her feet wide apart and her hands held in fists in front of her.

"Stand up."

"Euwae..."

"Stand *up*."

He reached down and picked up his jug. "Al'Aith, you're drunk. Sit down, before – "

"Before what, then?"

He took a deep breath. "That's not what I meant, Euwae." He held up his jug to her. "Please..."

Her chest rose and fell as she stared at him.

"Please." He said gently.

Her right hand shot out and swept the jug out of his hand. With a ragged smile she raised it to her lips.

"Shitesan you," she toasted.

"-Sas," he muttered as she took a deep drink.

"And what of you, then?" She asked, waiving the jug at him. "If you fight not for your own glory, then why would you fight at all? To my way of thinking, you may as well be some shop keeping bua'Theu as a true ath'Ale if you have no heart for it."

Slowly, Brand stood as well. Euwae stood less than an arm's reach away when she found herself staring at his sternum. With a spreading grin she looked up into his face.

"Are you *challenging* me, Brand Eastlander?"

Very slowly, he reached out and took away the jug from her. He raised it to his lips and took a long drink; when he finished, he looked down into her face with an stubborn expression.

"Get your own."

They stared at each other for a long moment, before a giggle began wracking Euwae's shoulders. Unable to contain it, she quickly succumbed to debilitating laughter. Brand watched as she bent at the waist, then sank to her knees trying to control her outburst.

Once the laughter started to subside, she looked up at her companion. His face was an amalgam of irritation and perplexed amusement.

"Finished?" He asked with a deeply acidulous tone.

She opened her mouth, but was consumed by a second fit of laughter. With a condescending grin, he sat back down and drained the rest of the jug.

The evening passed quickly enough. Euwae soon fell prey to the call of the strong mead and curled up upon a bench of smooth boulders near the outdoor hearth to sleep. Brand removed himself and sat down upon the ground with his legs crossed, Crows Call across his lap.

Through the red hues of firelight, he watched Euwae as she slept, her rhythmic breathing shot through with an occasional gentle snore. His own eyes heavy from the mead, he rocked his head from side to side to stretch his neck and relax his body. Then, he looked up at a cluster of stars that had crept into a break in the black clouds above them.

"I haven't forgotten," he said softly, "but I never expected something like this." A sad smile swept across his face and his eyes dropped back to Euwae.

"Shitesat en'Och." He said as a yawn pulled down his jaw. Then he let out a snort and shook his head. "It'll probably get us both killed anyway."

Turning away to put his back to the fire, Brand swept the span of the river one last time before he closed his eyes and allowed sleep to pull him away at the last.

Summersford

They started out late the next morning, after seeing to the animals on behalf of the missing family, packing some supplies and making a quick breakfast. The pair had taken a change of what clothes would fit them; Brand made sure to take a pair of water skins, as well, despite Euwae's protests given the proximity of the river. He also took two more jugs of the mead, about which his companion made no protest at all.

After leaving the homestead and following the river eastward a short way, it soon became clear that they would be unable to make good time at the river's edge. Unlike the southern side which was mostly low and flat, here the river cut into the banks. Any exposed shoreline was mostly tumbled rock which provided little open ground on which to walk and fording between them proved to be difficult given their need to make haste. Once they reached a lower point in the bluff they scrambled to the top, having decided to leave the side of the flow and move inland a bit to avoid another tumble through an undercut like they had experienced a week before.

In fact, this choice proved to make their travel easier by far. The ground was even and reasonably level a few hundred yards from the water. There were also frequent pools of clear fresh water lining the long dell at fairly regular intervals to provide refreshment. So, with the sun shining and a cool breeze coming off the river they made good time in their march towards Summersford.

They camped that evening beside a wide, narrow pool a bow shot from the river. There was no wood for a fire and the night was unexpectedly cool. They took a cold meal and settled down on a lee slope overlooking the pool to stay out of the gentle breeze.

After the sun had set, Brand stretched out on his back looking up at the stars, while Euwae sat beside the edge of the water with her boots off and running her feet back and forth through the tall grass that grew there.

"What a most wondrous night..." She sighed.

"Uh." Brand grunted with distracted consent. Euwae twisted and gazed back at him.

""Do you not think it so?"

"What?" He asked sitting up and looking back at her.

"Bird Club. Are you listening to me?"

"Of course –" Suddenly he shot to his feet. "Euwae... Move away from there. *Now*."

The al'Aith's head whipped back as she looked at the pool.

"Oh, my!" She said in wonder.

The surface of the pool shimmered as if it were bathed in moonlight... But there was no moon in the sky.

"Euwae. Back away!" Brand rushed down the slope and pulled her to her feet.

"What?" She cried out in dismay. "Are you gone mad?"

"That's a magic pool!" Brand said with temerity. "Back off!"

Her head tilted to the left as she studied him in the darkness.

"Stay clear of it? But why? It is a moon pool and no mistake."

"A – Moon pool?"

"Aye, water so pure as to hold the light of day... And sacred to the priests and such oracles as make use of it."

"*This* is a moon pool?"

He studied it with obvious distaste as Euwae shook her head in dismissal.

"Aye, they do to be common enough near about Summersford. In truth, it is why the druids of twoth'Ba lay such a hard claim to these lands... To be nigh to them."

He looked up from the water towards his companion.

"So we're close to Summersford, then?"

"Aye, given this we must be."

Brand turned towards the direction of the river. "So we've beaten them." He said quietly. "That's good... We should be able to reach the outer baileys of twoth'Ba and get word to the ree that cu'Kullah and his war band are coming."

"Get word – To the ree..." Euwae's voice trailed off as she considered that statement as Brand nodded.

"You're almost home, Euwae."

"Aye," she said flatly, "almost indeed."

*   *   *

The next day went much like the first. The sun was setting in glorious golden fire against the high clouds when Brand let out a grunt and pointed skyward. Running against the line of cloud rose a thin column of a much darker hue.

Euwae didn't have to ask this time, but rather inquired, "Are you thinking it to be another hearth?"

Brand scowled and shook his head.

"Not this time... The color's too dark."

He trotted off to the right and up a rise to get a better view of the river. Euwae watched as his head jerked down in frustration and he started to jog off instead of coming back to join her. Sprinting after, she soon caught up to the ath'Ale and slowed to match his pace.

"What was it that you did to see?" She asked between breaths.

He turned a dark face to her.

"We're too late. Cu'Kullah's at Summersford now."

"What! How?"

"They must've just passed us today... We probably missed them over the banks. There's a few outbuildings on fire – I don't think that they're into the main compound yet. At least, I didn't see any fire coming from inside the wall."

He looked Euwae up and down as she trotted beside him.

"Can you keep this pace up?"

"As long as you, sure enough!"

Brand kicked out his left foot and stopped short. Euwae trotted on for a bit before she stopped too. Brand just stood there with his arms hanging by his sides, but his fists clenched slowly. His breathing was slow and steady as he looked across the distance at the al'Aith.

"This is no game, Euwae. You may think that these men are no Red Caps or trolls. But don't underestimate them.

"I've fought beside them against the shitesannus marauds and against them when they tore down the best men that the River Prince could rally to him. They're smart and brave and they crap out en'Och with breakfast."

"Now – "

Brand cut her off by closing the distance between them with two long strides, his right hand raised in dismissal.

"No. If we can't fight them at our best we will lose." He said with utter conviction.

"If you – "

He took another step so that she was less than an arms length from his chest, forcing her to look up into his face as he loomed over her.

"Euwae, these men have already beaten me. *Twice.* If we are going to fight them now, we can't give them any shitesan advantage."

She opened her mouth but again he interrupted.

"None."

Euwae snapped her mouth shut and breathed furiously through her nose as she stared into Brand's eyes, but his demeanor didn't change. Unlike his companion, the ath'Ale was cool and fully in control, standing like an agent of death awaiting the word of his master to begin his harvest.

Slowly Euwae's shoulders ceased rocking up and down as her body seemed to absorb the glacial resolve from the warrior before her. But while her breathing ebbed, the fire in her eyes flared all the brighter as they stayed locked with his.

At last she nodded and turned to the pillar of smoke.

"Fine. We walk as swiftly as we may. But do not think that we do so for any sign that I am the weaker of us, Bird Club. It is well that you know much of this foe. For have I been shown that such wisdom is precious in battle.

"But – as *we* are saving our strength for the battle – you had best be telling me all that there is to be knowing of these men, that they fall all the swifter to the feet of their betters."

She turned back to him with an arch look.

"Well, then? What are you waiting upon?"

With a nod Brand resumed their march at a brisk pace, telling the al'Aith all that he could remember of the war band of cu'Kullah and their deeds against both the marauds and twoth'Shan'n as they followed the glow on the eastern sky to Summersford.

When the smoke started to get thick in their noses Brand slowed their pace further, carefully following the line of hills to stay wide of the settlement below. Once they had reached a suitable position out of the line of smoke the pair crept to the crown of the ridge and surveyed the town below.

Fires had been set to the buildings nearest the river, storehouses and small stalls of tradesmen looted and put to the torch simply for the sake of violence. Of the village itself – perhaps thirty houses – there was little sign of fire damage visible through the turf roofs, although armed men with torches moved warily through the streets, walking in low stances with weapons drawn.

The grand house and court at landward side of the village was ringed by a earth and log wall of twice a man's height. From their current vantage the pair could see both the warriors manning the walls at the gate and the mass of villagers huddled by the well in the center of the open ground. The gate was still intact, although the ugly black scars at the top gave obvious testament to the use of fire against it.

Four ships lay about the ford. Three were wide, laid out for oarsmen and two of these were further fitted with fore and aft castles from which to fight as well. One of the latter was anchored in the middle of the river; the other two warships were tied off at the wide pier that jutted out into the flow of the channel. Only a few men could be seen on the warships, but there was no sign of any encampment on the beach.

The fourth vessel was a sleek merchant cog, nearly forty feet long with the stylized horse of twoth'Ba carved like a figurehead on the prow. It was moored upriver in the channel fifteen feet from the shore. On that vessel, there was no sign of a crew.

Having taken the measure of the situation, Brand tapped Euwae on the shoulder and closed his right fist. Together they slipped back to the far side of the hill to construct their tactics. Once they were safely out of sight, the al'Aith balled her fists in fury as the two of them crouched together to plan their approach on the village.

"How *DARE* they?"

Brand rocked back onto his haunches.

"They dare because cu'Kullah is crazy and they've sworn to follow him. I told you, he sees himself as some ancient king... He sees all this as his way to en'Och and power."

Euwae said nothing as her eyes bored into visions of retributions yet to be dispensed. Brand looked at her face and scowled.

But, softly he said, "Euwae... I told you before: I need you focused. Right here, right now. If you go out there like this, you'll kill a lot of them before you die – But you'll never see the hit that kills you, either, because you're too shitesan angry. If you can't get your head back into this fight, you've not only killed us, but you've killed everyone left alive in that village.

"So, if you don't want to hand Summersford over to cu'Kullah on a plate, look at me and take a deep breath – Help me save those people down there."

Euwae shot to her feet, her falcata a dull gleam in the night.

Brand didn't move.

"*Don't* do this." In the same steady voice, he pushed her back to the ground; as if waking from a dream, Euwae shuddered and her sword nearly fell from her hand as her eyelids slammed shut to dam up the tears of rage.

Brand waited as the anger drained out of the young woman, never taking his eyes from her face. Finally her breath, while shallow, hit a constant rhythm and her eyes twitched open. He immediately locked his gaze to hers; after a moment, she swept away the water on her face and nodded.

"Good to have you back, Euwae." He leaned forward and offered her his hand. She swallowed and took it by the wrist, her head bobbing up and down once more. Brand dropped back into his crouch and rocked his head in the direction of Summersford.

"So, now that a frontal charge is out, let's go over what we've got. They're still roaming the streets, so there's still active resistance outside the court – But not enough to make them guard the boats..."

"So, there are but a few men that they do to be chasing."

"Agreed."

Euwae's breathing steadied as she examined the circumstances of what they had seen.

"I remind you that this court is the home of Konner Knot-Spender, the priest of twoth'Ba. He will be having no fear of fire, for his bonds to the sacred lakes run deep indeed. Nor is he any stranger to the field of battle, for he stands beside the ree of the twoth more boldly than any three ath'Ales of good worth."

"Konner? The druid with the braids?" Brand made a vague gesture around his head with his fingers. "Yeah, him I remember. If he's still alive, we're in better shape already."

"Should we be seeking to join him, then?"

Brand thought about that before he replied. Finally, he shook his head.

"No. I know the ath'Ales of twoth'Fhee. Our only chance is to break up their momentum tonight, before they get settled in – They won't be expecting any resistance in force at this point. If we can surprise them and make them think they've been had, they'll run and we've saved the village out of the gate... That's an advantage we can't pass on."

Euwae smiled coldly, swiftly becoming a mirror of Brand's disquieting calm.

"Have you a plan?"

He nodded.

"I do. But cu'Kullah's men will have to help us make some headway there."

Euwae's head tilted in an unspoken question, before the tight smile split into a truly frightening grin of understanding.

"When do we begin, then?" She asked with dark anticipation.

They made their way further around the village to keep the shadows from the fire around them before they made their way out of the hills and across the open fields to the village. They walked in the same crouched posture of the warriors raiding the village, as if they, too, were searching the terrain for something in the darkness. Thus concealed, they made their cautious way into the rows of houses that surrounded the wall of the court of Summersford.

They ducked into the first open house they found just as three men rounded the corner and began to make their way in the pair's direction from the far corner of the lane. They were tall and thin, dressed in a loose cloth that draped around them. Each carried a short bow and quiver, with a pair of clubs hanging from their belts. Brand nodded and he and Euwae both moved into the dark recesses just inside the door, where the light from the street refused to reach. As soon as the men passed, Brand slipped out behind them and Euwae followed close behind.

Crows Call let out an eerie whistle as Brand brought the beak across and into the back of the first man's skull. As the others turned, Euwae flicked out her sword and pulled it across the throat of the second man in line and spun in a circle as the third threw down his bow with a snarl and reached down to pull the clubs from his belt. Before he could clear them, however, Brand's weapon caught him in an upward stroke beneath the jaw and sprayed ruin across himself and Euwae.

"Bird Club!" Euwae hissed.

He scowled. "What? Don't tell me you're angry about me stealing the glory."

She waved her sword at him. "Do not be so touched." She whispered with frustration. "These men are of no good to us now!"

Brand looked at the bodies. The man that had taken the blade to the throat still thrashed about; he brought up his bec de corbin to end his suffering but Euwae seized the weapon and pulled it so that he had to turn and face her.

"NOT in the head!" She said as she fought to keep her voice down. "We will not be able to lay claim to the tathlum if you are going about smashing all of their skulls rather than taking a harvest of their heads!"

Brand looked at her askance.

"What?"

Behind her the warrior on the ground struggled to rise. Brand swung absently and brought the hammer head down on the back of his neck with a loud snap, looked at Euwae and made an apologetic gesture with his free hand. She rolled her eyes in frustration before she rocked her head back towards the doorway.

"Just you take those two there and be getting them inside," she muttered.

Once the bodies had been dragged into the house, she grabbed the man she'd injured by the hair and raised her sword. However, rather than decapitate him she looked at him for a moment, pursed her lips in frustration and let the body back gently to the floor. Brand spoke from the darkness.

"Second thoughts about that?" He asked casually.

"They are worthless dicenn." She said with disappointment, paying no heed to Brand's scowl. "Not a man of them is worthy of a torc."

"What does *that* have to do with anything?"

"You told the tale that cu'Kullah sees himself as a ree of ancient legend, did you not?"

Brand nodded.

"And you wished for his war band to be broken and flee?"

"It'll be a shitesan easier than killing all two hundred of them."

"Then we need the heads of true ath'Ale. In the stories of the kings of the Old Ages, they took the heads of their foemen and used them as a weapon: the *tathlum*."

She waited for a response, but Brand said nothing.

"To be struck with the tathlum brings instant death." She explained with a sigh of frustration.

Brand's left eye tightened in skepticism.

"So this... Tathlam – "

"Tathlum."

"These heads actually kill people when they hit them?"

"So the tales say."

"Sounds like it's more sorcery to me..." He shrugged. "Have you ever seen it work?"

"Well, no. It is a weapon of *legend*."

"Great. That wasn't my plan, you know."

"It was not?"

"No – "

Suddenly a dark shadow filled the doorway. "By the twelve skulls – What have I now..." Growled the voice of the warrior who discovered them as he slowly entered the room.

Brand looked at Euwae.

"*Not* in the *head*." She entreated him. With a sigh, he turned and swung Crows Call in a wicked upswing that caught the raider between the legs; as he sagged, a falcata dropped from his numb fingers and his silver torc glinted red in the wan glow of the fire. Brand pursed his lips.

"Not in the head." He muttered as he brought the weapon around and drove it into the center of the ath'Ale's chest and sent the body tumbling back into the street. As cries of surprise arose from the group of men outside the house, Brand was still shaking his head as he leaped over the corpse to begin the grim harvest.

The pair worked in an unspoken agreement; as Brand knocked them down with Crows Call, Euwae decapitated them with her sword. After three men had fallen, the rest of the warriors turned and fled, calling for aid from their fellows.

"We don't have a lot of time, here." Brand admonished as Euwae gathered her gruesome trophies. "So you get one shot at this. If it doesn't work out, then we do things my way."

Euwae nodded distractedly, unable to pull her eyes away from the heads.

"Bird Club – I am thinking that I am soon to be..." She swallowed hard enough for him to hear in the darkness.

He shook his head again disparagingly.

"This was *your* plan." He snorted.

"But..." Euwae looked up at him, visibly sickened by what she had done.

His gaze softened as he saw her expression.

"Never mind. Look. Give them to me – "

"They do to be there – Around this corner!"

Euwae and Brand exchanged a look, then he grabbed her under the arms and hoisted her onto the turf roof of the house. Before he could join her, however, the men who had fled careened back around the corner with a dozen of their fellows at their heels. With a shout they rushed at Brand, who turned to face them.

Forming a line that filled the narrow street, the raiders drew up well beyond his reach but stared past Brand, up at Euwae who stood just above him on the eve, the three heads hanging from her right hand, her falcata in her left. The gore spattered across her face and clothes shone wetly in the ebbing light of the fire from the far side of the village as she pointed her sword at the men in the street.

"YOU HAVE BROKEN THE SACRED LAWS LAID OUT FOR YOU IN ARD'REE'S OWN HAND." She cried out in a near scream. "NOW WILL YOU SUFFER TORMENT UNENDING FOR YOUR TREACHERY!"

She let two of the heads drop beside her, being careful to keep them from rolling off the roof as she lifted the third into the air.
"DEATH TO THOSE WHO HAVE RAISED THEIR HANDS

AGAINST TWOTH'BA! DEATH TO THOSE WHO HAVE DARED DEFY ARD'REE'S LAW!"

With that, she threw the tathlum at the crowd of men below as even more of them rounded the corner and began to charge up the street. The head arched up slightly before it tumbled down amongst the first group, striking their leader squarely in the chest. He flinched and turned his face away for several seconds.

Nothing happened.

Brand backed up and shot Euwae a dark look as the man chuckled at his own temerity and reached down to pick up the head. Brand prepared to scramble onto the roof; the men at the corner had nearly closed ranks with the first group when the man holding the tathlum let out a shrill noise and let the head go.

But the tathlum did not fall to the ground.

Rather, Brand watched as a flickering bluish-white light began to radiate out from the eyes and mouth. The men in the first group backed away and stumbled into their reinforcements as the light became a sphere too bright to look upon, before it expanded like a wave and engulfed them all.

A wail of desperate grief and pain echoed out of the brilliance as Brand turned his back to the intense glare, shielding his eyes and cringing at the mournful cacophony. Framed by his hands, he saw Euwae stand unmoved upon the edge of the roof, a second head in her hand, poised to send it into the press of raiders should a target emerge from the impenetrable luminosity that shielded them.

Then, the light was gone.

Crushing his lids to try to clear his vision, Brand heard rather than saw the few survivors fleeing back the way they had come, shouting the word "Morrigen!" as they stumbled in blind panic through the street.

As his vision cleared he turned to face more than a dozen corpses lying in the road. The flesh of each of the bodies had contracted and turned the color of ancient leather; some had clawed at their eyes while others covered their ears in a futile attempt to ward off the fate that had consumed them.

"Sacred shitesan." Brand muttered and swallowed hard against his own gorge as he looked at the forlorn postures of what had once been brave men which now littered the street.

With a concerned look, Brand turned back to Euwae. She stood as still as the men who had suffered and died at her hand, her eyes locked on the place from which the mob of raiders had scattered. With concern he rushed back to the edge of the roof and reached up to touch her leg.

"Euwae..?"

Like the melting of bitter ice her head slowly dropped while her gaze shifted towards him. A second tathlum dropped from her numb fingers and rolled down the roof; despite himself, Brand gasped reflexively as he ducked away from it in fear, but it simply hit the ground with a hollow thud and lay still. He exhaled slowly and looked back at Euwae. Her face was drawn, her eyes vacant.

Brand quickly vaulted up and took Euwae into his arms. After a moment, he felt her begin to sob, but otherwise she made no move to seek his comfort. He shifted his position upon the roof to keep her from falling should she collapse, but also to move his vantage so that he could see the street once the inevitable return of the ath'Ale of the war band commenced. But the only people he saw were a few dumbfounded defenders of the great house, who stood behind the log parapet of the wall across the way with a vantage to have seen the light... And they looked nearly as shocked as the al'Aith in his arms.

The defenders further away from the scene, however, quickly raised the cry that the attackers were falling back to the village green. Brand looked fully upon Euwae, then took a final look down the street before he gently helped her sit down and crouched beside her protectively.

"Hey," he asked gently, "How're you doing?"

Euwae's shoulders shook with her ragged breathing; her eyes refused to focus as he took her chin in his hand and rotated her face towards his.

"Are you all right?"

Brand's face puckered at her weak nod. He turned his eyes back to the great house as the nearest defenders started to run off towards the gate and recomposed his demeanor before he turned back to his companion.

"Things are starting to move, Euwae. We need to keep pushing the flanks. Are you – " He shook his head.

"No, you're not." He let out a sharp exhalation through his nose, stood up and offered her his hand.

"Come on, al'Aith. Let's get you off of this roof."

Brand helped her up and escorted her over to the eve. He dismounted first, took her about the thighs and lifted her down. Once Euwae had her footing, he took the last head out of her hand and set it gingerly on the street beside the other. Brand started to lead her back into the house, but after looking at the blood trails clotting on the threshold he led her to the next building down the street.

The door was locked, but Crows Call made short work of it. Brand scanned the chamber once to make sure it was empty before he led Euwae to the low bench along the wall inside the chamber.

"Here. Lay down," he admonished gently as he led her to the bench. "You've done good work, Euwae – You've got them on the run. But the town still needs our help."

He helped her sit, tucked her legs up and threw his cloak across Euwae to both warm and conceal her.

"So, you rest here for a little while. I'll be back as soon as I'm done."

As he stood, she made a noise deep in her throat and her eyes slowly shut. Brand turned and studied the room one more time, then strode out towards the street, leaning the battered door back into the frame as best he could after he stalked outside.

Moving quickly, he jogged past the brittle looking victims of the tathlum and rounded the corner from which they had both advanced and fled. Before him milled a knot of the northern mercenaries that he and Euwae had first encountered. They huddled in nervous conversation, their attention focused on the gateway into the defenders wall.

Without breaking his stride Brand jogged up casually towards them. A few took notice, but didn't recognize the threat that sauntered into their midst until he brought up his weapon and began to rain blows into them.

There were too many to make a coordinated response to this unexpected assault. Those closest to him shouted in dismay as they pulled out their clubs and sought to get at their attacker, but in the narrow street their numbers worked against them. With his first few strikes, Brand was able to clear himself enough room to fight, but the mercenaries had little success in doing the same. Quickly, the men at the rear of their group began to retreat, rather than wait for a chance to fight. As the men in front of them heard them flee and weighed it against the cries of their injured and dying comrades at the front of the line, they quickly turned to join them. And so it went.

After the last of them had made a few feeble feints at Brand before they ran off, he ducked into the shadows between two houses and looked further down the street. There, the real threat emerged like rocks from the torrent of fleeing men: the ath'Ales of twoth'Fhee held fast to their weapons and blocked any further advance towards the gate. In the front, Brand recognized Angus, as always leading the men in cu'Kullah's absence. Once the mercenaries had cleared the street, Brand counted at least thirty men in his path and swore bitterly.

"Did you to say, 'shitesan,' ath'Ale?" A voice behind him quietly asked.

Brand turned slowly to face the man in the deep shadows, Crows Call held low between them.

"I know, too, that weapon," said the man, gesturing towards the weapon as he stepped forward into the poor light. "It served famously enough beside the rees of three twoths when joined together to put down the disease of del'Ath.

"And I am most sure that – were the dead to rise to our defense – I should stand most pleased that this one had come free of the dark world to see to it."

He held out his right hand, palm up.

"I am Konner, priest of twoth'Ba and master of Summersford."

Cautiously Brand reached out and accepted the wrist clasp. When he pulled his hand away, it was slick with blood. Konner winced and nodded.

"Aye. These hiel were upon us like mad wasps..." He grimaced. "And, more is the pity, I was stung."

Brand looked at him in concern. "How bad is it?"

The druid's face pinched as he took a step to the side and leaned against the wall to his right.

"It will grow grander with the re-telling of it in my old age." He replied.

Despite himself, Brand smirked.

"That's good to hear, Konner. We can use a magician's touch right about now." But the other man shook his head.

"The wounds may not be the death of me, but my weavings will be spited by them, worse is the luck. But I will do what can be done to aid to you, Eastlander."

Brand hefted Crows Call with a conciliatory gesture, leaned back and peeked around the corner. Angus and his men still stood firm at the gate, having paid no heed to the flight of their allies. Brand turned back into the alley to look over Konner. The priest's left hand was clamped firmly to his side; blood stained his shirt and pants below the wound.

"Blade or bow?"

"Arrow, straight away."

"How's your head?"

Konner licked his lips.

"In truth, it spins unkindly. But fear not... I am no coward. I will not fail these people, who have so well served me."

Brand was quiet for a moment.

"Can you come up with something that'll keep them distracted?"

Konner's eyes moved as he considered his options. Finally, he nodded.

"That is the way of it. Yet the weaving requires focus, so time will not be well met should your dance be over long."

Brand chuckled darkly.

"It won't if I can help it."

"Then give me but a moment to prepare, ath'Ale and you shall be having your distraction."

Then the priest slipped back into the darkness.

Brand returned his attention to the street. Angus had his back towards him and was gesturing sharply.

"Your men aren't too happy, Angus." Brand nodded with satisfaction as he looked them over. "Good."

The light from the docks was brighter here and beyond this house there was little useful cover. With no other good option, he simply shrugged and crouched down to wait for Konner's word.

When he heard the druid chanting behind him, he shifted forward to keep his gaze locked on the group in the street. Soon he realized that the light was taking on an odd color, as if it were being reflected off of gently moving water. Angus noted it, too, for he started to gesture to the men when all of their weapons were jerked from their hands and cascaded to the street.

Brand grinned and tossed a salute towards the priest as he charged out into the light. He ran as fast as he could to close the gap between himself and the ath'Ale of twoth'Fhee, who tried vainly to pull their weapons off the ground and stared at their attacker in shock. All but Angus: he turned to face the oncoming threat with his bare hands and rushed headlong to face the lone warrior who charged them.

They met roughly twenty feet from where the men of the war band vainly tried to pry free their weapons. Brand swung Crows Call in a shallow arc at shoulder height, but Angus spun left and slipped inside the blow, throwing a punch with his right hand that caught Brand on the side of the chest. He grunted at the pain but kept his grip on the bec de corbin, catching it below the head with his left hand and using the long shaft to strike Angus under the chin and snap his head back with brutal force.

Angus stumbled, but now his men had given up on their swords and were starting to follow his lead. Three ran forward and circled around Brand, looking for an opening. He faced the one to his left and made an obvious stamping motion, followed by a sharp thrust with Crows Call to the right. The man on that side fell for the feint; the weapon caught him on the side of the knee and sent him tumbling back into the wall of the building behind him.

Brand used the momentum and pivoted on his right foot, leaning into the blow to get even greater extension and struck the man behind him in the arm. The heavy hammer head glanced off with a crack as the forearm shattered beneath it.

The third man wisely stepped back until more of his allies joined the circle. Two of them tried to close the distance and were quickly dispatched. The rest began to slowly press forward when Angus cried out hoarsely, "Hold! Back away!"

The men were well trained and followed orders, falling back four paces towards their leader and setting Angus, who had not moved, in their front rank once again. He stared through the strange flickering glow at the single warrior who faced down his men.

"Dicenn..." He questioned in quiet shock. "But – I saw you drown, and no mistake!"

The men behind him suddenly let out a gasp of dismay and began to back away, forcing back their fellows. But they were not looking at Brand. He half turned to see what frightened them and saw Euwae walking slowly up the street with a fatigued shuffle. In her right hand, a naked falcata glistened... While her left clutched the pair of severed heads so fiercely that her knuckles had drained of blood. The shifting light caught her eyes, which reflected the odd glare as she looked upon the men in front of her.

Angus held up his left fist to steady them. Even as they stopped giving up ground, Euwae lifted the heads towards the sky.

"The Morrigan..." Some of the men muttered.

"No!" Shouted Angus. "It is but some trick! STAND YOUR GROUND!"

Euwae started to advance on them once again, but stumbled; she fell to her knees, losing her grip on the heads, although she managed to keep hold of her sword. Her hair was loose and spilled forward over her face, concealing it to the nervous men who stood against her... But her eyes caught the bloody glow of the fires, glaring out from beneath the wild mane with unbridled menace. In the hush that followed, Euwae lifted the heads.

"I have come." She said raggedly.

Shouting in horror, the men behind Angus began to turn and run.

Angus looked from Brand to Euwae.

"But – What *trick* is this, then..?" Moving his eyes between the two of them, Angus studied the two of them. Finally he backed away until he could safely turn and make a full retreat with the men who had already fled back up the street, crying out that Morrigen was upon them. As they headed for their ships, Euwae levered herself to her feet and made her way to Brand with the shuffle of bone weary fatigue.

"Well then," she asked quietly, "what was that all for?"

137

Brand still gazed at where the al'Aith had stumbled, but at the sound of her voice suddenly turned his head to face her and took a ragged breath, shaking his head.

"I don't think they liked the look of you, Euwae." He chided quietly. "Maybe it's your hair."

"Oh? And what about my hair is so displeasing?" She said self consciously, trying without success to clear her red locks from her face.

Brand turned and walked away from her to where the men had lost their weapons. Once he reached the spot where Angus had stood, a broad grin lit his face.

"Shitesa!" He said in pleased surprise. "Remind me to thank Angus the next time I see him."

Brand reached down towards the street and tried to retrieve the long, chisel tipped knife Angus had taken from him on the shores of Ers'Elb. He gave the handle several long tugs, before he stood up and looked towards the alley to the left of the street.

"Konner!" He cried. "That's enough! They've gone... Drop the spell!"

After several seconds, the eldritch flickering faded back to the aching throb of normal fire. Brand reached down again and picked up the wicked looking scramasax.

"That is a fine looking knife..." Said Euwae quietly as she finally gave up on pulling her hair back into place. Brand looked from the knife to his companion.

"Yes, al'Aith... It's good to have it back."

"So, the war band of cu'Kullah is in flight. What steps are we taking, then?"

"We keep pushing them, Euwae." He said grimly. "They'll rally once they get back to the ships – Once cu'Kullah takes charge of this mess. We can't give him the time to do it."

Her chin trembled as she nodded her ascent.

"You sure you're up for this?"

Her chest swelled as she drew back her shoulders and raised herself to her full height. But Brand raised his hands in apology before she could voice a protest.

"Let's get going." He said firmly as he began to jog after Angus and his men, with Euwae trotting heavily beside him.

As they turned the corner, Konner staggered out of the alley. He opened his mouth to call after them, but the sound was choked out of his throat when he saw that the two severed heads that Euwae had dropped still hovered roughly six feet off the street, their luminescent eyes steaming with the drowning weight of the damned.

      Smoke from the burning buildings stung the pair's eyes but concealed their advance as they covered the open space towards the men huddled together on the docks. Angus was pushing his way through the press along the length of the pier, towards the war ship which had anchored in the flow of the river rather than being properly docked. At the end of the dock he climbed a mooring post so that he could see the vessel clearly, cupped his hands around his mouth and cried out to the ship.

      "My ree! We must abandon the shore and take to the longships!"

      "No." The voice of cu'Kullah pealed like the menace of distant thunder across the water.

      Angus swallowed. Twice.

      At last he shook his head and called out again.

      "My ree! The priest here has raised nothing less than the dead and their queen! She stands with her very tathlum against us!" Around him, the men muttered their consent.

      "Impossible."

      Angus took a quick breath. "I have seen her, my ree!"

      "Aye!" cried out some of the men behind him. Once added in piteous terror, "I did to see those who fell to the heads of the doomed!"

      The men on the pier surged forward towards their ships, but the voice of cu'Kullah dammed their retreat.

      "You dare to *fail* me?"

      Euwae shuddered and came to an abrupt stop at the sound of that voice. All of the men of the war band turned their eyes to Angus.

      Heavy with reluctance, his eyes lowered and he shook his head.

      Brand screamed and ran forward, tearing off through the smoke and into the morass of men on the pier. As he crashed against them he cried out, "Not the heads! Save HER the heads!"

      The men who still possessed weapons raised them in their own defense but fought without the resolve that drove their attacker. Those who were closer to safety began to jump from the dock onto the pair of long ships that were tied off to it. The rest began to slowly back away from the town towards the far end of the pier as best they could.

      From beyond the smoke came a dull crash, followed by shrieks of hatred from a great chorus of throats hidden in the pall of smoking ruin towards the center of the village.

Slowly, the smoke parted long enough to reveal a lone woman standing motionless in the middle of the road, as if awaiting an invitation to bring destruction upon them all. As she took a single step forward the shroud of the fires wrapped about her again, but the wailing, maddened voices filled the air with sounds as harsh to the ear as smoke is to the chest...

Then dark forms began to rush like a river from the fog of war towards the men of twoth'Fhee. The last vestiges of their bravery were slaughtered. They threw down their weapons and made for their ships; soon those who had reached them safely began to cast off, stranding a score of their fellows on the pier.

These men decided to take their chances with the river and jumped into the water in the hopes that they might swim to safety... Heedless of the thought that the weight of their armor might prove just as deadly as the ghostly horde streaming out of the flames to doom them.

While his comrades panicked, Angus turned to meet his fate at the hands of the oncoming threat and quickly realized it was only Brand and the peasants of the village who faced them. He looked across the faces of his terrified men, rolled his eyes and dropped down off the piling, pushing against their retreat, back towards the shore of the river. As Brand came within earshot, Angus called out, "Dicenn! There is one who does not fear you! Fight ME!"

Brand reached out with Crows Club and took one man in the stomach while he pushed a second opponent aside and sent him toppling into the water. Angus wove through the men into the gap that Brand had cleared, picking up a falcata that the second man had dropped when he had futilely tried to catch his balance. Both men looked at the other...

Angus' shoulder sagged in resignation. He threw the sword into the river with a shrug.

"I cannot slay them what are already dead." Angus said heavily. "But I would as soon die by the hand of such, as suffer what fate awaits me at the hands of cu'Kullah should I flee."

A man pushed into Brand from behind; the warrior swung Crows Call over his head and brought it down behind him with a crunching thud. Ignoring the injured man stumbling away behind him, Brand looked at his unarmed adversary with dispassion.

"Angus – Don't be an idiot. I'm not dead."

The other man shrugged weakly.

"I saw the way of it. Saw you drown that night at –" A tremor ran through him. "And now here you be... And like as the herald of the queen of the dead, no less."

140

Brand scowled but Angus charged at him. Brand brought up Crows Call and held it across his chest, using it to force the bigger warrior back as Angus tried to get a hold of him. Two more men shook off their fear and pushed in to help their leader; Brand turned to face them, deflecting the blow of one sword away and catching the other man's sword with the beak of his bec de corbin as he followed through with the swing. The first man closed again; Brand kicked him savagely in the knee. Howling in pain, he overbalanced and fell into the river. The man whose weapon was bound against Crows Call released it and plunged into the water after his comrade.

Brand cursed and turned back to Angus, but the leader of the war band was on his knees, blood spreading across the front of his tunic. Brand stepped forward and reached out to him, but Angus lifted the scramsax which he had taken from Brand in the charge, slowly turned it over in his hand and passed it to back to its owner, hilt first.

"A goodly knife, indeed..." Angus stammered through the pain, before he sagged back into one of the dock pilings.

"That's just shitesat." Brand said bitterly.

Euwae shuddered while the men from the village rushed past her through the smoke, as if she were waking from a dream. Glancing from side to side, the al'Aith quickly realized that the folk of the village had rallied. Crying out to the glory of twoth'Ba, she joined their headlong charge towards the war band on the dock. To her utter surprise, the warriors who had so brazenly attacked were now in full retreat, cutting loose the two long ships rather than casting them off properly... Those who were too far or too late to make the crossing as they were pushed off from the pier jumped into the river in a vain attempt to reach their fleeing comrades.

As the smoke thinned in the breeze she saw Brand had driven far into the thinning press of men, while the villagers moved to follow him; he did not stop his relentless advance until the villagers stormed past to force the last of the raiders into the water. Near the end of the pier he turned and scanned through the crowd of people around him until he saw her towards the rear of the throng.

They locked eyes.

Brand nodded solemnly towards the al'Aith; with a trembling lower lip, Euwae responded in kind. Thus distracted, neither one seemed to hear the the cries of victory which burst out around them, nor the harsh splash of the oars as the three warships took to the river current and pulled away from both their drowning brethren and the weavings of the dead that had pushed them from Summersford.

Euwae slipped through the press of cheering villagers to stand before Brand. He reached out slowly and pushed the hair away from her face.

"How're you doing?" He asked quietly, his voice thick with emotion.

"In truth?"

He nodded once, slowly, in response.

"I am thinking I am..." Euwae looked at the people around her, then slowly drew herself up, making a show of casting off the fatigue with a dramatic raise of her chin. Brand exhaled with a shake of his head and dropped his hand.

"I think you are, too." He said as lightly as he could.

Euwae tried to keep her lips set, but couldn't hide the smirk that pulled at the corners of her mouth. Brand exhaled gently and shook his head once again.

"Yeah, you are... No doubt about it."

From back towards the town, a horn sounded three sharp, high notes. Around the pair, the cheering villagers stopped in their tracks. After a moment, the horn called out again, the notes sounding clearly above the diffuse sounds of the fires and the dying men to echo off of the far banks of the river.

"The Priest of Summersford!" Cried a man by the shore. "He is in need!"

With their cries of victory now shouts of concern, the villagers turned and charged back into the billows of smoke that obscured their homes from the vantage of the river. As the press of bodies ebbed about them, Bran turned back towards the river and watched with consternation as the three warships receded into the darkness of night as well.

"Shitesan." He muttered. "Now we've lost him."

Euwae stepped over a fallen raider and stood beside him.

"They have not gone far. Surely we can follow? The Great River soon winds into the hills of twoth'Ba and becomes much harder to follow for a ship of any size. Once they come upon the gorges –" She stopped abruptly as she considered the path of the river. At last, she spoke again, her voice crusted with frustration.

"Aye. Then we would have to be making a great turn ourselves, lest we become lost in the ruts of the land as well. It is shitesant indeed."

The left corner of Brand's mouth rolled up, but he shook his head, knelt down and cleaned his knife on the clothing of the body in front of him.

"Well," he said dispassionately, "at least I got my knife back."

"Much good may it do you, dicenn..." Moaned Angus in reply.

Brand finished wiping off the blade, then turned and walked over to the wounded man.

"Angus..." He exclaimed sadly. "Maybe you should've gone for the throat, eh?"

The burly warrior turned his head, spat loudly and convulsed at the effort.

"My armor... Turned the blade of your cursed knife across my guts, rather than striking up and true." He was pale, the blood stain obvious in the tunic below the boiled leather plates. "It is my fate to die now in pain, for choosing a weapon so treacherous."

Brand pulled back the hand that Angus pressed over the wound and grimaced.

"With any luck, you'll survive it."

"I see no luck in that." Angus said hoarsely. "The bua'Theu of this village will offer no aid to the likes of me."

Brand glanced back at the buildings; the fires were guttering out at last. The villagers cries had faded, but there was no doubt that they would soon be back to dispatch the last of the surviving attackers. Angus followed his gaze and nodded weakly.

"Aye." He admonished. His hand shot out and grabbed Brand's wrist. "Finish the work, dicenn. Better by far to die by the hand of an ath'Ale than be rolled into the river to be a banquet for the eels..."

Brand pulled off Angus' right hand with his left and rose up, hefting Crows Call off of the planks of the dock and testing its weight as he stood over the fallen warrior. Angus closed his eyes and drew a ragged breath as he waited for the blow to fall. Brand opened his mouth and turned towards Euwae – But she was no longer on the dock.

He finally caught sight of her running across the strand just before she waded out into the water towards the cog that lay moored upriver from the pier.

"Good job, Euwae." He said with satisfaction as he watched her swim through the dark water towards the waiting vessel.

Angus moaned and slipped to the planks of the pier. Brand turned and knelt down, stripping the armor off of the fallen warrior and ripping the man's tunic to make a crude dressing. Once that was done, he stepped away from Angus to the edge of the wharf, placing a hand on a piling as he watched Euwae begin to make sail.

Against his will, his gaze was pulled towards the river. His eyes grew wide, as he looked down inexorably into the depths of the water where the bodies of the dead lay littered below the surface.

He coarsely whispered "Ers'Elb..." before his vision was stretched far away from Summersford; his eyes lost their focus and his face went pale as he teetered at the edge of the pier over the black waters.

Euwae reached the cog and with difficulty climbed over the side. Once on the deck, she lay for a moment, catching her breath and looking up at the fires of the stars, a grin of satisfaction chiseled upon her face. Finally, she reached out and patted the gunwale of the ship affectionately.

"Well met, Foamsmare," she said proudly, "it has been long since I have taken to the waters upon your decks... But somehow it is only right that you should bear us in this pursuit."

She rolled to her feet and quickly looked about the ship. The stores were well stocked in their jars and cases; the spare mast was in place and the sheets and sails well secured. She turned to the town and nodded politely.

"Konner, you have kept well this gift of my father's and that is the way of it." She said towards the shore. "I thank you for that! But the clan of the ree has need of it now and no mistake. Foamsmare shall be as safe as I can keep her while we are gone..."

Turning her eyes back towards the pier, she could make out Brand standing on the pier awaiting her return. Throwing him a grand salute, she set about raising the sail. Foamsmare quickly took to the wind as she went forward and released the line to the mooring buoy. But the wind was fairly strong from the west; Euwae cursed as the ship began to drift slowly down river and away from Summersford. As Euwae struggled, she saw Brand stand impassively at the pier, watching as the ship and the al'Aith began to sail away...

Yet it wasn't long before her time at the steering oar awoke in her memory and her confidence with the vessel grew. Although it took Euwae nearly ten minutes to sheet the sail correctly and tack back into the wind, eventually she was able to direct the cog upriver towards the pier where her companion awaited.

She waived to him a few times as the boat drew closer to the dock, rolling her eyes with frustration as Brand refused to respond in kind and finally retaliating by turning all of her attention to the task at hand. With a final flourish at the steering oar she brought the ship broadside into the pilings and landed against them with a heavy knock. Rather than jump aboard, however, Brand pitched over and fell into the boat.

"Bird Club!" Euwae exclaimed as she ran amidships to his side. "Are you wounded, then?"

As she began to run her hands over him in search of an injury, a man coughed loudly beside her.

"The dicenn is not stung by wounds," he said thickly, "he is *long* dead."

Euwae shrieked and leaped over Brand to tower over the fallen warrior. He lay on his left side, his right clutching a wad of cloth to stem the flow of blood from a wound in his abdomen. She reached out with her left leg and pushed against the man's shoulder to roll him onto his back. With a grunt, he relaxed and let her do so. His face was flushed, despite his wounds; his eyes were still bright. A thick torc of silver capped with ornately shaped balls of brass sat proudly upon his neck and seemed to almost glow in the light of the fires on the shore as she brought her weight down upon her foot and pinned him against the coarse wooden planks.

"Did you strike him down?" She asked coldly.

She felt the man shudder beneath her boot as he made a choking sound, which might have been a sign of his distress – Or an attempt at a laugh.

"DID YOU?" She shouted, drawing her falcata slowly and letting the fires catch its edge as well. She watched his mouth open and close several times, before his eyes grew wide and his chin trembled.

Finally, he forced his throat to choke out the words "I cannot... Speak of it..."

The pitch of her voice rose to a shriek as she drew her sword up in front of her chest and readied to thrust into the man's chest. But she was interrupted as she poised at the apex of the strike by Brand calling out her name.

She spun and leaped back to his side, the wounded enemy forgotten.

"Bird Club..." She said desperately, "where is the wound..?"

In response, he cocked his head forcefully to the left and rolled it to his chest, his eyes squeezed shut. But before she could ask again he reached up, placed a hand upon her shoulder and pulled himself into a sitting position. Euwae cradled his shoulders as she helped him rise, her eyes frantically looking for any sign of an injury.

"Your time in the world of men is done and gone, dicenn..." said the man on the docks behind them. "You have had your revenge. Now the land of the dead calls – "

"No!" Shouted Euwae violently as she rocked back on her heels to face him.

"*Speak* again and you *die*!"

"I am dead already," he muttered weakly, "the ghost of the Eastlander there has seen to that."

Euwae picked up her sword from the deck and walked resolutely back towards the wounded raider, her knuckles white as her fingers locked around the hilt of the weapon.

Brand's eyes unclenched and opened slowly. "Shitesat." He said almost to himself.

Euwae froze in place, pointing her falcata at the man on the planks. He opened his mouth, but after taking in her expression closed both his mouth and his eyes. With a snort of disdainful satisfaction, she turned back to Brand. He was now on his feet, although he swayed unsteadily as he raised his hand to her placatingly.

"I'm not hurt, Euwae..."

"Not HURT!?!?" She waived at the deck where he had lain. "And just what might that have been, then?"

His head rocked slightly from side to side in passive denial.

"I'm not really sure – I've never..." His gaze slid towards the dark waters of the river. "I guess I've got something I need to think about."

"Something... To *think* about."

His head rocked slightly again, but this time in affirmation. Euwae's eyes rolled in vague disgust. Brand chose not to discuss it further, but turned to look at the retreating ships, only to jerk in shock at the sight of the boat that was now docked at the pier.

"How'd that get over here?"

The al'Aith let out another disdainful grunt and sheathed her falcata.

"It was the fairies, to be sure."

"That's not funny, Euwae."

"Oh? And I am supposing now – just supposing, mind – that watching you drop like a dead man upon the deck was your way of saying 'Well done' then?"

He shrugged. "Well done, then. Sorry I missed it."

"Bah."

She walked past him towards the stern of the cog, letting her shoulder hit him roughly as she passed. Brand recovered his balance and smirked as she stormed down the deck.

"No, really," he said contritely as he started to cross the distance between them. "I am..." Then, he stopped and looked back at the pier. Euwae paid him no attention as she made her way to the steering oar.

"Just cast us off, Bird Club. I will have no more of your excuses this night."

She raised the gaff to push the stern off into the current. She looked forward towards Brand, then fiercely shook her head no.

"And just *what* are you doing? You will be putting THAT back, straight away!"

Brand dropped Angus down to the deck as gently as he could before he hopped back aboard. Despite her protest, he pushed off from the wharf to move the ship out into the current. Only then did Brand face the stern, where Euwae stood rooted in disbelief. Taking a deep breath, he moved astern to join her.

"We need to take him with us, Euwae."

"*We* do not."

His face went hard as he looked down at her.

"Angus is a leader of cu'Kullah's war band. He'll know what they're doing, and why... Once we get him to talk, then *we'll* have the advantage over *them*."

"He will not speak to us of his al'Aith's plans and that is the way of it."

Brand's face went from stern to grim.

"I'm betting he will."

"But he tried to KILL you!"

"Us."

"So much the better, then! Us!"

Brand nodded.

"I know. But I've – " He looked at Euwae and his expression softened. "But *we've* got scores to settle and there are only two of us."

"There are but only the two of you..?" Called Angus weakly from amidships.

"SHUT UP!" The pair shouted together from the stern. Brand looked back at Euwae and grinned. She rolled her face away in consternation, but looked back up to him with her lips pursed curtly.

"So be it, then, Brand Eastlander. But know this: should your captive so much as raise a hand against you, you shall be at your own devices to save yourself. I will not come to your rescue a second time. Does this ring clearly enough even to your ears?"

Brand made a flourishing salute.

"Absolutely, al'Aith."

"Go and see to your prisoner. His blood is staining the decks of this noble vessel." Euwae nodded in cold dismissal.

With a bow, Brand backed away from her before he turned and walked to Angus, who had pulled himself into a seated position against the gunwale of the ship. As he approached Brand nodded once to the ath'Ale.

"Let's take a look at that wound, Angus."

The injured man looked him over with wide eyes and shook his head.

"I did see you drown that night." He growled. "How is it that you came to haunt me here?"

Brand looked back at him without any hint of emotion.

"I told you, Angus... I'm *not* dead."

"Cursed dicenn..."

"Yeah, I missed you too, you old hiel. But the lady's right – I can't have you bleeding to death for nothing. So let's see if we can – "

Angus's eyes rolled up in his head as his consciousness fled away. Brand exhaled sharply through his nose and shook his head.

"Shitesan... Forget it." He muttered, as he began to strip off Angus' shirt and see to the wound his knife had made.

New Courses

For six days, Foamsmare made steady progress down the wide channel of the Great River. The vessels of cu'Kullah proved to be faster, however, as the oarsmen worked methodically to give the ships additional speed. By the dawn of the seventh day, they were long out of sight of their pursuers.

Brand spent the days under Euwae's direction, familiarizing himself to the tasks at hand. While she professed not to be a sailor herself, she was familiar enough with the ways of the seamen and the needs of the vessel to tersely guide him through the working of the sail and steering oar. Once they reached the river's estuary, it was wide and smooth as it neared the sea; with the winds steady from the west, their voyage was largely without urgent need for skillful handling.

Angus' wound had proven not to be beyond Brand's skill to tend; the blade of the scramasax had been turned by the padding of the armor so that the cut was long, but not deep. Brand had closed it as best he could and bandaged it well before securing the prisoner to the shaded area under the tent forward of the mast. Other than feeding the sullen captive, Brand let him be... And Euwae refused to pay any heed to Angus at all.

Yet, even amongst the two companions, the easy banter exchanged in Northmoors eluded them after their victory at Summersford. The cover of cloud grew ever closer as they neared the coast and the shadows that they threw upon the earth seemed to give absolution to the moods of those on the ship. It was increasingly obvious that Brand was very uncomfortable about being aboard Foamsmare, while Euwae's mood for reasons kept closely held had not brightened since the voyage began.

As the sunrise of the seventh day shot seams of red across the cloudy sky, Euwae shielded her eyes against the glare on the water and swept them across the ship. Brand sat sleeping on the center of the deck halfway between herself and their captive, his beaked club resting across his folded legs. His head bobbed up and down fitfully as his dreams began to retreat to his waking... With an exaggerated sigh, she tied off the steering oar and stretched, then tugged at the pin holding the cloak fast around her neck to pull it off now that day had come.

A wicked hiss sucked past her ear and a tug threw back the hood of her cloak.

With a start, she pulled it off and threw it to the deck. A thick, ugly arrow shaft protruded from its folds.

"Brand!" She cried as a second arrow whisked past her from the opposite bank of the river from which the first had come.

The warrior was already in motion, rolling into a low crouch with his weapon at the ready as the al'Aith took cover by simply dropping low to the deck. Brand looked at Euwae with his head turned to the side; in response she grabbed the arrow sticking out of her cloak and raised it so that he could see, while she circled her other fist to sign that they were surrounded.

He lifted his head to scan the banks of the river around them. While each shore was a good distance away, they rose in a pair of eroded, steep bluffs on either side – An excellent location for such an attack. The archers would need to have had some skill to shoot accurately at this distance... But the shot that nearly hit Euwae was testament enough to their ability.

Another pair of shots came from the near side of the ship towards Brand, both striking the gunwale within a foot of him. He ducked back down and shook his head with a scowl. As a third shaft from the far side of the boat buried itself into the wood next to him, he gave Euwae a desperate wave.

"Get below!" He urged her adamantly as he slipped down and crawled for the main hatch himself.

Once she joined him, the two listened intently.

"It looks like cu'Kullah's a bit worried about us after all." Brand said quietly.

"Oh, are you thinking so?"

He ignored the sarcasm and reached up a hand to steady himself on the frame of the hull while he continued. "It's a good place for an ambush – Those hills afford a full view of the deck from both sides. But they're being pretty careful with their arrows... Either they don't have many of them, or they're just trying to keep our heads down."

"And why would they be doing that?"

Brand ground his teeth once and swallowed.

"Because that'll make it easier for them to board us."

Euwae's face contorted through the range of emotions that she felt as Brand listened again and scowled.

"Where's your bara'Ba?"

"It is next to the steering oar, where I can get to it quickly, should there be the need." She said obviously.

Brand sucked in his lips.

"Do you think there's a need now?"

She opened her mouth but snapped it shut in frustration as Brand levered himself back up to gaze out through the hatch.

"It looks like we're almost clear of those hills... We should have a – Oh, shitesant!" He pulled himself up and onto the deck, calling back to her as he did so.

"Get your sword! NOW!"

Brand ran forward towards the bow as Euwae slid up onto the deck. Throwing a glance in that direction, she saw that four men had already climbed aboard over the bowsprit and that more were following. Quickly she pulled her feet underneath her and ran in a low crouch towards the stern. As she picked up her weapon and whipped back her arm to let the force of the movement free it from the scabbard, she heard a wet thud beside her.

Spinning about, she saw that one of the raiders had come aboard aft, directly beside her. He had caught the sheath of her sword as she had flung it off the blade and now stood there, examining it with curiosity. In his off hand he loosely held the haft of a long ax, which he rested upon the deck as he looked over the scabbard in his hand.

Euwae screamed as she brought up her sword in a low strike towards his abdomen, but the warrior responded without taking his eyes from her scabbard and blocked the swing with the upper shaft of the ax handle. The al'Aith's brow furrowed in surprise as she recovered and brought the falcata back around for a heavy riposte towards his arm, but again he blocked the strike by casually flipping the heavy ax around and catching her sword in the hook of its head.

Thus bound, her foe leaned forward slowly and forced Euwae to shift her feet awkwardly to keep from toppling over backwards; yet by doing so she was unable to move any further. Once he had her immobilized through the weight of the parry, the man looked into her face.

Euwae gasped.

His lips and cheeks were cut away, exposing his raw teeth and gums. Deep grooves ran across his face, brutal tattoos of scar stained with soot while the wounds were fresh in his flesh. But his eyes burned with a wild light that could only be sparked by truly violent insanity.

"Marauds..." The al'Aith's voice was seized in her throat by the terror that shot through her body, once that single word escaped through her lips.

Almost as an afterthought the maraud pushed forward and toppled her forcefully to the deck of the ship. As Euwae scuttled back on all fours he made a mockery of a bow before he swung the ax up over his head and brought it down in a blur towards the woman before him.

Euwae rolled to the left, then swung her legs around so that she was on all fours but facing her opponent. As the ax bit into the planks of the deck she sprang forward and landed her shoulder just above his hips, pushed up with all her strength and rolled him over her back. Before the maraud crashed into the deck she lunged down to recover her falcata with a spin so she was facing the man who lay before her.

He stared up at her, the corners of his eyes wrinkled into what must pass as a smile across his ruined face. Euwae kicked him in the side of the head and watched with grim satisfaction as his head snapped to the right; his eyes rolled back as consciousness left his body.

A deep shadow fell over her and Euwae leaped forward as another ax whistled through the air over her back. Spinning on her left foot, she brought the sword up into a defensive hold just as the new maraud corrected for the swing and redirected the weapon into hers. The shock of it sent ripples though the flesh on her arm, but she took the blow and turned her own blade to bind the ax head and rolled her arm back, managing to make the disarm, pulling the weapon free and sending it sailing over the side of the ship.

The maraud howled through filed teeth and stalked towards her, drawing an ugly thick bladed knife. Euwae moved to her right and kept her sword low, expecting another wild rush. She had only covered roughly six feet of her circle, however, when her opponent threw himself onto the unconscious maraud and began hacking at his chest and abdomen...

Euwae's throat worked as she felt her stomach turn. Swallowing back the bile in her throat she moved away from the butchery taking place astern and ran towards the center of the ship. Another maraud had climbed aboard Foamsmare's port side and launched himself at her as she stumbled away; grabbing around her arms and stomach he lifted the al'Aith from behind and raised her into the air.

With a shout of rage, Euwae flailed out with her feet, catching him in the midriff and knocking the wind from the maraud. They tumbled to the deck together, but the al'Aith was the quicker to recover and drove her blade deeply into his chest before he could rise against her.

Her chin lowered to her chest, she stormed back to the stern and killed the maraud that continued to savage its fallen comrade. Then she backed away from the bodies as two more of the foemen clambered over the rail and onto the deck. They separated, circling her like wolves, their mutilated faces and scarred bodies twitching with the anticipation of the kill.

Euwae kept her sword out towards the maraud on her right while her left arm was extended towards the other, should he be the first to attack. Instead, the two screamed and rushed in together, their large axes whirling in a fearsome circle of destruction as they came. Euwae spun in a mortal pirouette and brought her heavy blade down on the left arm of the first attacker, stepped right to pivot behind him and allowed the maraud's momentum to carry him into her blade. As he stumbled forward in shock she kicked out with her left foot and pushed him into the larger maraud, who screamed again in rage and cuffed his injured comrade across the face with the shaft of his ax to move him out of the way.

Euwae dropped back into her low crouch as he rushed forward and ducked under the arc of his weapon, slashing the burly man across both thighs as she dodged to his right and slipped behind him as well. She took two long steps to give herself some distance between herself and her attackers before she took a cross step to face them.

Both of the marauds were standing where she had wounded them, their guards down and their shoulders twitching oddly. They reached out and touched each others wounds - then their own - before they turned to face her. Horrid laughter spilled out of them as they flung themselves with crazed delight at the woman who had inflicted this pain upon them.

Her face screwed tightly in disgust, Euwae ducked and wove in a left hand arc as she was forced wholly to the defensive. The marauds gave no further sign of their injuries but threw themselves entirely into the assault against her. They cut off her retreat to the forward section of the ship and drove her further and further astern, until with a cry of shock she stumbled into the bodies of the first two which had attacked her. Failing to catch her balance, Euwae fell over them and landed hard onto her back, knocking the wind out of her and sending her sword spinning well out of reach across the deck to her right.

The two marauds tossed aside their own weapons and fell on top of her, pinning her limbs beneath the weight of their bodies, their bloody hands leaving grotesque stains on her clothing where they groped at her body as they sought to immobilize her.

Desperately Euwae managed to get her left leg free and repeatedly kicked the gashed thighs of the bigger maraud, but this only caused him to laugh with hysterical delight as he rolled back and grabbed her leg, shifting back so his own legs wrapped around Euwae's, locking her into a submission hold. With a grotesquely blissful expression, the other managed to get a purchase on her arms at last, his flayed mouth just inches from her throat.

Slowly, his tongue snaked out of his mouth and across the front of his rotting teeth...

Euwae flailed about in a frantic attempt to reach freedom. In desperation her hand seized upon the hilt of the knife in the body of the mutilated maraud. Contorting herself to gain leverage, she brought the clumsy weapon up in a wide slash, striking the maraud holding her leg squarely in the chest with the back of the blade and pushing it into his ribs with what strength she could manage.

As soon as his grip loosened, Euwae yanked her leg free and rolled beneath the maraud above her, reversing her hold on the knife and stabbing upwards into his stomach repeatedly she did so. With each strike the maraud let out a cry of guttural pleasure, but his grip quickly weakened until Euwae could slip free and roll across the deck, out of his reach.

Across from her, the maraud she had stabbed in the chest was also sitting up, blood bubbling out in a froth from the wound. With a feral growl, he hunched over and began to crawl towards her on all fours. Euwae's mouth curled in hatred as she flipped the knife over in her hand and flung it into the maraud's shoulder. His right arm went limp and he tumbled onto his face, but relentlessly he struggled back to his feet.

With labored breath Euwae rose as well, scanning about her for another weapon. As the maraud stumbled towards her, his left arm extended, she reached to her left and wrenched an ax free from the deck, bringing it down with a wet crunch into the maraud's skull. As he collapsed she turned towards the bow, only to find herself staring at the chest of yet another maraud, his ax already raised above his head to kill her, just as she had done to his comrade seconds before.

She tried to bring the ax she held up to parry the strike, but it was too heavy and she only managed to clumsily deflect the blow; the side of his ax head slammed into her shoulder and drove her down to the deck in pain. Yet rather than follow up the blow, he dropped the ax and clutched at his throat. Euwae watched him stagger and fall face forward to the deck in front of her.

The sun shattered the cloud cover. From the back of his neck protruded Brand's scramasax, the blade burning in the reflected light from the sky above.

With a long exhalation, Euwae slumped back onto the deck with relief before the pain and fatigue drowned her senses and she collapsed at last.

As Angus began to clear the bodies from the deck of Foamsmare, Brand ran back to the stern to see to the al'Aith. He scanned her quickly as he knelt by her side and gently took her arm.

"Euwae, were you hit anywhere else?"

She opened her eyes with effort.

"In what wise is that, then? I was not hit at all."

"Uh-huh."

"No, it is the way of it. This blood is not mine."

She tried to sit up, but her head suddenly spun.

"Ach." She raised her hands to her temples. "That was some sport."

Brand gently lowered her back to the deck.

"Yeah, it was." He turned towards the bow.

"Angus! Bring me the healer's bag from the tent!"

Euwae scowled and tried to rise again, but Brand kept her down.

154

"Healer's bag? Oh!" Her face was shot with concern. "You are like to be wounded!"

He nodded.

"Yeah, like to be. But you stay still."

Angus came running back to the stern with the bag in his hands.

"What is this, then?" He asked with some concern.

"Just give me the bag."

Angus passed him the satchel and Brand dropped it to the deck to rummage through it. Angus stepped closer, looking over his shoulder.

"Aye, that is a wicked cut, indeed."

Euwae rolled her eyes.

"And what is he doing, up and wandering free as you please upon the decks of – AAH!"

"Sorry about that, Euwae. But this is going to hurt soon. I need to see to it before it does."

"See to WHAT?" She asked and brought her hands to her side where Brand had poked her. Her fingers brushed against a ragged tear in her flesh and she pulled them back in shock, staring at the blood on her hand.

Brand nodded.

"Looks like one of them got a piece of you, Euwae..."

"Aye; the beak of the ax, eh, dicenn?"

"SHUT IT!" Euwae's voice trembled with indignation. "You have NO right speaking to him so!"

"It's all right, Euwae." Brand's voice was even as he interrupted. "Angus – "

"Should be bound and thrown back into the river with these marauds." She said with bitter conviction. "Were it not for you, he would be dead there already."

Angus straightened up. He looked at Brand.

"I will be seeing to the last of the dead, then..." he said resignedly and walked off towards the bow.

After he was out of ear shot, Brand shook his head and spoke quietly to the Al'Aith.

"Were it not for Angus, you'd be dead, too."

Euwae scowled at him, then flinched in pain as he tended to her wound. She made to speak, but Brand continued his dialog without giving her the chance to interrupt.

155

"He's the one who took out that last maraud – The one that had gotten behind you. Shitesast good throw, too – Hit him in the side of the neck, not off the top of the spine.

"He didn't have to help you. I didn't even realize that you were in trouble until I saw him make the throw."

"You did not realize... Were you not watching over me?"

Brand shook his head.

"Why?"

"I didn't think you needed it."

Euwae's brow lowered in a scowl, but her face smoothed over as the meaning of his compliment became clear. With a nod to the ath'Ale, she closed her eyes again and let him finish tending to her wound without further distraction as the clouds once again shrouded the heavens in damp gray.

                    *   *   *

With Euwae injured, Brand ran about carrying the double duty of the steering oar and minding the sails over the next few days as they slid into the wide marshy lands where the Great River fed into the cold waters of the sea of isle'Eh. The water level of the river was low in its shallow summer bed and most of the shoals were easily discernible. Still, Brand was mindful of his lack of skill and kept Angus at the bow of the ship to call out when the brown waters of the river turned to leathery froth above the shallows, to be sure that they avoided them.

The insects, a plague on the shores at this time of year, were less abundant on the open water, but there were still enough of them to be a powerful distraction in the early morning and late afternoon. Euwae swatted at them distractedly as she sat with her back against the aft gunwale and watched Brand struggle with the tall handle of the rudder oar. Finally, she closed her eyes roughly, blinked and cleared her throat.

"Bird Club..."

He kept his feet planted and his shoulder to the oar as his eyes swiveled towards her.

She let out a quick breath and raised her chin towards him.

"It is – " She stopped and dropped her eyes for more appropriate words. After biting the inside of her lip, she rose with some difficulty and walked across the deck to him.

"Here," she said quietly as she reached out to touch the very end of the oar, "is the way to the wings of Foamsmare..." Her eyes swept from the oar across the ship and finally back to Brand. "You are trying to command her, to force her to do your bidding." Euwae shook her head.

156

"But this ship is nothing less than a noble lady. You must make her your companion, for she will never be your willing servant." She tried to take his place, but he stood there watching her with his face locked in a rigid mask. Finally, she scowled.

"May I?" She pushed, with her voice cloaked with noble pique.

Brand looked down at Euwae, nodded and stepped aside, allowing her to slide her hand up the length of the oar and pull it slowly down to her as she moved to the end of the leather wrapped wood. She clenched her teeth behind her lips as the pain of her wound sent a tremor through her body, but held fast to the stout pole and lightly maneuvered it through the water slipping beneath the ship.

Brand shook his head and looked at his feet.

"I don't know if that's really fair," he said with a trace of reconciliation woven into his voice. "I think she likes you more than she likes me."

Euwae beamed. "It *could* be." She said mischievously. "After all, I am the daughter of Lohvtreu, who is ree of all twoth'Ba and al'Aith over the Confederation of the Pirates of isle'Eh."

"Yeah, I know." He said with a kindly rebuke.

Despite the pain in her side, Euwae's face glossed over with personal pleasure as she held the oar. "Aye, Bird Club. And so, too, does she..."

From the bow, Angus turned to call out that there was shallow water ahead, but the breath dropped out of his chest as the spied the two of them standing together. He gave his head a quick jerk as he fought off the scorn that braided his lip, lifted his chin and cried, "Bring the ship around to leeward!"

Turning back to the river, he added bitterly, "Aye. The *pair* of you."

The light of the sun was all but drained from the cloudy ceiling of the sky as Brand heaved the ship's anchor into the river. As Foamsmare swung about in the current, he nodded to Angus, turned and made his way astern.

There, Euwae was setting out clay jars of food from the ship's locker. Brand smiled wearily and settled into his usual crouch near the center line of the ship. As he joined her, the al'Aith closed her eyes and took a deep breath through her nose against the shudder of discomfort from her wound, although a wide smile stretched across her face.

Brand tossed her a look of curiosity through heavy lidded eyes.

"Catching cold?"

She opened her eyes and shook her head at the jibe, refusing to play along.

"Can you not smell it?" She said, her voice hazy with personal pleasure.

"The marshes?" He wrinkled his nose. "Yeah, I sure can..." He waived his hand in front of his face, but she shook her head and rolled her eyes.

"No! Not the marshes, you old 'scra." She closed her eyes and made a show of breathing deeply once again. Brand sat patiently, affording her his attention.

Finally, her eyes opened; she looked over at him, lowered her face and scowled playfully.

"New Courses?" She asked openly. When he just shrugged, she craned her neck forward at him incredulously. "Where the Great River comes to rest?

"*The sea*!" Euwae finally said emphatically, before she dropped her head further between her shoulders with a sigh. "I have missed it so..."

Brand took a quick sniff, but shook his head.

"I've got nothing."

"That is the truth of it and no mistake, Bird Club."

The left corner of his mouth rose up in acquiescence.

"What's on the menu tonight, al'Aith?" He asked mildly.

"It is the same fare as you have taken every other meal since we loosed Foamsmare from her moorings:" Euwae replied, "cheese, brine fish and oat cake."

"Just pass me the mead." Called Angus, stepping across the shadowed deck. "That will do for me tonight."

Euwae's face curdled, but she held her tongue and tossed him a bottle. He caught it by the neck, touched it to his forehead and retreated back to the shelter of the tent amidships.

"You are welcome, certainly!" Euwae called out, then shook her head. "He has not a respectful bone in all his body."

Brand shrugged and gestured towards the crock of fish.

"No, I guess he doesn't. At least not for me – So, I guess that means not for you, either."

Euwae's eyes narrowed as she watched him settle in.

"We would be better without him. His en'Och turns on no useful course."

"He saved your life."

"To what end? Had he not been aboard, I am of the mind that you would have stepped up to the cause, just as well."

Brand gave a weak shrug.

"Maybe." He added after too long a pause. "But he knows what cu'Kullah is planning... And 'til he's willing to clue us in, I don't want to cut him loose."

She looked at Brand, suspicion pulling at her eyes.

"But – if you are indeed of such a mind – why is he free to wander where he will? Is he so afraid of your wrath that he will lift no hand against you, or seek the shores of the river in the midst of some dark night?"

Brands eyes chained her gaze to his for just a few seconds, before she swallowed hard and looked away.

"Yeah," her companion said without any trace of emotion coloring his response, "he is."

Euwae scooped up a crock of the oat cakes and passed one to Brand. He set aside the fish and nodded in acceptance. As he chewed at the dry biscuit, he made a vague gesture towards the steering oar. Euwae squinted into the darkness, then looked back at him as he swallowed the first mouthful.

"Where'd you learn that trick, about working the very end of the tiller?"

She rolled her head as she asked, "What, then, is a tiller?" Then she followed the direction of his motion back towards the steering oar.

"Oh, the oar? The seamen showed me the way of it when I sailed to isle'Eh with my father aboard Bayl'Ors Eye to take our tribute from the pirates."

"Take your tribute, eh?" He chuckled. I doubt the Confederation sees it in quite that way."

"Then they would have been the wiser to leave our shores alone!" Euwae bristled. "It was they who –"

Brand held up a conciliatory hand and waved it in consent.

"I'm not saying they didn't have it coming. From what I've seen, I'm sure they started the whole thing. I was just..." his eyes searched the air for the right words, but they proved elusive. Finally, he just shrugged.

"I just saw some irony in the way you said the word 'tribute,' I guess."

"Irony!"

Brand scowled at the retort and Euwae's lips snapped shut with a sullen pout. She poked at her oat cake for a bit, before asking distractedly, "What do you know of the pirates?"

Brand smirked as he decided to answer the rhetorical question.

"Well, they *were* the ones who got me to Cord'Or, Euwae."

She looked up, her voice still hued with her frustration.

"Oh, in truth – So your triumphant arrival among my folk was brought upon us by the Confederation? What a grand day that must have been for you both."

"Yeah..." Brand's eyes left her and focused on the middle distance between them as he responded quietly. "I'd taken a berth on a Darksail as a marine. "

"And was it a Cutter or a Reme to which you cast your lot?"

"Hmm?" His eyes snapped back into focus.

"If you are not even going to do me the courtesy of listening –"

"A Cutter. Under the flag of a captain named Ronan."

"Ronan?" She searched her memory, but shook her head in the negative. "He is not one of whom the tales I have been told recount any deeds, amongst his folk or my own."

Brand shrugged again.

"He was good enough to get me all the way across isle'Eh."

Euwae looked at Brand and searched his face; her own was smooth as she went back to her food.

Quietly, she replied "He was good enough, then, if that is the way of it."

Brand looked at the al'Aith, a gentle smile on his face.

"Agreed." He said quietly as he resumed finishing his own meal.

*   *   *

Late the following afternoon, Euwae took over at the oar while Foamsmare danced over the rips at the mouth of the Great River and guided her slowly onto the pale grey waves of isle'Eh. Where the brown waters of the river eddied into the heavy waters of the sea, great white birds swung lazily through the air and yelped haunting cries that echoed off the bluffs of the shore and back out across the seas beyond.

The sun tore through clouds that mocked the undulating waters below, while the waves returned the gesture by throwing cloaks of white froth across their peaks as they made their inevitable course towards the rocky shore.

Brand pulled at the sheets of the mainsail, drawing the tall spar across the deck to make the best use of the wind that now shifted towards the open seas. As he made them fast, his gaze came to rest on Euwae. She stood beneath the steering oar, but her hand guided it without the need for its support as her weight shifted in perfect time to the rocking of the boat upon the waves. Her light skirt was pushed forward and her hair was loose on the wind, reaching out towards the bow of the ship as if to embrace it.

Yet, if her face had shown joy at the scent of the sea last evening, now it glowed with a deeper blush of a raw passion as she guided the nimble ship from the gentle path of the river and through the first throes of isle'Eh's embrace...

Unconsciously, Brand was smiling.

The shadow of the sail threw a chill into Brand as Angus wove his way to him unsteadily across the gently pitching deck. He caught the rail behind the Eastlander and looked towards the woman at the stern with a hard expression. Leaning forward, he nudged Brand, who turned to face him. Angus raised his bearded chin towards the al'Aith, lowered it and looked at Brand without dropping his bitter expression.

"Were this a game of crossed sticks, dicenn, your next moves could be no less obvious."

Slowly, the emotion seeped from Brand's face as well.

"I know the game, Angus – But I've never been that good at it."

"No?" The ath'Ale's eyes burned into his. "Then think well upon the actions you now take. You may still see yourself a mighty champion of twoth'Shan'n, but I have seen you cast down into your place, to lie in the dirt like all of the cuhm'l I've left behind me. You would do well to keep that to your mind."

Brands head rotated slightly to the left. Through tight lips, he asked quietly, "Shitesat. You want to play a game? Because I'm just about ready to settle this with you, Angus."

The other man's lip curled scornfully.

"So, this is the truth of it, then?"

"What?"

Angus gestured towards Euwae again with his chin.

"She has an eye for you and no mistake." Brand's brow furrowed as he mulled that over; Angus parried with a dismissive gesture. "Surely even a dicenn such as you can not have been so blind to that?"

Brand spat over the side of the ship.

"You're a shitesas idiot, Angus."

"Am I in truth?" He asked conspiratorially. "Or are your fancies not of a kind that let you dream of a twoth of your own one day?"

"You've been serving cu'Kullah too long, Angus." Said Brand coldly. "He's the only one with fancies like that around here."

"Is he, now?" Angus smirked, but his discomfort was plainly obvious; the mention of his al'Aith was clearly painful to him.

"He is – As you ought to know."

The warriors both looked back at Euwae as the wind finally released her from its caress. With a laugh, she made an off handed salute to the sky and began to secure the steering oar in its place to the side of the ship.

"And I *suggest* that you keep your shitesannus ideas to yourself from here on out, Angus." Brand concluded without turning to face the other man, although Angus looked back at him once he had spoken.

"Oh? And tell me plain, then, why this is so?"

"Because if you don't, this is going to end very badly."

"Badly for who, dicenn? Me? Or you?"

Brand's back went stiff and his shoulders dropped. Angus heard him swallow as Euwae approached them.

"Well then!" She said brightly. "That was –" The contentment split away from her voice as she looked at Brand. "What is this, then?"

Angus let out a snort.

"The dicenn and I were discussing crossed sticks."

As quickly as the sun ducked back behind the clouds, the high notes of joy were flushed from her face by the lividity of anger.

"How DARE you!" She cried, ducking around Brand's shoulder to throw herself angrily in front of Angus. "Were it not for him –"

"Aye, were it not for him more ills would have never troubled my life than you will have the pain to be knowing!" Angus hurled back at the woman before him. "It were better still that I had died than to be left to – "

"It is death that you are seeking?" Euwae shrieked as she plucked Brand's scramasax from his belt. "Then so –" She pulled her arm back to strike Angus, but Brand caught her wrist and pulled it back to stop her, nearly spinning her across the deck.

"SHITESAT!" She screamed at the top of her lungs.

Brand looked at her strangely, nodding slowly.

"You're right, Euwae..." He said with a detached tone.

Both Angus and Euwae looked at him, their eyes wide with mutual confusion. Brand took two steps forward and gently took the long knife away from Euwae.

"You said it right." He said gently to her. She blinked and her head trembled slightly as she tried to make sense of his calm demeanor.

"And you were right about Angus, too, I guess." He said softly, before he turned to the taller warrior.

"I was hoping that you'd – " Brand rolled his lips to the left and shrugged. "I was hoping that we wouldn't have to go here. But now that we've reached New Courses, it's time to settle this."

He reversed his grip on the weapon, so that the blade ran along his forearm as Brand looked into Angus' face.

"We need to know where cu'Kullah is going, Angus." He said with that same, displaced serenity. "So I need you to tell us, now: where is he headed?"

Angus looked away.

Brand took a deep breath.

"Uh-uh, buddy... Not this time. cu'Kullah's got days on us, already; there's no way to track him on the open sea. You know where he's going, don't you?"

Angus turned a pale face to Brand. His response was haggard.

"You cannot understand, *dicenn.*"

Euwae tried to duck past Brand, but he reached out and stopped her with his free hand against her stomach. Her chin trembled, but she kept her voice in check as Brand spoke again, without a trace of menace in his voice.

"Angus: cu'Kullah's got days on us, already; there's no way to track him on the open sea. You know where he's going, *don't* you?"

The muscles at the sides of the ath'Ale's jaw worked furiously, his clenched lips were pale. But he shook his head in denial.

"Shitesa," Brand said at last, resignation finally giving a coarse timbre to his words. "All right. If your damned en'Och says it's better for you to die, then I'm through talking about it."

Angus took a deep breath through his nose, his chest swelling as he braced for the thrust of the blade. Brand's left hand shot out -

And pulled the torc from around Angus' throat.

"NO!" the warrior shrieked wildly.

He lunged for Brand, who lifted his foot and kicked him in the center of the abdomen, pushing the air from his lungs and sending him sprawling against the gunwale.

Brand's face began to flush with anger as he stepped past Euwae and towered over the fallen warrior.

"NOW!" he cried, looking down at Angus. "Either you tell me what cu'Kullah is up to, or so help me Angus, I am going to pitch this necklace of yours into the shitesat sea, the same way you were going to toss me into that shitesat lake."

The wind gusted, throwing the ship off to starboard. Waves began to slap at the front of the ship, causing it to jump convulsively.

Euwae gasped as Angus struggled to pull air into his lungs again. "P-please..." he choked out, "I cannot speak of it!"

Brand's cheeks burned red with his fury.

"Angus!"

"I have said it –"

"You haven't said shitesa!"

"Please –"

Brand's chin tucked quickly into his chest as he pushed out the air inside him through his nose. Then he drew a long, slow, shuddering breath.

"Fine," he said, nodding at the terrified man before him. "You want to die?" He cocked back his arm and started to hurl the torc out into the waiting arms of the sea.

But Euwae seized his wrist in both of her hands, preventing him from doing so.

Brand stepped back and stared at her. Euwae gently shook her head to the negative, relaxed her hold on his arm and pulled lightly at the torc. At the third tug, Brand released it to her custody.

She stepped up to Brand and placed a hand upon his chest. In a smooth, soft voice, she said calmly, "Now, I think I see some truth in this..."

The color faded from Brand's cheeks as he looked into her eyes.

"Euwae..?" He asked in a small voice. "What are you –"

She raised a hand, pressing a finger to his lips.

"This is not the way, Bird Club... No boon will come of it."

She looked deeply into his eyes and said quietly, "*I* ask that you show him mercy..."

His hand shot up and pulled hers away.

"WHAT?" He cried. "A minute ago, you were ready to kill him *yourself*!"

"But he cannot *speak* of it." She replied earnestly.

Brand stared at her without comprehension. The wind shifted further, rolling the boat broadside to the waves. Foamsmare began to roll deeply as the ship slid from trough to crest of each wave that slapped against it.

"See to the oar, Bird Club," Euwae said firmly. "I will finish here."

With an snort, Brand tossed his hands into the air to fend off his frustration and stalked off to the stern of the ship, muttering to himself. Once he was out of earshot, Euwae rolled Angus' torc over in her hands, before she lowered it down to him.

As he slipped it around his neck, she spoke to him coolly, but averted her eyes respectfully.

"Right you were, in one thing, Angus of twoth'Fhee. Brand is not of our folk; he does not know of the Fate to which you and all your line would have been cast, had he sacrificed the torc of your kin to the hunger of the seas. And, as little as I - regard you - and as like I was to see you die, in my heart I could not let you fall so low as that.

"I did not know that your oaths to cu'Kullah were such so even in death your en'Och would be bound to his, that you can speak no word nor raise no hand against him. I had thought such oaths were just tales the shaman told around the hearth, to stir our minds with the legends of ages gone and our hearts to understand them...

"And, too, Brand has never heard the call of the torc that fires the en'Och within us, nor felt the heat of the honor it brings, just as all of our deeds temper it ever further with their memory. But you should know the truth beyond this, ath'Ale: even without this, Brand knows such honor just as truly as I or you – And is all the greater for finding it without the song in our hearts that calls us."

When she finally looked down at Angus, his head hung in shame.

"I will speak to him of the truth of it as our folk know it, ath'Ale of 'Fhee. And as for you – "

Her shoulders rose and fell.

"You may sleep peacefully tonight, knowing well that there may be not so great a need of it."

She turned and walked away across the rolling deck as Brand corrected for the shift winds and swung the bow of the ship back into the waves that had sought to upset them.

Angus lifted his head and wiped harshly at the water in his eyes, his jaw slowly setting with grim determination.

Brand watched Euwae cross the deck to him smoothly, despite the way Foamsmare still pulled through the exuberant sea. Once she stood beside

165

him, Brand rocked back on the balls of his feet and stepped beneath the steering oar to put it between them. The princess furrowed her brow and slid around the front of the oar to face him.

Brand shook his head.

"I thought you were on my side." He remarked without spirit.

"Brand –"

He interrupted her with a wave of his hand.

"Now I *know* I don't want to hear it."

Their gazes locked: his, cold and emotionless, hers slowly building from placating to resolute. Finally, he exhaled through his nose and shook his head.

"You know, Euwae, it could be shitesat well that cu'Kullah and his band are going after your family as we speak."

"I know."

"Don't you care?" He asked incredulously.

"Aye." Her gaze never wavered.

Brand lifted his chin towards the bow of the ship. "He *knows*."

"But he *cannot* speak of it."

"And you're fine with that?"

Euwae didn't respond. She simply closed her eyes and took a deep breath. The left corner of Brand's mouth twitched as he threw his shoulder into the oar and Foamsmare reared across the peak of the next wave and came down upon the water with a clap that shook the whole of the ship.

Euwae's eyes shot open as she was rocked off balance and had to seize the gunwale beside her to keep from falling down.

"What was THAT then?" She demanded as she regained her footing.

"Well, one of us cares what the shitesat cu'Kullah is up to. You may not want to face him down before he reaches twoth'Ba, but I do."

"Bird Club – "

"Too late, al'Aith. You made your choice. Now it's time to do the best we can with what we've got left."

"But you have no idea where he has gone!"

"No. And, thanks to nobody else around here speaking up, neither do you."

The ship was now taking the surf across the beam once again, causing the rails to bite deeply into the oncoming waves as Angus grappled his way down the rail towards them.

166

"Dicenn!" He called out with concern. "What are you seeking to do then? Sink us now?"

Brand shot him a dark glance.

"Don't get me going, Angus – Or you'll be swimming home."

Again, the ship took a hard blow from the rough seas; the sails went slack, having lost their impetus from the wind which now blew fully across the deck. Euwae planted her feet and stood in front of Brand.

"Give me the oar!"

"Go fix the sails."

"Bird Club!"

Angus finally reached them and said darkly, "Give her the oar, Outlander."

Brand just stared at him.

"Give her the oar," Angus repeated with a growl, "because you are taking us all the wrong way."

Brand scowled and spat "Oh, *that* you can say?"

Angus stared into the other man's face without remorse.

"Aye, in truth... That much I *can* say."

Brand looked from Angus to Euwae and back again as the ship took two more rough slaps broadsides. Finally, his shoulders dropped in defeat.

"Take the shitesat tiller." He said with pained aggravation and let go of the thick handle of the oar. "*I'll* go fix the sails."

Euwae reached up and seized the oar, bringing Foamsmare back to rein as her companion wove away from the stern up the pitching deck. As she guided the ship into the wind once again, Angus rocked his head towards Brand.

"He would like have drowned us, acting so."

Euwae didn't bother to face him as she replied sternly, "You are not speaking of it."

Angus eyed her, then looked down at the blood stains on the deck where she had held her own against the repeated charge of the marauds. Pursing his lips, he glacially nodded twice.

"Aye, al'Aith." He finally agreed.

Seasgift

For three days, Foamsmare fought against the cruel ambition of the waves as the three people aboard her struggled to keep an eastward course into isle'Eh. They soon realized after setting out upon the ocean they would have to rotate tasks between the three of them, with one at the tiller while another toiled and kept at the corrections to the sails and the third slept. Both Euwae and Brand had misgivings about putting their trust in Angus, who was still committed to the service of an al'Aith who had succumbed to madness... But the warrior was true to his word and kept their vessel on as fair a course as either of them could manage, allaying their concerns and making their interactions more amicable.

Yet, despite the ceaseless aid of a favorable wind, it slowly became obvious to each of them that the voyage was getting ever more perilous. The swells near the shore had been enough to throw those on deck about with dangerous ease. Now, out at sea, the waves rose far above their shorebound kin; Brand lost count of the number of them that were near or greater to half the length of the ship – And more than once they had been far larger still. Luckily, Euwae had been at the oar each time; she seemed able to time the tack up the face of a wave and the quick turn at its crest as if she had been born to it.

Two hours ago, he had remarked as much to Euwae – And grumbled that it was only a matter of time before she would be asleep when one of these mountains of water would stalk them... And the outcome of *that* climb would be a much closer contest indeed.

Now, she was sleeping.

Brand had grown accustomed to the way Foamsmare would shift as she started to come into large swell. The ship did so now as he was trying to shake off the perpetual ache in his shoulder; he braced his feet and slipped his hand out to the tip of the oar, scanning the deck to make sure that everyone was ready to take the shock of the ship as it crested the waves.

Angus screamed, waiving his arms towards the starboard side. There, moving at a near right angle to the rest of the swell was the biggest wave Brand had ever seen. He tried to swing the ship towards it, but it was already cresting the rough seas that he had previously anticipated; the stern was out of the water for several long, tortuous seconds before the oar could bite back into the ocean.

But now they were riding across the face of the wave, rather than up it. The sound at the top where the wind churned the sea water to foam was like that of the rapids on a river. The ship rolled further and further to port as the wall of water reached up to vertical... Beyond it... Turning the ship over onto its side and shattering the mast with an explosive crack as the frothy peak of the wave consumed it.

Brand swore he could hear cu'Kullah's laughter as the air burned out his lungs and a blackness darker even than Ers'Elb ripped his senses from him.

Angus looked at Brand as he twitched in his sleep while he sat in the center of the deck.

"It is not natural, that." He said to himself. "Sleeping in that way. Why is it that he cannot bring himself to lay flat, like any normal man?"

Euwae turned back from gazing at the horizon over the stern, down at Brand, and finally at Angus.

"He does it out of strength. To his cause."

"And, tell me then, what cause is it that makes a man refuse the comforts of a warm bed or a moment's peace when he is finally alone?"

Euwae looked back at Brand, her eyes soft, but shook her head.

"Foolish dice-" Angus bit back the word. "Foolish Outlander ones, to be sure."

She looked back at the way they had come. "To *some*, perhaps." She said with foreboding.

Angus swallowed his retort, instead turning to follow Euwae's gaze.

"A storm, you are thinking?"

She sighed. "Aye, to be sure. And a grand one... We have been lucky, these last three days to be riding upon the skirts of it. But we will not be outrunning it much longer."

He studied the sky as he said slowly, "By tonight, you think?"

Her face fell.

"Perhaps... Certainly no longer than the rising of the sun tomorrow."

"If we are in so happy a place to see the sun, through all of that."

Euwae simply nodded.

Brand awoke with a start, rolling across the deck and ending in a low crouch with his bec de corbin held in a cross parry above his head. With a wild eyed expression he looked around him, before he lowered the weapon, slumped onto his haunches and took a series of deep, deep breaths.

Then he looked slowly about the boat, before his eyes settled on Euwae and Angus standing beside the tiller, looking at the ominous bank of clouds that had been relentlessly pursuing them as they had made their way across the sea; neither was looking in his direction.

With an uncomfortable chuckle, he set down his weapon, stood and stretched, pressing his hands against the small of his back with a grimace.

"Well, that's not good..." He said to himself ruefully. Shaking his head, he retrieved Crows Call and made his way to the stern as well.

Euwae's face lit up as he joined them.

"So, good day to you, Bird Club. Did you sleep well, then?"

"Yeah, just great." He replied, with a tone that indicated the statement was pure fabrication. Although she didn't prompt him, Euwae's brow dropped in concern. Finally he relented and continued.

"I dreamed we got caught in a big storm." He tilted his head towards the high bank of clouds behind them.

"Oh! That would be a troubled dream, indeed..."

Brand grimaced.

"Yeah; let's just say it didn't end well."

After Angus rolled his eyes and moved off to check the sheets and sails before he turned in, Euwae reached up and placed her hand upon Brand's chest. He looked at it, nodding at the concern in her eyes.

"You know," he said with dark humor, "I don't know what it is, but since I've been on this little quest with you, I'm getting pretty concerned about the way my dreams have been going."

"It was so dire, then?"

"If I'd have had *this* dream the night we ended up on the far side of the river, this time none of us would have woken up."

He felt her hand clench with apprehension, but her voice was steady and solemn.

"Was it *that* sort of a dream, Bird Club?"

He shrugged.

"Well, we haven't drowned... Yet. But, if I had to compare them, I'd say that they were pretty close."

She dropped her hand and nodded.

"Then we must make harbor. And soon."

He looked at her and chuckled.

"Shouldn't be a problem, out here in the middle of the sea like this."

Her eyes lashed out at his implied rebuke.

"I would have you know, Outlander – "

"Outlander?"

"– that we have hardly but left the shoals and rips so beloved of the fisherfolk of twoth'Ba. There are a number of safe harbors on the islands just east of Cord'Or. With a good wind and a knowing hand upon the oar, we should reach them before the sun drops from the sky on this very day."

"Well, that's good." He grinned. "Outlander?"

She shrugged.

"Huh. Maybe I should have left Angus to the mercy of the folk of Summersford after all."

"As I would have had it done."

"Not going to let me live that down, are you?"

"Such is the way of it."

"But I can't just kill him now."

"I would not have it done."

"So you're happy that he's here..?"

"His company most certainly does not cause my heart to sing, Bird Club."

She scanned his face for some sign. He shook his head.

"No – I suppose it doesn't." He watched Angus settle down beneath the tent amidships. "But we're stuck with him... At least for now."

Euwae looked back behind them with an excellent imitation of Brand's non-committal shrug.

"You should get to the mast, Bird Club. Call out, as soon as you spy any land ahead and we shall make our way to it as swiftly as Foamsmare will bear us. We should be coming upon the island of Seasgift soon enough; there we can take a harbor that will prove safe enough."

He nodded reassuringly.

"We've both seen worse shitesan than this, Euwae. We'll get through this one. I've got to say I never expected you to be such the sailor. They really teach you al'Aith's well in twoth'Ba! I wish I'd spent more time there... I would have – "

Brand looked into her eyes. He smiled, leaving the thought unspoken. He reached out to squeeze her shoulder gently before he walked to the food locker and fished out a crock of honeyed fruit. He offered it up to Euwae, but she shook her head. He smiled again as he moved off to take his post on the seat near the top of the mast.

The al'Aith looked off to the menace clutching at the western sky, her confident facade cracking as she bit at her lower lip.

"Aye, they taught me well enough. Never sail isle'Eh in the summer without the weavings of the priest, they say, lest the deceitful waters drag you down.

"And yet, here we are..."

She reached out and stroked Foamsmare's aft rail.

"And never set foot upon the shores of Seasgift, should you hope to trod again the lands of living men... Is that not the tale that old Raf'Em spins to make the seamen – for all their time voyaging – shrink like children into their cups at feasting?" But no reply came, save the cool, damp wind that ran its touch across her skin and through her hair.

She turned her back to the storm, her chest rising and falling as she steeled herself for the final race of the voyage ahead.

It was not long after that Brand spied the highest points of Seasgift on the horizon off to port. He slid down the mast and re-set the sails while Euwae guided the ship onto that tack. Brand corrected the sails before he returned to his perch and remained diligent until he no longer had to hand sign course corrections to her, after which he reclined in the woven seat and casually watched the island begin to crawl over the skyline.

A central ridge dominated the spine of the island, running across the length of it from his current perspective. This dropped in a sheer wall of roughly fifty feet to a series of three deep terraces covered with forests; each terrace, like the ridge, ended in an abrupt drop to the next. The lowest rode perhaps twelve feet above the waterline; this final abutment had far fewer trees, but sported dunes of black sands and thickets of scrub oak and low brush.

After several hours, the clouds had consumed the blue sky and left only dull gray ruin across the heavens while Foamsmare made her final dash for Seasgift. Beneath the clouds, the ruins of an ancient castle could be seen, jutting like broken teeth from the far left of the ridgeline. There, the trees which had managed to find purchase along the roof of the island had long ago been cleared and now spitefully refused to return, despite the retreat of the men who had cleared that land to build the ancient fortification. The stone of the collapsed walls played odd tricks on the eye, catching the light reflected off the water far below and giving the impression that they were chiseled from a black ice rather than having been stripped from a quarry by long forgotten hands.

As they approached, the waters hue shifted from the green grey of the open sea to a darker tone like that of oil-rich slate. The winds drove the waves directly into the final cliff of the lowest terrace, without any sign of a beach or portage. The water slid relentlessly into the dark hued rock, sending the crests of foam nearly three quarters of the way to the top, where it clung like a garter of dirty cloth to the stone.

Brand looked back towards Euwae. Once he caught her eye, he placed his right fist to his chin, pointed towards his eyes with his first and last fingers and swung his hand around so that his fingers pointed towards the front of the ship. She nodded once, at which time he clambered down the rope ladder that ran up the mast and made his way up the gently buffeting deck to the bow.

Leaning forward, he quickly realized that the darker water was not a deeper channel, but was instead where the menacing stone from which the island was carved rose in furtive shoals towards the surface. He flagged Euwae's attention again and guided her with broad gestures to keep Foamsmare from charging over and aground one of these unexpected reefs. But the wind – which had driven them with haste towards this refuge – now sought to keep them from avoiding these submerged threats. Brand was forced to wake Angus and direct him to work the sheets as Euwae danced with the steering oar to keep the ship free of this threat.

Finally they reached a point roughly a half mile from the lower cliffs when the grey-water channel they were following narrowed abruptly and sheared off to port. The three of them were barely able to keep their ship from careening into the far side of the shoal, which actually stood exposed in the troughs of the taller waves that raced to their dramatic ends on the wall of stone ahead.

As Foamsmare listed hard to starboard and the mast creaked as Angus fought desperately to keep the boom out of the water, Brand spied a gap in the cliffs up ahead which had been naturally concealed by the contours of the surrounding stone. He shouted above the gusts of the wind to Euwae and frantically waved his hands towards it.

As soon as she understood the commotion she shouted back, "Angus! At my call, let free the sails!"

The ath'Ale looked back at her, his eyes wide as he balked at her command.

"But the ship... She will reef and no mistake!"

"Aye," Euwae shot back, "In truth! On my word!"

"It is mad!"

Euwae's head was bobbing in time with the rise and fall of the deck as the ship rode the surf which raced towards the cliffs.

"On my word!" She ordered without heed to his responses.

"But – " In the distance, thunder tolled across the open sea.

Brand's face lit with understanding as he watched the shifting contours of the cliffs ahead. "Just do it!" He encouraged from the bow.

With unguarded dismay, Angus made ready to release the ropes that held the sail in place and – in turn – was the only sure way to safely propel the vessel. Foamsmare's deck lurched in a shallow trough and rolled steeply once more to starboard as Euwae cried, "Now! Angus!"

Pulling his head into his shoulders with a stark grimace, the warrior released the pair of ropes from the cleat that held the sail at a near right angle to the wind. The ship completed the pitch up the wave; at the crest, the pressure of the wind on the sail swung it wide across the deck towards shore. Without the momentum supplied by the bite of the storm wind, the ship immediately began to lose speed. By the time the second wave struck the side of the hull, the force of the water began to drive the ship directly towards the cliff...

Or, rather, towards the tall, narrow gap in the face of it.

Euwae began to fight the oar for control. She looked wide eyed towards the two men.

"I cannot turn the bow! Move to the rails – Keep us off the rocks!"

Both men jumped to the starboard side and seized docking gaffs, prepared to lean out over the side to try to catch the edge of the rocks should the ship be swept too close. Foamsmare slowed her glide, until the waves held more control of her direction than the wind. The two warriors slowly walked to the stern, keeping pace with the jutting edge of the corner of the channel in the cliff; while it took them both to finally force the stern clear of the rock, they managed to do so without any great damage to the side of the ship as it was drawn into the channel between the walls of rock by the force of the tide and into the wide harbor beyond.

The two men let out a howl and jumped the short distance to where Euwae stood beside the oar. Brand scooped her up off the deck with an exuberant hug and Angus slapped his knee.

"Most WELL!" Angus cried. "You have the makings of a true captain, and no mistake!"

Euwae pushed on Brand's chest. "Put me down, Bird Club!" She extolled with relief.

Brand spun her about once, then set her down gently on the deck with a grin.

"Well done, al'Aith," he said respectfully, "I'm shitesa impressed."

Euwae blushed furiously.

"Well, I am thankful for all that and no mistake." She said with awkward humility. "It was a fair idea, but it put all of us to the work of making the passage."

Brand beamed, while Angus shook his head.
"Oh!" Euwae called out and leaped back to the steering oar.

"We may be pleased, but we must not forget Foamsmare, eh?"

She patted the oar as she swung the ship back to the middle of the channel. The two men grinned as they looked from Euwae to each other.

Angus continued to shake his head and made his way forward. Brand stepped back and leaned on the rail, watching her as she guided the ship. Euwae tried to make a point of ignoring him, but could not fight down the flush in her cheeks.

"WHAT!!!"

Brand's right hand shot to his weapon as Angus came rushing back down the deck.

"What were you THINKING then?" He howled as he stormed up to Euwae. "This is to be the deaths of us!"

Euwae swallowed hard as Brand stepped between them.

"Back off, Angus."

"Back off? Back OFF? Aye, I would that I could do so! Better would it have been had we been dashed against the cliff, than be so daft as sail to our very Fates!"

Brand stepped back and looked from Angus to Euwae. Her head hung low; she made no attempt to refute his wild ranting.

"What's the problem here?" Brand asked with honest discomfiture. "We got to Seasgift with no problems..?"

"ACH!" yelped Angus as he turned to Brand. "Just how did your folk SURVIVE the evils of the world to spawn you?"

Brand's lips pursed at the insult, but Angus could not be cowed.

"Just LOOK if you need to see the truth of it!" He wailed and gestured over the side of the ship. Brand turned to look and his jaw almost dropped in astonishment.

"Sacred shitesan..." He said under his breath.

Foamsmare had slipped into a wide harbor, deeper than he would have guessed by looking at the stark cliffs that protected it. The tracks of ancient roads were still visible leading away from the ends of grass covered stone quays, while tumbled stone rings laid out the graves of the houses that stood upon the ancient foundations.

But from the water spouted the boles of a hundred masts, like timber stripped of bark and left to drown in an inevitable tide. Some were bleached almost white by long years of exposure, while others wore the brown stain of worn wood in a wretched tribute to the once proud ships that now lay in their watery necropolis.

Brand looked back at Euwae.

"What's this?" He asked in bewilderment, waving his bec de corbin out across the harbor at the vessels' corpses.

"It is Seasgift, in truth..." She said, almost too weakly to hear.

Brand lowered Crows Call and looked back out across the span of the harbor.

"It's not what I expected..." He said with black humor.

"Some of these ships look like they've gone down pretty recently."

"Aye, that they have, dicenn." Spat out Angus reflexively. "For this is the very place where all those who die beneath the waves of isle'Eh are drawn to suffer out their dooms."

Brand's head leaned to the left as he grimaced.

"What is it with you people and water?" He asked ironically.

Angus ignored him pointedly and turned back to shake his fist at Euwae.

"We are now no more than dead, having dared sail to this cursed place! What were you THINKING, woman!"

Brand's lips peeled back with a retort, but Euwae was the faster.

"Mind your PLACE, Angus of twoth'Fhee!" She parried regally, her pride of station wholly restored by the ath'Ale's accusations. "I am no *wench*, who lives by the mean generosity of wayward men; I am living heir to the blood and geasa of the very ree's of twoth'Ba." She finished hotly, stepping forward into his raised fist until it was just before her face and then pushing it aside to close with him while she continued her rebuke.

"We risked sailing upon isle'Eh without the weavings of a priest to protect us... And we are at it too late in the season to fly free of the seas wrath. The storm that chased us was no fall tempest! And in truth, were we to try to ride out the ire of it, we would now find ourselves here not as living folk, but as those who are gathered by ancient ways that still lay claim to all sailors in death.

"So I thought it wise to seek out the one harbor which is known to be proof from the fury of the sea."

Angus looked down at the woman before him.

"This is no reprieve of our doom, *woman*." He growled ominously. "You have but led us to it."

She glared back at him with the armor of her superiority wrapped fully around her.

"We are not yet fallen, *ath'Ale*."

Angus struck her hard, his fist coming up and cracking against the bottom of her jaw. Euwae's head snapped back and her long hair spun out in a halo as she tumbled backwards and fell to the deck.

"You may be born of the blood of a ree," he said with caustic fury, "but you are no al'Aith of *mine*."

176

Euwae shook her head with a remedial tremor, shot to her feet and pushed hard against the big man's chest. Rage twisted her features as her right fist shot out and hammered into Angus' nose; with a startled yelp he leaped back, his hands flying up to his face.

She raised her hands again to follow up on the initial blow, but Brand stepped between them and looked at Angus coolly.

"So, she's no al'Aith of yours, eh?" He said calmly. "Well, maybe it's time we did something about that."

Euwae tried to rush past Brand and get to Angus, but he reached out and held her back. She relented and stood beside him, her fury chained only by the strength of Brand's demeanor as he began to circle the other man slowly.

"Do you remember the night that you first took me down?" He continued. "You and the rest of cu'Kullah's band... He asked me if I understood what it meant to be beaten by warriors of another twoth. Do you remember?"

Angus still held his hand to his bleeding nose while he shook his head no.

Brand ignored him and continued.

"Well, back then, I suppose it meant you could toss me into a lake. But, if I remember all those stories about en'Och, once you get your tail handed to you it's supposed to mean that your duty to your old ree is forfeit – And that your shitesas hide belongs to the one who beat you, if they care enough to claim it."

By now, he had circled the other man twice. He stopped short behind the other warrior and said darkly, "cu'Kullah also said a few things to me beside that lake. So you can thank him for whats about to happen.

"Now *kneel*."

Angus started to protest, but Brand seized his shoulders and pushed him to the deck of the ship. "I said KNEEL!" He called out as the other man was forced to his knees.

"Now, Angus of twoth'Fhee: you've been beaten by the al'Aith of twoth'Ba and the champion in her service. By that en'Och you hold so dear; on everything that torc means to you...

"Swear to follow Euwae instead."

Angus was silent. So was Euwae. Brand shook his head.

"By the Ard'Ree, you *nothus*... SWEAR."

The storm roared against the island with a blinding flash of light and the shattering voice of thunder. Angus' head bobbed; his eyes bulged. His lips moved, but no sound was pulled through them. Brand's brow furrowed and his head drew back. Both he and Euwae stepped away from Angus as wracking shakes spread through the kneeling man's body with growing force.

"I – Swear – " Angus croaked hoarsely, then let out a choked scream that was strangled by the rush of foulness from his throat.

Angus doubled over in pain as his body spasmed. Thin fluid poured from his mouth, as if he had gagged on the water of an ancient pond; black flecks swirled within it as it poured out of his body and spilled around him on the deck. With his right hand he clawed at his torc and jerked it off his neck as if it were strangling him... Then he jerked backwards, as more of the repugnant ichor cascaded out of his mouth and nose, flowing down his throat and chest and staining his flesh with its dark pallor before one last, awful shudder broke his spent body, which collapsed to the deck and was still.

Euwae shot Brand a look, but he pulled his head between his shoulders and quickly shook it no.

After a moment, the fluid began to steam.

The tendrils reached up, almost imperceptibly at first. But as more of the rank moisture rose and began to coalesce into a column, Brand circled around it and stood beside Euwae, their weapons instinctively drawn.

The cloud continued to expand, until it swirled into a roughly man shaped fog above the deck. The wafting tendril where the head might have been on a man swiveled slowly about until it locked on Euwae.

Then, the figure of polluted mist began to waft inexorably towards her.

"Shitesan!" Brand cried in surprise. "Get BACK!"

Keeping just a short distance between them, they moved to the centerline of the deck. The black flecked apparition followed. Brand risked a glance at his companion.

"I've got nothing. You?"

"In truth, I have heard of no tale that gives mention of such a thing."

"All right, then. Looks like we do it the hard way. You ready?"

"I am."

The pair lunged in unison at the figure. Brand kept his attack high, drawing Crows Call out and through the figure's chest while Euwae ducked and swept her falcata across the area where it draped across the deck. Both weapons sung through the air but failed to do more than leave a gap in the form where they passed through it.

Wisps of the creature trailed the weapons, but both warriors were careful to stay well clear of them as they withdrew. Each, in turn, took a few more exploratory strikes before they backpedaled further down the deck towards the mast.

"Well, that's not gonna work." Brand said flatly. "How about you? Any new ideas?"

Euwae scowled, lowered her weapon and drew herself to her full height.

"In the name of Ard'Ree and the ree of twoth'Ba, I command you: BE GONE!"

The mist continued to approach.

"That did to be my guess, then." Euwae sulked. "I pass the matter back to you."

Brand nodded.

"Not a bad guess, Euwae. It was worth a shot."

"Perhaps we could make a great wind and so banish it?"

"I doubt it. It's coming at us upwind already."

"Ah, so it does. That still does leave you to make the next – AH!"

The cloud-figure suddenly whipped forward. Euwae ducked and rolled to the left, but Brand stepped directly into its path to defend her. As they touched, the warrior was pushed back through the air and down onto the deck with enough force to drive the wind from his body. As he lay there on the deck struggling to breathe it glided over him and continued to stalk the al'Aith, who paused only long enough to see that Brand was not badly injured before she turned and sprinted off towards the bow of the ship.

As he struggled to rise, Brand noticed that Angus, too, had levered himself to his hands and knees. With effort, Brand got to his feet and staggered to the other warrior, helping him find his own feet before he pointed at the apparition which floated across the deck.

"What IS that?" He demanded.

Angus lifted his head with effort, squinted and shook it in denial. Brand exhaled sharply through his nose and watched sourly as the other man tried to stand without his assistance.

"Great." He muttered. "That was a big help."

He bent over and picked up Angus' torc.

"You dropped this..."

Angus' hands trembled as he took it back.

"Thank you, Outlander..." He replied, his voice a harsh whisper grating on his raw throat.

From the bow of the ship, Euwae gave a frustrated shriek of effort as she leaped from the bow rail past her pursuer and sprinted back down the deck towards the two men. Brand started as she leaped, but as soon as she made the jump safely he turned back to Angus.

"This is all about you," he said roughly. "This thing came out of you... And you've got no idea why?"

"I have an idea *why*." He said, the accusation clear even through the raspy abrasion in his voice. "But none as to *how*."

Euwae was gasping for breath as she reached them at the rear of the ship. Another flash and clap of thunder threw hard shadows across her delicate face and under the swollen lip where Angus had struck her.

"How – How fares he?" She asked with concern.

Brand scowled. "He fares, but that's about it."

She grinned bitterly.

"The next choices are to be yours, then..."

"Choice-es?"

"Aye," she nodded as she fought to force the air into her lungs. "I have sought to strike, banish and outrun the beasty. That leaves you a choice behind."

"I guess Angus doesn't count then?"

She shook her head and bent over, placing her hands on her knees to try catching her breath more quickly. Brand bit the inside of his lip and shrugged as he watched the thing float towards them. Angus finished seating the torc around his throat and pulled in a bracing lungful of air.

"What is the order, then?" He asked resolutely.

"Bird Club..?"

"Yeah?"

"Where did the waters go, then?"

"Huh?"

Brand's eyes shifted from the phantasm to the deck. While the wood was stained where the ichor that had spewed from Angus had touched it, there was otherwise no liquid to be seen. He turned to Angus, his jaw set.

"I've got an idea... But you're gonna have to trust me."

The other man's face contracted in suspicion. Brand ignored him and knelt down in front of Euwae.

"Can you buy us enough time to get him out of his armor?"

She flashed an impish smile.

"Aye... I can circle about the deck like a spring doe, if needs I must."

"Then do it." He rose and turned back to Angus, stripping the straps from the buckles of his curiass. "As for you..."

Despite her claim, Euwae was having trouble keeping her feet as she finished the third lap across the deck. The thing that pursued her was getting faster, but was not clever; it made no attempt to trap her or cut towards her at angles where the deck narrowed.

At last, Brand signaled her to join them and she sprinted towards them on wings of true relief.

"Catch your breath," Brand said gently. Then, turning to face Angus, "You ready?"

The barrel-chested ath'Ale nodded grimly.

"Are you sure of this, then?"

"Nope."

"Fair enough, then. Outlander. I am ready to act as best as I may."

Brand nodded respectfully.

"Good enough for me. When it comes, it's gonna come fast. I'm not sure how long I can hold onto it... So make it good, Angus."

Euwae looked at them blankly. "Hold fast to it? And just how will you do that?"

Brand opened his mouth, then snapped it shut as the miasma bore down on them.

"Euwae – Get behind me."

Still panting, she stepped back and allowed Brand to move between her and the pursuer... Time seemed to slow to a crawl for them as the creature surged forward and struck him in the chest.

But Brand had moved over his center of balance and kept his feet. The tendrils of fog coalesced and lost their transparency, wrapping around him like cables of steel. Suddenly, Brand had the wild sensation that he was drowning... His lungs burned and his sight began to blur. He reached out and clenched his hands upon the things neck, but they burned with a freezing cold that left them cruelly numb and all but useless. At last he could not ignore the need for air in his chest; against his will his mouth opened and the fog began to flow into his throat.

And then Angus reached them with a leap.

Wrapping his arms around and through the mists he tore away its grasp on Brand, before the pair of them tumbled to the rail of the ship and over the side.

The creature wailed as Angus' weight pulled them both into the salty waters of the harbor. The parts of it that touched the bay were sucked down and those mists were devoured. But much of the creature returned to its immaterial form and avoided the doom that the warriors had planned for it, while Angus dropped headlong into the cold waters and vanished from sight.

Brand dropped to his knees, while the wailing thing shot away from the water and hovered above the deck. He lifted his head to follow its movements, but was unable to do more than watch what follwed.

Euwae stepped forward and stood over him, her blade gleaming in the dull light. Black smoke wafted out of the places where the creature had touched the water but were sucked away by the gusting wind. The two studied each other for a long moment, before the al'Aith nodded to her opponent and braced herself for the final attack.

She was deafened as a crack of lightning burned out of the sky and struck the mast of a sunken ship within the bay, while the thunder that followed sent ripples across the waves in the harbor. As she crushed her eyes shut and tried to clear her vision, the vapor circled behind her and raced out of the sky towards its quarry as the first, cold drops of rain began to fall.

Just above them, the creature wailed again with haunting despair as the rain drops seared smoking holes through its body. Thus restrained, it began to stretch further apart as the initial shower burst out into a full torrential downpour.

From the deck, just beyond its dissipating grasp, Euwae and Brand watched without emotion as each drop brought the creature one more agonized wound closer to dissolution, until it had been torn completely asunder and was gone.

When there was no more trace of it, Euwae turned to Brand and helped him to his feet. As he stiffly clambered upright, he gave her a lopsided grin.

"Guess I made the right choice... I just wish I'd known it was gonna rain."

Euwae dropped her sword and hugged him fiercely.

At first, he stood there uncertainly, but at the last his hands lifted and patted her gently on the back. They stood in that pose for a moment, before Angus' voice could be heard above the pouring rain.

"Do you live?" He cried. "Al'Aith? Outlander?"

Euwae leaned back and looked up at Brand, who shrugged and wiped the rain from his eyes.

"I guess we should probably get him back aboard," Brand said lightly, "before he drowns."

Euwae chuckled.

"Aye, Bird Club... Let us find him the ladder."

She moved to the rail and called down for him to be patient, while Brand moved amidships to break out the rope boarding ladder and lower it over the side to allow Angus to return to the safety of the ship once again.

After they helped him up, he pulled at his long hair to wring the water from it and a feeble grin cracked his lips.

"So, we did it then." He croaked. "Most well, indeed."

Brand reached out and clasped him on the shoulder.

"Most well." He replied. Then, he turned his hand palm up to the rain. "We should do something about this, though." He rolled his head towards the canopy that sheltered the deck ahead of the mast. Both he and Euwae turned to get out of the rain, but Brand put a restraining hand on Euwae's shoulder.

"Why don't you get over there, Angus... We'll be over in a minute."

The warrior looked from Brand, to Euwae and at last towards the shelter.

"Aye." Was all he said, before he shuffled off.

Euwae beamed.

"Brand Eastlander," she said with a smile, "Although the moment was such that I had no chance to speak my mind, I tell you now that I am most pleased to accept your pledge."

"What?"

"Your pledge. When you proclaimed yourself to be the champion to my service."

Brand looked confused.

"No I didn't."

"Aye, but you did! Back when you forced Angus to yield to me! Do you not recall?"

His eyes moved back and forth as he sought for the events of which she spoke in the recesses of his mind. Finally, he sighed.

"Now, wait a minute. I said that I helped you defeat – "

"No. You said that Angus was brought to his defeat by an al'Aith," she curtsied "and the Champion who stood in the right cause of her service."

"That's not exactly – "

"It is the way of it. You spoke the words yourself!"

Brand's shoulders slumped in defeat.

"Ach!" Euwae clapped him on the shoulder. "And I accept your pledge, Brand Eastlander."

He looked down at her hand; his gaze traversed the span of her arm and drove into her eyes. Her brow fluttered with sudden uncertainty, yet he did not draw down the intensity of his stare.

"All right," he said coolly, "Then you won't mind if I spout off a little bit, then."

"Spout off..?"

He nodded, never taking his eyes off of hers.

"You seem pretty sure of yourself, Euwae. Sometimes, it works out for you. But sometimes, not so much."

"What is your meaning, then?"

He made a sweeping gesture across the harbor. Another bolt of lightning and crash of thunder shot across the harbor from further inland.

"You knew all about this place. Before we came here. You *knew*. But you kept it a secret.

"Why?"

She tried to look away, but found her eyes were riveted to his. A faint tremor shook her lip, but she pursed them to hide it.

"As I told Angus – We were sailing isle'Eh with no priest to guide us, nor to make the right weavings to see our passage safely made. And with the rise of the storm – "

"Shitesan." Said Brand flatly.

Her eyes slipped across his face like the rain which streamed across his countenance, but it was hard as stone.

"In my homeland, we've got nobles, too. Most are born to it; and I can tell you, there are times when you'd fit right in with them."

A smile started to light her face, but he extinguished it with a shake of his head.

"I came here to get away from all that."

At last, his eyes freed her as he turned away to face the forgotten ruins that lined the shore.

"There's a big difference between being 'noble' and being 'worthy.' On that one, Angus had it right. You might be the daughter of the ree of twoth'Ba. But that blood doesn't give you the right to do whatever you shitesas want.

"But – "

"I'm not finished." He said, refusing to relinquish his momentum.

"You're the one who said you accepted my service – So don't think I am cheap. If nothing else, then maybe you'll think twice before you try that one again. And if you want it, you're going to accept it for everything it means.

184

"*Do* you want it, Euwae?"

She nodded, almost timidly. "Yes, Bird Club..."

His shoulders rose and fell before he turned back to her.

"Then you need to realize that being an al'Aith isn't just about how you're born. Your family might have all the power in the world. But the people around you aren't going to judge you for that. They're going to judge you for what you do with it.

"And you aren't just issuing orders from your feast hall, here, Euwae. We're depending on you and everything you bring to the table. But your choices'll cost us a lot more than our trust if they're wrong."

He took a breath for emphasis.

"Angus was right when he said you knew what might happen if we sailed to Seasgift. And you did it. But without telling us – " he closed his eyes, then opened them again, "Without trusting *me* with what you were up to."

"I thought you would well understand – "

"Shitesan. You knew I would have no idea. Otherwise you would have told Angus, too. Right?"

Euwae stood stiffly, with her arms locked to her sides.

Brand's voice softened. "Look. I know you did it because you thought it was the right thing to do. And I can't fault you for that.

"But if you don't think that – your champion – is worth trusting, *don't* be surprised if I'm not willing to follow you.

"You go around proclaiming to everybody that you are full of the blood of the rees, so you should start acting like it. Because if you don't, you'll find out pretty quick just how important that heritage is when no one has any faith in who you are, or what you stand for."

Euwae's eyes were liquid. The rain ran down her face and buried her tears.

Brand stood just outside of arms reach; he spun his weapon around in his hand with anxious tension.

Finally, Euwae broke the silence, her voice thick with emotion.

"I am thinking that I – " She faltered, searching for the words.

"I – " Her voice cracked. As Brand watched the tension drained out of her body. Her shoulders shook with her sobbing. He closed his eyes, took a deep breath, opened them again and clenched his jaw.

Her head was nodding up and down, in answer to an unstated question. Finally she steeled herself and pushed the water off her face.

"So, then."

"So, then." He replied.

"You have been a fine and worthy companion, Brand Eastlander." Her voice cracked again as the sorrow fought through her resolve.

"Have been?" He asked frankly.

"Aye. You have. We have made a worthy tale of it. I am – " She searched his eyes "It was my *honor* to have fought at your side."

Crows Call stopped spinning in his hand.

"I don't think you understand, Euwae."

"Aye, I do. You are done with me."

Brand shook his head.

"Is that what you want?"

"No! Why would it serve me to cast you aside? It is you who have taken your leave..."

Brand flipped his weapon over and rested it on his shoulder.

"Yeah... Why indeed?" He said to himself. Then he closed half the distance between them.

"Euwae," he said firmly, "You said you've accepted my choice, right?"

Her head bobbed up and down. "Aye... You are your own man, by any and all rights."

He shook his head, the ghost of a grin on his lips.

"Not any more."

He inverted his weapon and let the head of it swing down, so the handle was in front of his face. He bowed his forehead to the bottom of the handle and lowered it between them.

"Habes brachium, meum obsequium et fidem meam." He said solemnly.

"You have my arm, my loyalty and my faith."

With that the warrior turned and started to walk back to the shelter. Euwae stood alone on the deck, staring at the space where he had been standing as a flood of emotions washed across her face. Just outside the shelter, Brand stopped and turned back towards her.

"Are you coming, my al'Aith?"

Euwae took a deep breath as a newfound strength flowed through her. Her shoulders rolled back; the next flash of lightning in the distance caught and burned in her eyes. Without a word, she turned away from Seasgift and walked across the deck to take her place at Brand's side.

the Way of It

The tempest besieged the island for several days. Although the three travelers aboard Foamsmare were protected by the cliffs from the direct threat of the surf, the wind still tormented the ships mast and rigging; during the most savage throes of the storm, the tide drew so much water out of the harbor that they had to allow the boat to drift back into the mouth of the bay to keep it from going aground or getting tangled in wrecks beneath them.

All the while, the thunder never ceased its ominous song around them. In the shadows of the lightning strikes, fleeting glimpses of dark forms seemed to be moving across the shoreline, but left no trace once the brilliance of the sky's wrath passed. First Angus, and later Euwae averted their eyes from the island whenever possible, but Brand found his gaze drawn towards it, as if he were trying to seek out a vision somewhere upon the barren empty ruins before him.

During the storm, Euwae and Brand spoke at length about the merits of trying to pursue cu'Kullah across isle'Eh without the protection of the weavings of a priest or any way to chart a course to their quarry beyond the inability of Angus to speak. At the last, they reluctantly decided that their only good option was to return to the shores of Cord'Or, where they could better prepare for the demands of the chase once word of cu'Kullah's deeds reached them.

Early on the morning of the fourth day, there was a distinct change in the wind. It blew in cool from the northeast, routing the storm clouds and forcing them to retreat back towards the lands of the Cord'Or. The three quickly agreed to risk making good time on the favorable wind and raised anchor on the outgoing tide to start the journey back to the twoths.

As they put Seasgift behind them, Brand spent the first few hours watching the island crawl back behind the horizon. Euwae stood beside him, keeping her hand on the tiller, but her furtive glances in his direction could not penetrate the depths of his ruminations. As a pale fog rose astern and cloaked all but the highest points of the island from sight, he finally turned and gave her a single methodical nod. Then he walked off towards the canopy pitched over the deck and sat down to sleep.

Angus was seeing to the sails as Brand sat down and began to focus on his meditation. The larger man's lower face and chest were still stained by the contamination that had been forced from him; the day before he had surrendered to it and, rather than continue to fail to scrub it away, had shaved off his beard instead in the hopes that the new growth of hair might help conceal it.

He thumped down onto the deck beside Brand and picked up a jar of mead. After a deep drink, he offered it to the other man. Brand's eyes swiveled from the jar, to Angus' face and back to the jar. He accepted with a nod and took a deep drink as well, before he returned it and closed his eyes.

"Well, then," said Angus cautiously, "I see now that there may be a bit of reckoning to be had between us."

"Huh."

Angus turned towards Brand, but the other warrior simply sat there with his eyes closed.

"By the skulls of the blessed, man!" Angus growled, "I am trying to make peace with you!"

At that, Brands eyes slowly opened once again. His head rotated towards Angus like a leaf blowing across a still pond. He studied the bigger man silently before nodding once.

"OK, Angus. Consider us at peace."

Then he turned away and closed his eyes once more.

"Just in such a way as that?!?!"

"Yeah; just in such a way."

"Had you tried to cast *me* away into Ers'Elb, I would not be so light as to absolve you then!"

"And if you had hurt Euwae, you would be dead now." Brand said calmly, without no change to his position.

"I – "

"Would be dead." Brand's eyes opened while his head swung towards the other man once more. "The point is, you served cu'Kullah faithfully; I'd be an idiot if I thought you were wrong for being everything that your en'Och demanded of you."

Angus' own eyes narrowed.

"Aye. She said you knew of en'Och."

"I'm not sure how you'd make a living in our line of work and not trip all over some idea like en'Och – No matter where you were born."

"That is the wisdom of an Outlander, right enough," Angus grumbled, "although I do not care to have you speak of it in that wise."

Brand nodded again, his eyes focusing on those of the ath'Ale.

"My only concern is what you do now that we're standing on the same side of the line, Angus. What's done is... " He pursed his lips with a methodical smile. "We can't change what's done, right? So I'm willing to let it go, if you are."

Angus shook his head.

"I know not how your people make their way, Outlander, that you would so quickly let a foeman cast off one banner for another. In this, or any wise."

But he clapped Brand on the shoulder and gave it a rough squeeze.

"Though let it be as you have spoken."

Brand nodded and returned to his sleeping posture. Angus rose and started to make his way out of the deck shelter.

"Angus!"

He turned. "Yes, Outlander?"

"If you are going to be fighting with us, you'll need this."

Brand tossed Angus his scramasax. The other man caught it deftly; his chin trembled as he studied the weapon.

"You keep it," Brand said approvingly. "It needs somebody to earn it a name."

Angus' chest swelled. With a nod he turned away and walked towards the mast, water welling in his eyes.

Brand took a last, calming breath and cloaked himself in sleep.

*   *   *

They were better than halfway back to the mainland before the winds finally failed them. Euwae had spent the time wisely, however, showing both Brand and Angus the trick of making wide tacks upon the wind, while keeping the sun or the stars of the High Crown in the right places to keep them headed along their line of sail. Now that the wind chose to swing against them once more, each was able to see to the steering oar in their turn and they continued to make good time towards their destination.

That night Angus was at the oar, while Brand took the watch upon the deck. Euwae had finished her evening meal, but sleep was not fast in coming. At last, she rolled out of her sleeping furs with a sigh and pulled on a long tunic. After belting it and slipping into her soft boots, she padded her way across the deck to join the two men who sat within a pool of lantern light in the stern of the ship.

Angus' deep laugh rolled past her across the deck.

"Is that in truth the way of if?"

Brand nodded with a hinge of embarrassment at the back of his skull.

"You should have seen it. That shitesat greyblood just reached down from off the roof, picked me up and tossed me over Euwae's head like I was a little doll."

"That must have been a most grand fight, indeed, Outlander... The pair of you fending off such a beast as that!"

Euwae beamed. "Oh, it was indeed!"

The two men turned to face the darkness. Brand flashed a lopsided smile.

"Yeah, it was." He confirmed.

"So, tell me then: which of you took the honor of slaying it?"

Brand shot a glance at Euwae.

"Neither one of us." He remarked, his voice weighed with irony.

"Not one of you?" Angus asked, astounded. "You fled?"

"NO!" Euwae cast back at him and nodded at Brand. "He did to beat it most soundly."

Angus chuckled and nodded.

"I suspected as much." He pronounced. Brand tried to wave off his next comment, but Angus continued blithely. "It is an ath'Ale's work, that and none other."

Euwae's tone dropped an octave.

"An ath'Ale's work, is it?"

"Aye!"

"So you think me not worthy of such a task, then?"

Brand grimaced and averted his eyes.

"Such a fair woman as you?" Angus said honestly. "You have shown well enough your talent with your ba. But a troll?" He shook his head.

"And what of you, then?" Asked Euwae with flagrant innocence. "Could *you* be laying low a troll, Angus of F'hee?"

"Myself?" Angus' eyes searched for an answer, before he added thoughtfully, "Oh, I would not be thinking such a feat would be *beyond* my reach..."

"No?"

Brand raised his right hand and closed his eyes as he rubbed the bridge of his nose.

"Oh, aye."

"Would you care, then, to be showing me just how you might be doing that?" Then, she added contritely, "Just so I might be shown such prowess, that I might tell the tale of having seen it..."

Brand opened his eyes and looked through the shadows at Euwae.

"I think we're good with that." He said diplomatically. "We can take Angus at his word on this one."

"But – " Chimed both the al'Aith and the ath'Ale together, as Brand raised his hands as a gesture of both peace and finality and shook his head.

"Uh-uh. Euwae, you are not going to take Angus to task over that."

"Take me to task?" Said the big man with surprise. "I will be reminding you that it was I who did to lay you low back at Bay Henge."

"Yeah, you and the thirty other men in cu'Kullah's war band did a great job of taking me down after I had fallen asleep." Brand said with self reproach.

"No!" Said Euwae with feigned shock in her voice and a twinkle in her eye. "In truth?"

"Oh, aye!" Beamed Angus proudly. "And, my plan it was, too. You should have seen him there. All – "

"Yeah, that's great, Angus. But don't push your luck."

"Luck? That has not to bring to bear to this. Are you claiming to be my better?"

Brand's head rotated until his flat stare engaged Angus' determined look. After a moment, the bigger man sighed and looked down at the deck.

"Oh, aye." He said with remorse. He raised his eyes again and looked at Euwae. "But surely she..."

Euwae's expression was just as emotionless as Brand's. Angus studied her face; his shoulders rose and fell unenthusiastically.

"I would not count the skills of Angus of F'hee so lightly, were I the two of you." He said with deflated bravado.

Brand reached across and squeezed his shoulder.

"Don't worry about that, Angus. I've seen you fight – We both have. And I'm a lot happier that you're sitting here beside me than on the other side facing me." He nodded in affirmation, while Euwae's expression softened and she smiled.

The ath'Ale's face flushed. He drew his lips tight across his face to hide his own feelings, but returned Brand's nod. His companion squeezed his shoulder once again, lowered his hand and leaned back, his face smooth once again as Euwae stepped lightly across the deck and stood over him.

"It is pleasing to know that you think so highly of the pair of us, then." She said softly.

Brand's gaze swung up to her and he gave a slight nod.

"Although the outcome was never in doubt." She grinned.

Angus started to protest, but Brand was quicker with his own rebuttal.

"Euwae..."

She tilted her head to the left and shrugged lightly.

"I am, as you yourself claimed, the better of Angus. And, as he defeated you..."

Brand sat up. Angus' gaze slid from him towards Euwae and back to Brand, a slight smirk now flitting across his lips.

"Huh." Said Brand, unimpressed. "I've seen you fight, Euwae – "

"As I have seen you."

"And you're not shitesas bad." He continued through her interruption. "But you aren't going to be taking down any trolls, all by yourself, either."

She grinned. "Oh, that may be the way of it... But I was not speaking of the trolls, here, Bird Club. I was only speaking of the two ath'Ales I see before me."

Brand's lips compressed.

"After all, am I not the al'Aith of the ship and daughter of the Ree of twoth'Ba?"

Brand's chest expanded as he breathed deeply. His eyes never shifted from hers; she, in turn, made no attempt to look away.

"You know, al'Aith, I am thinking that you are right in one wise," ventured Angus. "He carries himself with the fires of en'Och right enough."

"You too?"

"I was but making plain what my eyes are seeing."

"Thank you, Angus." Said Euwae politely. "And well timed it is, too."

"You want to see some en'Och?" Brand said, sinuously rising to his feet. Behind his back, Angus gave an overt wink to Euwae, who stifled a giggle in response. Brand looked at her and scowled. "I'll show you some shitesat en'Och."

He loosed Crows Call from his belt and hefted it lightly.

"All right, al'Aith of the ship and daughter of the Ree of twoth'Ba. But I'm warning you, my people take this kind of dancing seriously. Are you sure you're up to this?"

Euwae's brows furrowed, her grin dropping from mischievous to wicked.

"I am as fine a dancer as ever you will meet, Brand Eastlander."

He exhaled sharply through his nose. "Fair enough." He raised his weapon vertically in front of him. "Ready for a bit of schooling?"

Euwae's voice was cool as she sought to copy his demeanor. "Are you, then?"

Brand nodded, a hard grin curling the left side of his mouth.

"Yeah, I think I am."

"Well, then," Euwae continued gravely, "let this be our pact. If you can show me – in any wise – the better of my skills, I shall in the same show you such steps, drawn from my people... Who have ruled by the blade for as long as there has been a sun that shines upon the lands in which we dwell."

Angus stood up.

"Al'Aith..."

"No, Angus. You are witness to this: my partner has called me to the deck to dance with him and I cannot refuse so bold a gesture as that.

"So, do you agree, as a true ath'Ale of mine, to keep this duty?"

Angus looked from Euwae to Brand.

"Outlander..."

Brand waived the comment away with his free hand.

"Don't worry about me, Angus. She wants to go a round or two, it's fine with me."

"In truth, it is not you for whom I worry."

"Oh?" Euwae interjected as she drew her falcata. "Then let us take the first steps together, then, shall we?"

Angus grimaced but stepped back, to the periphery of the pool of light shed by the lamp. Brand and Euwae stepped back as well, leaving four feet of critical distance between them.

"So, then, teacher," purred Euwae, "what are the first steps of this?"

Brand studied her posture, his eyes slipping from the tilt of her head, past the ready sword to her wide stance and the angles of her feet.

"How about this?" He asked casually, flipping the head of his heavy weapon out gracefully. As Euwae brought up her own blade to catch the strike, he shifted the turn of his wrist so that the beak of Crows Call slipped over the back edge of Euwae's sword; shifting his feet to a much wider stance as he turned at the hip, pulling both weapons back towards him. As she began to lean forward he stepped around her and gave the al'Aith a shove from behind that almost toppled her to the deck.

Euwae's shoulders dropped as she stood back up, her chin rising as she turned with regal disdain towards Brand.

"That is but one step, Bird Club. In truth, I know many."

Brand grinned.

"So do I."

She shed any traces of play as she dropped into a low crouch and began to circle him slowly.

Brand nodded and slipped towards the center of the pool of light, so that Euwae was always forced to face into it; but the glare did nothing to distract her. Tossing her head to keep the hair out of her face, she stalked him as she orbited his location.

With a sudden shout that echoed back from the far end of the ship she leaped out and slashed down at him, but Brand stepped aside from the blow, catching her belt in the beak of his weapon as she passed by. Using the full length of the bec de corbin as a lever he leaned back and redirected her trajectory, sending her crashing to the deck beside him.

He turned his wrist and freed Crows Call as she fell and followed up with a gentle touch to her back as she tried to rise.

"That's a great move." He said honestly. "Your father teach you that?"

She looked at him darkly.

"Aye." She shot back. "And that is but two steps of the dance!"

She lashed out with her feet and caught Brand behind the right knee. As he toppled over she shot to her feet to cover the distance between them, but rather than stop his fall Brand rolled twice over and let his own momentum pull him up. His weapon was out in a low parry that stopped Euwae's blow just as he regained his feet.

Angus whistled softly.

"No help from you, then!" Euwae scolded him. To Brand, she added, "And I suppose you would be counting that as three, then?"

Brand shrugged.

"I'll let it go if you will."

"Three it is, then. And *no* mistake."

Brand nodded. "Three it is..."

Euwae disengaged her weapon and stalked back, until she regained her critical distance. Once more she sank into a deep stance that minimized her exposed body. Her hair now hung wildly across her face, but her smoldering eyes were torches of utter resolve as she searched her opponent's position for every possible opening.

For the next several minutes the contest continued: Euwae sought to test Brand's defenses, or he would test hers. Often the al'Aith came close to striking him, but he would manage to evade those strikes at the last moment. She quickly became aware of the way in which he used his weapon to move past her own and managed to adapt to its curious and heavy blows, but Brand's experience proved to be greater than her own talents and technique could conquer.

At the last, her clothes were disheveled and sweat flowed freely across her skin to stain her garb despite the cool night air. She was not alone in this, however, as Brand's breath came harder as well and he was equally sheened with perspiration.

As they faced each other across the dimming circle of light, Brand made to take a step back but mistimed the shifting of the deck and lost his footing. Seeing her final bid for victory, Euwae once again leaped forward to land a blow against him. However, as her lunge carried her into the air she realized that Brand was smiling... His stumble shifted to a roll and as she sailed over him, Brand reached out and snatched away her sword as she tried futilely to recover from the stab at the space where he should have fallen.

She hit the deck with a roll and slowly got to her feet, her expression as dark as the night around her. He extended the falcata to her, hilt first.

"You knew, did you not?" She said without humor as she snatched the weapon back.

His head tilted to the left, as that shoulder rose in agreement.

"You're getting pretty tired. I figured we'd be done soon, so it seemed likely that you were going to try something fancy... "

"A grand lesson, then, indeed." She said sourly as she dropped into a squat on the deck. The al'Aith caught her breath for a moment, while Brand stood warily nearby. At last, she waived him away.

"No, Bird Club," she said with an edge of fatigue blunting her frustration, "your point is well made. I am conceding this lesson to you; well and hard earned it was, too."

She rose unsteadily and looked at Angus.

"How many then?"

His brow furrowed, so she repeated, "How many? Steps did he best me at?"

"Al'Aith," Angus looked almost embarrassed, "in truth, I lost the count of them watching the two of you in your contest.

"But I fear it was most, if not all."

Her shoulders rose and fell.

"The whole of it, eh? Very well... It would seem that I have a great deal to strive for, if my debt is to be repaid in full."

She picked up her sword; Brand raised his own weapon slightly, but she shook her head.

"No, Brand Eastlander. This night is yours and no mistake." Her falcata whispered as it returned to its sheath.

"Once I have slept and the sun has flown back into the sky, I shall see to my debt and we two make an end of this lesson."

Euwae's eyes were heavy as she levered a smile onto her face.

"In Ard'Ree's name, good ath'Ales, I bid you both a most gentle night."

With that, she made her way back to her bed.

Angus looked at Brand and nodded.

"That was most well fought, Outlander. And you are to be right in this: she, too, is my better. You have my thanks for saving me from the lesson that she herself received this night."

Brand accepted the thanks with a gracious nod, but his eyes were locked on Euwae as she glided across the dark deck of Foamsmare. She became little more than a shadow as she ducked into the shelter, doffed the tunic and boots and dropped down into her sleeping furs; yet he did not look away until she was well and fast asleep.

*   *   *

Once the sun's climb carried it above the height of the deck, Euwae rose and stretched languorously before slipping into her traveling dress and boots. Properly attired, the al'Aith made her way aft to join her companions. Angus had already spread a group of crocks upon the deck and was taking his final meal before he would retire. Brand now sat on the high bench beside the steering oar, his arm resting lightly upon it as he sipped from a mug of mead.

"Well met, the two of you." Euwae said with a tone as bright as the sunlight upon the waves around them. Angus grunted around a mouthful of fish; Brand nodded in acceptance. She looked at the jars Angus had laid out, took some of the oat cake for herself and sat down opposite the big man as she began to eat.

Brand swung the ship to port, well into the wind. Euwae closed her eyes and listened to Foamsmare's song as she shifted across the crests of the waves; the boom creaked as it shifted over the deck until the sheets held it fast on the opposite side of the ship; the sail let out a pair of thumps as the tension was lost from the cloth, only to be regained once the breeze caught it again. As the ship threw itself into the new tack, Euwae opened her eyes again and looked at Brand approvingly.

"You have come a ways, in truth, since you first took hold of that oar back at New Courses."

He nodded once again in response, but accorded "I had a good teacher."

196

"Did you then?" Euwae beamed.

Angus looked up from his food with a grin and studied her. The big man smirked, shrugged and helped himself to the mead.

"I think he's waiting for the other shoe to drop." Brand added politely.

"Other shoe?"

"Yeah. From last night."

"Ah." Euwae's focus dropped to her own meal. Taking the jug of mead from Angus, she took a deep drink and muttered astringently "I had no idea I was so lacking as that. There has never been a one to stand aside from my weapon as you have done..."

She took another drink.

"Were you to have placed a purse on the outcome of your lesson, I gladly would have placed twice more with the thought that it was you who would have tasted the sour juice of defeat."

"And lost..." Added Angus, although he did not face her as he said it, knowing full well the curses her dark looks would bring him. But before she could protest, Brand called her attention back to him.

"Euwae," he said tactfully, "don't be like that. You know shitesan well how good you are in a fight." His head rocked towards Angus. "And so does he.

"You're young, but you've got a lot of hours under your belt with that Bara'ba... You've got a great stance and you don't make the mistake that most of your folk do by keeping the blade low when you're defending yourself."

Angus' brow furrowed and he opened his mouth to protest, but the al'Aith was well ahead of him.

"Well, if that is the way of it," she shot back, "how does it come to be that you laid me so low?"

Brand smiled insightfully.

"That's fair enough." He said quietly.

"You're quick, but the bara'Ba is a heavy blade and requires a big arm to hold it back if you over-commit. You've learned to use that to your advantage for the first few strikes, but if you don't take down your enemy right away, you let the momentum of the weapon do the work, not your technique. As soon as you're doing that, it's a lot easier to knock the blade aside and get at you."

She thought about that for a moment, her eyes shifting as she did so.

"Aye, that is the truth of it and no mistake – Although, were I the size of Angus, you might not be saying such."

197

"If you were the size of Angus, we'd have other things to be talking about, I'm sure."

Angus looked from one to the other, unsure of the direction of the comment, but the others continued without granting him a say in the matter.

"You're also still favoring your wounds." Brand said delicately, but Euwae just sighed.

"Aye, Bird Club. *That* much I did know."

Brand nodded. "That's all right, Euwae. We all do it; it's rough to have to fight over an injury."

"Aye..." Angus nodded and secured himself another jug of mead.

Brand locked eyes with Euwae.

"But, the big thing is that you let yourself get angry."

"Now, WAIT then!" Interjected Angus, who nearly spilled his drink as his head whipped up at Brand. He looked at the jug ruefully and continued.

"You needs be cautious as to what you are saying, then, Outlander. A warrior needs fire in his blood, if he is to stand strong against the foeman. It is rage that pushes out the fear and no mistake – If you do not feel the heat of it and the other man does...

"Well, then it is your blood that will be spilling, not his. Right enough."

The corners of Brand's mouth were pulled down with his rebuff.

"Angus, that might work if you're as big as you are and you've got others who're willing to watch your back. But if you're alone, or you're the weaker opponent, you can't afford to get blinded like that."

Euwae looked at Brand, her eyes working out the truth of his words in the lines of his face. Angus waived the other man's words away and muttered into his drink.

"But what," she said at last, "do you do, in such a moment as that? If you cannot trust to your righteous fury to give you strength, from where can you call the will to do what must be done?"

Brand's eyes softened.

"You watch; you learn." He smiled respectfully. "You set aside all of the distractions and focus on what's going on around you, right then and there.

"You're shitesas good, Euwae," he said gently. "All you need to do is remember that. You know what to do and how to do it. Don't think that arrogance is confidence...

"If you get over that, I don't know if anyone will touch you."

"Get over that?" She said, consternation struggling with understanding in her voice. "And just how do you go about doing that, then?" She finally asked earnestly.

Brand pursed his lips and took a deep breath.

"It's the hardest thing you'll ever learn to understand, Euwae." He said softly, but with utter commitment. "You just *do* it."

She sat back and looked at him.

"That does not sound to me to be helpful, in the least."

He pursed his lips and his head rocked gently to the right.

"Yeah, I know. But that's the only real answer."

"I simply am to not be angry. To not be afraid. To not – " She looked over at Angus, but he just shrugged.

"That's about it, Euwae. Once you've got that, you'll see what I mean...

"And I'm looking forward to that day, my al'Aith."

Euwae pursed her lips.

"Are you then?" She asked, her tone buoyed by pride.

She sat up and set her dishes on the deck. "It is my turn to show *you* the way of it."

She looked over at Angus.

"Would you take the steering oar from Bird Club?" She asked rhetorically.

"Well, my watch is over and no mistake." Angus said coolly, his eyes steady upon her. "And yet..."

His face lit up and he turned to face Brand.

"If the Outlander is to be taught the *way* of it, then I feel my arm has strength enough to bear the burden a while more, yet."

He rose and took Brand's place. As the other man climbed off the bench, he clapped him hard on the back and stage whispered, "Just remember: do not be letting your anger blind you!"

Brand looked at Euwae and rolled his eyes.

"Thanks." He said dubiously.

"It is a hard lesson," said Angus as he climbed onto the bench, his accent copying that of the other man as best he could, "But once you have learned it, you will be the better for it."

"Yeah, got that."

Euwae took several steps back towards the center of the deck and bid Brand to follow. Once he arrived, he stood warily, conscious of her movements and location as she circled him twice. At last, she stopped a few paces in front of him and nodded.

"It will do, as well as any."

"What will do?"

"Shoosh, then."

She took a step forward; Brand flinched back. Euwae's hands flew to her hips as she glared up into his face.

"STOP that, Brand Eastlander!" She scolded.

He relaxed as she stood in front of him once again.

"It'd help if I knew just what *way* you were going to show me..."

She pointedly ignored him. "Now, then. Put your right hand into a fist, like this."

She made a fist. Brand copied her but shook his head.

"Euwae... I don't think this is such – "

"SHOOSH!"

Brand held his tongue with a bemused expression as Euwae continued her demonstration. She took his right arm and raised it above his head, while placing the left upon his hip. She stepped back and held her left arm in front of her chest, while the right hand gathered her dress at the thigh and pulled it a few inches above her ankle.

She looked at Brand and nodded. He looked at her, when his eyes suddenly grew wide.

"Oooh, no." He raised his hands and waived Euwae off. "Not gonna happen."

"BIRD CLUB! You return to your place straight away!" Euwae demanded regally.

Brand shook his head.

"Sorry. If this is the way you meant..."

Her response was slick with frost.

"Was it not *you* who said last night that you would show me your ability to keep with your en'Och?"

"Well – "

"And was it *not* you who said that your people take your dancing seriously?"

"What I meant was – "

200

"And was it not you who claimed to know more steps to the dance than I?"

"She has you there and no mistake." Chimed in Angus supportively.

Brand ignored him.

"I'm not getting out of this, am I?"

Euwae's expression melted almost immediately.

"You have shown me new steps to *your* dance, my ath'Ale... Is it so fraught with danger that you fear to learn mine?"

Brand's lips curved downwards in an expression that was close to pain. But finally, he relented with a resigned "No."

Euwae nodded primly.

"It is most well. Now: stand as I have shown you..."

Euwae walked him through the steps of the Reel of the Ba. From the starting position, he dropped his arm as if drawing a sword; Euwae's steps mimed a parry of his strike. Locked arm to arm, they advanced. He moved her back; she swung about, pulling the pair back together, before they faced each other once again.

She showed him how to take her left hand and pull her forward so that they spun and swapped places, then to make another spin which brought them back to their respective sides.

At last, she showed him how to lead her in a series of spins that brought her across his right side and around him, so that they started back in the poses in which the dance had begun.

After several repetitions, Euwae looked back at Angus, who was grinning so fiercely that his cheeks were flushed above the black stains on his lower face.

"Angus of 'Fhee!" She commanded. "You may as well make yourself of some use, there! You count the beat of the reel, so that Bird Club's ear will hear the way of it and his feet will be more inclined to follow."

Angus stopped grinning.

"Ach..."

Euwae's eyes rolled.

"Men!" She muttered. "Count in this wise: One; two. One; two. One; two. One-two-three. Is that a thing that you can be doing then?"

Brand chuckled. "I can do that."

She turned and pointed a finger into his face.

"Mind your place and be ready to make the steps." She ordered.

Brand raised his hands in surrender and she turned back to Angus, who promptly began to knock out the beat on the oar. Once he had the tempo to her satisfaction, she turned back to Brand.

"Now, then, Bird Club..." She said with a gently exhaled breath, "It is time that we danced again, you and me."

Brand looked into her eyes and finally nodded without pulling them away as they took their places.

As Angus beat out the time, they began to move through the steps once again. At first, Brand was still hesitant. But as they made pass after pass, he soon found the rhyme of the motion. His tenuous movements became punctuation to the language of each element of the dance, matching Euwae's sinuous turns with precise steps and gestures as the pace of the tempo grew steadily faster.

And as they danced, the dynamic between them changed as well. As Brand became more familiar with the steps, Euwae's role as the instructor fell away. She threw more of herself into the movements, her regal facade stripped away by the freedom she felt while she stepped and swung around the deck. Once Brand no longer was focused on the steps of the reel, he executed them with increasing precision; but more and more his eyes focused on his partner.

At first, Euwae was given over to her own indulgence and failed to notice his gaze engaging her. But once she was aware of his attention, she returned it without hesitation. The dynamic between them turned yet again: their eyes now locked each time they faced each other, their expressions as aligned as their bodies when they spiraled through the reel together.

At last, the tempo that Angus rapped out on the oar grew too fast for Brand to follow. He missed a turn and reached out too quickly, accidentally taking a hold of Euwae's shoulder as she turned to face him.

They froze in place.

Euwae looked up into Brand's face, studying his eyes.

Angus stopped clapping the oar and slowly turned his attention to the horizon, his mouth stretched thin as she started to reach up with her right hand...

Suddenly he cried out.

"Ach! Look there, then, to port!"

Both refused to look away, so Brand finally answered.

"What is it, Angus?" He asked, his voice oddly calm.

"Just there," the bigger man said, pointing well to the south of them. "Sails. And no mistake."

Euwae slipped away from Brand and rushed to the gunwale. Brand walked coolly to the stern of the ship and picked up his weapon before he joined her. Together, the three of them studied the distant specks that caught the morning sunlight from where they poised on the horizon. As it became obvious that the other vessels were riding fast before the wind, making good speed towards them, Brand looked to Euwae. But she continued to lean out over the side of the ship, trying to close all the distance possible to discern any clue about the three ships.

"Is it cu'Kullah?" Angus finally asked quietly.

"What do you think?" Brand enjoined Euwae, shaking his head.

"No, Bird Club... Not cu'Kullah." She said with resignation.

"Pirates, then?" Angus continued. "Who else would be so mad as to set sail to isle'Eh in the season of storms?"

Brand shaded his eyes and studied the sails, but Euwae turned away from them and slumped against Foamsmare in search of solace.

"No, it is no gang of the confederation that bears down upon us." She said quietly.

Brand stepped away from the rail to face her. When she refused to look at him, he raised his chin and looked at the ships one more time, then back at the al'Aith.

"Euwae?" He asked quietly.

She took a deep breath.

"I know them, as well as I know myself." She said, finally raising her head to look at Brand. "The ship at the fore is none other than Bayl'Ors Eye... The warship of the ree of twoth'Ba."

Brand looked from her back towards the ships as they steadily drove through the seas towards them. Euwae said calmly, "They are searching me out and no mistake."

Angus looked confused.

"But, this is a good tiding..." He asked, his voice awash with a lack of understanding. "Is it not?"

She turned to Angus. "Let loose the oar... There will be no outrunning them." She turned back to Brand. "I am sorry, for that."

The al'Aith rose and took hold of the streering oar from Angus, bringing the bow well into the wind and slowing their advance to a drift against the rush of the three oncoming ships. Angus stood beside her, his fingers running nervously now over the handle of the scramasax.

Brand stalked back to the port side, his eyes hard as he watched the ree's approach, but he said nothing more.

203

Tidings

Roughly four hundred yards out, the two trailing ships turned before the wind and began to maneuver in the aft quarter of Foamsmare. These were also cogs, like the vessel that bore Euwae and the two warriors; however, the decks of these vessels held two tight groups of ten ath'Ale each, in addition to the sailors who deftly brought them to bear on their target.

The third vessel turned sharply into the wind, bearing down on Foamsmare with little heed to its direction. There could be no doubt that this was Bayl'Ors Eye: she was half again as long as the others, but only slightly wider in the beam across the deck. Rather than have the mast amidships, as it was for the other craft, it was located just a third of the way from the bow. Shields hung along the seaward side of the gunwale, providing some protection to the oarsmen along the level of the deck. Brand counted twenty shields per side, each adorned with a different stylized head of a horse; his lips tightened as he hoped that there would be just two men to each of those 40 oars and not three.

Beyond the might of the ship, there was a grand beauty to it, as well... The sail was the green of wild grass, traced with wide white lines that wove together to form the stylized head of the horse of twoth'Ba. The forward spar arched up high above the prow of the ship, carved in the likeness of a swan, with intricate knot-work in lieu of feathers carved lovingly into the wood. Where the neck of the swan merged with the bow rode a massive bronze torc, capped with the heads of horses whose eyes glimmered with pale warmth of gold.

As Bayl'Ors Eye drew closer, Brand spied a man in a wide sleeved blue robe directly behind the neck of that swan. His arms were outstretched; ribbons of blue light formed intricate pattens between his hands. His long hair was woven into tight braids bound with ribbons and wrapped like a turban around his head.

Brand studied him for a moment, his eyes searching for something within the reach of his memory. Once he grasped it, he smiled grimly and raised his hands to his lips.

"Konner Knot-Spender, priest of Summersford!" He called out across the water.

"And none other!" the druid called back with satisfaction. "Well met, are you, Brand of the Condotterai, Master of Horses and last Champion of twoth'Shan'n!"

The priest's fingers moved quickly, as if he were tying the waves of light that flowed through them to the air itself; when he finished, the pattern hung suspended before him like a signature of woven moonlight. He stepped closer to the bow and called out again.

"Does the daughter of Lohvtreu still cross your shadow with her own?"

Brand looked aft towards Euwae and Angus. The woman rocked her head forward once in acquiescence. He pursed his lips together ruefully and turned back towards Bayl'Ors Eye.

"Yeah, she's here."

Konner's shoulders fell with relief.

"Most well!" He called back. "Be prepared, then, to receive us... The ree of twoth'Ba would have words with you both."

Out of sight behind the gunwale, Brand's fingers worked their way around the handle of his bec de corbin. To Konner, he nodded and tossed a wave with his free hand before he turned and stalked to the stern of the ship to join his two companions and looked down at Euwae.

"This is your call," he said quietly, "but you'll need to make up your mind right now."

Angus looked from one to the other, his actions burnished by confusion and near panic.

"You are mad, the pair of you and no mistake!" He said fiercely.

"The better part of the war band of *twoth'Ba* sails down upon us." He continued. "In truth, you cannot be of a mind to fight them all!"

"It would not be the first time." Said Euwae ruefully, rolling her eyes back towards the big ath'Ale.

"But, be at peace, Angus. I have no mind to do so here upon isle'Eh."

Brand clenched his jaw.

"If this goes – "

Euwae turned back to Brand stiffly.

"You will not be raising your hand against my father, *or* those who serve him." She said flatly. "Do you understand?"

Foamsmare shuddered as Bayl'Ors Eye shouldered against her with the brusque thud of heavy hulls meeting upon the waves. As the warriors of twoth'Ba leaped across to her deck and made the two ships fast together, Brand finally conceded with a bitter nod.

"Yeah, understood."

"Very well, then."

Three warriors of twoth'Ba quickly made their way aft and after a quick courtesy took the steering oar from Euwae. She nodded in thanks and made her way towards where the two ships were joined, with her own retinue in her wake.

Konner had already made his way to the deck of Foamsmare. Two ath'ales stood beside him, their hands resting lightly on the hilts of their falcata. The warrior on the left was a lithe woman with long braided hair and a crooked nose; Euwae recognized her from the fight with her sister at the pells, took a deep breath and gave her a slow nod.

The woman's face was not softened by the courtesy.

Konner took a step towards them.

"My lady," he said quietly, "it would seem that you have done well, in *recovering* my ship." He put deep emphasis on the word 'recovering.' "I had feared it lost in the raid upon my folk."

Euwae sighed.

"The foe was in flight," she said quietly, "and there was – "

"Need." Brand finished for her. She looked over at him, her eyes watering, but her face a mask of calm.

"And, what is this, then?" A regal woman's voice rolled across the deck. "These seem not so much like blood thirsty curs to me..."

"MOTHER!"

Euwae shouldered past Konner and threw herself into Meeruen's arms. The ree folded her head down to her daughter's shoulder as she reached out to return the embrace.

"So, then," she said, her voice choked with emotion, "you are well, still. Even with the wild tale that Konner laid before us, I was fearing a less than bright ending to it."

Euwae's voice was broken by sobs.

"I am – Sorry..."

"Hush, then; say no more of it... There will be a great deal to discuss, but now is not the place of it."

Euwae finally nodded. She extracted herself from her mother's arms, wiping her own fiercely across her eyes while the ree stepped forward to face Brand and Angus.

"Champion of twoth'Shan'n and ath'Ale of the Condotterai, well met are you, once again."

Brand made a fist and struck himself over the heart in a salute to her authority.

"You honor me, ree, with your words." He said formally.

Meeruen blinked twice as her head tilted imperceptibly to the left, an unspoken question in her eyes.

Brand lowered his hand and forced himself to exhale.

The ree's eyes slipped from Brand to Angus.

The jewels in the mouths of her torc flashed with bloody light as her eyes narrowed.

"You are no ath'Ale who serves a friend." She said coolly.

The two warriors behind Konner were startled and drew their weapons, but Angus was oblivious to them. He swallowed hard under the bright gaze of Meeruen's green eyes, his own distracted by the light that danced across her golden torc and over her bright red hair.

The ree slowly reached up and lightly touched the ugly black stains on his face.

"This is Angus," Euwae interjected, "ath'Ale of twoth'Fhee."

Her mother studied the blots intently.

"How came you by these?" She asked quietly.

"Don't ask." Brand said darkly, "He can't speak of it."

As one, all of the Cord'Or folk within earshot turned a stunned expression towards Brand. He looked from the ree, to Konner, to the warriors before him; even those who stood in earshot on the deck of the other vessel at the ready for their ree's command stared at him in open shock.

"Whoa..." Brand said gently, his eyes going a bit wide at their reaction. He raised his hands in front of his chest as a gesture of amity.

Meeruen's eyes ripped into Angus' and remained fixed as she asked, "Is this the way of it?"

Angus' nod seemed to be drawn from him.

"For much of the tale, that is the truth, aye." He said, transfixed.

Brand shook his head.

"Yeah, it is."

Most of the warriors around Brand looked at him fiercely, but Meeruen dropped her hand, her eyes visibly softened.

"Angus, ath'Ale of twoth'Fhee... You have the sympathies of the ree of twoth'Ba and all our folk besides."

Brand's eyes rolled, but this time he held his tongue under the withering gaze of the warriors around him. Angus shook his head as if waking from a dream while Meeruen stepped back and turned to Euwae.

"I am pleased to see you well and in fine company, Euwae." She said gently. "From all those fears, I stand relieved."

Euwae studied her mother closely, slowly turned and swept her eyes across the deck of Bayl'Ors Eye. After a moment, she turned back to the ree.

"But..." She swallowed with painful reluctance.

"Why have you come, then... And not father?"

Meeruen rubbed her thumbs against the insides of her fingers and looked at her daughter for a long moment. Konner took a half step forward, but the ree shook her head and he returned to his place behind her.

"The ree – My husband was unable to undertake this task, little one."

Euwae gasped and buried her face into her hands. Meeruen stepped over to her and wrapped her arms around her daughter, her own eyes suddenly awash as well.

"Have heart, have heart; he lives... And is strong of mind, still. But he misses your return as the shore awaits the tide, too long dry before the rush of the winds of the storm."

"But, mother..."

"Hush."

Konner stepped forward again.

"It is well as it may be, Euwae; glad we are, that the two of you were not put to the sword the night that you were taken."

Euwae's chin shook as she tried to pull away from Meeruen's embrace.

"Taken..?" She asked, her voice frosted with ignorance.

Her mother pulled her back and lifted her chin to look her daughter in the eye with dark comprehension. Euwae stifled a cry and buried her face into the ree's shoulder as Konner continued the tale with full conviction.

"Aye... And a hateful thing it was, to be stealing the horses of the ree on the very night that all were gathered to celebrate his return from the Confederation.

"Once he was able, he told all the folk of your bravery: how the both of you saw the men at the stable and tried to stand them off... And, that he, having been struck down by them bade you take his horse and give chase."

"We found all but three of the steeds," said ad'Ah – the warrior with the broken nose – as she nodded with affirmation. "But of Courser and two others, there was no sign to be seen scattered across the shore, where the rest of the herd was tracked and found."

"But Courser made his way home upon the Night of Fires," said Meeruen quietly, "with a goodly burden of travelers' needs. And, then, we all feared the worst..."

Konner took up the narrative. "Until I was able enough to take to the road, bringing the truth of the raid upon my hall and the arrival of such unexpected aid as was provided by the pair of you. Then, all began to come into its place; those who attacked the halls of twoth'Ba had obviously come once more by ship to Summersford and there sought again to strike out against us."

Angus started to protest, but closed his mouth, his eyes sorting through the tale for some truth that proved too elusive to his ear, while Konner brought his discourse to a close.

"Upon that word, did Lohvtreu send us forth to find the hiel who dared raise their hand against the folk of the twoth and put an end to it. I had feared Foamsmare was now captive, so I made my weavings to seek her out...

"And, so it seems, you as well."

Euwae blotted the tears from her eyes and looked up at her mother. But Meeruen shook her head gently.

"Aye," she acknowledged, "I do to know the way of *it*, in full."

Euwae started to speak, but the ree quickly interrupted.

"But, my daughter, never forget this: your father is still the al'Aith of the Great Hall of our twoth; *we* will ever stand by his word and live to see his will is done... Our ree who would still give his very life for each one of us. Once spoken, his word is not to be opposed.

"Do *you* understand this?"

Euwae nodded, her chin still plagued by tremors. Her mother took her face in her fingers to soothe the raw emotions that bruised her daughters countenance.

"Then, for now, let us set ill tidings of deeds done aside." She said gently. "This matter of the attacks upon Summersford is what draws us; to that – and that alone – we must set our full attention."

Euwae looked into her mother's face once more, then buried her own against the queen's shoulder in a fierce hug.

"Yes, my ree," she said without releasing Meeruen, "You have my oath upon it."

At that, Meeruen's body gave a sharp twitch. Her eyes wide with surprise, she looked down first at Euwae, then at Konner, who gave a cryptic nod.

Brand watched the exchange from the side of the group, his mouth still set with grim determination. Angus noted the heavy expression and raised his shoulders in an unspoken question, but Brand shook his head, watching the ree and her daughter as they finally broke their embrace and Meeruen led Euwae from Foamsmare's deck and back to Bayl'Ors Eye.

With a deep breath, Brand followed; Angus slid into his wake and did the same.

Konner's eyes moved from the back of one man to the other, then grew unfocused as they turned inward for a breath of time. A scowl turned down the corners of his mouth as he bid the two warriors beside him to see that no one returned to Foamsmare without his permission before returning to the ree's ship as well.

A raised tower a third of the ship's length from the stern doubled as a cabin for the ree and the most important ath'Ale aboard. Meeruen led Euwae and her companions into the low room and bade them sit on the benches fixed to the walls, while she had mead fetched up from below. Once everyone was comfortable, she took her own place on a bench next to her daughter and closed her eyes with satisfaction in the warmth of a shaft of sunlight streaming in through the open shutters of a window.

The ree tucked her legs up beneath her and looked at the men in the room.

"So, then... These men, who have arrayed themselves against us. Who calls them to this purpose? And to what wise?"

Brand looked at Angus, but everyone else in the cabin looked at Brand. With a snort of resignation he shook his head, but to everyone's surprise Angus stood up and looked at Meeruen squarely.

"You need look no further for the villains than to me." He said hoarsely, as if the words themselves fought to stay locked in his chest. Konner's eyes narrowed, but Meeruen's calm voice seemed to soothe the tension in the room as she replied.

"The ree of twoth'Ba has no quarrel with Angus of twoth'Fhee... It is plain that you have found a path away from the deeds that brought you into our company."

Angus' hand stroked his stubbled chin self consciously as he nodded in thanks.

"In truth, I was a captain of the unwelcome guests who came to Summersford uninvited. We sought to take the hall and drive out the hold of twoth'Ba on the Northmoors as part of our claim. But you proved you were a worthy host: death was gifted out to both our parties, given and taken... But the folk of Summersford proved in the end to be the more generous and no mistake."

"Claim?" Konner interjected. Angus turned to him with watering eyes.

"It is spoken that you are a priest of no small strength..." He said with difficulty. "Yet no priest, no conjurer" he turned back to Meeruen "no druid can weave away the storm that comes upon you now.

"My - *The* al'Aith, cu'Kullah of twoth'Fhee, lays claim to the halls and twoth of the River Prince."

"By what RIGHT?" Shouted Konner as he shot to his feet. Angus shrank back; Brand started to come to his feet as well, but Meeruen was the faster.

"SIT." She commanded. "This man has endured much, Konner Knot-Spender, priest of the ree of twoth'Ba and master of Summersford. I would have your counsel in this wise; yet, if you cannot set aside this lust for your reprisal, I will send you forth now from this place upon your ship and call for you no more.

"Do you understand?"

Konner looked at Meeruen. He swallowed hard.

"I see the way of it, aye..." He said at last. "It was not in my mind to lay challenge to your judgment."

He slowly returned to his bench along the starboard wall next to Euwae. Unnoticed on the opposite side of the cabin, Brand lowered himself back down slowly as well, while the ree turned to Angus.

"Continue, ath'Ale, as best you may."

Angus nodded, his resolve crawling up his spine and into his throat once again.

"He has - " Angus looked now to Brand, who nodded once in encouragement. "He has cast offerings into the black depths of the Lake of Geasa and called upon it for the gift to rule by right of conquest and sacrifice..."

The shattering of pottery at the door of the cabin drew everyone to their feet.

There, a thin young man stood staring at Angus, a tray of mead and cups laying forgotten on the deck at his feet.

"*Kelleu*..." Hissed Euwae. But he ignored her and took two blind steps towards Angus.

"The Lake of – Ers'Elb. You – "

Meeruen glided across the distance between them and gently took the young druid's arm.

"What is it that you see..?"

He briskly shook his head, both in the negative and to clear his thoughts.

"The night before father was struck down, I dreamed of the Black Waters." He swallowed hard. "A dream of the end of life, of the end of hope."

Konner looked at him fiercely. "A dream of death?" He prodded.

"No," Kelleu responded fearfully, "a dream of waking... And no mistake."

Konner exhaled and sank back to the bench.

"So," he said quietly, "the shaman have seen this." He shook his head. "It would have been better to have known the way of this from the start."

Kelleu blushed and looked at the floor. Meeruen turned her gaze out the door of the cabin and across the waters as a mantle of bitter despondency cloaked the room. After a moment of bleak silence, Brand cleared his throat.

"I'm sorry, but there's something here I'm not getting... This lake – Ers'Elb – it was used ages ago to determine who could become a ree, right? *Believe* me, I get that it's not the nicest of places. But the Ard'Ree has the handle on all this now. If cu'Kullah's breaking the laws, then his claims are shitesan. We find him, we put him down, right?"

No one else moved.

"Right." Brand exhaled sharply and rolled his right hand in a circle as he prompted them to speak. "So, would someone fill me in on what it is that I'm missing, here?"

Konner and Kelleu looked at the warrior, but it was Meeruen who answered without turning to face him.

"This *place* is more than just a gateway to an ancient way of being." She said quietly. "Have you not heard of geasa?"

Brand nodded slowly.

"Yeah, I have... The rules you say you can't break, or you'll die." He shrugged. "That's still a hard one for me to work my head around, but I've heard of them."

"Each geas carries more weight than that of simple belief," Euwae said quietly. "They are knotted and woven to the en'Och; woe to any and all who think naught of them."

Brand sighed.

"Tied to the en'Och, huh?" He shook his head. "That figures."

"But, more upon the mark, there is a strand of the geas that ties each of us to the powers that lie at the heart of the black lake." Said Angus, his voice hollow and emotionless. "When into this world we come, it touches us... And, for some, calls back upon them once the tie is broken."

Brand scowled as Kelleu spoke up.

"In your eyes, think of the pattern of life as a great knot; the strands that form it are drawn from many places... But the first is Ers'Elb."

Meeruen lowered her head as she resumed speaking. "So, Brand Eastlander, you now come to see that the deep places of Ers'Elb hold the banes and ends of many things, many times over... Hidden as they are in the darkness that lies beneath those still waters. What Ard'Ree brought to the Cord'Or was a freedom from the way of life that wholly bound us to these shadows... Undisturbed, their will slept across the generations who grew and passed, their weavings left at peace."

Kelleu's chin trembled.

"Now," he added quietly, "the ancient rites have been called out and upon. The rise of a ree from the depths of Ers'Elb will pluck upon the geas that binds us all. No one, since the hand of Ard'Ree lay this threat, has sought to end it, as it would well mean the end of the Cord'Or as well."

Brand tossed himself back against the wall in frustration and looked from Kelleu to Euwae.

"Seriously?" He managed to get out at last. But the funereal looks on the faces of those around him were his only response.

Brand shot to his feet and stood in front of Euwae.

"Hey, look..." He said quietly. When she refused to look up at him, he demanded. "LOOK."

She raised her eyes to his, her lips pursed and trembling gently with unspoken emotion.

Brand ducked his head slightly in supplication.

"Euwae... Think about it." He turned and swept his gaze across everyone else in the room.

"Cu'Kullah did this two months ago, right?" He paused; no one responded. His face knotting in frustration, he turned back to Euwae.

"You *aren't* dead yet, are you." He said obviously. "So, maybe this curse *is* real. Maybe it isn't. But, in all honesty, it hasn't happened *yet*. So, you can brood about this geas all you want, but the truth is you've still got time to do *something* about it."

He stepped back and looked deeply into her eyes.

"So, *do* it." He finished with a heavy exhalation.

Slowly, Euwae's expression thawed to hard determination.

"Mother..." She said quietly.

With a measured turn, Meeruen rotated in place and gazed from Brand to her daughter, a vivid smile of liberation marching across her face.

"Kelleu," the ree said calmly, "be good enough to fetch us up more mead... There is new council to be had here and we are yet waiting upon the hospitality of the first."

The young shaman looked from his mother to the tumble of broken pottery and spilled honey wine at the threshold of the room. He flushed again with embarrassment.

Euwae's fist shot out and struck him on the arm.

"The ree has spoken, Kelleu. Here... Let me help you with that."

Kelleu rubbed his arm as his sister began to clean up the broken jars, then joined her. Once the two were distracted, Meeruen stepped closer to Brand and laid two fingers upon his arm, guiding him from the center of the room to the far bench.

"A champion, indeed, you have proven yourself to be this day." She said quietly. "And more, I think, though we conjurers are not so gifted with prophesy as some."

Brand shook his head.

"I've got a score to settle with cu'Kullah..." He looked over at Euwae as she assisted Kelleu. "That's all I care about."

Meeruen's eyes dropped politely.

"Is it, then?"

After a pause, Brand nodded. As her children left the cabin to see to the mead, the ree's expression changed subtly, from confident to confidant.

"So be it, Brand Eastlander... That you will have and more."

After Euwae and Kelleu had gone to the gunwale of the ship and tossed the broken mugs and bottles over the side, she looked him up and down with a critical eye.

"Of all those I had been thinking to be seeing on the decks of Bayl'Ors Eye, you did not number amongst them." She said at last. "Your arm has never been long for the ba, nor your legs sturdy upon the strake."

Kelleu winced.

"In truth," he admitted, "I wanted little of this voyage; my heart still aches to be away from father's side. Yet, when I made this known to Raf'Em, he was overtaken by sadness. I asked him to tell me in what wise I had made this so... But he was loathe to look upon me, saying only that I had yet to see the way of it. So, now it is he who stays by father's bed, while for my part, I sail upon this venture."

Euwae's expression softened.

"In truth - The old druid was displeased with you? I cannot recall such a thing, in all the days you have wandered the halls of my family."

Kelleu nodded forlornly.

"Had I but known in what wise I had failed him, I would leap like the salmon to see my misdeed done. But, now that I am here and the tale is being woven about us, I have a sharper eye upon the matter... And why my blindness took his heart to such a place of distress."

Euwae shook her head slightly and rocked it to the left. Kelleu forced a smile to his face and stood up resolutely.

"You will forgive me, sister, for saying so... But there are times when the strength of your arm is so great as to keep your thoughts pulled far from your mind."

Kelleu took a deep breath and held it in his chest. His sister bristled, but the tone of her retort was as cool as the breezes of the Northmoors in the late autumn.

"If you think to paint yourself so much the wiser than I, then find what contentment in such words as you may and color the world for me."

After a few seconds, her brother visibly startled, his eyes wide. Euwae scowled and looked him up and down.

Kelleu shook his head and exhaled through his teeth.

"I thought, sure, that you would strike me for that!" He sputtered with surprise.

Euwae rolled her eyes and shook her head.

"And what, if ask I might, put such a notion into you as that?"

Now, it was his turn to study her closely.

"At what time and in what wise, since I have come to live in the halls of our father have you not availed yourself of any chance to do so?"

Euwae stared at him, her mouth a thin line. But, at the last, she dropped her shoulders and shook her head.

"Perhaps, that was the way of it." She said, her eyes focusing inwards. They locked into his with poignant need. "But, as you say: if you see now with a sharper eye having come upon this journey, might not that be the way of it for others, as well?"

Kelleu blinked.

"Why..! Is that, then, an – Apology?"

Euwae scowled.

"Let not your fancies wander too far afield."

Kelleu exhaled through pursed lips and smiled reassuringly.

"Ah, then," he said with a tone of discretion, "Now I see too that seasons change, if slowly, and no mistake."

They looked at each other for a long moment, before Kelleu nodded back towards the cabin.

"Mother will be expecting that mead any time, now..." He said quietly. "Was it in your mind to lend your arm to that task, as well?"

Euwae tossed her head.

"The daughter of the ree? Serve the ath'Ales?" She rolled the taste of the words in her mouth. "Do you not see that as the place of the bua'Theu to service the hall?"

Kelleu raised his left hand to shade his eyes and made a show of surveying the decks of all of the ships around them.

"I think them to be in short stock, here-abouts." He said and shrugged. "I will meet you back in the cabin, then."

He started to make his way towards the hatch amidships. Euwae watched him for a moment, sighed and jogged across the deck to join him. As she slowed to pace Kelleu on his right side, he turned his head and looked at her quizzically.

"The last time you were entrusted with a task in such wise, I seem to recall you proved less than able at the doing of it... I would not want my ath'Ales to be of the mind that the folk of my house were all of the same weaving."

Her brother looked at her and beamed.

"*Your* ath'Ales?" He chided as they walked off chatting together.

From the shadow of the inside of the cabin, Meeruen watched her children as they spoke at the side of the ship. Konner moved up to join her, his face lined with preoccupation.

"You felt it, then?" He asked cryptically.

The ree nodded.

"I saw the tathlum and no mistake." He said flatly. "And now this. And, in the shadow of the tale of cu'Kullah's wickedness..."

He shrugged. "The *way* of it all is yet beyond me."

"I am still of a mind to doubt what I see, Konner..." She replied. "For all that she was and for the world has been... Does she come to this?"

From the back of the room, Brand scowled.

"Come to what?"

The ree and her priest turned to look at Brand and Angus.

"There is much of this tale that has yet to be woven for us," said Meeruen, her tone an urgent prompt. Konner nodded, the priest adding his authority to that of the ree.

"She has the face of my daughter," added Meeruen quietly, "but this woman is someone new to me. What wise can be spoken of this?" She entreated.

"Good ree – " Angus started to speak, but Brand stood up and blocked the space between them, shaking his head.

"I think that's between you and her," Brand said flatly. "Euwae's not the only one around here who's not laying out everything she knows. And, even if it was my place to say something – and I'm pretty sure it's not – I don't know enough about all this 'weaving' not to be drawing the wrong conclusions. So, if you want answers, you'll have to ask her."

Konner's chin drew back to his chest.

"You would speak to the ree of twoth'Ba in such wise?" He asked with dismay.

Angus looked at the floor, but Brand stood his ground.

"That's about the way of it, Knot-Spender." His shoulders rose and dropped once as a humble apology. "And – no offense – but I've given my word to serve Euwae. At least where I come from, that service doesn't end just because someone higher up the ladder calls down to you from on high."

Meeruen stepped to the side, so that she could clearly see Angus.

"And what of you, ath'Ale? Have you, under the weight of your torc and the stains on your chin, given such a pledge to my daughter as well?"

Slowly, the big warrior stood up and stepped forward so that he stood beside Brand. Dropping his hand to the hilt of the scramasax tucked into his belt, he looked at Meeruen full on and nodded solemnly.

"I have. And for me as well, that is the way of it."

Meeruen closed her eyes, a weighty concern visibly sliding off her neck and away from her shoulders like a sodden wool cloak. When she opened her eyes, they shone with a fiery resolve that made Konner look at her askance.

"My ree..?" He asked gently.

Brand stepped forward and clapped him on the shoulder.

"Don't worry, Knot-Spender. It's all good. I've seen that look before."

Konner turned his face towards Brand.

"When you fought with her at the side of Lohvtreu?"

Brand shook his head.

"Nope... When I fought beside her daughter."

Konner gave a start, but the ree nodded, her lips drawn back in a luminous smile.

"I would say, Konner Knot-Spender, priest of the ree of twoth'Ba and master of Summersford, that this is answer enough and no mistake."

Konner looked at her with pursed lips and nodded his consent.

*   *   *

Once the mead had been successfully dispensed, the group sat quietly upon the benches in the cabin. Euwae sat on the left of her mother nearest the door, while Konner took up the place of honor to her right. Opposite them sat Angus and Brand; Kelleu sat alone with his thoughts on the bench along the port side of the room.

There had been little more than polite thanks and a quiet word to Kelleu from Meeruen since the two had returned, but it was obvious to Euwae that a change in the dynamic of the group had grown in her absence none the less. The ree and the priest sat in pools of contemplation, while the two ath'Ales seemed almost agitated and shifted fitfully in their places. Twice, Euwae had cast questioning looks at Brand; the first he had ignored with all but a single, quick nod. The second time, he had parried her exasperated expression with hand-speak to wait; if anyone saw the gesture, however, no one commented upon it.

At last, Brand tossed back the dregs of his mead. Euwae started to reach for the jar at her side, but he shook his head and set down the mug on the bench. Reaching further to his right he picked up Crows Call and examined the damage to the weapon idly, raising covert glances towards the ree and the priest as he did so. Finally, he sighed, set the weapon back down and stood once more. After rolling his head to ease the tension in his neck, he swept up his mug and stalked over to Euwae; hefting the clay jar in his hand, he poured himself another mug while looking hard at Meeruen.

As he topped off the drink, her eyes finally found his.

He raised the glass to her as a toast, then took a deep drink. The ree smiled in response, but her expression conveyed little warmth. Brand exhaled through his nose and finally gave voice to his impatience.

"So," he said as casually as possible, "what's the plan?"

Meeruen's smile quirked towards empathy.

"We are searching out cu'Kullah, Champion of twoth'Shan'n and ath'Ale of the Condotterai."

"We are?"

"We are, indeed."

"Hmph." He grunted. "Sorry – I guess I missed it."

"We look in this wise," Meeruen explained patiently. "Kelleu, as a shaman, is the keeper of our history and myth... He is unraveling the weaves of this knowledge as you would track a man through the forest, comparing the signs you are seeing now to those which you know to have been there long before any foot was set upon it.

"Konner, my priest, likewise uses the knots and bindings of our law to see the wise in the actions cu'Kullah has made which touch upon us, as the stone cast into the river sends its ripples far down the course to either shore."

Brand looked from one to the other, then back at the ree.

"I've seen Konner weaving. I always thought he – You know..." Brand waived his hands in the air, dropped them and shrugged.

"I thought that was how it worked for you."

Euwae laughed.

"Bird Club," she said gently, "such weavings are, in truth, to be had. But – as I understand such things – the druid must first know the knots to be woven, before they can set to it and begin. Much as you did not take to force of arms without the *practice* of them, so the druids must first know what is to be done."

"You will have to forgive him," Angus said, his voice a parody of Brand's, "he cannot think on it."

Brand turned back to the ath'Ale and jabbed a finger in his direction.

"Don't *you* start with me." He said coolly. "When I said you couldn't speak of it, I was *trying* to do you a favor."

Angus shrugged but made no attempt to drop the smirk from his face, when Brand started as Meeruen rested a hand on his shoulder.

"Your defense of the ath'Ale of twoth'Fhee was wise," she said quietly. "It may not have gone so well for him, had you not spoken when you did."

Brand turned and her hand fell away.

"What? I don't see the point. He's been talking the whole time."

The ree smiled coyly.

"Aye, that is the truth. Yet it is not the way of it. That was the doings of my weavings upon him... As one who walks the paths of the conjurer, the banishing of shadows and dark ways is my gift to the halls of twoth'Ba."

Brand looked at her torc, then into the lady's eyes.

"I'd heard you were a conjurer... I just never knew that meant you were a wi- A druid." He tilted his head towards Konner.

"Like that."

Euwae looked at Brand curiously.

"Are there no druids, then, in the east of the world?"

He snorted.

"Druids? No. We've got men to the north who claim to be shitesannus sorcerers. And I've heard of some odd things that really weren't what I'd call normal when they're around. I had a friend who claimed to see one of them in action, but his story was a lot more – " Brand cast about for the right word, but gave up with a halfhearted shrug. "Dramatic, than this."

"Was it, indeed?" Meeruen chuckled and returned to her seat, slipping her arm around her daughter. "Once this hunt is come and gone, you must tell us the way of this sorcery."

Brand studied the ree's posture, but there was no sign of condescension in it. With a self deprecating grimace he turned and stalked back to his seat. As he leaned against the wall, Angus clapped him on the knee.

"So then, Outlander... Now you know the way of it, eh?"

"You know, Angus. I think I liked it better when you couldn't speak of it after all." He turned to Meeruen. "Would you mind shutting him back up?"

Angus blushed as the two women giggled. He opened his mouth, but Brand raised a hand and waved a finger before him as a warning. As his mouth snapped shut, Euwae clapped her hands.

"Bird Club!" She exclaimed. "You have made your first weaving!"

The two ath'Ales exchanged glances. As one, they rose and left the cabin, followed by the laughter of the two women inside.

Once on the deck, Angus shook his head.

"It is well, Outlander, that you were here. Were it not for you, we would like as not still be waiting for the doom of the lake to take us all."

He held offered his hand to Brand.

"There has been a bitter harvest between us and I was the worse for the sowing of it. I would have you plow that back into the graves we leave behind, so you and I might feast together in what ever hall the al'Aith sees fit to keep us."

Brand looked him in the eye and took his arm by the wrist.

"Fratrum ad gladio; fratrum de gladio." Brand said solemnly.

Angus buried his confusion, wrapped his thick hand around Brand's wrist and shook it decorously.

"It's good to have you on our side again, Angus." Brand said sincerely. The bigger man beamed, but said nothing.

Euwae stepped out of the cabin and swept smoothly towards them across the gently rolling deck.

"Bird Club..." She said lightly, her face still echoing the lilt of her laughter, "In truth, I meant no insult to you."

"Yeah, no worries." He confirmed quickly. "I really just needed to get up for a minute."

Angus chewed the inside of his lower lip.

"My al'Aith, I should stand watch with the ree..."

"Shitesan that!"

"Shitesat."

"Shitesat that!" Euwae shot a glance at Brand. "Shitesat? In truth?"

"In truth."

"Shitesat that. Are you not *my* ath'Ale?"

"That is the way of it and no other."

"Then stand with me."

Angus shifted uncomfortably, but nodded curtly. Brand studied his face as Euwae returned the nod with approval.

"It is well, then." She said with honest confidence.

Turning so that she could face the two men equally, Euwae glanced about to be sure they would not be overheard, then motioned them both closer.

"Kelleu is of a mind that he has found the weaving he has been seeking," She said quiet earnest. "And Konner is willing to lend what aid he may to the making of it."

Brand stopped looking at Angus and turned to her instead.

"Then – What's the problem?" He asked with concern.

"Mother will not allow it."

The two men exchanged glances.

"What's the problem?" Brand asked again coolly. "I thought she wanted to bring cu'Kullah down as much as we did?"

Euwae looked at him earnestly.

"It may be the death of Kelleu to tie this weaving to him."

Angus' head rolled back in frustration, but Brand nodded, staying focused on Euwae.

"OK, that's bad. What are our other options?"

She shook her head.

"None, in truth, that they are seeing. Kelleu would take on this task and no mistake. But the ree feels the hopes are of less weight than the sorrows that lie upon them."

"So – Why are we whispering?" Brand said adamantly.

"Because my daughter, no matter what guise she may wear, has suffered less beneath the burdens of selfishness than I had hoped." Called the ree from behind them, her voice numb with the predisposition of long experience.

Slowly, the three turned to face Meeruen. Although her face gave little hint of her anger, her fists were clenched so tightly that her knuckles were bloodless.

Euwae straightened and turned slowly to face her.

"Mother – " Euwae began; but the ree would have none of it.

"All these years, your brother has been fostered in our hall. He has never wronged us, nor you, nor any who have come under our roof by action or word. His sense of the Ancient Forest is keen: Raf'em has spoken, time and again, that his skills as shaman may be worthy of service to Ard'Ree himself.

"Yet you, who is born of the blood and en'Och of the rees of twoth'Ba and twoth'Bur alike are heedless of your cruelty for just the very sight of your brother. And now it seems as well, if it pleased you, you would cast his life aside for whatever it may be that you were of a mind to set about.

"For if your *beloved* father – "

"MOTHER!" Euwae shouted, charging towards the ree. She leaned forward and stared up into Meeruen's face, her arms out from her sides, her fists clenched. Bitterly, she continued. "You have no need to be calling out my wickedness to *me*...

"My dreaming casts me back, time and again to the dark night that feast cast all I knew to ruin. Time and again I wished it were my body rusting with such wounds as would slay me dead and not those of my father!

"And so it should have been, had he not set his weapon aside..." Euwae began to sob. "It was me that should have died and no mistake... Me..."

Her mothers frigid expression softened, but her tone was winters ice.

"In what wise am I to see the way of this?" Meeruen asked. "If it is as you say, then your heart is cruel to want for death's company... Yet that is the better path of the two, the other being the blackness of a truly wicked heart, that would try to earn forgiveness through such lies as this."

Euwae straightened up, dropping her shoulders and raising her chin. Although her lips trembled gently, the noble bearing of her posture divulged no trace of self doubt.

"I am the daughter of the ree of twoth'Ba," she said quietly, "and no liar."

Her mother looked down at her daughter, her eyes watering.

"Then in what wise do you condemn your brother so?"

Euwae shook her head.

"It was never in my heart."

Meeruen shook her head and started to turn away, but Euwae's hands shot out and seized the back of her mothers head, forcing her to look back at her. Across the deck of Bayl'Ors Eye, thirty ath'Ale drew their weapons and began to race towards the cabin.

Brand gave Angus an elbow to the ribs; when the warrior shot him a furious glance, Brand rocked his head towards the charging warriors. Without a word, the pair drew their own weapons as one and stepped forward to protect Euwae, standing almost back to back to provide her with a shield of their own bodies against any attack.

The royal women of twoth'Ba were oblivious to the commotion. The ree stared into her daughter's eyes and spoke in a voice no longer devoid of warmth, but tarnished with menace.

"Unhand me. *Now*."

"Look at me." Euwae said calmly.

"I will not ask again."

"*Look* at me."

"If you do not let loose your – "

"*Mother*," Euwae said quietly, "you have left no doubt that you are of a mind to which I am lost, no matter what befalls me. But it is not in me to leave this be."

Slowly, she relaxed her grip, so that her hands slid forward and came to rest gently upon the ree's cheeks.

"I would have you know the way of my heart, for – For my father... For my *brother*." Euwae took a shallow breath.

"If your weavings go the worse for me, then it was I who was truly blind... And I have no fear of taking on the weight of the shame you would strike upon my body and mind for the keeping of it.

"But I *must* have you know the way of it... As a child of the ree of twoth'Ba and of any hope I am to have for the coming of my days yet to be."

Euwae nodded once, with no less composure than that her parents had shown to her so often in her youth.

Meeruen took in a long breath through her nose, then locked her eyes palpably upon those of her daughter.

The rubies binding the mouths of the serpents in the torc at the ree's throat threw out more light than they gathered in; the reflection of them became embers in Euwae's eyes. The young woman began to shake as if she might collapse, but for the strength of will that chained her mind to the weaving of her mother. Slowly, Euwae's lips moved soundlessly and tears flooded her eyes, but even as the tension became pain and the pain became torment, she would not look away, until the ree reached up and took her daughter's hands into her own.

"My daughter..." Meeruen said gently as Euwae collapsed into her arms.

"I see, now, the way of it in truth." She looked to Brand. "Champion of twoth'Shan'n and of Euwae of twoth'Ba, ath'Ale of the Condotterai... Take her inside and tend her."

Brand swept in and caught Euwae in his arms. Without a glance towards the ree or the warriors of twoth'Ba still arrayed around them, he carried her into the cabin.

Now, tears streamed down Meeruen's cheeks as well. The other warriors looked cautiously from their ree towards Angus, until ad'Ah stepped forward and nodded towards him. At this, the ree seemed to notice their presence at last and bobbed her head with a fatigued denial.

"There is not to be done, nor seen here." She said firmly, despite the expression on her face. "My thanks to all of you and your eye for duties call.

"Please, be at peace... Return to your tasks at hand. All here is well."

Slowly, the ath'Ale of twoth'Ba returned to their stations, save for ad'Ah, who stood defiantly before Angus, blocking his path to the ree and staring at him with grave suspicion.

Once it was clear that she would not leave the ree's side, the big warrior pulled his broad smirk onto his face.

"Well met, again." He rumbled.

The ath'Ale ignored his pleasantry and kept her hand to her weapon as Konner came out of the cabin.

"What did to pass here?" He asked with jagged concern.

"Konner," the ree replied disconsolately, "There was a truth here that, for all the knowing of it, was never in my mind."

He turned from Meeruen towards the cabin and watched Euwae as Brand set her down lightly onto a bench in the shadows of the room. Kelleu stood over them, his face twisted in concern. Konner blinked several times, before he looked back at the ree.

"You – " He blinked again. "You *wove* upon your own?" His face was a mask of disbelief. "What exorcism did you wrap about her?"

"The choice was hers. She *called* me to it... And, for my part, there was naught to be done but her wish in it."

Konner gasped; his retort was little more than whispered exasperation.

"You *opened* her?"

Ad'Ah's jaw dropped, but Meeruen shook her head.

"I tried, Konner, but I could not... There is iron there that lies beyond my skills to work without proper seeking. But much lay open to the fires of it. And the one wise I had expected to find, was most noted in absence and just cause."

Konner nodded, his face troubled.

"And what was that, my ree?"

"My daughter had no plan to carry forth the weavings Kelleu had set forth, from love alone and the fear for the death of him."

In the cabin, Euwae reached out and took Kelleu's hand. As the youth bent over her and spoke to her in hushed tones, Angus stepped forward so that he could speak to the two druids as quietly as possible.

"What is the way of this weaving, ree, that it goes so ill against him?"

"It is not the weaving." Replied the ree to Angus in kind.

Konner shook his head, but the ree waived him off and continued furtively.

"Rather, my fostered son is the child of cu'Kullah, al'Aith of twoth'Fhee and that is the way of it."

Despite himself, Angus' jaw dropped as well.

"Come," Meeruen prompted as the color returned to her cheeks, "we have yet a hunt to make – And now there is all the more need to see the kill made."

Once again every inch the ree, she turned and walked back into the cabin. Konner cocked his head in curiosity as she passed and walked beside her as she strode inside. Angus and ad'Ah, both stepped forward to follow but bumped shoulders as they did so. The big warrior looked down at her and nodded, but she shook her head and motioned for him to go first.

A broad smile splitting the black stains on his lower face, he did as he was bid; with unguarded skepticism, she followed him inside.

Meeruen took her place on the port bench with Konner at her side. Euwae tugged Kelleu's hand and pulled him aside so that she could see the ree fully.

"Mother..?"

Meeruen smiled softly and shook her head. The corners of Euwae's mouth fought for ground on her cheeks against the corners of her weary eyes, before she nodded back and lowered her head back onto the bench. As raw fatigue unlimbered the strength from her neck and shoulders, Euwae's eyes turned to Brand.

He nodded once, solemnly.

Content with that response, her eyes ground shut and her head rolled off to the side as sleep drowned her at last.

As Kelleu bent down to compose her comfortably on the bench, Brand turned to the druids.

His head rocking unconsciously towards Euwae and her brother, he rolled up the left corner of his mouth and shrugged.

"So much for all that." His eyes flipped from Meeruen to Konner and back.

"Now what? If Kelleu can't do his thing, where does that leave us? The ocean's a pretty big place to be looking for cu'Kullah, assuming he's even out here... But I've got a hunch that he's not. At least not this far out."

"And why, ath'Ale of the Condotterai, might that be the way of it? Did he not sail out in ships fitted for facing the sea?"

"He did – And that might have been his plan, until we laid out the better part of his men at Summersford. He hasn't got the crew he needs for whatever he'd originally planned. So I figure at this point he'll be up to his neck in plan B."

Angus moved away to a covered arrow loop on the starboard side of the cabin and idly pushed aside the heavy linen curtain to view the distant horizon. Konner leaned back against the wall and nodded.

"Plan B is it? A curious turn of phrase – Yet apt and no mistake. But what of it? We are no less wise of the first, setting aside the latter."

"Oh, but we are." Meeruen said quietly. "Think upon this. We are wise to his notion to take up the mantle of the ree, by way of the ancient weavings. He, for his doings, was wise to the demands of Ers'Elb – Both in preparation and execution of those weavings so needed."

Brand made a sour face at the word 'execution,' but made no comment. Instead, he added quietly, "And he had these ships lined up and ready to go once he was done. So this was definitely part of the plan.

"I don't know shitesan about these – Weavings." He continued. "But a sea voyage is obviously next on the agenda. Where would he need to sail to?"

Konner looked across the cabin at Kelleu, who perched lightly on the bench at Euwae's feet.

"Shaman?" He asked after the young man failed to notice his gaze.

"Hmm?" Kelleu replied. "Oh, yes... Ers'Elb..."

"Well, what comes *after* that." Brand coaxed gently.

"The night of father's return, was the first Red Moon." The shaman replied, his voice taking on a hollow timber. "I dreamed that night of the Black Lake... Or, in its slumber it called out to me. 'Beyond mortal days,' it sang, 'Lost Hopes' artesian artery... Draught and wine of Fate.' That is the way of what I dreamed."

Brand turned to look at Kelleu.

"Sacred shitesan." He murmured. "I can't believe I forgot."

All of the faces in the room save Euwae and Angus now locked with his. His brow furrowed and he shrugged.

"Well, it's *been* pretty busy..." He waived off the excuse and continued, his eyes moving back and forth slowly as he looked through his thoughts to find the words he required.

"I met Euwae at twoth'Shan'n. But there was an army of ghosts, there, too." Meeruen and Konner exchanged a tight glance, but said nothing; Brand seemed too lost in his narrative to pay them any heed.

"They spoke to us," he continued, "about finding a lost name on the east wind; they said darkness would fail, once the –"

Kelleu leaned forward.

"Once the what, Eastlander..?"

Brand suddenly set his jaw. He turned and looked down at Kelleu.

"Once the shaman opened the cairn." Brand said with foreboding. "Opened the cairn and the torcs sang."

Everyone in the room but Brand stirred uncomfortably.

"So," he concluded, "I take it that means something to you."

Konner looked at Kelleu.

"He means to raid a twoth's House and no mistake."

"Aye... But which? And why the need to set sail to it?"

Brand raised his chin.

"Twoth's house?" He interjected.

Meeruen nodded. "The heart of any twoth, Champion of the Condotterai, is the place where the memories of its ancestors reside... A special tomb, which holds the skulls of all the rees who have seen to the stewardship of the lands and folk who dwell there."

Brand nodded. Very slowly.

"Yeah – I've heard of them."

Konner nodded as well.

"But there are no twoth's to be found off the shores of Cord'Or, no matter the breadth of isle'Eh you hope to span."

Brand turned back to Konner.

"What about Seasgift?"

"Madness!"exclaimed ad'Ah, as Konner rocked back against the wall of the cabin. Even Meeruen went a bit pale. Kelleu simply hung his head and hid his expression altogether.

A dark smirk stole onto Brand's face.

"Well, this is cu'Kullah we're talking about..."

Meeruen looked from Brand to Kelleu, then took up the discussion.

"But, you did to say he lacked the men to make such a sailing, once the giftings of Summersford were done."

Brand let out a relieved breath. "True enough. So, the question is; if not Seasgift, then where? I'll be honest, I don't really get what singing torcs have to do with all this... And I'm kinda sure I don't *want* to know." Meeruen smiled sympathetically as he continued. "So this one is gonna have to be on you."

The discussion of the various twoth's Houses began in earnest, but no firm choice seemed to be clear. Finally, the sun was kneading the horizon of the sea when Angus turned cleared his throat self consciously and looked at Meeruen.

"When we met this day, you wove speech into me." He said quietly. "I know the way of the tales cu'Kullah would have left unsung. But the words will not come to me."

Konner looked at Angus with pity. "What of it, then?" The priest asked quietly. "The weaving is true, though the geas that binds you cannot be unmade... What mind you have to speak, is freely yours; that which is bound to the al'Aith you have departed will ever be his."

Angus shook his head.

"The ree can take them from me... She could open me, as she did her daughter. Then, all would be freely known... And that is the way of it."

Brand sat up and looked at Angus as Meeruen replied gently through the shadows that climbed across the cabin as the light of day failed beyond them.

"This is no small thing you are asking of yourself," she said quietly. "My daughter was both open to the weaving and innocent of any wrongs that might have wrought worse of her.

"Can you say the same?"

Angus sat there for a long moment, before he took a deep breath and looked at the floor.

"No."

"Then what you ask is as like to be the death of you as not."

Angus looked up and turned to look at Brand.

"Since Summersford, I have not lived but on the moment of another's word." He said, his statement dull with memories. "If I am to die now, then it was in the call of a true al'Aith and by the hand of a ree.

"If there is better to be had, then I'll live to find it – And no mistake."

Brand stood up and walked over to Angus. Clasping his shoulder, he looked down into the big warrior's eyes.

"Don't quit on me, you shitesas." He said reassuringly. "I'll need you here, once we track cu'Kullah down."

Angus nodded. His mouth worked, but no words could push their way past his emotions.

Meeruen rose delicately and crossed through the pools of darkness that filled the room to stand before the big warrior.

"Are you of no other mind, then?"

Angus swallowed hard. His lips were pursed as he shook his head no.

"Aye." He responded gutturally.

Meeruen touched Brand on the shoulder. Reluctantly, he stepped away.

The ree stood fully before Angus now. She reached out and gently took him by the chin, her pale skin almost glowing in contrast to the black stain blotted across his jaw. The ath'Ale's eyes were slowly drawn up to hers as the rubies in her torc took on a baleful glow, casting phantom glimmers across his face.

"Angus, ath'Ale of Euwae of twoth'Ba, do not look away." She said quietly. "The cause you serve is just and in the way of the ancient rites..."

Out of respect, the others slowly made their way out of the room. Konner led Kelleu towards the bow of the ship, while ad'Ah took a place by the door to prevent anyone from entering. Only Brand stayed, standing between where Euwae slept dreamlessly and the power of the weaving as it filled the room with a dark fire which the natural shadows of night now fled, as surely as the people in the cabin had done.

Yet even Brand was forced to look away, well before Angus choked out the secrets of his former master while the weaving took its final toll upon him.

Three Rees

The gray-green waves of isle'Eh pushed foam and detritus up to the high water line etched into the reddish sands as Bayl'Ors Eye slid smoothly up onto the beach. Following her lead, the other three ships did the same; last to lay a keel to the earth was Foamsmare, once again under the hand of her Master, the priest of Summersford.

While the ath'Ale from twoth'Ba began to debark, Meeruen moved to the bow and joined Euwae and her companions as they scanned the shore from that elevated vantage. The strand here was fairly steep, offering fair harbor for the ships. After fifteen yards of sand, dunes quickly gave way to steep bluffs which sported armor of gravel and stone from long years of erosion. These, in turn, were crowned by a thick pelt of grey scrub oak that rolled off down the far side of the slope.

Angus waived his hand at the tops of the bluffs.

"The whole of the south of del'Ath is in such wise... Hills round as a buttocks clad in brambles and brush that is as like to flay the skin as let you pass in peace."

Brand shook his head and scowled.

"This might be the shortest route to take, but it'll be hard going. Getting through that brush is gonna take some work."

Meeruen smiled reassuringly in response.

"If that is the worst of it, we shall make quick work of this indeed Bird Club."

Brand grunted, but kept studying the terrain. Euwae looked up and down the shore, then turned to Brand.

"I know that tone, right enough... You should be wise to the wiles of the women of twoth'Ba by this time and no mistake."

The ree's eyes narrowed slightly as she looked from Euwae to Brand, but she made no further comment. Now, Konner was making his way across the beach towards them through the press of warriors as they made the ships fast or broke ground for the camps that would house those who would stay behind to guard the vessels. The four in the bow slid over the side to join him, followed at the last by Kelleu as he rushed from the cabin of Bayl'Ors Eye to join the others.

Konner looked from Meeruen to Kelleu.

"And what was the way of the last weaving, then?"

"The twoth's House of del'Ath is, as yet, undisturbed." Kelleu's head bobbed breathlessly as he replied. "But there have been hands laid upon it and weavings besides. I have no wise to how long it may take them to pass the threshold, for there is blindness upon all those who seek to do so."

Euwae studied her brother.

"Weavings?"

With difficulty, Angus cleared his throat.

"There is one." He rolled his chin towards Konner.

"Genna?" Brand asked coolly. Once Angus was able to wrest a single nod of confirmation from his reluctant chin, Brand turned to the rest of the group.

"Genna is cu'Kullah's priest. He's – "

Brand's face locked up in bitter memories.

"He's the one who did the sorcery at the black lake."

Kelleu gasped, but Konner spoke first.

"If their druid is a priest, it will take them some time to unbind the weavings upon the house."

Kelleu shook his head.

"Yet, if he has the skills to open the waters of Ers'Elb – " the young man said, as Angus flinched and Brand looked away down the beach "– then he has a mind to the ways of things even the shaman fear to touch. More so, the will to risk the geasa that comes of doing so."

He turned to his mother.

"We must make haste and no mistake. If this priest cares so little for the law and I can see that they are about the threshold, no matter the shroud that hides them, they must be closer to crossing than we know."

Konner inhaled deeply, closed his eyes and exhaled very slowly. Brand's expression softened. He closed the distance between them and clasped the priest's upper arm.

"No worries, Konner," he confided, "I've felt that way since Euwae loaded me onto your ship." He lowered his hand and shrugged.

"We've got three druids to their one;" his eyes ranged across the magicians and came to rest on Angus, "better warriors and experience. The men who stand with cu'Kullah are swept up in his quest... He's the key.

"Once we take him down, the rest will break – Or we'll *break* them."

Everyone save Kelleu nodded in mutual understanding. As the six separated to prepare for the hard march ahead, Brand caught Euwae's shoulder gently and held her back.

"Your brother," Brand said quietly, "doesn't look like he's too happy about this. Is he gonna be all right, once we find them?"

Doubt stole across Euwae's face, but she closed her eyes and swept it away before she turned to face Brand.

"He is the son of the ree of twoth'Ba and wise in the weavings of the shaman, besides. He will be true to his destiny."

Brand looked into her eyes and nodded.

"Fair enough."

He let her go; she trotted off to join Kelleu as he clambered back into the Bayl'Ors Eye to gather his things. With a deflated smirk, he shook his head slightly and followed them to the ship.

*   *   *

The ree chose to leave half of the ath'Ale with the ships, to protect their swift return home while she led the rest of the men up the crumbling cliffs and into the thick brush that crowned them. These sentinels were instructed to make no fires and to keep close watch upon the shore... For del'Ath had fallen into ruin from the predation of marauds and no living Cord'Or felt safe passing through this broken twoth.

Night was well upon them as Kelleu made the first ascent, while the others still gathered on the beach below the bluff. Once he crested the overhanging eave of root and sparse soil that jutted out from the top of the rise, he approached the wall of thick brush with outstretched hands.

His fingers gently brushing against the outermost branches, he began to move them in an interlaced pattern, singing wordlessly as he did so. Around him, a gentle breeze tousled his hair and pulled at his tunic before it carried his song off into the bracken before him. He closed his eyes and smiled, his hands expanding the diameter of his gestures and rotating the plane of the figure he wove from a vertical to the horizontal.

The low trees began to rustle. Their branches shook and began to pull apart, swinging to his left and right, or arching above his head to form a narrow but open track that snaked forward and down the hill.

Nodding his thanks to the nature of the wood, he began to follow the path, his hands never ceasing, nor his song pausing in its haunting melody.

Brand was next to reach the summit; by that time, Kelleu was already walking at a brisk pace well ahead of him down the far side of the hill. Whistling softly in appreciation, he hefted Crows Call onto his shoulder and trotted off down the easy track after the shaman. One by one, the rest of the band of twoth'Ba followed.

The ree, fourth up the hill, was none the less the last to take to the trail. Once she was on it, the winds behind her faded and the gnarled branches reached out to each other and clasped their fellows in an unrelenting embrace once more.

The trail that Kelleu made traced like a river through the valleys of the hills that rose about them. Euwae and Angus followed Brand directly; more than once, he cast them an appreciative glance for the ease of their advance as they wound through the maze of thickets that had conquered the abandoned fields and pastures of del'Ath. Each time they found themselves crossing one of the low stone walls which had once formed a boundary between prosperous families in days now forgotten, Konner studied it with a deep sorrow, replacing any stones that were dislodged in their passing before he followed the line ahead of him.

As the light filtering through the arches of the branches began to soften with the first touches of dawn, the tight confines of the bracken forest abruptly fell away to a wide expanse of sparsely turfed earth. In the distance, a pair of campfires flickered fitfully around a high berm over worked stone and tumbled rocks that surrounded the ruins of the great hall of del'Ath.

Brand stopped short and looked at the landmarks in astonishment.

"*Shitesa!*" He exclaimed. "How did we get *here*?"

Euwae stepped past Angus and surveyed the area around them as she replied coyly, "Bird Club, did you not see Kelleu walking before you?"

He shot her a dark glance.

"No, that's *not* what I meant. That old fort is four days hard march from the coast. I remember *how* hard it was, when your father lead the men of the River Prince here to beat back the marauds that were raiding our southern border. We made our stand right there – " He pointed to a low escarpment of stone that jutted from the ground like an ugly scar, "while your father set the ath'Ale of twoth'Ba in the ruins themselves.

"There's a nasty bog, just out of sight at the base of that rise. Cu'Kullah..."

Brand's voice dropped an octave with the sorrow of the memory.

"Cu'Kullah led the warriors of twoth'Fhee and formed them up in a spear hedge between the two in that open space there."

Angus nodded proudly.

"Aye. A grand day that was, indeed. The hiel were anxious to be giving us gifts of death and no mistake... But, by the time the sun had had enough of the day, we had served *them* up such a feast of it that the crows themselves went hungry for it."

Euwae looked confused.

"Surely, you mean that the crows had more than their fill of it?"

Brand and Angus exchanged a look; the bigger man looked away. Brand hefted a grin onto his face and nodded once.

"Yeah, that's what he meant." He said disingenuously.

"Look," he continued on with a lighter tone to his voice, "we should get something to eat. I'm famished and I've had enough walking for now... Let's see what your mother has planned for today, all right?"

Euwae's face contracted at his obvious evasion, but Brand was already walking off to join the ree where she spoke in hushed tones with Konner and ad'Ah. Euwae looked darkly at Angus, who was still making a distinct point of studying the camp of cu'Kullah's men in the far distance.

"Fine, then." She spat out. "Be of such wise."

The princess turned stiffly and followed Brand, before Angus exhaled slowly in relief.

After the ath'Ale were given word to take food and drink, it was decided that it would be best to wait for a time and give them a much needed rest. While Meeruen dispatched a pathfinder to scout ahead and see if the strength of cu'Kullah's force could be ascertained, the other warriors of twoth'Ba kept low with their backs to the forest of scrub oak and briers, to keep themselves from being seen or approached unawares.

While they waited for the scout's return, most of the ath'Ale wrapped their eyes and took some sleep beneath the warm rays of the sun. A few saw to their weapons, or kept a watch on the camp far ahead of them or to their flanks for any sign of an enemy. Kelleu was exhausted and slept like a stone beside his mother, who wrapped them both in her wide cloak. Brand slept, as always, sitting with his face towards the enemy. Euwae stretched out beside him with a soft smile on her face.

Well away from the warriors of twoth'Ba, Angus sat stiffly, his eyes burning with a strange light and fixed on visions no one else could see.

*   *   *

When the sun settled reluctantly upon the broken shoulders of the hills to the west, the nobility of twoth'Ba gathered to hear the pathfinder's report. Inside the ruin, cu'Kullah's band numbered only thirty men, all told. Most were ath'Ale of twoth'Fhee; however, a group of a dozen marauds kept to themselves on the far side of the ancient forts vanquished walls. Between them cu'Kullah had laid his own camp in the jagged remains of a tower atop a low mound at the keeps center. There were others with him as well; their numbers were unknown, though likely few.

Angus and Brand supplied that Genna, the war band's priest, would be there amongst them. Konner volunteered to face him, but Angus immediately demanded the right to do so. When the druid began to protest, Meeruen raised a hand to silence the debate and charged Angus to the task. The big man nodded gravely in thanks and the rest of the plan was laid.

Two thirds of the men would head for the larger camp at the gate, while the remaining twenty warriors would set out to separate and destroy the marauds. The ree, the druids and Euwae's band were responsible for taking cu'Kullah and his retinue; after a cool protest about the safety of the ree, ad'Ah was taken into this last company as well. Given the presence of a druid amongst the enemy, the ree's party would ensure that there were no subtle weavings against attack before the final push was made: the two larger groups would wait for a signal from the ree before they charged into their foe.

As they all picked their way slowly through what cover the sparse vegetation provided, ad'Ah kept the middle distance between the ree and Angus. Once the big warrior noticed this, he made some sport of his movements, forcing her to pay ever closer attention to him – At least until Brand seized him by the shoulder and whispered something harsh into his ear. Crestfallen, he dropped back behind his companions until they reached the gap in the eastern wall which provided the closest access to the tower from their line of approach.

There, Kelleu placed his hands gently upon the few stones which stubbornly stood in hopeless defense of the perimeter and sang gently to himself. His eyes became unfocused for a brief time, while his fingers traced the faults in the fractured blocks. His breath caught twice in his chest, but he remained on task until his song softly trailed off on the evening breeze.

Closing his eyes to clear his sight, he shook his head quickly before he turned to face the others. Brand started at the verdant green color of the young man's eyes, but listened intently as he spoke in hushed tones.

"There are weavings all about us and no mistake." He said gently, his voice soft with sorrow. "Some are like as the moss on the stones; these are all but broken, now, and pose no threat.

"Two more, I see, that are the songs of RafEm, shaman of twoth'Ba. These are drowned out in a weaving the like of which I have never seen, in waking..." He shuddered once at some unpleasant memory. Behind him, Brand unexpectedly did the same. Euwae's brows lowered in concern, but he shook his head once in denial; she flashed an angry glare in rebuttal before she turned her attention back to the rest of the group.

"In what wise?" Konner had asked sharply, but Kelleu just hung his head. Meeruen circled around them and reached out to lift his chin.

"Find peace in this, my son," she said gently, "your vision served us well, even so."

Euwae looked from Meeruen to Konner in confusion.

"I am at a loss, then," she admitted. "What was spoken?"

Konner looked at her with frustration and his voice was cool as an autumn pond as he replied.

"The last two weavings," he said brusquely, "of which wise the shaman knows nothing, save that they exist at all."

The ree lowered her hand and turned to face the gap in the wall. The jewels at the ends of her torc burned with the reflection of the dying sun as she lifted first her left hand, then her right and twisted them around the shape of the tower on the hill. Suddenly, her eyes grew wide with understanding, but grew wider still with growing fear. Her chin trembled and her arms shook with the effort it took to pull her hands away and drop them to her sides.

"Kelleu," she said starkly, her breath ragged in her chest, "send out the word to the ath'Ale...

"We are discovered."

In the gaping mouth of a passage that led into the tower, the wan light of a dismal fire was blotted out.

"Now..." the ree implored. "DO IT NOW."

Kelleu cupped his hands to his mouth and uttered a piercing sound like the call of a hawk in stoop. Off to either side, the war cries of twoth'Ba erupted and echoed like drunken phantoms off of the ruins around them. Meeruen gritted her teeth and levered her arms back up to her chest, her fingers clawing at the air for a purchase on her power as the light of her torc blazed around her.

"This – task..." She choked out painfully, "does to be – Mine...

"Now. Go... Now."

Without a word, Brand vaulted into the breach in the wall and shot up the slope. Startled, Euwae quickly followed with Angus shouldering his way through directly behind her. Konner looked from the ree to the tower, drew his falcata and slipped into the gap to run up the slope. Kelleu and ad'Ah continued to stare at the ree in concern.

"GO!" Her command erupted as violently as spasms rippling across her hands and up through the flesh of her arms. Pulling her own weapon free of the scabbard, ad'Ah nodded and chased after the others. But Kelleu simply took a calming breath, before he took a shaft of alderwood, polished smooth by years of handling, from a bag at his hip and thrust it into the earth beside his mother.

Meeruen looked at her son and smiled proudly.

"Kelleu, shaman of twoth'Ba... I am proud that you stand with me."

Her son nodded once.

"You have seen the twoth's House is opened..." he said with his quiet reserve. "Only a ree may take the torc of another and cast him down. Without you, mother, all this will fail to end what he has begun."

237

Angus easily outstripped the pace of Euwae and even overtook Brand on the charge up the hill. Together, they reached the gap in the wall just as licks of blue flame snaked up the inside of the passage and blossomed into columns of fire that traced along the walls and rolled up to engulf the ceiling. From the throaty hiss of the flames, they heard the voice of Meeruen whisper to them encouragingly.

"Do not linger!" The flames entreated. "The moment slips away!"

They exchanged a glance, lifted their arms to shield themselves from the heat and raced on into the tunnel just as Euwae reached them. Her eyes rolled to the sky in frustration as she followed after them, with Konner and ad'Ah at her heels.

They emerged into the rubble of the open space left by the upper floors where the tower had surrendered to the paired violence of man and nature and collapsed, covering the lowest floor below in a cacophony of rubble. From the light of the fire behind them, they could see that a space near the far wall had been cleared of detritus, revealing an open bronze door in an outcropping of the far wall. Atop the threshold stood a figure in a dirty blue robe, above whose unkempt beard nested a pair of burning blue eyes. From his left hand trailed long strands of string, while his right arm ended in an ugly, scarred stump.

"Begone, you!" He cried out haggardly. "This is the hall of the ree of del'Ath and you are of no right to enter without his word!"

Angus stepped forward, his stained face weighed down with pity.

"This is not the way of it, Genna..." Angus said sadly. "Old friend, this is no hall, nor fit place for any ree to call out for the bua'Theu to tend him."

Genna's eyes looked around the tumbled ruin expansively.

"Is it not, then?" He called out grandly. "Your sight is as lost to you as my arm is to me, Angus..."

He looked down at the ath'Ale and added cruelly, "Oathbreaker."

But Angus was not shamed by the accusation.

"Come down from there, Genna. This is no place for you, priest, either... Come down and see the way of it."

"The way of it?" Genna parroted. "The WAY OF IT?

"YOU have no place here, Angus Black Face. In no wise are you to live for raising your hand against your ree!"

"Genna – "

But ad'Ah strode forward and cut him off.

"Del'Ath is lost, by word of Ard'Ree!" She shouted, her words as hot as her anger. "It has no hall – And it has NO ree!"

A great shadow plummeted like a stone from the splintered wreckage of the floor above and struck the earth behind ad'Ah like an avalanche of flesh. An arm as big around as her thigh whipped across the distance between them and effortlessly lifted her from the floor, tossing her onto the pile of debris that surrounded them. As she struck the wreckage of stone, an impossibly deep voice taunted her with its response.

"That is not the way of it, little ath'Ale..." Said the massive figure with ironic sarcasm. "It does, in truth, serve a ree."

Brand started.

"Cu'Kullah..?" The name slipped from his throat unbidden.

The figure before them was graven into their minds by the relentless blaze of the fire behind them. Twice the height of Brand, he wore only a kilt of rough cloth, bound at the waist with thick rope. His swollen chest was a grotesque mockery of idealized strength and his corded limbs were thick enough to match. Only the pitifully small skull bore any resemblance to the warrior who had once stood at his side, perched atop a torc of stained leather that strained like a noose around his neck. Hands nearly the size of Euwae's chest opened and clenched with cracking joints that echoed through the tower as it turned to face him.

"Outlander..." The mockery of the tone reeked of hatred. "Somehow, I knew I was not done with you.

"Yet."

Ad'Ah moaned, tried to rise, but only managed to slide down the pitch of the rubble and onto to the paved floor.

Cu'Kullah ignored her.

"And – *Angus*." His voice drew out the word, as if there was something pleasant about the bile that filled the pronunciation of it. "You would have served me better to have died on the banks of Summersford, *ath'Ale*."

"Aye." Angus swallowed hard, his fist tightening around the sword that he had borrowed and the knife that Brand had given him in equal measure.

"And who, then, is *this*?" The words of cu'Kullah were poisoned as much by a stirring desire as raw, violent hatred. "Have we met, little one?"

Euwae's face was a mask of disinterested scorn.

"I take it, then," she mocked, "that you are cu'Kullah, al'Aith of twoth'Fhee – "

"Ree of del'ATH!" He roared in anger.

239

"Al'Aith of twoth'Fhee,"she continued in the same condescending tone, "and outlaw to the customs of Cord'or and Ard'Ree."

The huge figure covered the distance between them in two steps and leaned forward so that he could study her over the bulwark of his chest.

"Al'Aith..." He cooed.

He lashed out, seized her with both hands and pulled her up to his face. "You talk too much – " He hurled her into the air back towards the entry. "And that is the way of it."

Brand was already in motion before Euwae hit the ground, clawing his way up the barricade of wreckage that surrounded them to reach her. Before he could mount the crest, cu'Kullah seized his leg and pulled him back, dangling the warrior upside down before him as Euwae hit the ground hard and made a boneless roll to a stop against the wall.

"Watch." Cu'Kullah rumbled.

He rotated his wrist so Brand was facing the door as well. Konner had made his way over to ad'Ah; now, he was helping her to her feet, his face a mask of confusion. Angus was still rooted to the spot, his knuckles white as they gripped his weapons while in the flames wreathing the doorway, something –

Moved.

Black mists coalesced into fangs and talons that shot out of the flames towards Euwae. But before they could reach her flames roared out behind the blackness and engulfed it in a blazing cloud. The creature within writhed furiously, but was unable to pull free of the fires as they receded back into the tunnel, drawing the furious creature back with it.

Euwae struggled to raise herself to her hands and knees, while cu'Kullah rocked back, his twisted face a mask of shock.

"Druid!" He roared.

Genna drew back his left hand and hurled the wad of strings high into the air. As they reached the apex of the throw, they shimmered and expanded, creating an intricate weave of blue light rippling high above them.

"NO!"

Konner cried out as he released ad'Ah and threw up his hands at the pattern. He made a slapping gesture which sent a ripple through the whole of the weaving. With a grin, he began to move his fingers around the edges of the knotted light and one of the strands moved out of alignment with the pattern.

Genna looked about furiously for the other priest. As he saw Konner unweaving his pattern, his left hand shot up and he began to pull the strand back into place.

Cu'Kullah raised Brand so that their heads were at the same level.

"You have brought a conjurer and a priest?" His voice rumbled like distant thunder as his pinched head moved minutely from side to side in disbelief. "I would not have thought you so wise, cuhm'l... But they will be of little use against the might of a true ree."

"You want to see the way of it, you shitesan?" Brand asked coolly before he jerked backwards, using the momentum to bring Crows Call forward and drive the beak savagely into cu'Kullah's groin.

With a howl of pain that echoed across the ruins of the keep, the giant staggered back and turned in a half circle as his knees convulsed together.

"You want to see the way of it, Outlander?" Cu'Kullah sputtered. "Learn this truth!"

Brand struggled to land a second blow, but his captor hurled him side-armed into the yawing darkness beyond the bronze door.

"Death to YOU!" he boomed with laughter as Brand tumbled down a narrow stairway and vanished in the darkness within them.

Euwae was oblivious to the forms of darkness that struggled to escape the bondage of flames as she slowly rose to her feet. Her eyes had been locked on Brand as he landed a wicked blow on the monster who held him, then went wide with horror as he was tossed into the shadowed twoth's House.

"TWOTH'BA!!!" She shrieked as she threw herself across the loose footing and leaped through the air towards cu'Kullah's back. He started to turn, but was too late. Her blade caught him on the shoulder and bit deeply into his flesh. Buried past the center of the blade, it was wrenched from her hand as her momentum carried her past the hideous giant and down to the floor. She rolled over twice before coming to her feet in a low crouch.

Beyond her, cu'Kullah made several desperate attempts to reach the weapon and pull it free, but his massive bulk worked against him and he could not reach it. With a snarl, he gave up trying to dislodge it and turned his attention to the woman who had struck him.

But, before he could reach her, ad'Ah and Angus charged in from either side and began to strike at his legs and arms with berserk abandon. They worked as a team, with one sweeping in to attack while cu'Kullah turned to try to seize the other. Slowly, they drew him away from Euwae, more than once saving the other from certain death at his hands as they did so. With the immediate threat at bay, Euwae shook her head to clear her vision, then turned and faced the dark stairway down which Brand had vanished.

She saw Genna still stood above the portal, working furiously to maintain the delicate pattern that Konner wrenched upon with a resolve that matched that of Angus and ad'Ah. Still in her three limbed crouch, she looked about frantically. Her eyes lit up and she scurried across the rubble to her left, where she reached out and seized Crows Call.

Standing to her full height, she gave the heavy weapon an experimental heft.

"Bird Club," she chided to herself, "what brings you to use so – "

Angus stumbled back into Euwae and sent them both sprawling onto the ground. Above them, Genna screamed for cu'Kullah; who, upon seeing two opponents down, took a broad step towards ad'Ah, but turned with impossible speed and lunged for the pair sprawled out on the floor instead.

Angus took Euwae by the waist and tossed her out of the way. Cu'Kullah's huge fist smashed into the ground where she had lay as Angus rolled in the opposite direction, so cu'Kullah swung his left leg around in a solid kick to the ath'Ale's lower back.

Angus grunted in pain as he rolled well across the open space; then he lay still.

Ad'Ah took the opening and rushed forward, driving the thick blade of her sword deeply into cu'Kullah's right leg behind the knee. The limb gave way and the huge man spun to the left and collapsed on his side; Euwae's blade snagged upon the ruined floor and was finally torn free from his body.

Seeing this, the al'Aith quickly retrieved her falcata and nodded to ad'Ah. Like wolves, the two women circled in upon their stricken foe. Rather than trying to rise and fight them, however, he just lay there, like wounded prey before the inexorable end of the hunt. As ad'Ah moved close enough to strike and raised her weapon, Euwae looked down at cu'Kullah and shuddered.

His eyes were closed. And he was smiling.

From across the room, Konner shouted at the two warriors.

"Ad'Ah! Stay your hand!"

But ad'Ah's reflexes had brought down the killing blow to cu'Kullah's chest. Just as the falcata touched his flesh, the blue energy above them fractured the air like lightning and grounded through the blade and into ad'Ah. Veins of power convulsed across and through her, lifted the warrior's body into the air and suspended her in the weaving of Genna's magic like an insect in a web.

Euwae could only watch in horror as the weaving continued to course through the other woman. She convulsed erratically as Konner frantically worked at the knots of energy. After several long, terrible seconds the strands slipped away and ad'Ah fell lifelessly onto the floor.

Euwae started to run towards her, but her feet were torn out from under her by cu'Kullah. As she stumbled and spun to the ground, he lurched to his feet and grabbed her with a single hand across the shoulders, drove her head into the floor with a thick thud and casually tossed the body aside. Cu'Kullah now turned to Konner, his low voice rebounding across the room imperiously in spite of its conversational tone.

242

"You should have brought more warriors, priest, and that is the way of it."

Konner tugged frantically at the weaving, but Genna's cackle was a knife in the back of the priest's final hopes. At the far end of the chamber, the flames that had warded the tunnel coughed and suddenly died out. Cu'Kullah bent over slightly, so that he could see the priest fully and chuckled.

"Many more..."

Brand slipped an arm out before him and painfully levered himself into a sitting position. Eldritch blue light filtered down the stairway behind him, creating a thick gloom that was barely enough to see by. He turned his head from left to right, then struggled to his feet.

The small chamber around him was roughly hewn from the rock foundations of the tower wall. Each was lined with a series of neat niches several inches high, from which glittered the ambient light of precious stones and metals. His eyes fluttering to clear his sight, Brand took one step closer when a chorus of whispers erupted around him.

"*CHOOSE,*" they called out as one.

"*CHOOSE.*"

"Choose what?" He called back. "Who's there?"

"*WE ARE.*" the whispers chimed back, their numbers making the response seem to echo in the gloom.

Brand shook his head with a scowl.

"That's not shitesast helpful." He muttered. "You sound like the dead from twoth'Shan'n..."

He blanched. "Is that who you are?"

"*WE ARE TO BE CHOSEN.*"

Brand's brow furrowed and he took a step forward. Every niche held a singular torc, each as fine in crafting as he had ever seen. He blinked again in understanding.

"This is the twoth's House. You're the torcs of the dead rees."

He pursed his lips and exhaled through his nose.

"I guess we're too late, after all..."

"*CHOOSE.*"

Brand's brow furrowed again. Quickly he turned, bending low, craning upward, looking in each of the niches.

All of the torcs were there.

"Shitesan..." He said with wonder. "He never made it down here."

"*YOU SHALL BE REE,*" the whispers enjoined together. "*CHOOSE.*"

Brand stepped back, his eyes scanning the niches once again until they locked upon a singular torc. It appeared at first to be made of thick bronze, but was actually woven strands of metal which was cunningly hammered to resemble scales; the finials were worked into the heads of dragons whose eyes glowed with pale gold.

Slowly his hand reached out for the torc, his eyes drawn to it and softening as if it were the most precious thing he would ever see again.

Just as his hand slid into the niche and hovered over the torc, it spoke to him alone; the rest of the chorus had fallen silent.

"*YOU HAVE CHOSEN ME.*"

Slowly, Brand nodded.

"I know what you are... To them you are en'Och and death."

"*AND TO YOU?*"

Brand answered without hesitation.

"En'Och. And death."

Konner lowered his hands.

"Strike, then, and be done with it." He said proudly. "If we are not Ard'Ree's hand in this, others will be and no mistake... You stand against the order of life, cu'Kullah of twoth'Fhee – "

"Enough of your tongue, priest."

As he started to cross towards Konner, however, a figure emerged from the tunnel out of the tower and stepped into the glow of the weaving above them.

Cu'Kullah raised his hand to strike the priest down, when Kelleu gently sang, "Stop."

The corded muscles of the arm swelled as it dragged downwards, finally being arrested in mid swing. The huge frame of cu'Kullah pivoted so that he could study the newcomer.

"A shaman as well?" He muttered, then shrugged. "No matter. Genna – Destroy it."

A wicked grin split Genna's face. He raised his left hand just as the scramasax flashed past him and drove deep into the flesh just below his left collar bone. He stared at the handle of the weapon projecting from his shoulder, before the arm spasmed and he screamed in pain.

As his priest sagged to his knees, cu'Kullah turned to see Angus levering himself off the floor, fighting the pain in his back that hobbled his limbs.

"I said Genna was mine to take," Angus chided Konner through gritted teeth as he stumbled forward to stand over Euwae. "The rest I care nothing for."

As the weaving above them began to dissipate through the air like ripples on a mirrored lake, cu'Kullah wrenched his arm free and took a swing at the priest. But Konner was already sprinting away from him towards the opened bronze door, where Brand was bending down to recover his bec de corbin. From the entryway to the tunnel, Kelleu scowled as he looked around the room.

"Euwae," the shaman said quietly, "arise... Arise."

Brand stood beside Konner across the room from cu'Kullah.

"Well met, Knot-Spender."

"Well met, Eastlander."

With a shout that shook dust from the ruined floor above them, cu'Kullah vented his rage and charged the pair of them. As he closed to arm's length, each stepped to the side, doing their best to stay well clear of his reach while trying to land counter-strikes on the massive arms as best they could.

Angus bent over Euwae and gently lifted her head.

"My al'Aith..?" He said quietly, then noticed the blood that streaked across his hand from the back of her head. "Euwae..."

"Angus!" Brand shouted from across the room. "Get her OUT of here!"

Angus tried to lift her, but sagged down to his knees, tears of pain streaming down his face as his back spasmed. Cu'Kullah looked frantically around the room and spied his former follower. But as he stormed off towards Angus, Konner and Brand raced around him and together managed to beat him back.

Angus started as he felt a pair of hands take hold of him from behind, but ad'Ah's agonized voice alleviated his fear as best she could.

"Get to your feet, ath'Ale," she commanded through gritted teeth, "there is work yet to be done!" While Konner and Brand bought them time, she helped Angus struggle to his feet and together they raised Euwae between them and tried to drag her up the slope of wreckage around them and out of harms way.

As they crested the top of the debris, Kelleu saw his sister at last. Reaching out a hand towards her, his request took on the quality of a song, his fingers moving in time with the rhythms of the music, while cu'Kullah finally shouldered his way through the defensive line of Konner and Brand, reached up to seize her and pulled her back to him.

With unity of purpose, ad'Ah and Angus wheeled and slid back down into the pit to face cu'Kullah while Brand and Konner struck blow after blow into him from behind. The bloated giant stumbled to his knees once again, but clutched Euwae to his chest like a doll with his good arm and refused to let her go.

Overcome by pain and fatigue, an unwilling lull settled upon the companions from twoth'Ba. Now well beyond the reach of cu'Kullah, Konner rocked his head to one side to get Brand's attention and gestured at cu'Kullah's back with his sword. Brand's shoulders sagged and his breathing turned ragged.

The wounds on their enemy were already starting to close.

"Shitesan..." Brand panted. "Sacred shitesan."

Euwae's eyes fluttered open.

A slight smile painted itself across her face, before she snuggled further into the tight embrace that held her. She closed her eyes again and said softly, "No... No shitesan."

The grip around her closed painfully and her head began to swim. Her eyes fluttered open again, but the pleasant expression bled out behind a wash of fear and anger as cu'Kullah rose back to his feet, turned his back to Kelleu and faced all of the others arrayed against him.

"*Now*, you know the way of it..." His massive voice crooned. "There are none here so worthy as me – Not champion, druid or ath'Ale.

"By ancient rite and by my choice," he thundered, "I am the REE of del'Ath!"

Brand shook his head.

"You should've gone down there, cu'Kullah... You might've learned something yourself."

The massive man bent slightly forward and faced Brand.

"You are *nothing*, cuhm'l... There is nothing I fear of you."

Brand swung Crows Call in quick circle.

"My geasa are sealed," cu'Kullah continued with a tone straight out of the grave. "Without a torc, you are nothing."

Suddenly, Euwae screamed as she pushed with all her might against the muscles of cu'Kullah's chest.

Everyone took a step forward, but the big man simply squeezed a bit harder and her yell of defiance turned to one of pain. With a chuckle, he relaxed his grip enough to pull her face up to his.

"Wench, you surprise me... You should by rights be dead." He chuckled again. "Your strength suits me; I have broken too many others."

"Have – You now..." Euwae managed to sputter. "My strength... Suits..."

The others tried to advance again, but he simply flexed the muscles in his arm; Euwae did her best to choke back the sob of pain he squeezed up from her chest. Brand whipped Crows Call around in another arc beside him, his breathing steady now.

"You're gonna have to put her down sometime, you hiel."

But cu'Kullah chuckled.

"I think not... She makes a fine shirt of mail at this moment and no mistake."

Euwae blinked.

Across the span of the room, her brother was waiving his hands frenetically. Despite her predicament, her face lined with disappointment at his pointless antics.

"... And I'll show you just how much nothing this cuhm'l really means."

Konner's brow furrowed and he shot an odd glance at Brand.

"But – Eastlander," he questioned, "we have seen – "

"We've seen his tricks," Brand retorted, "but I've got a few left, too."

Genna collapsed off of his perch and fell in a heap to the floor below. Cu'Kullah scowled.

"Worthless," he said to the fallen priest with bland displeasure, "and no mistake."

Once he had caught his sister's eye, Kelleu continued his odd little pantomime by moving his hands to his throat. Euwae's expression slowly shifted from pity to exasperation, when suddenly her eyes went wide. Cu'Kullah shifted his stance slightly; in response she craned her neck to one side so that she could continue to watch her brothers hands as they cut through the air.

With a bored sneer, cu'Kullah shifted his grip on his prisoner and started to slowly stalk towards his attackers.

"Angus?" Brand coaxed.

The big ath'Ale shot him a look, but after a nod from ad'Ah beside him he squeezed his shoulders together as best he could and nodded as well. Konner took three quick breaths and hefted his sword up to a high defense.

Brand looked at them and nodded in response, when Euwae took a deep breath and spoke as best she could.

"You are ree?" She said breathlessly.

Without breaking his stride, cu'Kullah's head pivoted in the affirmative as best it could.

"Aye, little one."

"The name," she replied, "is Euwae!"

With that, she wrenched her arms free and wrapped her hands around cu'Kullah's neck.

He stopped his advance and shifted his grip.

"What is this?" He asked jovially. "You *are* spirited and no mistake!"

But, as he pulled her away, her hands remained firmly locked at his throat. First with a pair of tugs and then with a single increasing effort he tried to pry her free. Euwae's shoulders rolled forward and she gasped in pain, but she refused to release her hold.

At last, with a deafening yell he tore her away, hurling her through the air and into Brand. As the pair went down in a tangle of limbs, cu'Kullah stepped forward and towered above them.

"ENOUGH!" He screamed. "It is time for this to *end*."

Euwae struggled free of Brand and rolled over to face cu'Kullah.

"In *truth*." She said imperiously.

Her face was tortured as she raised her right arm and held out the contents of her hand: a broken loop of boiled leather, woven artfully with luxurious lengths of golden blond hair.

His hands shot to his throat as cu'Kullah's expression careened from recognition to horror. The big warrior dropped to his knees, as black waters began to pour from his mouth and wounds... The torrent flowed across his flesh like the scarf of death, wrapping about the man's shriveling body until only a limp, dry husk of a corpse lay in the pool of poison, its mouth wrenched open in a silent scream and the sunken eyes locked on terrors outside the world of living men.

Final Words

"Show me! Show me! Show me!"

Finara pulled at the long sleeve of Euwae's dress as she sat on the rocks overlooking the pass down to the beach from the court of twoth'Ba. The sea breezes were tugging just as hard at her hair; with a dramatic sigh she pulled it down and rolled it into a loose knot behind her head.

"Show you what, then?" She asked innocently.

"The torc of the evil ree!" Finara stamped his foot impatiently. "I want to see it!"

Euwae's face took on a mask of feigned indignation.

"And what would an al'Aith such as me be doing with such a thing as that? I ask you!"

Finara puffed up his chest and waived his finger at his sister.

"You are the ree of twoth'Shan'n." He corrected her. "You won it in battle."

Euwae laughed.

"I am not the ree yet, Finara of twoth'Ba... There is much to be done, yet, before I can claim such an honor as that."

"But you *do* to be the ree... Just like mother. Kelleu said so."

"Did he now?"

"He did. He said such wise to father, after the priest of Ard'Ree made his weavings and took his leave." Finara raised his chin and crossed his arms before adding gravely, "and that is the way of it."

Euwae could no longer keep the delight from her face. As soon as she began to smile, Finara knew he had won... A grin of elation dawned on his face as well as he stood and waited for the spoils of his inevitable victory.

"I did not win it alone, you know..." She explained as she reached down and began to release the cord that secured the claps of a thick leather pouch at her hip.

"I know!" Finara said excitedly, bouncing up and down with each response. "As the evil ree made to grab you, Kelleu used the warrior's hand-sign to tell you to take away his torc..."

"And you wouldn't want to be losing your torc, now, would you?"

"Brand!"

The object of his quest momentarily forgotten, Finara raced back up the path to give the warrior an expansive hug. Brand chuckled and tousled

Finara's hair, then stepped back and dropped down onto one knee to look at him directly.

"Your mother is looking for you, Finara."

"Aww..."

"She said something about a march."

Finara's eyes lit up, but they narrowed as he studied Brand.

"But, Brand Eastlander – Where is *your* torc?"

Brand looked from the boy to Euwae, then back to Finara.

"I've never had one, my al'Aith."

"Never? But... I thought everyone had a torc."

Euwae slid down from the rock and gave her brother a hug from behind.

"Not everyone has a torc, Fin," she said softly, her eyes locked on Brand's. "Some people are born... Special. And no mistake."

Finara snuggled into his sisters embrace, released her and looked at Brand seriously.

"You should be getting one, Brand." He advised knowingly. "They are important," he said, emulating his sister's tone, "and no mistake."

Brand nodded graciously.

"I will remember that, my al'Aith."

Euwae stood and gave her brother a gentle push.

"Mother is waiting, Fin."

"What of you, then?"

"We will be along."

Finara started to trot up the path for a few steps, but slowly came to a stop. He turned and looked at his sister with a sad expression.

"I hope no one comes after the feast tonight." He said quietly. "You will not go outside the walls of the grounds, will you?"

Moisture thickened Euwae's eyes as she quickly closed the distance to Finara and gave him another bracing hug.

"You need not worry of such things, Fin..." She said gently. "I promise."

Reassured, the young boy finally raced up the pathway and off to the great hall. Brand watched him go in the fading light, then offered a hand to Euwae and helped her rise.

"How're the shoulders?"

"No worse than my head or hips or my knees." She said without sarcasm. "The next time we are off to some grand adventures, we should be wise to the bounties that await us at the journey's end..."

"The next time?"

She looked at him and grinned.

"You are still my ath'Ale, champion of twoth'Shan'n... And I am of a mind that there *will* be much to be done, before our hearth is as grand as it was in the days of the River Prince."

"Fair enough." Brand conceded. "It was nice of your father to offer up men and supplies to you. I half expected we'd..." He looked at her and his voice trailed off. He smiled gently. "He really loves you."

The knot in her hair slipped loose, freeing it to the pull of the wind once more. Looking away from Brand towards the pillars of smoke rising from the bonfires around the great hall, she only nodded once in reply. At last, he took her arm and led her back up the path as well.

"At least you don't have to marry Kelleu..." He cajoled.

She punched him in the arm, but winced at the pain of the motion in her shoulder.

"I bet that hurt." He said with feigned regret.

"It did," she shot back, "but was worth the cost in full."

They both laughed as they made their way back to the gate and joined the revels in the courtyard beyond.

Within hours, the celebration was at its fullest measure. Warriors who had attended the ree on the voyage regaled their comrades with their deeds in arms, or embellished the successes – or failures – of their fellows. Some toasted the fallen, while a few sought company and took to quiet places to see to the generations to come... Angus and ad'Ah, together, the first amongst them.

For all, there was food enough to spare and mead enough to make generous rounds. For the al'Aith, the tables had been plucked from the hall and set outside between the two large bonfires. Euwae had been offered the seat next to her father, but she chose to keep her old place at the table. Behind her stood Brand, quiet and vigilant now that they were in the company of others once again.

Once he had eaten his fill, Finara soon grew distracted and set out to play with the other boys. After he left, the rees of twoth'Ba called for another round of mead and set the stage for the stories of their own. Lohvtreu plied his family for details of all their adventures. Those that were willingly given, he took keen measure of; those that were set aside, he allowed to pass for the time being.

After he had complimented and honored those deeds Lohvtreu deemed worthy, he also complimented the skills of Una for seeing to the running of the household, so that she would not be left out of the praise that those who had traveled abroad now enjoyed.

Euwae paid the greatest heed to all that was said, although she herself said little, save for what was directly asked of her. Brand was asked even less, but when Euwae commented on this, he reassured her that he understood the nature of the moment and was content with his place in it.

As the night drew on, Lohvtreu finally called for his youngest son to return to his side. Finara raced to the head table, as fast as youthful enthusiasm could carry him. Once he stood before his father, he gave a grand salute.

"My ree!" He said proudly.

Lohvtreu nodded from his seat.

"The time for the March has come, my son." He said proudly. "Are the piper's at the ready?"

Finara looked about and saw that the pipers were, in fact, still in their cups... In a flawless imitation of his sister Euwae he marched off to their benches and roused them to the task straight away. Once they had been herded and marshaled to his satisfaction, he called back across the field to the high table.

"Father! The pipers do stand at the ready... *Now*." He turned and gave them a baleful look, which they played well to and seemed either abashed or fully turned out, as was their want... Much to the amusement of those who could see them.

"Most well, then!" his father replied. Raising his voice to its most commanding, Finara called out, "Folk of twoth'Ba! Your ree calls you now to the March!

"Stand and be counted amongst the ready!"

As the young prince mounted an empty bench to look over the warriors and nobles as they gathered to their places, Lohvtreu leaned back in his seat. Meeruen reached over, took his hand and said quietly, "I will not leave you."

He turned to her, his eyes soft, but only nodded. Without looking away, he called to his daughters.

"Una – You shall dance in our places with your brother today."

Una rose and nodded gracefully. With her father's broad smile, she swept off to join the dancers, Kelleu walking just as proudly beside her. As she watched them go, Meeruen gave her husband's hand a gentle squeeze. He turned in his seat and looked down the table at his younger daughter.

"Euwae... Any man here would count himself prized, were you to take his hand this night for the March of the Ba. But – I suspect that you have chosen your partner already.

"Is this the way of it?"

She nodded without hesitation. Her father smiled, his eyes moist with pride.

"You have come into your en'Och and your destiny, daughter of twoth'Ba.

"Now, take your place before us as ree of twoth'Shan'n."

Euwae rose, stepped away from her seat and slowly took a knee in utter respect for her father. Pursing his lips to hide his emotions, he reached out from his chair and guided her to her feet. Then, as Una had done, she lowered her head in a graceful nod and began to walk around the table.

She had closed half the distance, before she stopped and turned to Brand.

"Well, Bird Club... Where are your manners?" She asked lightly.

He titled his head in response.

"We are off to *March*," she explained dryly. "I would have you by my side and no mistake."

He looked at her with a perplexed expression.

"Me?"

"Whom else would you be thinking? Now, come along." She ended the conversation with an abrupt turn and resumed walking towards the center of the crowd. Brand rolled his eyes and took a deep breath. As the two rees of twoth'Ba watched in amusement, he set Crows Call down upon the table and followed her into the throng.

As they watched their children take their places, Meeruen's left hand traced the familiar tracks of scar and muscle along her husband's forearm.

"She has changed much, this last year away from hearth and kin." Meeruen said quietly.

"Aye, my love, that she has." Lohvtreu said with gentle pride. "That her heart was bursting within her for the want of glory, there was never a mistake... But it was beyond dreaming to think that she would rise in such a wise as this."

Meeruen's fingers paused at his wrist.

"The call of Ard'Ree to send her to the halls of twoth'Shan'n?"

Her husband shook his head.

"Oh! That is the gift of gifts and no mistake..." He turned at last from watching his children to address his wife. "But she has found peace with herself, at the last of it - For me, that treasure is greater still, by far. For all my hoping, I never thought to see the day it would come to pass."

Meeruen's voice dropped to a near whisper.

"You, my ree, had all reason to have fear for such a thing... After you tried to stop her fleeing from the twoth and she struck you down – "

Lohvtreu raised his hand and gently placed it upon his wife's full lips. Slowly tracing his finger along their contours, his own mouth curled in enjoyment as he soothed away the lines of concern at the corners of her eyes.

"The en'Och in her was so great..." He said, just as quietly. "Too much to bear for anyone and all the worse for one so young.

"The night of *that* feast," he continued, "the call of destiny was on her at the last. Only a blind man or a fool has the lack of wits to stand and face the tide sweeping up the shores before the storm."

Meeruen scowled and pulled his hand away, wrapping it in her own.

"You are neither blind nor witless fool, Lohvtreu of twoth'Ba." She said reproachfully.

He looked deeply into her eyes, the light of the bonfires casting the shadows from his own.

"I was young once, too, Meeruen of twoth'Ba. Seasons come and pass and that is the way of it."

She smiled at that; keeping hold of his hand, they turned together to watch the Dance of the Sword unfold before them.

After reaching Una, Euwae took a moment to straighten the heavy pouch at her side. Her sister stepped even closer, however and whispered to her confidentially.

"So, then, sister of mine... Who shall you be facing on the March?"

Euwae rolled her head twice to gesture behind her as she fiddled with her pouch. Una looked confused, until Brand ducked out of the crowd and joined them.

"Hi..." He said uncomfortably.

"Ach!" Una piped. "Surely not!" She stepped back and pulled her sister with her. Euwae gasped at the pain of the movement and looked at Una with deep annoyance.

"And what was *that*, then?" She asked hotly.

"Euwae," Una said almost frantically, "What are you thinking, woman?"

"What was that?" She asked, now confused enough to forgo the thought of her own discomfort.

"*Him.*" Una said coolly. "Surely, you are kind enough to let him stand for your cause. But to bring him here, to the center of the March?"

"And what is wrong with *him*?"

"Pipers!" Cried Finara. "Stand at the ready!"

Una looked at her aghast.

"Euwae... He is an Outlander!"

"What?"

"He has no torc!" Una said bitterly. "You cannot – "

Euwae raised her hand and placed a finger against her sisters lips. Looking deeply into her eyes, she said quietly, "He has honor enough for any two men – And that is as good a burden as any who bear their en'Och in wise of tradition alone!"

Finara called out again, his high voice carrying across the dancers on the wind.

"The al'Aiths and rees of twoth'Ba stand assembled for the March of the Ba!"

Euwae stepped back and held her arm across her chest, taking her place beside Brand. Kelleu drew the dumfounded Una into place.

"But... He has no torc..." She stammered again. Kelleu smiled gently.

"No... But we are all none the worse for it." He said quietly, then turned to Euwae. "At the start of this, you sought nothing less than an aes'ree of your own. Are you taken, at the last, by what you have now?" The shaman said cryptically.

"My Bird Club?" Euwae beamed and smiled. "Aye... No more worthy a weapon is to be found in all Cord'Or and that is the way of it."

Brand actually blushed as Finara began to count the measure ceremoniously and the dancers set off on their way.

Once the March had run its course, the pipers took up another wild reel. Brand quickly excused himself and made for the outside of the rings of dancers. With a chuckle, Euwae followed.

After they had moved beyond the crowd, Brand turned to watch as the folk of twoth'Ba made merry. Without looking at Euwae, he spoke in a low voice.

"Well, that could have gone better."

"What? You missed none but the last steps and that was on the first pass alone. You take to the March better than most of the folk here."

"Maybe... But I think most of the folk here have had a few more bowls of mead than I have."

"Fair enough."

He paused, glanced at Euwae, then looked back at the revelers.

"That's not what I meant, though."

"I know in what wise you speak."

"Huh." He paused again, and continued a bit ruefully. "Maybe I should have picked up the shitesat torc... It might have made your life a lot easier, having a champion who wasn't a – An outsider."

Euwae stepped forward and turned to face him full on.

"Brand Eastlander, I would as much prefer to have cu'Kullah at my back as a man who lacks the heart that you possess and no mistake. No torc, no en'Och, no aes'ree stands as true as you stand now, without any of these things."

She looked into his face, continuing on with a softer tone carrying her voice.

"I have seen the way of it, because you are the man you are. And that is shitesan fair enough for me."

Brand looked at her with a clouded expression.

"Huh." He said at last. "Really?"

"Aye."

"Ah." He nodded at last. He looked at her once more for a long moment. Finally, he nodded again.

She turned at that and stood beside him. Together, they watched the dancers wheeling lightly across the field. As one reel ended, another just as quickly began. Once it was well underway, Euwae turned her head and looked at Brand.

"Bird Club," she said quizzically, "there is one truth that I am keen to be knowing."

His expression shifted subtly towards apprehension; he took a deep breath and blew it out through puffed cheeks before replying quietly.

"Yeah, fine. What is it you want to know?"

She looked at him earnestly.

"What *does* shitesa mean?"

He opened his mouth, started and quickly clamped it shut. With a spreading grin, he leaned over and whispered the answer into her ear.

Euwae blushed furiously.

"No! In truth?" she gasped.

"In truth..." He replied with a knowing chuckle.

the Reel of the Ba

> The men and women form a circle, with the men on the inside facing out and the women outside facing their partner

> The man stands with the right arm held up, with the right hand in a fist and the left hand on his hip; the woman's left arm is held across her chest, left hand in a vertical fist, her right hand at her thigh gathering her dress

> The man's extended hand is brought to the opposite hip, then moved forward with the palm facing left and the thumb tucked in over it as the arm is rotated towards the partner and the right elbow locked at the side; the woman brings her hand up in front of the man's, so that their wrists touch

> Both partners make a quarter turn (he to the left, she to the right) so that they are facing forward with their joined arms held between them

> Starting with the right foot, the partners take 3 steps forward

> The man then makes a half turn and tucking his left thumb against his palm places his left wrist against his partners

> He takes 3 steps forward, she takes 3 steps back

> The woman then performs a half turn and makes a vertical fist with her right hand before placing her right wrist against her partners

> They both take 3 steps back

- ➢ **B**oth partners make a quarter turn so that they are facing each other

- ➢ They join left hands, step towards each other, make a half turn and swap their places on the outside of the circle and then step away

- ➢ They join both hands, step towards each other making another half turn to swap their places on the outside of the circle again, then step away; the left hands are released

- ➢ The woman then steps forward under the man's right hand with two spins and passes from his right side to his left, to join the next partner with a third; when the woman steps behind him and releases his hand, the man returns to the starting position and cries "Bara!"

- ➢ **P**lacing her hands in the starting position, the woman calls out "Ba!" and moves forward to the next partner

- ➢ Once the woman joins the next partner, the steps are repeated

www.ingramcontent.com/pod-product-compliance
Lightning Source LLC
Chambersburg PA
CBHW050501260626
47157CB00004B/1139